D0800315

POOR TOM

Other novels by Martin Drapkin:

Now and at the Hour

Ten Nobodies (and their somebodies)

The Cat Tender

POOR TOM

Martin Drapkin

Three Towers Press

Milwaukee, Wisconsin

Published by
Three Towers Press
An imprint of HenschelHAUS Publishing, Inc.
Milwaukee, Wisconsin
www.henschelHAUSbooks.com

ISBN: 978159598-932-1
E-ISBN: 978159598-933-8
LCCN: 2022946690

Printed in the United States

*"The lamentable change is from the best;
the worst returns to laughter."*

—Edgar

King Lear

ONE

THE FIRST TIME I NOTICED THAT my father had stopped laughing was five days ago when I came over to his house for our monthly Sunday morning bagels and lox and Marx Brothers brunch. Well, the lox was for him; I find it disgusting. Dad was sitting in his beige La-Z-Boy, slumped forward and looking a bit frazzled—unshaven, white hair uncombed. I noticed that his normally clear gray eyes were murky. He hardly spoke. He was wearing the ratty green bathrobe that my mother'd given him for a Chanukah present the year before she killed herself. It occurred to me that this was the worst my father'd looked in the past few weeks. When I asked him how his back was feeling, he stared at me for a few moments and shrugged and said, in an uncharacteristic monotone, barely audibly, "I guess it could be worse." His voice was still a bit hoarse from all the yelling and shouting he'd had to do in the play. I noticed that he half-heartedly buttered his sesame bagel but didn't slather cream cheese on it. In all our long brunching history, I don't recall my father not *shmearing* cream cheese on his bagel. It worried me.

The movie we watched while we ate was *Duck Soup*, one of our longtime favorites. Soon came the scene where Margaret Dumont, as imperious Mrs. Teasdale, says to Groucho, as Rufus T. Firefly, "Notables from every country are gathered here in your honor. This is a gala day for you." Groucho replies, "Well, a gal a day is enough for me. I don't think I could handle any more." I laughed on cue, but Dad didn't. He didn't even chuckle. He just stared, stone-faced, at the screen. *What's up here?* I remember thinking. *Is this the Herbert Dickman I've known so well for the forty years of my life on the planet so far?* In all our years together of enjoying Groucho and Chico and Harpo, all those Sunday mornings, the man had never not guffawed at that scene.

Nor did he laugh at anything else in *Duck Soup*, including when Firefly proposes marriage to Mrs. Teasdale and, wagging his black painted-on eyebrows, says, "Married! I can see you right now in the kitchen, bending over a hot stove ... but I can't see the stove." Even though we'd heard that line dozens of times over the years, my father'd always slapped his knee and pointed at the screen and at least chuckled, but more often laughed heartily.

I love Groucho, but I wish he'd had a better given first name because I was named after that given, Julius. It's not a name I'm fond of, particularly when paired with our unfortunate surname. Dad told me that it was his choice to name me that, and that if he'd had two more sons he'd have named them Leonard, Chico's name, and Arthur, after Harpo. I asked him once if Mom had gone along with his choice, and he furrowed his brow and looked at the floor and hesitated. "I, uh, don't remember that," he muttered. "I guess she was okay with it." I've often wished I could ask her. But I can't.

Sometimes I wish they'd given me a nice, short, masculine, one-syllable name—Bob, maybe, or Biff. Al would be okay. I think I'd have been more successful with women that way.

Just three Sundays ago my old man was on top of the world. The matinee of *King Lear* that day was the final performance of his long theater career. He'd announced his pending retirement before casting for the play started. Lear was the role he'd waited all his life to play, but had for years insisted that he wouldn't do until he was "close to the old tyrant's fourscore years," as he said. "When you're young you play Hamlet and when you're old you play Lear," he'd noted many times. He said he wanted to be old enough to understand the wacko king's desire to step down from his long life's work and to "shake all cares and business ... and unburdened crawl toward death."

Crawl unburdened toward death. Yikes! I didn't want to hear that. Maybe that's a noble goal, but unfortunately the old man's not quite unburdened yet. He's been suffering with pain from his back injury for three weeks now, and I'm worried that it's even worse than he's admitted. I remember exactly when it happened. It was at the end of Act V, the final act of *Lear*, that Sunday. Dad was carrying the corpse of poor hanged Cordelia onstage, howling in grief and agony. Just before he was getting ready to lay her body down in front of Kent and Albany and Edgar, I saw him stumble and slip and grimace with pain. Bad luck there, to hurt himself like that at the very end of the very last performance of his long acting career. Damn!

At least Celeste is a small actress. If she were bigger, maybe his stumble would have been worse. There's that.

Plus, the old man clunked his noggin a week or so ago. He told me that he went to the basement to do a load of wash and there was just one dim light and he put the clothes in the washing machine and, when he straightened up, banged his head hard against the bottom of the wooden cabinet with all the detergent and bleach and fabric softener and lint traps. Now he has a headache and a knot on top of his head. It's not huge, but still a knot. I asked him if he wanted me to take him to urgent care or the emergency room or at least to go see Dr. Ansfield, but he said he didn't. "Men must endure," he intoned.

And I know he hasn't been sleeping well for the last few weeks. He told me that when I called him earlier this week. "I can't get comfortable," he said, his voice still a bit strained from all the yelling he'd done in *Lear*, particularly in the storm scene. "I move from my back to my left side and then to my right side and then to my stomach. I get up and walk around. I'm gobbling Ibuprofen. It's terrible!" He paused. "Nothing works. Nothing." A few moments later, he looked up at me, almost bewildered, and said softly, "Nothing will come of nothing, right?"

So now I have my father to worry about. That's not my only worry. Yesterday I managed to irritate my live-with girlfriend, certainly not for the first time, and this morning she's still mad. It was Thanksgiving and Naomi'd invited her cousin Lydia for dinner. I'd been looking forward to the day, mainly because Lydia was coming. I hadn't seen her since Naomi's birthday dinner in March. The woman's magnificent: heart-shaped pale face with big dark eyes and pouty lips, framed by fluffy black hair. She has a cute upturned nose with a dusting of freckles, not like Naomi's big hooked Yid shnoz. When Lydia arrived, she gave her cousin a warm hug and hugged Naomi's kids, Benji and Elise, and then handed me the bottle of Beaujolais she'd brought and gave me a cursory hug. "Julius," she murmured. "Nice to see you again." She took off her coat and handed it to me and I saw that she was wearing one of those sexy little black dresses that show a lot of skin, including cleavage. I recall thinking that a little black dress seemed a strange choice for Thanksgiving. But what do I know?

During dinner, while Naomi was going on and on to her cousin about how her boss at Jewish Social Services, Arthur, is such a jerk—some grievance about how he plays favorites among the female social workers—Lydia glanced at me and held her gaze for a moment and, I think, gave me a subtle little smile. Just then I had forbidden fantasies. Sitting there at Naomi's dining room table, eating the turkey that my girlfriend had so competently prepared, and mashed potatoes and dressing and cranberries, sipping the Beaujolais, I imagined being upstairs in our bedroom, or some bedroom, with little Lydia and kissing her passionately and unzipping and slipping off that black dress and then her bra and panties and tossing them unceremoniously to the floor. "Julius," she'd murmur, "I've thought about this for so long!" I'd rip off my own clothes and the two of us would tumble together onto the bed, naked and sweating, and make mad passionate love. I imagined running my hands through her fluffy black hair and maybe gently kissing the tip of that sweet freckled little nose. "Oh, God," she'd moan. "Oh, *Julius!*"

But then I thought: *Who am I kidding?* Really, who would I be kidding? Lydia's a highly regarded personal injury attorney with a reputation, according to Naomi, for ferocity in representing her clients. She talks on equal terms with judges and opposing attorneys and jurors and the like. She negotiates settlements for big bucks. She's competent and has self-confidence. She's out of my league. She's *way* out of my league. Someone like her could never, I'm sure, be interested in a stuttering nobody *schlemiel* like me.

The schlemiel designation is according to Naomi. That's what she called me last night after Lydia'd left and the kids had gone to bed. We were getting ready to go to bed ourselves and she gave me one of her wonted bad looks, with hardened eyes and arched eyebrows and a wrinkled nose and the right corner of her mouth turned down, and rebuked me for staring at her cousin over dinner. "Could you have been any more *obvious?*" she scolded. "Why didn't you just invite her to sit on your goddamned lap and feed her precious little bites of turkey?"

I told her that I didn't realize I was being inappropriate but apologized anyway, and then tried to change the subject by telling her about the uncomfortable episode I'd had in the Culver's drive-through two days ago. I'd wanted to get a cod fillet and a large root beer and noticed that there was only one car, a blue Dodge Caravan, ahead of me in the drive-through lane. I'd been planning to play it safe and go inside to order but thought I'd be okay with just that one car ahead and scrapped my go-inside plan. But almost immediately after I pulled my Honda Civic into the lane behind the Dodge, a huge black Ford pickup, maybe one of those F-350s, pulled in behind me and a moment later a silver-colored SUV got in line behind the Ford. So I was trapped—couldn't move forward or backward and had zero control over any timetable for progress. There was a curb to the right, so I couldn't pull out of the lane. There's no such curb when you go to McDonald's or Hardee's or Burger King, so a guy can withdraw from the fray if he needs to. I panicked and began sweating and breathing hard and my heart started pounding. I was majorly *verklempt*. I opened all the windows and turned off the heater. I thought about turning on the air-conditioner full blast, even though it was freezing out. I tried taking deep breaths, slowly and evenly, in through my nose and out through my mouth. My panic lasted until the jerk in the Dodge moved forward and got his order and drove away from the window and I pulled up to pay and get my food, and there was no one in front of me. "F-Free at last, Naomi," I said. "Thank God almighty, I was f-f-free at l-last." When I finally got my sandwich and root beer and was driving away, I thought to myself: *You idiot! From now on just go inside to order and forget about the damned drive-through.* I told Naomi that thought, hoping for maybe a bit of understanding, even sympathy. But no. She just stared coldly, brow furrowed, and shook her head slowly. "Not only are you *indeed* an idiot, Julius Dickman," she practically hissed, "but you're also a first-class schlemiel!"

She's probably right. How stupid can a guy be? When you've lived with a woman for three years you should know what she's like, should know how she's going to react when you tell her about having a panic attack in a Culver's drive-through. You should be able to anticipate her tendencies in given situations, like a football coach calling the defense's plays anticipates the opposing offense's tendencies on third and long. My cousin Herschel gave me that idea; he calls it his "game plan" approach to dealing with women. So a guy should be smart enough to learn from experience a little—just a little, anyway. He should know when to keep his stupid mouth shut.

Then she raked me over the coals again this morning. I was making the coffee and Naomi came into the kitchen and I looked at her hardened face, jaw clenched, and immediately wished I were elsewhere—New Zealand, say, or Argentina. She walked over and got right in my face. I noticed, not for the first time, that her nose seems bigger than usual when she's angry and has a purplish hue. "Are you having an affair with Lydia?" she hissed.

I didn't say anything.

"*ARE* you?" she yelled.

I shook my head. I was sweating. "N-n-no," I muttered. "I'd never d-do that. I'm n-n-not." I think she believed me, but who knows?

She just glared at me for a long moment. "Well," she said, "see that you don't."

I had to go to the bathroom and when I got back to the kitchen I saw that Naomi had my cellphone and was studying it closely. She put it down quickly when she saw me. "What's up?" I asked. She shook her head and gave me a hardened look and walked away, still in a huff.

Why do I stay with that woman? That's almost always one of my issues, obsessions, in the middle of the night when I have my damned insomnia. It's on my mind every day, particularly when she's badmouthed me or chastised me for some ridiculous thing I did or didn't do—usually something earth-shattering, like starting the dishwasher before it's full or not emptying it in a timely manner once the dishes have dried, or not getting the cans out to the curb early enough on garbage day—or otherwise tongue-lashed me. We're not married, so I can leave any time. I guess I can. Herschel thinks I should leave. He's said so many times. He's never liked Naomi. He said once that she's "a shrew who needs some serious taming."

But as bitchy as she can be, it's not all bad. Sometimes—not that often, but now and again—she's nice and even warm, affectionate. She's comforting during my tough nights when I've popped awake at two or three and my fevered brain's immediately commenced to ruminating and worrying and obsessing. Well, she's not comforting but her body is. She always falls asleep easily and sleeps quite nicely through the night, apparently untroubled by worries or concerns. I'm envious. The woman rarely stirs. Sometimes she makes endearing little "m-m-m" sounds when sleeping. She must have nice dreams because she now and again smiles in her sleep. I don't imagine she's dreaming about me, though. Maybe, but not likely. Happily, she usually sleeps on her left side, with her back to me, so I can snuggle against her and even spoon with her, scrunching my groin against her soft buttocks. It's comforting. I especially like to reach under the blanket and run my hand over the feminine curve of her right hip, usually covered with one of the flannel nightgowns she favors in the winter. Last night she wore a red-and-black-checked nightgown. Sometimes I cup a breast. She's usually not aware of what I'm doing because she rarely reacts. Now and again she'll wake up and is okay with my touching and snuggling, as long as it doesn't go on too long or get too intrusive. Sometimes, though, she tells me right away to cease: "Move over and leave me the fuck *alone!*" she'll growl.

And I'm usually okay with our twice-a-week morning ritual. Naomi got the idea at one of her social worker in-service trainings that couples should proactively set aside scheduled time—each day or every other day, say—to just sit together and talk about things on their minds, to share ideas and thoughts and dreams, blah blah, so as to stay connected and to hash out any issues or problems in their relationship. "It's a couple's check-in," she said. So she chose Monday and Thursday mornings, at the kitchen table over coffee, before her kids get started on their days. On the one hand, it's a pain in the ass because I have to get up earlier than I want to on those days and start the Keurig and I'm usually tired because of having been awake during the night with my damned insomnia. On the other hand, it's okay. She does most of the talking, and I can just sit there and sip coffee and listen to her familiar voice, which, when she's not mad at me, is nice enough. I've always been okay with Naomi's voice, with its slight melodious lilt, when she's not unduly agitated. And I get to look at her face, which I'm also okay with except when it's all tense and purple with rage. The only issue I have is that she usually devotes most of the conversation to her work gripes, mostly regarding Arthur, rather than to checking in as to our relationship. "I'm just so pissed at him," she said on Monday. "He asked that little bitch Amanda to chair a committee on disabilities outreach when he knew I wanted to do that, and he knows I have eight years of seniority on her. Oh, she's always sucked up to him. And not only that, but … " And on and on in such tedious vein for ten or fifteen minutes.

I always nod and try to look interested and sometimes say "Um-hmm" or "Well, that wasn't f-fair," but, really, I could care less about most of her issues. I'd never tell her this, but sometimes I sit there and fantasize about other women. I met Amanda once at a Jewish Social Services Purim party, was favorably impressed, and, when Naomi mentioned her, had the brief vision of meeting up with her at some sleazy motel near the highway, one with bad lighting and suspicious stains on the sheets, and having a secret little rendezvous. "Oh, Julius," Amanda'd murmur. "That Purim party was the best day of my life, because, of course, I met *you!*"

Saying "Um-hmm" and the like is something I learned from Naomi. After she's gone on for a while with whatever's on *her* mind, it occurs to her that she should ask me about what may be on *mine*. "Well," she'll say after she's yapped nonstop for a long while, "I've talked a lot. Anything you'd like to bring up?" Usually there isn't. For one thing, there's the damned stutter. For another, I can't imagine she'd actually be interested in most things I might have on my mind, including my feeble attempts to change the subject when necessary, like with the Culver's incident. I certainly can't tell my girlfriend about my fantasy life. "W-Well, Naomi," one can imagine me saying, "yesterday I s-saw an amazingly scrumptious b-b-blonde at the g-grocery store and wished I could g-g-get to know her b-better and m-maybe even p-p-pork her sometime." But, to hold up my end of the bargain, I'll maybe talk about a painting job I worked on or a wedding I photographed. On Monday I'd told her about a wedding I'd done a few months ago in which the bride was quietly but visibly weeping as she was being escorted down the aisle by her father and I didn't know if she was crying because she was happy or because she knew she was making a gigantic mistake by going through with marrying this particular doofus, but did it anyway because she didn't want to disappoint her family and the guests. Naomi, as usual, used her social worker's active listening skills, making eye contact and nodding now and again and going "Um-hmm," and saying things like "How did that make you feel?" and "Help me to under-stand why that affected you so much." On the one hand I appreciate her doing that, but on the other hand it's tedious and annoying and seems rote after a while.

The other thing about Naomi is that I almost always melt when that woman cries. She has that going. She cries sometimes when we've had an argument and she's all hyper-emotional. Usually it's tears of anger or exasperation with me. But even so I usually want to put my arms around her and hold her when her dark eyes start to moisten. On the one hand, I think that's fine; it's good to comfort your woman when she's upset. On the other hand, it's sick. There's Naomi pissed at me yet again and calling me the nastiest names and wanting to rip my head off, or rip *something* off, and crying, and there's me wanting to comfort her for that. That seems crazy.

And she cries at movies and silly television shows too. Soon it'll be December and *It's a Wonderful Life* will be on TV and Naomi will predicta-bly turn on her waterworks when George Bailey, with Clarence the guardian angel's help, realizes on Christmas Eve that he's had a wonderful life after all and decides he wants to live rather than jump in the river and rushes home to his family. His goody-goody wife, Mary, has put out the word that George needs help and all the upstanding citizens of Bedford Falls come dashing through the snow to the Bailey house, overflowing with the spirit of the season and their love for George for the wonderful life he's led, and bring money so that George won't go to jail for embezzlement of the eight thousand dollars that hapless Uncle Billy lost and nasty Mr. Potter found and kept. They all drink wine and sing "Hark the Herald Angels Sing" and "Auld Lang Syne" and a bell on the Christmas tree tinkles and little curly-haired Zuzu preciously notes, "Teacher says that every time a bell rings an angel gets his wings." Naomi loves that stupid movie and always weeps on cue at that scene. I always put an arm around her shoulder and hold her while we're sitting on the couch, and sometimes I'll even lean over and kiss away a tear. It's maybe our best moment of the year. Things might turn to doo-doo again the next morning, or even ten minutes later, but at least there was that moment.

Well, one reason I stay is Benji. Maybe he's the main reason. Poor kid. I feel bad for him. His mother's a nasty bigmouth and his older sister's a carbon copy. Sometimes those two get along okay and even watch stupid *Bravo* reality TV shows together, particularly the ridiculous "Real House-wives" ones, but my God, the screaming matches at other times! *Vey iz mir!* Yesterday Naomi and Elise were in the kitchen working on the Thanksgiving dinner and Naomi told Elise to cut some celery for the dressing and Elise made a face and rolled her eyes and said, "Why do *I* have to do that? Tell Benji to get off his ass and do something!" and Naomi turned purple and screamed, "Because I *told* you to do it, do you fucking understand?" And it escalated from there for another ten horrible minutes, with obscenity-laced accusations and insults bouncing off the walls and ceiling of the kitchen. "Mom, you're such a *cunt!*" was one.

Benji was in the living room watching football, Detroit versus someone, and I saw his pained expression as he had to yet again endure those two harpies going at each other full-bore. He's a quiet twelve-year-old kid. He doesn't talk much. He keeps to himself most of the time. He likes to read books and watch movies about prehistoric times, cavemen and mastodons and the like. Last week he was in his room watching *The Clan of the Cave Bear*. He also likes to play video games in his room or scroll his phone. He loves his X-Box. He dreads having to go to his dad's house on alternate weekends. I'd like to get to know him better, maybe help him somehow. I'd even like to be a buffer, if possible, between him and those obnoxious, bigmouthed women. Maybe that could be a *mitzvah*, a good deed. Rabbi Twersky said that God wants and expects us to do mitzvahs. I'm down with that.

TWO

WHO DREAMS ABOUT SOUP? I guess I do. I never did before, but last night I had a wonderful such dream. I'd fallen asleep shortly after ten, next to already-asleep Naomi, and soon found myself dreaming about matzo ball soup. In my dream, I was sitting alone at the counter at Izzy's Deli. Magda was working the counter. "Vhat vould you like today, my goot man?" she asked pleasantly. I remember that I studied the menu intently, brow furrowed, before ordering my usual. "Oh, just b-b-bring me a c-cup … no, make it a *b-bowl* … of m-matzo ball soup. Yes, a bowl. Definitely a b-bowl today." Magda smiled and nodded and walked away. I watched her hips swaying pleasantly beneath her green uniform. Soon she returned and set the bowl down in front of me. "I hope you vill enjoy, *ja?*" she said. I stared down at the soup and then lowered my face to take a whiff. It was heavenly, that familiar chicken odor. I looked at the soup for maybe thirty seconds before taking my first spoonful. I noticed the tiny squares of translucent onion suspended in the broth. The three matzo balls seemed to rise part way out of the bowl—floaters, not sinkers. With my spoon, I carved off a chunk of one and let it slide into my waiting mouth. It was dense and overwhelming with wonderful *schmaltzy* flavor. I remember Izzy once saying that he always uses schmaltz—rendered chicken fat—instead of vegetable oil, the oil being perhaps more convenient but definitely a lesser option tastewise. He considers himself a purist in such matters. Yet despite the density of the matzo ball, it tasted somehow light, with tiny pockets of air. I remember that I ate slowly, savoring each spoonful for the heavenly treat it was. My custom has always been to eat a chunk of a matzo ball and then follow with two spoonsful of just broth, and then repeat. Now and again I'll eat one of the thinly-sliced carrot pieces or a morsel of celery. In my dream, I recall the sensation of being happy and satisfied, sitting there alone at the counter in Izzy's, glancing now and again at big-boned Magda going about her tasks, her muscular rear end bulging pleasantly, with my steaming, oh-so comforting soup. My world, just then, seemed right. It was a disappointment to awaken from that dream.

Herschel's a mild soup fan too. He only now and again orders soup when we go to Izzy's, usually preferring just one of their overstuffed sandwiches, but when he does his favorite is Isadore's Mishmosh—chicken soup fully loaded with matzo balls, kreplach, noodles, rice, chicken and vegetables. Herschel says that he's a big fan of kreplach. "Better than sex," is how he once characterized those little dumplings with paper-thin sheets of dough rolled neatly around soft minced beef and onion. "Or almost as good. You down a bowl or two of that and you don't have to eat again for a week."

My cousin's short and arguably ugly—a poor man's version of Danny DeVito, with the same stumpy physique and barrel chest, though with a bit more hair on top. He has just enough hair to keep his always-on-his-head blue beanie yarmulke attached with a bobby pin. Despite his appearance, he somehow has a way with women. He's not intimidated by them, like I am. I'm envious. Herschel's accomplished at flirting. He thinks he's charming, and women—some, at least—apparently find him so. Why, I don't know. I think Magda even likes him a little. He kids around with her and can get her to giggle now and again. He claims to have bedded dozens of females, lauding his seduction skills, but he's probably exaggerating.

He did a nice job as the Fool in *Lear*, I'll give him that. My father thought that Herschel's dwarfiness actually helped him be a wonderful Fool. He looked the part of a jester, as opposed, say, to that conceited well-coifed hunk Donny, who played Edmund. He was even able to carry a tune when singing the Fool's various witty songs—"*With hey, ho, the wind and the rain ... for the rain it raineth every day,*" for one. I liked that one. For a short, maybe ugly man, my cousin has a decent singing voice. I'm envious of that, too.

As to Herschel's seduction skills, his ethics may or may not be admirable but he certainly has imagination and *chutzpah*. I've seen it. Last summer he asked me to help him out in a scheme involving his ugly little Corgi-shepherd mutt, Ajax. His idea was that he and I would walk around downtown, usually on Main Street, and on the Square with Ajax on his red retractable leash and I'd bring my camera. Invariably, people—mostly women—stopped to admire Ajax. "Oh, what a cutie!" some would say. Sometimes it'd be a mother and her young daughter and the little girl, often with her mommy's prompting, would ask, "Can I pet your dog?" Herschel would smile sweetly at the child and say, "Oh, *sure*, honey," and then smile at the mother as well, and in a bit the standard questions would commence:

"Oh, what kind of dog is he?" and "What's his name?" and, sometimes, "How old is he?" Herschel would answer each question patiently and politely, being sure to make eye contact with both the kid and the mother. Sometimes, based on his assessment of a situation, he'd look down at Ajax and be quiet for a moment and then a sad, worried look would spread across his dwarfy face. It's the same look that the Fool had in the Act III storm-on-the-heath scene, when he's cold and wet and shivering and seeing Lear, his beloved master, wild-eyed and raging and acting bonkers and talking craziness with Poor Tom. Perhaps the woman would notice and ask Herschel if everything was okay. He'd shrug and keep looking sad and maybe his eyes would puddle up. "Oh," he'd say, his voice quivering a bit, "I just learned that Ajax has some growths on his chest. The vet said it could be cancer. I'll get the test results in a few days." He'd pause and look deeply into her eyes. "I'm *very* worried," he'd whisper. Her face would soften and sometimes her eyes would moisten as well. Maybe she'd put a soft hand on his arm and squeeze lightly. "It'll be okay," she'd offer, all concerned and warmly sympathetic. "Try to be optimistic." He'd nod, bravely, and after a few moments his face would brighten a bit. "Hey," he'd say, "would it be okay if my cousin takes a picture of us with Ajax? I really want to have good memories in case … in case … " She'd nod. "Oh, of course," she'd reply. "That'd be fine." Sometimes he'd put an arm around the woman's shoulder while posing for the photo. He'd usually ask for her contact information so he could send her a print later. That was his scheme, his *in*, with a female object of desire.

Later, he'd tell me if it worked out with any particular woman, and, if so, how. Usually the narrative involved sexual conquest. Sometimes there was even mention of her having arched-back multiple orgasms, which he took credit for bringing about. I never knew how much to believe, but was usually inclined to give Herschel the benefit of the doubt. Maybe that wasn't the way to go.

My guess is that Herschel isn't as bothered as I am about our mutual surname. Maybe, given his predilections, he even considers it a badge of honor.

Part of me regrets agreeing to be Herschel's seduction photographer. He always asked me to make five-by-seven prints for him, which he keeps in a file folder labeled "WOMEN WITH ME AND AJAX." He writes notes on the back of each photo, including ratings, on a scale of one to ten, of lustful encounters. If he asks me to do it again next summer, though, I hope

I have the courage to say no. I love my cousin, but the whole *cockamamie* deal's too creepy, even for me.

I'll say this for Herschel: he's a good dog daddy. He named the mutt after one of the characters in his favorite Shakespeare play, *Troilus and Cressida*. He said his dream role would be to do Thersites in that play, "a deformed, foul-mouthed, cynical servant of a big, dim-witted Greek warrior named Ajax," as he described him. Herschel has his favorite quote by his dream character printed in nice script, framed in black metal, in the living room of his apartment: *"Lechery, lechery, still wars and lechery! Nothing else holds fashion."* Two years ago, he even bought a green parrot and named it Thersites and taught the damned bird to scream "Lechery! Lechery!" as well as "Chuck you, Farley!" and "Eat shit, Ajax!" It's an ordeal for me to visit my cousin, when I do, and have to listen to that annoying bird squawking out his disgusting brainless phrases. But at least Herschel's kind and attentive to Ajax, taking him for a daily walk in the park and giving him rawhide bones to chew on and squeak toys to play with. So there's that.

Thersites wasn't the dog's original name. That was Happy, and he belonged to Herschel's father, my Uncle Norman. But Herschel changed it when poor Norman tipped over three years ago from lung cancer—a horrible death—and my cousin kindly took the mutt. His mom, my Aunt Bessie, had died eight years ago from a ruptured aneurism. Like me, Herschel's an only child. Unlike me, he's an orphan.

Herschel's kind to street folks, too. Last summer he and I were browsing in Lieberman's Bookshop and soon in came a stocky, elderly black guy with a fluffy white beard, wearing ancient railroad stripe overalls and a puffy beige parka with a faux fur hood and heavy brown scuffed work shoes. It was maybe eighty degrees out and he was wearing that parka. The parka was partially open and I could see that he had a dozen or so assorted pens and one yellow pencil in the top left pocket of his overalls. Herschel and I were near the checkout counter, and the black guy went up to the clerk and asked if the latest *Gentlemen's Quarterly* had come in yet. "*GQ*'s been in for a week now," the prissy clerk intoned haughtily, his chin raised and mouth in a downturned scowl. The old man's eyes widened and his eyebrows arched and he extended to his full height and slowly shook his head. "You don't mean to *tell* me!" he said. He paused and looked at Herschel and nodded. "Well," he went on, "I guess it's true what they say: 'Time and the river wait for no man.'"

Herschel nodded. "Very true, Snowball," he said. "Very true indeed." It turned out that Herschel knew the man, had conversed with him before. "This is my cousin Julius," he said. "He's a world-class photographer and a mediocre house painter." I offered my hand and Snowball grasped it firmly in both of his and pumped up and down. "A true honor and a pleasure to make your acquaintance, sir," he said, grinning hugely. "A *true* honor, indeed." I noticed that several of his front teeth were missing.

Snowball. I wondered what the guy's real name is. I don't know if I'd be too comfortable calling a grown man *Snowball*.

I'm a mediocre house painter? Maybe Herschel was right. What do I know? Maybe I'm not exactly a master craftsman, not yet anyway, but I'd like to think I'm at least a step above mediocre—not a big step, necessarily, but a step. I've been doing it for almost twenty years, on and off, helping Perry Schwartz, my best friend in high school, when he needs an extra hand with a brush or roller. *Schwartz's Fine Painting* is the name of his business. If he'd asked my advice, I'd have suggested zapping the "Fine." Slap the paint on and let folks judge for themselves, would be my idea. But he's never asked my opinion.

Perry's another with many seduction narratives, in his case of female painting clients. Not all the seductions were by him, though. His famous story, if he was telling the truth, is that he was painting a married woman's living and dining rooms, a soothing light-blue, and she asked if he wanted to take a break and have coffee and they were sitting on the sofa and at one point she looked at him sweetly and smiled a bit and put her hand on his knee. "I'm thinking of a state that starts with the letter 'I,'" she whispered. "Can you guess what it is?" Perry thought for a moment. "Illinois?" he asked. "No," she replied softly and slid her hand up his thigh a bit. "Iowa?" She slid her hand further up his thigh and murmured, "No, guess again." "Indiana?" he tried, in a higher register. "Not that one," and her hand progressed further yet. Perry strained and tried to think of another state. "Idaho?" he finally offered. "That's *it*," the woman whispered, smiling, and her hand traveled as far as it could up his thigh and cupped his now-alert privates. "You've got it!" she said. "And so have I." That led to, as Perry described it, "a memorable fornication."

In all my years painting for Perry, I've never had such an opportunity. I wish I had, and still hope to, but won't hold my breath. It might not work out well. "I'm thinking of a state that starts with the letter 'M,'" some lonely, sex-starved woman might say to me during a break, her hand on my knee. "Can you guess what it is?" I'd probably start sweating profusely. "M-M-Michigan?" She'd look at me askance. "M-Maine?" She'd sigh and say, "No, that's not it." By then I'd probably have turned red and commenced to shaking and maybe my eyes would have started to water. "Well, c-could it be M-M-Maryland? Oh, I just d-don't *know*." She'd probably stand up and raise her arms toward the ceiling in exasperation and stride out of the room. "Oh, *forget* about it!" she'd mutter. "Jesus Christ, what a schlemiel!"

Perry has a contract with a leasing company to paint apartments between tenants and he told me that he sometimes tries to commune with the spirits of people whose apartments he paints after they've tipped over. He said that now and again he's been able to get a feeling for a person's spirit. I've never tried that, and don't think I will. The whole deal seems too creepy.

Naomi's had little use for Herschel, nor he for her, but she's said she likes Perry. She sees him and his anorexic wife, Arlene, with her purple-streaked hair, each year at the high holidays—Rosh Hashanah and Yom Kippur—at Beth El. "Oh, he's so handsome and so *polite*," Naomi said once, during our first year together. She even likes it that Perry has one of those strong chins with a dent in the middle, like Kirk Douglas had. She disapproves of Herschel's sawed-off appearance and his wrinkled, stained clothing, often gray sweatshirts, and his sloppy eating habits. She has a point there; my cousin always chomps off huge bites and chews with his mouth open and now and again dribbles food. She also thinks he's rude and too cynical. But Schwartz, she likes. She thinks he's refined and well-mannered. He's tall and athletic, with clear skin and friendly hazel eyes. Maybe she likes his big hooked nose, too, since it resembles her own. He also has a somewhat receding hairline. I guess Naomi thinks Perry's not rude or cynical, like Herschel, and maybe that's accurate. I've never thought much about it one way or the other. Perry's my long-time friend, he has good stories, he's tolerant of my stutter, and working for him supplements my meager photography income. So there's that.

I've sometimes wondered if Naomi and Perry ever did the deed. She also seems to like that he's taller than she is, that she has to look up at him when they talk. With me, she can't do that. We're the same height. Well, maybe I'm even an inch shorter than she—two at most. She stands erect and throws her shoulders back and sticks out her chest while looking up at

Perry's face. Her eyes sparkle. So I can't say I'd faint with surprise to learn they'd *shtupped.*

I like it best when Perry has me do a painting job alone, rather than with him or any of his other part-time guys. I don't have to talk with anyone, and I like to listen to Naxos AudioBooks CDs of the plays Dad's been in so I can understand them better—not easy, for me—and maybe even be able to talk with him semi-intelligently, though that hasn't happened much. I started listening to the plays when he was in *Hamlet* four years ago, playing Claudius. I thought my father was good in that role. I don't remember him as Hamlet because I was just in grade school when he played that annoying prince. I like *Hamlet* the play, I guess, but I'm not crazy about Hamlet the character. I didn't like the way he treated poor Ophelia and her dowdy father, Polonius. I didn't like the way he treated his friends Rosencrantz and Guildenstern and even that pompous but harmless Osric. He was haughty and condescending and too damned moody. Oh, I'm sure he was a smart and clever guy, Hamlet, a complex guy, a deep thinker, a philosopher, blah blah, but he's not my cup of tea. A guy can be witty and bright and philosophical, but still be overly self-centered and even mean. I preferred Herschel as the gravedigger four years ago, especially when he held up Yorick's skull and said it was the skull of "a whoreson mad fellow."

But I had trouble understanding a lot about *Hamlet* when Dad did Claudius, and still didn't when it was over. That's when I had the idea of listening to the CDs, so I could maybe get smarter by hearing the dialogue over and over. I'm not sure that's worked too well. For one thing, there's always a lot going on that I just don't grasp. For another, when you're listening to a CD of a play you don't always know which character's speaking. Sometimes you do, particularly the main characters, but at other times you don't. Many sound alike. I guess if you were someone who was very familiar with the text in advance, like Dad and Herschel or Howie or Jake, you'd know who's talking. I was a little familiar due to helping Dad memorize his lines before rehearsals started, but not enough to make much sense of the whole deal. Maybe it would be better if a soft voice definitively announced each character before they spoke their lines—"*Hamlet*" or "*Horatio*" or "*Gertrude*" and so on. That way a person with limitations, like me, could make better sense of what he was listening to

It's interesting that my father's career goal has been to play all these high-faluting big-time roles—Romeo, Hamlet, Macbeth, Iago, Lear—

whereas Herschel's just wanted to play lesser roles, particularly the more eccentric minor characters like the gravedigger, that nasty little twerp Thersites, the drunken porter in *Macbeth*, the Fool in *Lear*, and even Caliban in *The Tempest*. Of course, when you're a balding sawed-off runt I suppose you can't realistically expect to play a prince or a king or a general or some other muckety-muck.

The big advantage of playing those minor roles, though, is that most of those characters are still taking breaths in and out at the end of the play, whereas the muckety-mucks have all tragically expired one way or another and are all stiff and cold. There's that.

Herschel's a serious little Jew. He goes to temple fairly regularly other than just on the high holidays, mostly for Friday evening Shabbat services. He has his own prayer shawl, his *tallis*, that he brings to services, in a blue felt carrying case with a gold-colored zipper, and wears faithfully. He always goes to the end of the aisle and touches the scrolled Torah with a lower fringed corner of the tallis and then touches that corner to his lips when the worshippers have removed the Torah from the ark and are parading it through the aisles while the congregation belts out the standard songs and prayers on that *constant* but tedious theme of God's greatness. We Jews must think that God is one of those guys, like King Lear, who requires never-ending praise and adulation. Enough "Oh, God, you are, like, SO great and almighty! You're definitely a KING! Oh, there is absolutely NO one like *you!*" is never, it seems, enough. Herschel's a believer. He's even good at doing *shuckling*, that sort of bizarre swaying—bending at the knees and bowing your torso forward and then backward and wagging your head— that many Jews do while *davening*, reciting the prayers.

I remember that about halfway through the run of *Lear,* I asked Herschel if he thinks there's really a god, Yahweh or Adonai or whoever, who's in charge, who sees all and knows all, who's the big and majestic boo -hoo over our little lives, like our faith says. Or are we just alone out there, flailing about—poor, pathetic nothingheads who live for a while, some longer than others, who eat and sleep and eliminate and, hopefully, copulate, and try to get through one dreary day and then another, who sweat and strain with a camera or a paintbrush just to earn a few modest shekels, who have to fuss and fret with Naomi over endless stupid stuff, such as loading and unloading the dishwasher or putting the cans out in a timely manner on garbage day, and then are gone and soon forgotten, sometimes quickly, and in a short time decomposed into fleshless Yoricks? Herschel furrowed his brow and looked irritated and said, "Yes, for Chrissake, God's out there. What the hell's the *matter* with you? Are you a fuckin' atheist?"

I don't know if I'm as serious a Jew, a believer, as Herschel is. I may have been once, sort of anyway, but probably less so now. Helping my father memorize his lines before the rehearsals for *Macbeth* three years ago put a dent in my belief. It was toward the end of the play, in Act V, when Macduff and Old Siward and those guys are about to attack Macbeth's castle, Dunsinane, and settle accounts with the homicidal king, and Macbeth hears women screaming, and my cue line to Dad was, "The q-queen, my lord, is d-dead." My father looked all glum and serious and nodded his head and solemnly, in his stentorian stage voice, recited his character's gloomy lines: "She should have died hereafter ... Tomorrow, and tomorrow, and tomorrow creeps in this petty pace from day to day to the last syllable of recorded time; and all our yesterdays have lighted fools the way to dusty death. Out, out, brief candle! Life's but a walking shadow, a poor player that struts and frets his hour upon the stage, and then is heard from no more. It is a tale told by an idiot, full of sound and fury, signifying nothing." Those lines gave me the heebie-jeebies, and thinking about them still does. "Signifying *nothing!*" Yikes! So I don't know if I'm an atheist, like Herschel said, but if nasty Macbeth was onto something, cynical and disillusioned though he was by later in the play, I don't see how a guy can be too optimistic. How can a guy *not* have a bleak outlook?

What do I know?

Well, what I know for sure is that in so many of the damned plays, the tragedies mostly, the stage is littered with corpses at the end. Macbeth ended up that way, and lost his head as part of the deal. Hamlet ended up a corpse, too, and so did his poor mother, Gertrude. His Uncle Claudius and Laertes became stiffs, too. Polonius and Ophelia had expired earlier, she probably a suicide. Lady Macbeth was reportedly a suicide too. So what was the damned point? Did their frantic little lives mean anything? Was there any larger purpose to those lives and deaths that the average dullard, like me, is supposed to understand? Or is it all indeed just "a tale told by an idiot ... signifying nothing"? If I was confused about such questions before Dad did *Lear*, I'm more confused now that it's done. A big pile of corpses in that one, too. Almost everyone's cold and rigid by the time the curtain goes down—the king, all three of his daughters, Gloucester, Edmund, Cornwall, that nasty little prick Oswald—and loyal Kent's likely next in line. So what's a guy supposed to get from that supposedly great play?

I remember that I asked Dad, after the premier, what he thought *Lear* was saying about why all those sad, tragic things happened. "What's the p-p-point, Dad? I m-mean, is someone c-calling the shots here or what?" He looked directly at me and stood ramrod straight and threw back his shoulders and stared at the ceiling and furrowed his brow and intoned, in that same stentorian voice, "There's a divinity that shapes our ends, rough-hew them how we will." At first I thought he'd said that there's "a divinity that shapes *rear* ends" and recall thinking: *Thank you, kind divinity, for shaping Naomi's rear end. It's been quite comforting during the long winter nights.*

Maybe Rabbi Twersky would know about such ponderings. He's a smart guy. He's isn't patient, at least with me, and not good-looking, but I'm sure he's learned.

Or maybe it's best not to worry so much and just enjoy matzo ball soup while I still can.

THREE

I WAS GLAD TO SEE MY father more animated when I saw him this morning, when I stopped over to bring him the Big Breakfast he'd requested. When I opened the door, he looked up at me from his La-Z-Boy and grinned foolishly. "Sirrah," he said cheerfully, "how dost? How dost, good sirrah?" I noticed that his eyes seemed less murky than the last time. I also noticed that the TV volume was unusually high.

But then he got weird. When I handed him the white McDonald's bag, he practically ripped it open and immediately devoured the biscuit in two big bites and then both the sausage and the hash-brown patty and washed it all down with huge gulps of McDonald's coffee. There were crumbs from the biscuit in his whiskers. Then he tackled those horrid scrambled eggs, and when they were gone he slathered butter on the stack of three hotcakes and poured the entire plastic container of syrup over them and furiously shoveled them down his gullet. He didn't offer me a bite. When he'd gulped down the last morsel he wiped his chin on his sleeve and looked up at me, smiling foolishly. "Breakfast was good, kid," he said. "A veritable feast, as it were. So when's the next repast?" He sat upright in his chair and assumed his haughty King Lear pose, chin pointed upwards, and raised his right hand high, index finger extended. "Dinner, ho, *dinner!*" he intoned loudly. His voice was still hoarse because of all the shouting he'd had to do in each performance, in Act I and then again in Act III, in the heath storm scene, to be heard above the simulated sounds of rain and thunder.

"You okay, Dad?" I asked. He furrowed his brow and raised his right index finger to his lips and shook his head and pointed with his left hand toward the TV. *The Jerry Springer Show* was on and Jerry was talking to some skinny, heavily tattooed guy who'd slept with his girlfriend's cousin. "I dunno," the guy said when Jerry, dressed in a navy-blue sport jacket and pink shirt with no tie, provocatively asked how that happened. "We was kissin' and stuff and next thing I know I'm, like, all naked in her bed." Pretty soon the girlfriend came out from backstage and the guy sheepishly confessed to her what occurred and she blubbered a bit on cue and then the chunky cousin was brought out and she, eyes blazing, wagged a stubby finger at the girlfriend and yelled, "He don't love you no more. He loves ME now! Get *over* it!" The two women started flailing away at each other with wild overhead swings, few of which landed with much effect, and a beefy black-shirted security guy, stifling a grin, stepped between them to break it up. The young audience members commenced to pump their upraised fists and shout "JER-RY! JER-RY!" and my father, grinning hugely, pumped his right fist and loudly shouted "JER-RY!" along with them. Then he hunched his shoulders and bent forward and covered his mouth with both hands and giggled like a silly little girl for a few moments.

On the one hand, that sight was disturbing, worrying. *Was this my father?* I again wondered. Was this the Herbert Dickman I've known, the serious guy, the well-known classically-trained actor with an M.F.A. from the Yale School of Drama, with a fat resumé and tons of accolades, the guy who'd just finished playing Lear and had also done the title roles in *Hamlet* and *Macbeth* and who'd played Iago in *Othello,* and Willy Loman too? Was this the man who'd always memorized all his lines before rehearsals started? And now he's reduced to *this?*

On the other hand, it was interesting, even amusing. There was my old man, a seventy-two-year-old *alter kacker* who's always lived his life as though he had a rod up his ass, oh-so important and well-regarded, always full of himself, with my many photographs of him in his various big roles on the walls all over his damned house, like a shrine to Herbert Dickman the Great Thespian, and in the albums I've put together for each play, prominently displayed in the middle shelf of the living room oak bookcase with the title of each play in 72-point bold capital letters—**HAMLET, OTHELLO, DEATH OF A SALESMAN** and so on—and here he is now, a pathetic old man in a ratty green bathrobe, his skinny calves sticking out from the bottom, crumbs in his whiskers, white hair askew, smelling bad, bent over, giggling at an idiotic TV show. And he still has a knot on his head from that noggin clunk. His forehead and both eyes still appear a bit discolored, purplish. At least he'd laughed a little, crazy though that was.

"D-D-Dad," I said, "why are you watching this c-crap?"

He stared at me, his eyes now a bit clearer. "Let me tell you something, Julius," he said, quietly, after a moment. "All the world's a stage—a stage of fools, if you will. It's all theater, high or low. We're all just those poor players strutting and fretting our hour upon that stage, and then are heard from no more." He paused and seemed more serious. He looked away. "My hour's over now, son," he said, softly. "I'm done strutting. I'll be heard from no more. I failed at the big one, you know. I tried, kiddo, but I failed." He paused again and grinned. "But yay for Jerry, huh?" he went on. "He's still out there strutting, huh?"

I looked at him. "Dad," I said, "what are you t-talking about? You've had a g-g-great career. You're a b-big success."

He shook his head and looked more serious. "No," he said, again softly. "Not this last time. Playing Lear was going to be the capstone to my many years treading the boards. But my big role eluded me, son. I couldn't get it right. I just couldn't … grasp my character well enough. Maybe I got close once or twice, but that's all. Scofield definitely got it. Derek Jacobi did, I think. Those two Ians, Holm and McKellen, probably. Gielgud. Others, I'm sure. But not me. I tried, son, but I failed." He nodded his head and looked away. He yawned and vigorously scratched his scrotum. "Oh, well. Let me tell you something, Julius," he said, more loudly. "It's all bullshit, anyway. Just a big … *nothing*."

I was startled to hear him say that and wanted to ask him what he meant, why he thought he'd failed, and who most of those guys he'd named were. Paul Scofield I knew from an incredibly dreary and depressing black-and-white film of *King Lear*, by some guy named Brook, that Dad had intently watched over and over while preparing to do his role. I watched it with him just once, and that was way more than enough; it was *so* bleak and joyless and the whole deal took place in a cold, wintry, monochromatic world. Plus, every damned character looked majorly sour and expression-less, as though chronically constipated, and most spoke in dread monotones, as though every ounce of joy had been sucked out of their guts by an industrial-sized vacuum cleaner. Watching it almost made me want to jump off a bridge.

I didn't recognize the names of those other guys he'd mentioned. But before I could ask, I saw his eyes flutter and he soon fell asleep in his La-Z-Boy. I turned off the TV and covered him with his white afghan and studied him. His mouth was open and he seemed to be taking shallow breaths. A trail of saliva drooled from the lower left corner of his mouth. He appeared smaller than I'd known him to be. I wanted to brush the crumbs from his whiskers, but didn't want to disturb and maybe awaken him. I wanted him to sleep. I felt affection, but also worry. I gathered up the remnants of his McDonald's breakfast and took them to the kitchen. I placed the dirty dishes piled in the sink in the dishwasher and disposed of the cardboard container of what was apparently his meal from last night, a Lean Cuisine Spaghetti with Meat Sauce frozen dinner, and also trashed the two empty giant-sized Doritos bags that were on the counter, next to his Metamucil.

I had a memory of another time when my father'd downed an entire large bag of Doritos. It was in early June this year, on my parents' anniversary. I'd gone over to his house for another of our monthly Sunday morning brunches and he was in the living room, again in that green bathrobe, sitting in his La-Z-Boy, holding the bag in his left hand and delicately extracting Doritos, one at a time, and shoving them into his mouth with his right. He was listening to his Whiffenpoofs record—a red vinyl LP with a photo on the jacket of fourteen clean-cut young men in tuxedos with crisp white shirts and vests and white bowties, mouths opened wide. Dad listened to that album every year on their anniversary but he never told me, when I asked, why he did that. I have a lingering childhood memory that he and Mom used to listen to it together now and again. The Whiffenpoofs were, and maybe still are, an *a cappela* singing group from Yale. What my parents mostly listened to, and what Dad was listening to that Sunday morning, was their signature song, "The Whiffenpoof Song." He'd stopped eating when it came on, and had set the almost-empty bag on the floor next to his chair. His eyes were closed and he was wagging his right index finger and silently mouthing the lyrics along with the recording:

> *To the tables down at Mory's*
> *To the place where Louie dwells*
> *To the dear old Temple bar we love so well,*
> *Sing the Whiffenpoofs assembled, with their glasses raised on high,*
> *And the magic of their singing casts its spell.*
>
> *Yes, the magic of their singing of the songs we love so well,*
> *"Shall I Wasting" and "Mavourneen" and the rest.*
> *We will serenade our Louie while life and voice shall last*
> *Then we'll pass and be forgotten with the rest.*

My first memory of hearing that song was when I was three or maybe four years old. I remember that I felt sad and got weepy when I heard one of the verses:

> *We are poor little lambs who have lost our way*

—25—

Baa, baa, baa.
We are little black sheep who have gone astray
Baa, baa, baa.

It was, I guess, the image of those poor lost little lambs with their *baa, baa, baa* that saddened my childish heart. I remember that Mom noticed I was sad and went "Aww!" and held me for a nice while.

"Then we'll pass and be forgotten with the rest." Now *there's* a happy damned thought.

Before leaving, I walked into the hallway between the living room and the bedrooms and looked at the black-metal-framed photographs on the wall—photos I'd taken, and of which I was proud for my composition and lighting and exposure—of my father in some of his big roles, all from dress rehearsals. There he was four years ago as Claudius in *Hamlet*, with a grizzled silvery beard and a bejeweled crown on his head and looking oh-so regal and self-important. And there he was as Macbeth, looking startled and maybe frightened upon hallucinating the ghost of murdered Banquo. There he was as poor doomed Willy Loman two years ago, brow furrowed. There he was as scheming, shifty-eyed Iago. And, at the end of the hall, there was my most recent photo, of Dad as Lear in the storm scene on the heath in Act III, inside the hovel, eyes wild in his madness and white hair askew, with Herschel as the soaked, shivering Fool and Howie as kneeling half-naked Poor Tom—Edgar in disguise—both staring up, wide-eyed, concerned, at Dad. That was my favorite of all the photos I'd done of my old man.

Looking at that last photo, something occurred to me: Where was Mrs. Lear, Queen Lear? There was no mention of her in the play. Why not? Had she kicked the bucket? If so, how? Or had Lear maybe impetuously dismissed her, the way he did poor Cordelia? Maybe he'd asked her to flatter him, to tell how very much she adored him and how unbelievably wonderful he was, to say how much she loved him, and she, like Cordelia, refused to go along with his childish request. Or maybe she'd just had enough of her husband's volatile temper and told him to pound sand. Maybe she'd had it with his riotous knights hanging around the castle, eating all the food in the pantry and drinking all the liquor and farting and burping and scratching their privates and yelling obscenities and insults— "Thou art a boil, a plague-sore, an embossed *carbuncle!*"—and telling raunchy jokes and playing grabass. For that matter, I wondered if there'd been more than one Queen Lear. Maybe Goneril and Regan had one mother and Cordelia a different one. That could explain why she, the youngest, was so different from her two horrible older sisters, so much more loving and forgiving. Or perhaps they'd each had a different mother, like Adam, Hoss and Little Joe did on *Bonanza*. Maybe Lear, like Ben Cartwright, was thrice-widowed, each wife tragically dying in childbirth. *Oy gevalt!* In any case, it just seemed that Queen Lear's absence was like a big hole, a gap, in the play, but we don't get to know the story behind that absence.

Or maybe Mrs. Lear ended it herself, like my mother did. If so, it could be that nobody talked about her death, just swept it under the rug. A taboo subject. I was twelve when Mom overdosed, and for almost thirty years now I've never known why she abandoned me—her only damned child. She didn't leave a note. I don't know if my father knows why, but if so he's never said. I used to ask him about it, but stopped. All he ever did when I asked was to look away and mutter some obscure thing that was neither helpful nor enlightening. "Well, people have their demons," he said once. Another time he said, "The heart is a lonely hunter, son." Or he'd just throw out Bard quotes. "The long day's task is done, and we must sleep," he mouthed on one occasion, noting oh-so proudly that the line was Antony's. Another time he said, "Life, being weary of these worldly bars, never lacks power to dismiss itself." I don't know where that one came from, and don't care. That was the last time I brought up the subject. The old man just won't talk about his first wife's—*my mother's!*—demise. So why should I torture myself?

So if he'd toss that damned robe, I'd be thrilled.

What's most galling is that my father rarely even mentioned Mom after he started dating Miriam, less than two years after Mom passed. They'd known each other for a while from theater stuff. I know that Miriam had auditioned for a part in *Julius Caesar*. Dad got to be Marc Antony, but she didn't get a role. I wasn't at all happy when they got hitched. She and I didn't click. I never warmed to her and vice versa. We tolerated each other, at best, and I suspect she wouldn't have minded much if I'd decided, as a teenager, to leave home and move to Tierra del Fuego. I didn't like it that she replaced all Mom's china and silverware and re-upholstered the sofa, a horrid baby-vomit yellowish-brown. Dad apparently didn't mind; he may not have even noticed. And what's worse is that Miriam had the gall to criticize my mother. "Well," she said, in my hearing, "I can't say much for Sarah's taste in upholstery." The one thing I'm glad about is that they never had kids together. There's that.

As I was walking to my car, I had the fleeting thought that I envied the skinny guy on *Springer* who'd slept with his girlfriend's cousin. At least he got to actually do it. Fantasies about Lydia were as far as I got or likely ever will.

Before going home, I stopped at Starbucks for a tall white chocolate mocha. There was an interesting, pretty young woman sitting two tables down from me. I'd seen her there before. She was alone at a table by the window, with an open Macbook Pro. She was slightly hunched over and had a brown coat draped over her shoulders and was sitting perfectly still, staring out the window, brow furrowed, right hand grasping a white paper cup. Her long brown hair was in a ponytail, held in by a lime-green scrunchie. She looked like she was thinking about something serious. I wondered what was going on inside that sweet head. For a moment I thought of approaching and asking if everything was okay. Maybe I'd reach over and gently grasp one of her hands in both of mine and squeeze just a bit to reassure her, to let her know that I was concerned, that I cared about her and wanted to help with whatever was troubling her soul. "What's going on today?" I'd ask in a soothing, masculine tone, sans stutter. "If you'd like to talk, I'm here to listen." She'd cautiously hesitate for a bit, but then see that I was sincere and caring, non-threatening and non-judgmental, and she'd open up. I'd listen to her troubles and concerns, looking always directly into her pretty eyes, nodding now and again, going "Um-hmm" and saying things like "I see" and "That must be hard" and "How painful!" or even "Help me to understand what you mean by that," to show that I heard her and to encourage her to keep talking. If I found her tale of woe boring or silly or petty in any way, I wouldn't say so. I'd just keep looking concerned and interested and empathetic. I'd maintain eye contact. I'd furrow my brow a bit and keep nodding. Maybe after a while she'd be so appreciative that someone finally cared and actually listened that she'd suggest that I come back to her apartment with her, where she'd rip off the lime-green scrunchie and shake her head to one side in an enchanting feminine gesture to let that lovely long brown hair fall free to her waist and then ask me to make beautiful love to her. I'd do that, if she wished.

FOUR

THIS DAMNED INSOMNIA is making me crazy. I'd hoped that the Ambien that Ansfield prescribed would help, and it did, a little, but also somehow made me feel jumpy. At least last night I didn't obsess too much about Naomi—why I stay with her—when I popped awake at two-thirty. I did a little, because of her predictable disproportionate outrage earlier over the Luigi's takeout screw-up, but not horribly.

Instead, my mind zoomed ahead to my doctor's appointment next Wednesday for my annual physical. Ansfield's office is on the eighth floor, which means elevator. Damn! The horrible thing about the elevator in that building is that it jerks a bit each time it starts moving, and then there's a pause when the damned thing stops at a floor before the door finally— *finally!*—opens. That's maybe the worst, that pause. It's probably not that long, but it seems long. It seems like forever. *What if the damned door doesn't open?* is what I always worry whenever the elevator stops. *What if I'm stuck?* During that moment, my heart beats faster and my face feels flushed. The main horrible thing is that if an elevator is stuck, you have zero control over how long it'll be before it gets unstuck. It could be minutes or hours.

I'm not sure what would be worse, being alone in a stuck elevator or being with people. Either prospect is a nightmare. Being with people is probably worse, particularly if it's a lot of people. What if we get stuck and they're all calm and collected and I'm a freaking-out mess, red-faced and breathing hard and sweating and maybe shaking or even crying? What if one of my fellow passengers is a pleasant-looking young woman whom I maybe briefly coveted and perhaps fantasized about and now she sees me as a ridiculous quaking neurotic and feels pity or even contempt? That wouldn't be good. So being alone would be better. At least that way a panicking guy can move around a bit and not be hemmed in, and if he weeps or begs God for help or pisses his pants nobody will be any the wiser.

Well, I guess I could just take the stairs. Eight flights, that's not horrible. It's not like having to go to the top of the Empire State Building or the Sears Tower. If anyone asks, I can lie and say I'm doing it for the exercise. So maybe doing stairs would be the better part of valor.

It would be nice if, when I awakened in the middle of the night, it could be more gradual and peaceful. I'd like it if I'd just wake up and feel warm and cozy and comfortable for a bit, even just a few minutes, before my mind started accelerating into overdrive. It would be nice to have some good thoughts or nice memories before the more worrisome ones started bombarding my overheated brain. Instead, I always just pop awake and immediately—*immediately!*—commence being assaulted with worries and negativities. It's upsetting. Sometimes it's simple worries, like what I have to do tomorrow, but more commonly it's more weighty issues, like why I put up with my girlfriend.

One nice thing I thought about when awake last night was Celeste. Sweet Celeste. I remembered staring at her, admiringly, during the table read for *King Lear*, and recalled the lovely moment when I took my first photo of her then. She was reading one of Cordelia's early lines: "Unhappy that I am, I cannot heave my heart into my mouth." I liked that line when I heard her say it, in her soft and feminine stage voice. I didn't understand it then and still don't, not completely, but it has a nice ring to it. I focused on her face in my viewfinder as she looked up at me after saying that, and immediately had the happy revelation that she, Celeste, is one of those rare women whom the camera naturally adores.

That's happened only a few times over the years, mostly at weddings I've done and once at a bar mitzvah with the petite mother of the sullen thirteen-year-old pimply-faced kid whose day it was. That mother seemed dull and ordinary enough and certainly didn't have an especially notable mug in general—a bit pasty, in fact, with a weak chin—but as soon as I saw her face through my viewfinder, I knew immediately that she was special, image-wise. I recall that I even sort of fell in love with the woman—Sylvia, her name was—just from taking her picture during the luncheon. She may have been a tedious dullard or a vindictive madwoman or some other horror as a human being, but her face as seen through my 28-105 mm. lens was enchanting. It seemed to glow with a special feminine charm that wasn't there at all when viewed in real life, so to speak.

But, of course, it came to nothing. I talked with Sylvia briefly—some silliness about how proud she must feel about her accomplished son, who was now a man in the eyes of our faith, ready and able to assume the duties of an observant Jew—but could tell she was impatient with my stutter and wanted our conversation to be over quickly and never saw her after that day. I made a five-by-seven print of Sylvia after the bar mitzvah so I could look at her face during my tough awake nights, to maybe savor a moment of beauty, even perfection, but it wasn't the same; she was just okay in the photo—better than in real life, I suppose, though nowhere near as sublime as when viewed through my lens. So, lying awake, I've had to be content with conjuring her through-the-viewfinder image now and again, and that's worked okay.

And I've often conjured Celeste's perfect face, too: those crinkly blue-green eyes, those delicate cheekbones, that smallish mouth with full lips, that feminine nose, her straight white teeth—all framed by short light-brown hair. Some woman. Thinking of her last night, I reached over and snuggled against Naomi's backside and ran my hand over the curve of her flannel-nightgown-covered right hip and happily fantasized that she was Celeste.

Celeste. Now and again I wonder if I could ever have a chance with her, if I were ever free of Naomi and she were available. She's not. Herschel told me that she's married to some lucky *goy* named Andrew, a certified public accountant—whatever that is. But that wondering doesn't last long. Who am I kidding? Celeste's another Lydia—*way* out of my class. Why would a beautiful, talented, well-regarded actress like her, who's played Cordelia, and Juliet when she was younger, and was the understudy for Lady Macbeth, give so much as a glance to a nothinghead *noodnik* like me? It's ridiculous to even ponder.

My one actual encounter with Celeste wasn't exactly a moment of glory. It was at the cast party after *Lear* had ended and I was taking candid photos and some posed ones and she approached, holding a long-stemmed glass half-full of white wine, and pointed a delicate index finger at my camera and asked why I was taking pictures now and had earlier, at the table reads and rehearsals and so on. I felt stunned that she was talking to me. "Well," I said, "I'm t-t-taking p-pictures for my father's, uh, my d-dad's, uh, album. We d-do an album for every p-p-play he's in. Also, to hang in his h-house." She smiled. "I see," she replied. "So you're his official memorialist? His photographic Boswell, as it were?" I just nodded. I couldn't think of anything else to say. My face felt warm and my heart was beating fast. I'm sure she could see how *farmisht* I was. After a moment, Celeste just nodded and said, "Well, that sounds like a nice thing. Good for you." Then she looked up at me and smiled again and walked away. I stared at her curvy butt for as long as possible without being too obvious or obnoxious.

I was irritated with my father at that party. Just after my nice encounter with Celeste, he gestured me over and directed me to take a photo of him with two of the actresses, Jewel and Alexis, who'd played Goneril and Regan. He stood between the pretty pair, posing, and put an arm around each of them and grinned. He was standing quite erect. His silver mane gleamed and his gray eyes were bright. Still, I noticed that he was wincing a bit, probably from his back injury. Both Jewel and Alexis smiled hugely, with very white teeth, and Alexis looked up at Dad adoringly. It was irritating because he'd done the same thing—posed oh-so proudly and gloriously with one or more actresses at almost every damned cast party before that. He even posed with four women after *Othello*, including the two beauties who'd played Desdemona and Emilia. I then had to make five-by-seven prints and some eight-by-tens and stick them into his albums. I don't know if Dad ever did more with any of those women than just pose for a photo.

I wonder, as far as that goes, if he ever shtupped pretty Elspeth. She was ambitious Lady Mac to his Macbeth. He'd asked me to take a picture of them at the cast party and, again, he snaked his arm tightly around her thin shoulder and then rubbed that shoulder sweetly and even squeezed a little, and she slid her arm tightly around his waist. She briefly leaned her tawny head against him and smiled mysteriously and closed her eyes. There were, I thought, vibes between them. But what do I know?

Not once did my father ever thank me for doing all that. Nor has he ever closely studied one of my pictures and commented one way or another on its quality as a photo. Instead, he'd maybe say something like, "Well, well, what a handsome rogue. Wouldn't you agree?"

Who's this Boswell person? I remember wondering after my brief encounter with Celeste at that party. Maybe he was a photographer too. That's what I've been doing on and off for almost twenty years, since I took pictures for the Roosevelt High School yearbook. It's a good deal. I'm an assistant to a woman, Liz Feldman, who's the head of Hadassah at Beth El and runs a photography business. She has a horrible blondish wig that now and again slips to the left side of her head and the phoniest big smile, showing yellowing teeth, when dealing with clients. She also has an off-putting laugh, *when* she laughs; it sounds like a cocker spaniel choking on a bone. Liz does most of the standard photography at the actual main events, the wedding and bar or bat mitzvah ceremonies and so on, including the formals, and I usually help with lighting, lenses, tripods and the like and take some photos, including backups or photos from different locations or angles than Liz's photos.

But she doesn't like to spend much time at wedding receptions or bar mitzvah parties. She comes to those events and stays for the first couple of hours, at most, and does some standard pictures and then packs her gear and exits. My job is to then stay late and do more pictures, mostly candids of the principals as well as of the dancing, toasts, table shots, bouquet tosses, various groups, and so on. It's good because I don't have to talk much. I get to look at women, including inebriated bridesmaids now and again, and certainly fantasize about some, mostly sexual fantasies featuring a liquored-up and horny maid of honor or other attendant losing her inhibitions and seducing me, or at least giving off unmistakable vibes that she's interested. Such a sensual encounter's always been my goal, though it's never happened—so far, anyway. But I don't have to interact with them much, or at all. That way they won't know how pathetic I am, though, of course, they might suspect that

The one success I had from my photography, I suppose, was meeting Naomi. I was helping Liz at Elise's bat mitzvah at Beth El almost four years ago, and immediately developed a little crush on Naomi. I'd seen her a few times before at the temple, but never talked to her. She was attractive, with her hair up, showing cute little ears with tiny lobes, and wearing a nice pink-and-white patterned dress. I took some candids and a few posed shots of her at the luncheon and party and she seemed to like that, maybe felt flattered. We talked a bit, and I recall being enchanted with her lilting voice. I even liked her hooked Yid shnoz. I surprised myself, toward the end of the evening, by asking her if she'd like to have coffee. We did, at my favorite Starbucks, and then started going out. I liked that she did most of the talking. She even, after four weeks, initiated our first copulation, which was quite pleasant. I recall that Naomi didn't actually kvetch about much or start giving me a mouth until we'd been going out for three or maybe even four months. After another five months, she suggested that I move in with her and the kids. I'd been living alone in a modest one-bedroom apartment in an eight-unit older building on the east side for years, and was mostly fine with that, but was so smitten by then that I thought it would be fine to change my circumstances, and agreed. I thought it would be nice to have a warm, loving woman to sleep next to every night instead of *always* being alone with the damned insomnia, particularly in winter with those endless, cold, dark nights.

So doing the events photography, even though some of the weddings lately have been disturbing, and helping Perry out with painting jobs here and there helps my checking account from drying out. I don't at all have a big profession that people can point to, like my father did, but it's something. I guess it is.

Sometimes at night, next to my asleep girlfriend, I wonder if Celeste the woman is as good as Cordelia the character. I don't know Celeste well at all, but I've thought a lot about the character she just played, Cordelia the Good. Well, who's *really* that good? Who'd be that caring, that loving, to a difficult, petulant father who'd treated her so badly, who'd pitched a childish fit and cursed her and disinherited her and said he never wanted to see her again just because she refused to flatter him? "Better thou hadst not been born," he snarls in Act I, "than not to have pleased me better." Yikes! Imagine hearing *that*. I doubt I could ever be as good a son as Cordelia was a daughter. I'd like to be, but doubt I have it in me. So is Celeste that good? Or is she just another crusty Naomi in real life? I'll never know. I'll almost surely never see her again, now that Dad's done with theater. Why would I?

Well, I'm *glad* he's done with theater. I can say that for sure. I've liked hanging around and seeing the plays with Dad in his big roles—*Macbeth* was probably my favorite, I guess, with those deceptive witches and their prophecies, other than that depressing "Tomorrow and tomorrow" spiel—and, mostly, getting to see and photograph the actresses and other female theater types, but having to be Dad's official photographer and also help him memorize his lines before rehearsals started has been a pain in the ass—a very *unappreciated* pain in the ass.

And I'm especially glad that *King Lear* is over. Overjoyed, really. I keep thinking that. It's a huge relief. I've never been so happy when one of Dad's plays ended. *Lear* put me in a bad mood, mostly. I'm sure it's a great play, a "treasure of Western literature," as Dad said, but it's way too bleak, too hopeless, and too many damned corpses at the end. And Cordelia's death is far and away the worst! Once, earlier this fall, while I was painting an apartment for Perry and playing my Naxos CD of *King Lear* and listening to the end, when Cordelia's been hanged and her father has the delusion that she's still alive, that her lips are moving—"*Look there! Look there!*"—just before he himself dies, I had to turn off my Sony.

And I guess I'm not smart enough to grasp a complex old guy like Lear. I get it that he was hugely upset with his three daughters, that he thought they were ungrateful, and I can understand that a father might be really angry with his kids for a while. But that guy went so *totally* nutso bonkers, so quickly, and stayed that way for such a long time, and talked crazy and adorned himself with flowers and weeds—fumiter and hemlock and nettle and even, appropriately, *cuckoo* flowers. It all just seemed so … disproportionate. And why? That's what's puzzling. Did the old fart have Alzheimer's or some other dementia? Maybe hardened arteries? Had he somehow gone psychotic? Bad concussion? Or was he just a very difficult and egotistical person, and had been his whole life, and got more that way the older he got? I don't know if the answers to those questions are obvious to others, but they're not to me.

And what's the takeaway? That's what eludes me, puzzles me, the most. Lear and Cordelia nicely reconciled toward the end and then she got murdered and then he died. So is a guy supposed to come away with the idea that love and redemption triumph at the end, so there's some hope, even though sad death may follow? Or is it that maybe there's really *nothing*, no love or redemption, just absurdity and cold oblivion, and that's it? Was my old man right when he said, "It's all bullshit"?

What do I know?

Still, I liked parts of *Lear*. I definitely like good old Edgar best of all, particularly when he's in disguise as Poor Tom. I like loyal tough-guy Kent and the Fool and, of course, wonderful Cordelia. My absolute favorite moment in the play was when Cordelia's rescued her wacko father and is taking care of him and he awakens from deep sleep after his rage and madness have passed and finally recognizes his youngest daughter and tells her that if she has poison for him he'll take it because he knows that she has "cause" to hate him, whereas her sisters, Goneril and Regan, didn't have reasons to treat him as horribly as they did—or, at least, as horribly as he *thought* they did. Cordelia just says, "No cause, no cause." That blew me away. *No cause!* Are you kidding? Just thinking about that line makes me shake my head in amazement. I can't imagine any real woman saying that, much less my girlfriend. With that harpy, everything's a cause.

Like last night. We'd ordered Italian carryout from Luigi's. It was just the two of us because the kids were with their father. Naomi'd told me what she wanted—the seafood tetrazzini with spinach fettucini noodles, with those little shrimps that she so loves—and my task was to call in the order on my way home and then pick it up. But when I called, I screwed up and ordered a different pasta dish for her. I had a brain fart and couldn't remember seafood tetrazzini and could only remember that she wanted some pasta dish with green noodles, so asked for that. When I got home and she took the foil lid off her container to put it in the micro to warm up, she examined it closely and furrowed her brow. "Hey," she shrilled, "*this* isn't what I ordered. Did you tell them seafood tetrazzini? With the shrimp? There's no shrimp in this." I knew right away I'd screwed up but instinctively nodded my head. "Yes," I lied. "Of c-c-course that's what I ordered. I know what you l-like."

She stared at me and scowled. "Well, goddamn it, I'm majorly pissed. I'm going to find out about this." She looked at the receipt to see the phone number of Luigi's and dialed it on her cellphone. "I want to talk to the manager!" she growled. After a moment he must have come on because she started right in on him. "Listen, I'm very unhappy. My boyfriend ordered the seafood tetrazzini and you sent some other crappy pasta instead. I had a very hard day at work, you know, with aggravation from my *schmuck* boss, and I was really looking forward to the shrimp, and there's no shrimp, and I'm *upset.* This has happened to me before…no, not with you, but other places, and I'm really sick of it … The order was under the name Julius … No, not *Julian*, JULIUS! … Yes, I'll hold." She cupped her hand and whispered to me, "He's checking the order." After a minute her face darkened even more and her already-shrill voice grew shriller. "Well, he told me that he *did* order the tetrazzini. I don't care what it says. The idiot taking the order must have gotten it wrong.…No, it's too late to get a different order. It's too damned late and I'm tired and hungry … Okay. Yeah, yeah. Goodbye." She put the phone on the counter, not gently, and turned to me. "They're going to send a gift certificate. The little twerp doesn't think they screwed up, but he apologized anyway. He didn't sound too goddamn *sincere*, though."

Listening to that exchange while twirling spaghetti around my fork, I felt bad that the manager was on the receiving end of Naomi's misplaced wrath. It occurred to me, after she hung up, that I should have been a man and spoken up. "Alright, Naomi," I should have said with masculine authority, sans stutter, "Put the damned phone down and listen. It was *my* fault, okay? I screwed up the order, okay? I'm sorry. I'm *very* sorry. We all make mistakes, right? You do too. So lay *off* the guy, for God's sake. It was *not* their fault."

But later last night, in bed, I thought that I'm glad I *didn't* speak up. I'm sorry that poor manager got tongue-lashed, but my thought was: *Better him than me.* I certainly don't need another debit added to Naomi's list of grievances. When it comes to my shortcomings or deficiencies, my many supposed acts of omission or commission, the woman has the memory of an elephant. Suppose I'd admitted, afterward, that I'd messed up her order. If somehow I stay with her for another three decades we'll both be gray and stooped and one night we'll order takeout from Luigi's and, as we're eating, her wrinkled face will harden and she'll glare at me from across the table, eyes blazing, and wag a bony finger at me and croak, "Hey, remember that time thirty years ago when you fucked up my seafood tetrazzini order and didn't have the balls to admit right off you'd screwed up? I haven't forgotten that! What a pathetic schlemiel you were then, and, by God, still *are!*" Do I need that?

For that matter, I wish I had the gonads to cut spaghetti instead of twirling it around the fork. Cutting is my clear preference, but Naomi always rebukes me if I do. "Hey," she'll say, with her wonted sour look, the right corner of her mouth downturned. "Refined human beings do not *cut* their spaghetti. Show some goddamn *class* once in a while!" If I had a pair, I'd just ignore her and keep on cutting and maybe, after a moment, sit up ramrod straight and look her directly in the eyes with a neutral though quite manly expression while chewing, while at the same time positioning the edge of my fork to cut the next bite. "Naomi," I'd say, slowly and deliberately in an authoritative voice, with no stutter, "I *am* refined and I *choose* to cut. Now you need to back off and let … it … *GO*. Understand?"

FIVE

LAST NIGHT, LYING IN BED wide awake yet again, I had the idea that I should take Benji to Izzy's some Saturday when I don't have a wedding or bar mitzvah to do and I have occasional lunch with Herschel and a few of the other actor guys, Herschel's buddies, as I did yesterday. Maybe he'd like that. Maybe he'd like the *menschkeit* and appreciate the opportunity to get away from the aggravation of his home life with Naomi and Elise. It would have to be a weekend when he isn't with his father. He wouldn't have to talk much, or at all. I think he'd like just hanging out with the guys. Of course, I'd have to warn him first about Herschel's disgusting eating habits.

Yesterday, Herschel got what he almost always gets: the Hear-O-Israel, a half-pound monster sandwich on rye with corned beef, pastrami, salami, pepper beef, Swiss cheese, coleslaw and Thousand Island dressing. He's said more than once that he appreciates that Izzy's corned beef and other meats are hand-carved. What was disgusting yesterday was that Herschel, as soon as Magda brought our orders, opened his sandwich and doused it with Dijon Grey Poupon mustard. So he had both mustard *and* Thousand Island dressing! I had to sit there and watch my quasi-dwarf cousin, his blue beanie yarmulke perched precariously atop his balding head, held on with a bobby pin, clutching his fat Hear-O-Israel in both stubby hands and opening his mouth wide to stuff huge bites into it. As usual, he dripped mustard and dressing back onto his plate or the table and even the sleeve of his gray hooded sweatshirt. He washed down those big sandwich bites with gulps of Dr. Brown's Cel-Ray Tonic. At one point, Herschel got a caraway seed stuck between two of his lower teeth and he somehow worked the thing out with the tip of his tongue and then rolled it around in his mouth and spat it out onto his plate. Well, the plate's what he aimed at but he missed and the seed bounced off the edge of the formica table and onto the black-and-white-tiled floor.

So I'll have to warn Benji, to maybe soften the horror.

I can't fault Herschel for rarely varying his order, except when he's in the mood for a bowl of Isadore's Mishmosh. I'm the same. I almost always get a cup of matzo ball soup and a corned beef on rye—Izzy's great hard-crusted caraway-seeded rye bread, particularly wonderful because it's double-baked: baked until almost ready, cooled, and then finished for a shorter time in a hot oven just before being sliced into inch-thick diagonals—with a side of potato salad and a chocolate phosphate that's flavored with, I believe, Bosco syrup. I'm not sure why I think he uses Bosco; maybe I dreamt that. Sometimes I get a bowl of soup instead of a cup, as in my recent dream. That's my only variety, other than the two times I ordered Izzy's great corned beef hash. I sometimes think I *should* get something else—maybe a roast beef sandwich or a hot pastrami or the Classic Reuben. Well, not that; I detest sauerkraut. So does my father. That's one of the few things we have in common, other than loving Groucho and his brothers. But I like my usual.

Naomi always asks what I had at Izzy's, and sometimes I tell her the truth but more often don't. If I told her that I always ordered the same thing each time, she'd give me a mouth. "Why the hell don't you try something *different* now and again?" she'd shrill. "What the hell's the *matter* with you?" Maybe she'd call me a schlemiel again. So I avoid that particular rebuke. Yesterday, when she asked what I ate, I lied: "Oh, I had a c-cup of cabbage b-b-borscht and a hard salami s-sandwich on challah." She thought about that for a few seconds and then nodded. "Well, that sounds okay," she said. "Good for you."

Loving Groucho and his brothers is a nice bond Dad and I've shared. We started doing that on one Sunday morning a month when I was, I think, nine or ten. Sometimes Mom sat in with us, at first. She liked cinnamon raisin bagels best, but never schmeared her bagels with cream cheese. She, too, liked lox. Yuck! I remember clearly that *Animal Crackers* was her favorite. I remember her tinkly laugh at her favorite scenes, including when Groucho, as Captain Geoffrey Spaulding, the famous African explorer, is describing his latest expedition and says, "One morning I shot an elephant in my pajamas. How he got in my pajamas, I don't know." I was too young, at first, to get most of Groucho's and Chico's puns, but I liked Harpo's sight gags and facial expressions, especially his trademark "Gookie" with the raised eyebrows and puffy cheeks and crossed eyes and mouth opened wide into an "O" and tongue curled upward. After Mom's death, Dad and I stopped doing our Sunday bagels and Marx Brothers brunches for a few years. I'm not sure why. I don't remember how we started back—I think it was my idea—but I'm glad we did.

I tried watching *Animal Crackers* with Naomi once, during our first year together. She tittered now and again, which was fine, but afterward said that she found their humor "way too juvenile." She didn't even smile, much less laugh, at "One morning I shot an elephant . . .."

Naomi. She can't be too critical of me for my deli preferences because at least I always remember to bring her two Joyva Halvah Bars from Izzy's, one marble and one chocolate-covered. She likes those. She's a big-time sesame fan. So there's that. Once I forgot, but lied and told her that they'd run out. I think she believed me because, though she looked at me askance, her face a bit hard, she didn't say anything.

Yesterday, I told Herschel and the guys that Naomi'd called me a schlemiel because of the Culver's incident and my cousin furrowed his brow. "I think the dumb broad got that wrong," he said. "A schlemiel's a guy that always spills his soup. You're more of a *shlimazel*—the guy who the schlemiel spills his soup on." He paused and gave me a sideways look. "Naomi!" he said, shaking his head. "Why do you care what *she* thinks?"

Just then Izzy shuffled over and wiped crumbs from a corner of the table with the edge of his stained white apron. I noticed that his piebald pate gleamed from the reflection of the overhead fluorescent lights. "Iz," Herschel said, looking up at him, "how long's it been since you washed that apron? That damned thing has to be almost as old as *you* are."

Izzy pursed his lips and shrugged. "*Nu?*" he said. "So all of a sudden you're particular?" He rubbed the left sleeve of Herschel's sweatshirt between his thumb and index fingers. "So you're wearing a *schmatte* like this and now you're a *gar*ment critic? Better you should worry about more important things."

Soon Magda came over to ask if anyone wanted dessert. "Ve have da cheesecake today," she said. "Good cheesecake, *ja?* Anyone vant?" Jake raised his hand and nodded, and Howie, in his good baritone, said, "Me too, Mag. Thank you much." Jake was a good Kent, and Howie was wonderful as Edgar—that great Edgar, particularly when he's in disguise as Poor Tom. If I could act, which I certainly can't, that'd be the role I'd want to do. I've even dreamt of doing Tom, being onstage practically naked, though hopefully with a better physique than the one I have, which isn't at all enviable—short, a bit pudgy, thinning hair, blah blah. Those have been nice dreams, but scary ones, too, because when you're in a play you have to talk, say your lines—unless you're a non-verbal extra or playing a mute. For me, that would, of course, be a huge problem.

Herschel looked up at Magda and gently touched her forearm. "Hey," he said softly, "did I ever tell you that you're the absolute love of my life? Do you know that I dream of you at night when I can't sleep? I have to admit, kid, I've got it bad. I hope you don't mind my telling you."

She looked down at him and pursed her lips. "Is dat true?" she said. "Vell, I love you too den. Vhen you are ready to support me in da style to vhich I hope to become accustomed, please let me know. I vill give Izzy my—how do you say?—my *resignation*, yes?" Herschel chuckled and squeezed her forearm and nodded. The guys laughed.

The funny thing is that I actually *do* sometimes dream about Magda at night. I doubt if Herschel really does, but I do. Well, I've never actually dreamt about her—at least not yet—but I've thought about her now and again, sometimes with lustful imaginings. That big Polish face. Those pale-blue eyes. That cornsilk-fine blond hair. Normally, I like smaller women—the smaller the better, in fact. Give me a waif, a spinner, like Lydia or Celeste, any day. But Magda's an exception. She's maybe five-ten and thick, solid. With her short hair cut in a sort of pageboy style and her broad shoulders and erect posture, she looks like she could have been a guard at Auschwitz or Bergen-Belsen. I visualize her dressed in a brown skirt and a white blouse with a beige clip-on tie and wearing one of those severe little caps and flicking a riding crop against her open left palm, authoritatively directing the Jews getting off the train. "*Achtung!*" she'd bray. "You men get in line over here and da vimen over dere. You must get ready for da shower, *ja*? You vill feel much better after da shower. Now *schnell!*" A real Aryan Magda is, with that blond hair and blue eyes. But somehow she appeals to me. I've even fantasized being in bed with her. She'd be calling the shots: "Now make mad passionate love to me right *now*, little man, and I vill tell you vhen to stop."

Magda. Herschel told me that she always works at the deli on Saturdays, so that some of the more observant Jews who work there can have that day off. He said that she's a sort of *Shabbos goy*, a gentile who's willing to help out and do things from sunset on Friday to sunset on Saturday that we Jews aren't supposed to do, per God's directives. Yahweh, I guess, wants his chosen people to just take it easy, not to exert themselves sweeping a floor or flipping on a light switch or turning on the air conditioner on the Sabbath, or to do other work. So good for Magda. She's doing a mitzvah.

As we were getting ready to leave, I noticed Big Art washing the exterior windows of the restaurant. Herschel saw him too. "Look at that fat fuck," he said. "He looks like he swallowed a watermelon." Art's huge stomach was bulging beneath his stained green parka, which was mostly open due to a broken zipper. He was wearing a dirty dark-red stocking cap and chewing on a toothpick. He wasn't exactly wearing himself out. Instead, he raised his squeegee pole and took a few perfunctory swipes at the window and then rested the pole on the ground and grasped it with both gloved hands and turned to stare through the window into the deli. He seemed to be looking at two bluehairs sitting near the front, both eating salads. I'd overheard one of them ordering a Cobb salad with a grilled salmon add-on. That sounds good. I might try that sometime if I can screw up the courage to vary my routine. One of the women noticed Art staring and looked down at her lap. I could see her whispering to her companion, and both looked uncomfortable.

I've seen Art do the same thing when he washes windows downtown in good weather. He'll swipe at a window a bit and then lean on his pole, seemingly exhausted from his efforts, and glare at women—always women—with his bulging dark eyes beneath wild brows. In the summer, he always wears a tattered blue baseball cap. Sometimes he calls out to women passing by. "Hey!" he'll growl. "Can't you smile?" Most of them lower their eyes and ignore him and quickly hurry past. He usually stares at them from behind for a long while, unblinking, most often while raising a brown paper bag to his mouth and taking a big swallow of whatever rotgut's in the bottle inside the bag.

But as we left Izzy's, Herschel walked over to Art and reached high to put a hand on his shoulder. "Artie," he said, "you're doing a hell of a job. And I *mean* that." Art didn't say anything at first, just cocked his big head and took off his red cap and scratched his dirty hair. His face turned a bit scarlet. After a few moments, he stared at Herschel and just nodded his big head.

Driving home, I wondered what Naomi would do if Big Art harassed her while she was walking down the street. She's not one to suffer fools gladly, so I don't imagine she'd just lower her eyes and quickly walk past. She'd probably have choice words: "Suck in that gut, douchebag, and give your nasty mouth a rest or I'll show you a smile you *won't* like! *Fershtaist?*"

While waiting at a light, I wondered if Big Art ever gets to sample the wares from Izzy's. I've had many wonderful Izzy's corned beef on rye sandwiches over the years, much potato salad, many lovely cups and bowls of matzo ball soup. In my coat pocket were the Joyva Halvah bars for Naomi. My girlfriend now and again likes hot dogs from Izzy's. My wife, Rivkah, did too. Naomi said that she appreciates that Izzy uses Hebrew National Kosher hot dogs exclusively. I wondered if Art's ever had one of those. If not, maybe he should. He may be obnoxious, he might be a hopeless drunkard, he may even be crazy, but I'm sure he deserves something of true quality now and again. Why not?

Now I'm wondering if Herschel was right. Am I the guy who spills his soup or the guy who gets the soup spilled on him? I'm certainly not above spilling soup on someone, though not on purpose, and I certainly wouldn't be shocked if some numbnuts did the same for me. I recall that Irwin Hillman spilled cream of tomato soup on my arm once during lunch at Wilbur Wright Middle School. We were at the losers' table at the back of the cafeteria and he tentatively raised the first spoonful to his mouth and it must have been too hot because he flinched just a bit and the spoonful went flying and most of it landed on the left sleeve of my nerdy pale-blue button-down shirt. I don't know if that incident made Irwin a schlemiel or qualified me as a shlimazel, but, if so, I won't deny the title.

Or maybe I'm just a run-of-the-mill *shmendrick*, a guy who ignorantly puts a tin can of cheesy broccoli soup in the microwave to warm it up and the can explodes and tin and broth and cheese and broccoli pieces fly everywhere, and you open the remnants of the micro door to look and just sigh, knowing that it'll take a week to clean up the horrible mess, and Naomi, having heard the explosion, comes running and screams, "What the *fuck* did you do, you ineffectual diddlehead? You ruined my goddamn microwave!" What can a guy do but stare at the floor and shrug?

SIX

I CAN'T BELIEVE MY LUCK! As I was getting ready to go over to Dad's this morning I got a text from Celeste. I'm not sure how she got my number. She asked if we could meet for coffee soon, that she has a favor to ask. I texted back and said sure, of course we could meet, and asked what the favor is. She replied that she'll tell me when she sees me. So now, if my luck holds, I actually get to see that amazing woman again and look at that sweet face and that pleasant little body. I didn't think I'd ever encounter her again, and now, out of the blue, she contacts me. What a turn! Well, what could the favor be? What might a lovely and accomplished woman like Celeste want with a clunkhead such as myself? Who knows? Is it even remotely possible that she's been thinking of me like I've been thinking of her and she likes me and wants to get to know me better? Hard to believe. It's likely something much more pedestrian; maybe she needs a ride to the airport.

So now I have something to look forward to in my otherwise drab life. I'm glad of that because I feel like I'm in a funk.

One reason is that I've been thinking about a wedding I helped Liz do in September. I haven't been able to stop thinking about that poor little bride, Debbie. She came into my head the other day when I saw Elise scarfing down an entire package of Little Debbie Honey Buns.

The ceremony was okay, a standard deal at a big Catholic church, with the soaring organ music and the readings and the priest's homily and the mass and the wafers, and now we were at the reception at an American Legion hall out in the sticks. Liz stayed for a little while and then left shortly after the arrival of the bridal party. It started out fine, with the guests, most enthusiastically consuming various alcoholic beverages, including foaming beer in translucent plastic cups, applauding and going "Woo-*hoo!*" when the newlyweds and the bridal party entered the building. Debbie and her new husband, Randy, looked happy enough. They were an interesting contrast, sizewise. She was maybe five-two at best and he was a lanky long-haired guy with a spiked goatee who towered over her by at least a foot. She had to strain her neck to look up at him.

Soon came the cake-cutting. Debbie, smiling sweetly, took a small piece of wedding cake and held it up to Randy's face and he obligingly opened his mouth to let her nicely feed it to him. He then picked up a bigger hunk of cake and made as if to follow suit. But, instead, he suddenly smooshed the cake against her mouth and she stumbled backwards from the force of the smoosh, stunned. Some cake decorated her mouth and chin and some dribbled down onto the bodice of her lovely off-white dress and into her cleavage. She looked down at her dress in horror and tried to wipe off the cake and started crying and ran to the ladies' room. The maid of honor, Debbie's friend Margie, gave Randy a dagger look, her face hard and eyes snapping, and followed the bride. "Hey," Randy muttered meekly, watching them go, "it was a joke, for Chrissake. I didn't mean nothin'."

Debbie somehow recovered and emerged from the ladies' room after about ten minutes. Her face was blotchy. Margie still looked furious, like she wanted to castrate Randy.

After a bit the bride and groom told me that their idea was for them and me to leave the reception and drive to the hotel where they'd be having their wedding night, about ten minutes away, to do some photos both outside the hotel and in their suite. We did that, and it was fine, but when we got back to the reception after forty-five minutes there were noticeable bad vibes. Randy's brother, Jack, the best man, immediately confronted the groom and commenced to yell at him. "What the *fuck?*" he screamed. "Where did you go? I wanted the freakin' wedding party to do a grand march, and nobody knew where the fuck you guys were! Now some people have already left." This guy was as tall as his brother, with deep-set dark eyes and a stubble of reddish whiskers, and now they were nose-to-nose. "Well, I didn't know you wanted to do a goddamn grand march," Randy said. "You never said nothin' about that." It escalated from there— increased volume, epithets, finger pointing, both gangly brothers red-faced—and at one point Debbie stepped between them. "Can you two please tone it down?" she said softly. "*Please?*" Jack backed up a step and looked down at her, still angry. "Shut the *fuck* up, you prissy little bitch!" he growled. She looked stunned and puddled up and again ran to the bathroom.

That was poor Debbie's wedding reception.

Remembering that event, I can't help conjuring Margie's hard face after the cake fiasco. The woman wasn't happy. I'm only glad she wasn't upset with me because angry women scare me in general and more so, of course, if it's me they're pissed at. Thinking of Margie makes me shudder and want to hide somewhere. I liked it, though, when she briefly turned to look directly at me as I stood to one side, holding my camera, watching the two stupid brothers bickering. Her expression just then was neutral, not angry, thank God. She held the glance for just a moment and then abruptly turned to follow the blubbering bride. I don't know what that was about. Maybe she was expecting me to be a man and stand up to Jack and berate him for his horrible treatment of Debbie, or even to punch his lights out. Perhaps she was thinking of asking me to leave the reception with her. "Listen," she'd maybe say, "I've had it with this idiot groom and his numbnuts brother. Let's you and me get the hell out of here and go back to the hotel and drink some champagne and … you know, have some *fun*." She'd again look directly into my eyes. Her face would soften. "Are you, uh, interested?" she'd murmur.

Another reason for my funk is my father. His appearance and behavior are more and more worrisome. I'd given him the rest of my Ambien prescription to help his sleeping problems due to his back pain, but he says it hasn't helped much so far—a little, maybe. Even though it didn't help me too much, I'd thought it'd maybe work for him. Oh, well. Still, I was happy to give Dad the rest of my prescription. Maybe if he keeps taking it, it'll help him sleep better. Howie said that Ambien helped with his mild insomnia. If it does help, my old man can get his own prescription from Dr. Ansfield. Or I'll get refills and just give him mine. That would be a good thing I can do for my father—that and maybe get him some over-the-counter stuff for his back. It could be a mitzvah. Herschel told me that he had back pain before *Lear* and had used Salonpas Pain Relieving Patches, the ones with Lidocaine. Herschel also likes rub-on pain creams, like Jointflex or Blue-Emu Super Strength. Maybe I'll get some of those. Even though my father's sometimes a worrisome meshugenner, I'd like to at least *try* to be a good son.

I hadn't seen Dad for a little while, and was … well, a bit shocked at his appearance. He opened the door to let me in, and I saw that his white hair was longer and uncombed and he hadn't shaved since I'd last seen him and had the start of a white beard. His lips were orange. His eyes were puffy and still had a tinge of purplish discoloration from when he'd clunked his noggin. He again smelled bad. He was still wearing the green robe, and I noticed that it had a stain in the chest area that looked to be spilled prune juice. All he said was a weak, "Welcome, sirrah." I saw, when he said it, that his tongue was orange as well. He lowered himself into his La-Z-Boy to resume watching TV and I noticed a large opened bag of Cheetos on the floor next to his chair. He reached down to scoop a handful and stuffed them into his mouth, adding to the orange motif.

Judge Judy was on and the judge, plucked eyebrows arched and looking severe, glasses perched halfway down her thin nose, with a white lacy collar frilling the top of her black robe, was rebuking the defendant. "Yup is not an answer, ma'am!" she shrilled. "YES is an answer. Do you understand?" The poor defendant, a sad-eyed middle-aged black woman with red and blue beads in her dreads, nodded slowly and muttered, "Yes, your honor. I understand." Judge Judy glared at her, "*Good!*" she practically yelled, leaning forward from the chair on her elevated bench. "Judgment for the plaintiff. That's all. We're *done!*"

Dad turned to look at me and grinned just a bit, his lips orange from the Cheetos. "This is good, right?" he said. "A millionaire bigmouthed Jewess with absolute power wagging her finger and yelling at all these poor guys and making them toe the line. Oh, brave new world!" He paused and smiled just a bit, with closed lips. "They're all strutting and fretting, eh? The judge and her slow bailiff, Mr. Byrd, and the … what's the word? … the *litigants*. It's all good, right?" He suddenly looked uncomfortable and squirmed a bit. "Uh, I'll be right back," he said. "Have to pee."

Soon after he returned from the bathroom, he leaned back in his chair and fell asleep. His mouth was partly opened and a bit of spittle drooled from one corner. His lips were still orange. I looked at my father and remembered how proud he'd looked at the start of *King Lear,* when the casting had been decided and the table reads were about to commence. That Herbert Dickman stood tall and straight, was clean-shaven and always well-groomed, every silver hair in place, and well-dressed, favoring dark-colored turtleneck sweaters. His back was fine. He was in his element—on the verge of playing the big Shakespeare role he'd been living for, had been waiting years to do, had been thinking would be his ultimate moment of glory. That wasn't long ago, but he seemed to have aged years since then. Now he seemed shrunken and bedraggled, a pathetic old man with nasty back pain that's been keeping him awake at night.

I have to say, though, that I keep wishing Dad would stop wearing that raggedy green robe. I can't look at the damned thing without thinking of my mother, and seeing him wear that just irritates me. One reason that *King Lear* gave me the heebie-jeebies was all the suicides. Goneril killed herself, Gloucester wanted to and tried to, and then, the last time I saw him, at Izzy's, Herschel said that his character, the Fool, probably offed himself because he was in despair over seeing his beloved master go bonkers, screaming at the thunder and lightning and huddling in a hovel while a storm raged and talking nonsense with Poor Tom. "He couldn't take it anymore," Herschel said. "Way too much bullshit, no relief in sight." The guys had been talking about the Fool, for some reason, and Howie, finishing the last of his disgusting pickled tongue sandwich on multi-grain bread, asked Herschel what the Fool's last line in the play—"And I'll go to bed at noon"—meant, and he said it was an old-time reference to doing yourself in. So, if Herschel's right, the Fool was a suicide. That lovely, clever character; that great, witty guy! I was stunned. I knew he'd disappeared from the play in Act III, after the storm scene, but never wondered why. And then all the suicides in those other plays: Cleopatra, Brutus, Othello, maybe Lady Macbeth, Juliet, probably Ophelia. Hamlet thought about it: "To be or not to be," blah, blah. Even old George Bailey considered jumping in the river on Christmas Eve. It's all too close to home.

One thing I wonder is if I could do for my father what Edgar in *Lear* did for his. Gloucester wanted to end it all by jumping off the high cliff at Dover because he was in big despair and blind—horrible Regan and her equally despicable husband, Cornwall, having spooned his eyes out—and he realized that his bastard son, Edmund, had deceived him about his legitimate son Edgar's supposed treachery, and now asshole Edmund sought his father's death so as to get his fortune, and Gloucester was hugely ashamed of himself for not realizing what was what, and now his beloved Lear was in extremis, and he felt that everything in his world had quickly and hugely gone to hell, turned absurd. Who *wouldn't* be in despair? Then Edgar, assuming his Poor Tom madman and beggar persona, tricked blind Gloucester into thinking that he was jumping off that cliff, whereas it was really level ground, and then comforted his deceived father and told him that his life was "a miracle." A *miracle!* What a good thing to say to your father, particularly considering that that father'd been suckered into declaring Edgar an outcast and proclaiming him a traitor, to be hunted down and killed.

That scene blew me away. Could I ever be that clever, that caring, that forgiving, that good if my father ever got so down that he wanted to do himself in? I doubt it. I don't think I have it in me. I'm not Edgar, not Cordelia. I could never measure up to that virtuous pair.

And sometimes I wonder if I could ever do myself in, if things came to cases. If my mother did it, maybe I could too. Maybe that sad tendency runs in families. I've felt pretty down here and there, for sure, and I've had fleeting thoughts now and again, but I don't think I've ever seriously considered ending it, even after one of my blood-curdling blow-ups with Naomi.

Well, last spring I was driving alone through a tunnel and traffic stalled while I was in the middle of it, so I couldn't see daylight either behind me or ahead, and had zero control, and after a few minutes of that I was so anxious that I wished I were dead and would have maybe welcomed oblivion. I was *quite* verklempt. I don't know how long the stall lasted; it seemed like an eternity, though it was likely only minutes. I recall that I unbuckled my seat belt and opened all the windows in my Honda and blasted the air-conditioner and did deep breathing, including alternate-nostril breathing, with my eyes closed except for opening them briefly now and again to see if traffic was moving. I hope I can avoid such tunnels for the rest of my life so, in that regard at least, I can keep from thoughts of self-extinction.

At least, thank God, I never told Naomi about the tunnel episode. I credit myself for that. When it comes to my issues, such as they are, the woman has the empathy of a gerbil.

And, thank God again, I've never heard my father say anything that made me worry that *he* was thinking of ending it. So far, anyway.

Dad woke from his nap just as I was putting my coat on and getting ready to leave. He looked at me for a moment, seemingly confused, as though he didn't know who I was. His eyes were hazy. He rubbed them with the back of his right hand and stared at my face again and a look of recognition slowly came into his eyes. "Oh," he said softly, "it's you, son." He paused and stared into my eyes. "Well, Julius, you see me here, a poor old man, more sinned against than sinning. Can you see that?" I didn't, but nodded to be affable.

I'm also in a bit of a funk about Benji. Poor kid. Last Sunday night he and Elise came back from their weekend with their father and I could tell right off that he was feeling down. His face was tight and his chin was trembling a bit. He didn't say anything, just plopped down on the living room sofa and pulled his sweatshirt hood over his head and hunched into himself and commenced scrolling through his phone. Naomi stared at him from the hallway, arms crossed, scowling. "So," she said, "how's your gaping asshole father?" Benji just shrugged, but didn't answer or even look up. "*Hey!*" she said, raising her voice, "I asked you a question."

Benji didn't look at her for a moment but then he did, briefly. "Okay, I guess," he said softly. He paused. "I mean, what can I tell you, Mom?" Thankfully, she didn't press it.

Later, after dinner, while Elise and Naomi were watching *Naked and Afraid* on Discovery Channel, eating potato chips, I knocked on Benji's bedroom door. "Come in," he answered softly. He was reading *The Mammoth Hunter*. I sat on the edge of his bed and asked how things were going. He shrugged. "Okay, I guess," he said.

At first, I couldn't think of anything to talk about. "Say," I finally said, "d-do you like chocolate ph-ph-phosphates?" He looked at me and nodded. "How about I take you to Izzy's some t-time? They have g-g-great phosphates. I think they use B-Bosco syrup. Isn't that g-good?"

Benji pursed his lips and looked at me for just a moment and then looked back at his book. "Sure," he said quietly. "Bosco. I like Bosco. That'd be fine." He paused. "Thanks, Julius."

Before going to bed, I paused outside the entrance to the living room. Naomi and Elise were still watching TV. Naomi was wearing her yellow-and-purple-checked flannel nightgown. Neither of their jaws, thank God, were flapping at the moment. A new episode of *Naked and Afraid* was starting and a voiceover was explaining that here we have one man and one woman, strangers to each other, who are about to be plucked down in a remote area of the Brazilian rain forest for twenty-one days, naked and with no food or water or shelter and only a few helpful items, and it's not going to be easy because the days are blisteringly hot and the nights freezing cold, and it rains huge amounts there, sometimes for days at a time, and flooding is a worry, and not only that but there are all kinds of nasty inhabitants of the neighborhood, such as snakes whose venom can quickly paralyze and kill you and huge, hairy poisonous spiders and millions of mosquitoes and fire ants and other miserable insects that long to pester you and dig into your skin, plus ugly long-jawed caimans that can grow to sixteen feet lurking in the rivers and various big cats that yearn to eat you for breakfast, to say nothing of bigmouthed howler monkeys who dwell in the trees and scream insults, disturbing what meager moments of sleep you might be able to snatch. Images of these worrisome creatures flash on the screen.

Then we see the actual pair, clothed and being boated down a river separately, each saying how much they're definitely up for this big-time challenge and how they're confident that their survivalist skills will help them prevail in this difficult three-week ordeal. Then the boats stop and each one jumps out and strips down to their birthday suit and they walk separately into the jungle, naked behinds on full display, while other private parts are blurred. Her bottom, round and dimpled, was pleasant enough. Then they meet and greet and, after a moment of subtly checking out the other's parts, show each other the one item they've chosen to aid in their ordeal. He'd brought a machete and she a pot for cooking and hauling and then boiling water. The *Naked and Afraid* people also nicely gave them a fire-starter.

Twenty-one days with a naked stranger? I wondered. That must be interesting. What would they find to talk about? I thought of how I might fare in that situation. Not well. My survivalist skills are zero, except for the fire-building merit badge I earned in Boy Scouts. And even that was undeserved because I secretly used a bit of gasoline to start the fire. Suppose I was out there in the harsh wilderness with my partner and a big storm came up—torrents of rain and raging wind, and the big cats and the spiders and the menacing snakes lurking and the monkeys howling—and she, trembling with worry and fear, looked to me for heroism and manliness in the dire situation, or at least minimal competence, and all I could do was to hunch over and shiver and cross my arms protectively over my unclothed torso. "P-Poor Tom's a-cold!" I'd squeal. She'd shake her head in disgust and turn her back to me. I'd sneak a peek at her sweet bare bottom. "Well," she'd sneer, "look who's all naked and *afraid!* I guess if anyone's going to wear the pants in this ordeal, it's going to have to be me!"

SEVEN

NAOMI SURPRISED ME twice yesterday. The first time was at breakfast when she asked me how my visit with Dr. Ansfield went. I hadn't said anything about it and thought she'd forgotten. "F-F-Fine," I said. She wanted to know if he'd listened to my heart and lungs. I said that he did, and they were normal. "That's good," she said. "I want you to stick around." That surprised me. I didn't tell her that Ansfield had suggested that I exercise more and eat better and maybe lose a few pounds.

I almost blurted out to my girlfriend that I took the stairs, all eight flights, both going up and coming down, instead of the elevator. That was true, but I was going to lie as to the real reason. But, thank God, I thought better of it just in time. Maybe Naomi would have said "Well, good for you," or "Nicely done," or even just "Oh, good boy!" But more likely she would have known the truth and pursed her lips and made a face and offered a disparaging comment. "'Exercise,' my *ass*," she might have said. "What a fucking wuss you are! Afraid of an elevator! Jesus Christ! A sad sack schlemiel from first to last."

The second time was when we watched that silly *It's a Wonderful Life* on the sofa after dinner. We were eating a bowl of Orville Redenbacher's Ultimate Butter microwaved popcorn and I had my arm around her and she now and again leaned her head against my shoulder. Soon came the scene where George Bailey is unhappy following his younger brother's wedding celebration party because his dreams of worldwide travel haven't come true and he feels stuck at the family building and loan business, and he wanders around town in a pissy mood and ends up at Mary's mother's house. Mary's home from college and they haven't seen one another for some time, though she's been in love with him since they were children together. They quarrel and he storms out of the house just as the phone rings. It's Sam Wainwright, George's old nemesis, who's now a rich *macher* in New York City and Mary's sort-of boyfriend. As Mary and Sam talk, George returns to retrieve his hat and Sam says to Mary that he wants to talk with George, and soon Mary and George are close to the phone receiver so that they can both hear

Sam, he taller than she and his face close to her pretty hair, and Sam talks about a great business deal that he wants George to invest in and Mary looks up at George's face and murmurs, "He says it's the chance of a lifetime … " and George drops the phone to the floor and grabs Mary by the shoulders and starts to angrily tell her that he doesn't want big business deals or to ever marry anyone, that he wants to do what *he* wants to do, and then he's overcome with emotion, maybe from sniffing her hair, and so is she, and they embrace and he blubbers, "Oh, Mary, Mary…" and she blubbers, "Oh, George, George … " and they kiss with long-pent-up passion and next thing you know, he's taken advantage of that chance of a lifetime and their wedding bells have chimed.

I'd seen the scene many times before and wasn't at all affected, but Naomi was and her lower lip quivered and tears were streaming down and then she leaned up and offered her wet face for a kiss. I accommodated her, but not with an "Oh, Naomi, N-N-Naomi … " and, thank God, she didn't sing out "Oh, Julius, Julius … " but she was moved, I guess, and snuggled close to me for the rest of the movie. We even held hands. Naomi, of course, got all misty again on cue at the end scene, with everyone all generous and warmhearted and beaming and drinking wine, and Zuzu blathering about angels getting their wings, and George looking heavenward and grinning and winking and going "Attaboy, Clarence," and I kissed away her tears and had warm feelings. But the best thing was that we went upstairs afterward and Naomi murmured, "Honey, let's make love." I couldn't believe it!

Unfortunately, things didn't advance from there. My thing wouldn't advance. It remained at rest. Well, it advanced a little, but not enough. Naomi furrowed her brow and gave me a look, but didn't say anything. She just sighed and turned over onto her left side and pulled the blanket over her head. At first I wasn't sure what to say or do, and then after a moment blurted out something I'd been thinking about. "You know, N-Naomi, the winter s-s-solstice was two d-days ago. Now the d-days will start getting l-longer. Won't that be n-n-nice?" She didn't say anything. I briefly considered telling her how glad I was about the days getting longer because I really hate it this time of year when the sun sets just after four-thirty and then doesn't rise until almost seven o'clock the next morning. That's almost fifteen hours with no daylight, and it's just cold and dark out, which sort of makes me feel trapped and helpless and even a little scared sometimes—no control over all that damned stifling darkness. And it's even worse if it's snowing because then I have to worry about shoveling in the morning and maybe even worry that the snow will be deep and will block the front door, which would make me feel temporarily trapped. I wanted Naomi to appreciate how very *glad* I was that after the solstice the days would start getting a bit longer, even if just for a few minutes a day. But, thank God, I caught myself from saying all that, thought better of saying anything more, and just turned over myself to go to sleep. I thought of maybe putting my arm around Naomi's shoulders or even stroking her right hip, but wasn't sure how she'd take it, given my erotic failings, so kept my hands to myself.

I had trouble falling asleep. I felt glad that things had worked out for George and Mary. Hopefully, they lived happily ever after and perhaps that nasty Mr. Potter would have keeled over from a massive heart attack and left George alone.

It occurred to me that maybe I should again ask Naomi to marry me. She's mentioned it now and again, and last spring, on the second night of Passover, we even had a fight because she said I should be asking her, after three years together, and what the hell was I waiting for? I thought about what she'd said, and two days later decided to broach the subject. Her response surprised me. "I need to think about this," she said. "Don't noodge me. My first marriage was a goddamned disaster, you know, and I don't know if I want to go there again." But I'd seen how moved she was by George and Mary being all romantic and kissy-face and getting hitched, so thought of maybe bringing it up yet again.

But after thinking about it for a bit, I dismissed the idea. *Do I really need the aggravation?* was my thought.

Who knows what's in anyone's head? As big a pain in the ass as Naomi can be, and as much as she routinely rakes me over the coals, and as irritating as she is to me and, I guess, I am to her, I'd still stand under a *huppah*, a canopy, with her if that's what would make her happy. I'd step on a white-cloth-covered wine glass, with Rabbi Twersky looking on with a half-assed smile on his face. I thought that nuptials are what she wanted, but maybe not. First she nags me to ask her and then, when I do, she's luke-warm at best and doesn't want to be noodged. I don't know how a guy's supposed to keep it all straight.

It's interesting how you can live with someone, maybe for a long time, but still not know them well, still be mistaken about them. Like in *Othello*, that Dad was in last year, playing Iago. He said he liked that role, that he thought he'd succeeded in it. I'm glad he felt that way, as opposed to how he said he felt about being a failure in *King Lear*. It made me think, though. Othello thought he knew his wife, Desdemona, but he didn't. He got her all wrong. He came to think that she was one kind of person, unfaithful and deceiving, but she wasn't at all like that. She was good and pure and loving. Then, thinking wrongly that she'd been unfaithful to him, he smothered her with a pillow. Oy gevalt! And Othello also completely misjudged Iago, his long-time trusted lieutenant. He thought the guy was loyal and trustworthy, not scheming and manipulative. Think again, pal. And Iago's wife, Emilia, had no idea that her husband was as foul as he was until it was too late. And then in *Lear*, Albany had no clue what an evil murderous wretch his wife, Goneril, had become until that was obvious, until he couldn't *not* see it. "Oh, Goneril," he sneered, "you are not worth the dust which the rude wind blows in your face." Yikes!

So maybe you can live intimately with another person for years— *decades!*—and still have no idea who they really are. You think you understand someone, but you can be wrong. You can be deluded. It's like that blind, head-wagging Ray Charles sang: *"You think you know me well, but you don't know me."*

It makes me wonder how well I knew Rivkah. Of course, that was a decade ago and our time together was brief, so I didn't have the chance to know her that well anyway. She was an exchange student from Tel Aviv who'd met Herschel at a Beth El Purim party and they went out a few times. He introduced me to her at a Shabbat dinner a few weeks later and we talked. Well, she talked, mostly about how much she loved America, particularly hot dogs and cheeseburgers, and that she really wanted to see the Grand Canyon. I listened, but mostly I stared. Oh, my goodness. That glossy black hair, that olive-colored skin, full lips, those big dark-brown eyes looking unblinking into mine. She called me shortly after that and asked if I wanted to go to lunch with her. We went to Culver's, my treat, where she downed two double Swissburgers and an order of onion rings and a large strawberry shake. A week later, she called again and asked if I'd go to the zoo with her. I agreed, and as we were standing outside the giraffe enclosure, staring at their absurdly long speckled necks, she asked me to marry her so she could get her green card. She said she wanted to eventually become a citizen and live in America. She said there'd be no strings attached and that we'd get a divorce afterward and go our separate ways. I asked her why she didn't approach Herschel for this high honor and she said she had but he'd declined.

After thinking about it a bit, I agreed and we got hitched by a munici-
pal judge for twenty-five dollars, which I paid. I thought of it as a mitzvah,
a good deed to help a fellow Jew—admittedly one with a magnificent face
and a luscious, though slightly *zaftig*, body—live her dream. She never
expressed a word of gratitude after the brief ceremony. I didn't expect
much, but I remember thinking that it would be nice if she'd offer just a
little payback—a perfunctory roll in the hay, say, or at least the next best
thing. But no. We never spent anything approaching an intimate moment.

Well, I did get a kiss—a brief one, but still a kiss. After we filed for
divorce, citing irreconcilable differences, and it was finalized, we went out
for lunch at Izzy's. Rivkah had the standard Izzy's Chicago Dog, a quarter-
pound Nathan's Hebrew National Kosher Beef Frank, grilled, on a poppy
seed bun, with relish, onion, sport peppers, tomato pickle and a sprinkling
of celery salt, and then asked for another. She got an order of fries with
each Chicago Dog. She doused her hot dogs with both ketchup and yellow
mustard, and also dipped each fry in both condiments—first the ketchup
each time, and then the mustard. While eating her dogs, she closed her eyes
and leaned her head a bit to the left. She had a look of near ecstasy on her
pretty face as she chewed. She even made a little moaning sound as she ate.
We didn't talk much. When we'd finished, I asked if she'd like dessert and
she said she wanted two orders of carrot cake. She quickly chowed down
one and asked for a box for the other. When the check came, I told her what
her share was and she stared at me as though I had two heads. "What are
you saying?" she asked. "We were married. The husband pays, always. You
didn't know this?" I didn't argue.

I drove her home, and she didn't have a high opinion of my Honda
Civic, which, then, was only two years old. "This is the piece of *dreck* you
have?" she said. I walked her to the door of her apartment building, still
hoping that she'd invite me in and we'd celebrate our marriage and divorce
with a memorable moment of passion. That didn't happen, but she did put
her hands on my shoulders and looked into my eyes and planted a moist
kiss that lasted maybe three seconds. Tongues weren't involved. I could
smell the relish and onion and maybe the sport peppers on her breath. "So I
am thanking you, Mr. Julius," she said. "So maybe I will see you somewhere, maybe at shul for the high holidays." At least there was that.

I thought of telling Rabbi Twersky about my mitzvah. I'm quite sure
he would have approved of my helping a young Israeli, perhaps particularly
one like Rivkah, with those big dark eyes and nice *toochis*. But I never got

around to that. I admire and respect the rabbi—he's learned and wise, I guess, though he has a somewhat off-putting wart on the right side of his nose—but his eyes always glaze over when we talk because of my stutter.

Just last week, I ran into him at Walgreens. He was there to buy toothpaste—Colgate Ultra White—and Excedrin Extra Strength and a large green package of Depend Guards. He was also buying two packages of Juicy Fruit gum, which surprised me; you don't think of a rabbi as a gum chewer. After exchanging pleasantries, I surprised myself by asking if God has a plan for us. "Is there a p-p-purpose to our lives, R-Rabbi?" He put his hand on my arm and said, a bit impatiently, "Of course, yes, there is meaning to our lives. Our purpose as Jews is to fulfill the mission that God has given us through His Torah, so that our lives are therefore meaningful. All that we do is part of that mission. So this is what gives us strength. Otherwise, it would all be just ... an absurd void, a nothing, yes?" Then he looked down at his cart, with the Depends and the rest, and walked away.

Again with the *nothing*. Twersky must have been talking with my father.

Rivkah, after our divorce was final, married an orthopedic surgeon, Arnie Berliant, who specializes in knees. I wasn't invited to their wedding. They went to Arizona for their honeymoon and Rivkah got to see the damned Grand Canyon. I didn't have the pleasure of hearing her review. I've seen Rivkah and Berliant at Beth El now and again over the years. He's short and stocky with a bit of a barrel chest, but has a wonderful head of curly silver hair and always wears highly-shined black dress shoes. He smiles a lot and has a hearty laugh, showing sparkling white teeth. He always wears a blue-and-white yarmulke and is constantly adjusting his tallis with his left hand so that it doesn't slip off his shoulders when he's been called to read a Torah portion.

Rivkah and I've exchanged mild pleasantries over the years—"Hello, how are you?" or "Good Shabbos" or "*Shanah Tovah*" on Rosh Hashanah—but that's all. The woman was briefly my wife—the only wife I've had, though, sadly, we were never intimate—and now we're acquaintances at best. At least I got that three-second kiss.

I hope Rivkah's happy. Her little dream came true and she became a citizen. She didn't invite me to that ceremony either. I wonder sometimes if she ever gives me a thought. I certainly give her some. I think of her at night now and again, when I'm awake with my damned insomnia. I conjure her dusky face. I sometimes wonder what my life would be like if we'd stayed married, if I were with her now rather than Naomi—assuming that she, Rivkah, hadn't gotten sick and tired of me at some point during the last ten years and discarded my schlemiel ass. Well, maybe we'd have been deliriously happy and had a torrid sex life, with loudly expressed enthusiasms on both of our parts. Maybe she'd have been daring and imaginative in bed and encouraged me to be the same. That would be good. We would have been active in Temple Beth El activities. We'd have gone to services together on the high holidays and maybe socialized with other couples. She'd likely have been active in Hadassah and led programs about life in Israel—kibbutzes and falafel and the Temple Mount and whatnot. Maybe we would have had kids. We could have had a son. That would have been lovely—a son. I'd have liked that. Probably it wouldn't have worked, though. The guy she's with has status and makes big bucks, which I'm sure she likes. I have zero status and make small bucks.

Dad wasn't happy when I married Rivkah, I could tell that, but all he ever said was, "That wasn't a smart move, Julius." But he never pushed it. Maybe I should have just not told him.

Herschel was more direct. "What the *hell!*" he said, stern-faced, his yarmulke slipped a bit to one side. "You could have gotten your pathetic ass in a sling if they found out you were scamming. Use your fuckin' *head,* cuz!"

And now Dad says the Ambien is helping him sleep better, a little anyway, but also making him jumpy, like it did me. But at least he's sleeping a bit better. Maybe the Ambien is kicking in more effectively. So maybe I did *something* right. When I told him, over the phone, that I was glad to hear he was sleeping better, he intoned, in his stentorian stage voice, *"Sleep!* Indeed. The death of each day's life, sore labor's bath, balm of hurt minds, great nature's second course, chief nourisher in life's feast."

And three days ago, I'd bought some Salonpas patches and Blue Emu for his back and had helped stick the patches on, carefully smoothing the edges and being sure the patches stuck to his pasty skin. I'd also, twice, rubbed the damned cream onto his back, where he said it hurt. But then I forgot to ask him if those things helped.

Two nights ago my father had said that sometime next summer, around his birthday, he'd like for the two of us to go for an airplane ride in one of those small single-engine planes that you can book rides in. "We can see the countryside in all its summer glory," he said. "Wouldn't that be fun?" I thought about that for a moment. *Really?* A very small airplane where you can't stand upright if you want to, where you can't escape, where the slightest breeze whips the plane around, where you're absolutely stuck, trapped, until the pilot lands the damned thing? Where a freakin' bird can fly into the engine and muck everything up and the plane might then crash into a school, killing everyone aboard as well as dozens of kids and teachers? Are you *kidding* me, Dad? Oh, my sweet *God!* But I just said, "Uh, I g-guess that would b-be okay."

EIGHT

EVEN THOUGH I NEVER GOT TO do the deed with Rivkah, it looks like I'm going to with Celeste. Oh, happy day! I met her for coffee yesterday at Starbucks and her favor was that she asked me to have sex with her. She said she'd had a big fight about money with Andrew a few days ago and it got ugly and then a bit physical and he'd pushed her and she fell backward down two stairs and strained her shoulder and wrist and, after a day of calming down, they tried to have make-up sex but it didn't work because, she blushingly said, she was "all closed-up down there." They tried again the next night, but same outcome. "Anyway," she said, her face a bit flushed and looking down, "I feel funny asking you this, but, well … would you sleep with me?" She said she needs to find out if her parts still work okay but thinks it needs to be with someone other than her husband— a neutral party, so to speak, someone "that I don't have emotional baggage with right now." I thought about it for a moment and then told her I'd be glad to help out. "I could d-do that," I said.

I can't believe my luck! Here I've spent countless hours over the years fantasizing about doing the deed with various women—real people such as Lydia and Magda and even Amanda or women I don't know but see, like that interesting woman at the same Starbucks recently, with the brown ponytail and the Macbook Pro, or maybe a drunken bridesmaid or the mother of a bar mitzvah here and there, and, certainly, many who exist only in my imagination—usually concluding that it's just a nice dream but unlikely to ever happen, stuttering schlemiel nobody that I am, whose own parts don't always work, and now, out of the blue, a woman actually *asks* me to sleep with her. And not just *any* woman, but a lovely, sexy, accomplished woman like Celeste. Who'd have thought? Maybe now and again God just smiles on a guy, regardless of his merits or lack of those. Fortune's wheel, for me, was down and now it's up. Some *nachas*—happiness—is coming my way, maybe to balance out all the *tsoris*.

The way I'm looking at it is that I'll be helping out an acquaintance, or maybe even a friend, helping her deal with a worrisome personal problem—

to learn if her ladyparts still work okay. I'm sure that has to be a concern; how could it not? I'll be doing a *mitzvah*, is how I see it. Doing good deeds is how you become a *mensch*, a decent person. So that seems a good rationale for agreeing to sleep with Celeste—that I'm doing a mitzvah for a friend in need. The fact that she's an amazingly beautiful woman with a perfect smallish body—my ideal—and is likely to be a magnificent and passionate lover is, of course, a secondary consideration.

I just worry that I won't be able to perform, to hold up my part of the agreement. I hope I won't be intimidated by being with a woman like her.

I should have asked Celeste why she chose me. I didn't think of that. Hell, she could have had anyone. She could have had that pretty boy Donny. I always thought there was chemistry between them when they did *Lear*, even though they didn't have any scenes together. I recall her staring at him during the table reads. They spent time together at the cast party, she looking up at him with big goo-goo eyes. Herschel once said that a key point about Edmund, as a character, is that he's very handsome. Both Goneril and Regan fell in love with him in the play and, I believe, he shtupped both of them, or hoped to, causing big jealousy and hard sisterly feelings. Donny's tall and muscular with broad shoulders and wavy light-brown hair and has one of those masculine chiseled faces with piercing blue eyes and a fine tenor voice. A perfect Edmund, I guess. So Celeste could have asked him to sleep with her. Or anyone from *Lear* who owns a functioning *shlong* and with whom she doesn't currently "have emotional baggage"—actors, directors, costume designers, set people, lighting technicians, anyone. So why me?

Well, maybe I'll ask her when we get together in a few days or maybe I'll never know. My guess is that she thinks I'm safe, unlikely to get weird or go wacko on her or make demands or to have expectations for repeat episodes or to blab to anyone afterwards. A guy with a bad stutter, she maybe thinks, isn't as likely to tell tales. She's probably right. "G-G-Guess what, Herschel?" one can imagine me saying. "Last n-night I p-porked Celeste. You know, the one who p-played C-C-Cordelia? It was g-g-good. She d-displayed a p-pleasant, uh, enthusiasm!" He'd probably fall asleep before I got it all out. So I may be a schlemiel or a shlimazel or even a shmendrick, but I think I can be a discreet one.

Still, maybe I was wrong to agree. I'm not married to Naomi, but I live with her and, I suppose, we're a couple. It may not be all roses and lollipops, our relationship, but we are together and, even though she regularly tongue-lashes me, her body at night is comforting, her tears sometimes flow, she can be loving and affectionate and even sexual now and again, and she's a decent cook. She makes a mean pot roast with boiled potatoes. She makes a lovely baked tuna casserole, always perfectly golden-brown on top. Now and again on a Friday evening, when the spirit moves her, she makes a nice boiled chicken and white rice Shabbat dinner, based on a recipe from her beloved though now-deceased Bubbeh Harriet. She makes a decent chicken soup, too, and always throws some of the rice into it as well. She's never made matzo ball soup for us, though. Our morning couple-check-in sessions have been okay, sort of anyway. We've never exchanged any vows to be faithful, but I guess that's assumed, part of the deal.

I don't know if Naomi's slept with anyone else during our three years together, though I've had my suspicions about her and Perry Schwartz, but I haven't strayed. Oh, I've thought about it, fantasized about it, hoped for it, but I've never actually done it—not mostly because I think it would be immoral or unethical or otherwise wrong or that Rabbi Twersky, with his disgusting nose wart, would disapprove, though those are considerations, but mostly for lack of opportunity.

I wonder how I'd feel if Naomi told me she'd slept with someone else. I guess it would depend. It would be one thing if she said, "Oh, Julius, I feel so bad about telling you this, but yesterday I was feeling sad and vulnerable and unattractive and I went out for a drink with one of my social work colleagues and one thing led to another, you know, and, well, we did it, just once, and I feel so terrible about it. I'm *so* sorry I cheated on you." But it would be another thing if she said, "Look, Mr. Schlemiel, I've been totally bored with you for three years now and there's no passion and I'm not getting younger and I'm a normal woman with needs, so I went out with one of my girlfriends and met a young stud at a bar, and, oh my God, we did it all night long and it was incredible and I actually felt satisfied, *really* satisfied, for the first time in years." She'd maybe pause. "And," she'd add, her face hard, "he could actually get it *up!*" That would probably be different.

Celeste left the Starbucks before I did yesterday, chirping that she needed to pick up a few things at Trader Joe's. She said she likes their frozen seafood, particularly tilapia, and refrigerated chicken marsala. She thinks that they have a great selection of trail mixes, and her favorite is one with almonds and cashews and tiny cubes of chocolate. I stayed for a while longer, nursing my tall white chocolate latte, and studied a sad little woman three tables down whom I've seen there a few times before. She's a short, stout middle-aged woman with dyed reddish hair who almost always dresses in a shiny black pantsuit and a white lacy blouse that's a bit tattered at the collar, and also a funny little black hat with a short brim all the way around and a narrow powder-blue ribbon above that brim. She has a distinct roll around her middle. She has very pale skin, almost translucent. With that skin, I had the thought that a good name for her might be *Blanche*. She always brings a tattered paperback romance novel with her, usually with a beautiful young couple on the cover lusting after each other—she with long flowing hair and distinct curves, including deep cleavage, and he with a strong facial profile and substantial shoulders and pecs and biceps—and sometimes she reads the book and sometimes she just holds it in one hand and sort of stares into the middle distance for a long time, perfectly still. She has big, liquidy pale-blue eyes and blinks a lot. Now and again I've seen her mumble to herself. She's always, *always* alone. I wondered who she was and what her story is and what her life is like. I wished that poor Blanche would be there at Starbucks with another human being, at least once.

I won't tell Dad about Celeste. What would be the point? Now, for God's sake, the *meshugenah* old man's actually started bringing out some of his King Lear costume, which he got to keep after the play as a token, I guess, of his glorious career. Maybe he pulled some strings to make that happen. I came over to his house this past Sunday for our bagels and lox brunch. I particularly wanted to see if he'd laugh at a different Marx Brothers movie. He was still in the green prune-juice-stained schmatte but I was surprised to see the sumptuous purple robe that Lear wore in the early scenes draped over the back of his chair. I thought of asking him what that was about, but decided to let it go. His white hair was longer yet and so was his white beard, and scragglier too. He was barefoot, and I noticed that he hadn't cut his toenails for a while. The nails on both big toes were horrid, sharp and jagged, and there were clumps of dirt in both. Thank God he wasn't orange from Cheetos, though I noticed two jumbo-sized unopened bags on the dining room table. There was a box of Skittles and a jar of Planter's Lightly Salted Dry Roasted Peanuts on the coffee table, and maybe a dozen spilled nuts were scattered on the floor in front of and to the right side of his La-Z-Boy.

I started the coffee and put the bagels and Dad's lox on plates and brought out the butter and cream cheese. I handed Dad a plate with his usual sesame bagel and he stared at it for a moment and then looked up at me. "What the hell is this?" he said. I told him it was his favorite bagel and he wrinkled his brow and his gray eyes narrowed. "You *know* I hate sesame," he said harshly. "For God's sake, Julius, you know that. I like onion. That's what I *always* get. You *know* that. Jesus!" I didn't argue. In all our time, all the years of brunching, he'd only eaten sesame bagels. I just shrugged and switched plates and gave him my onion and took his sesame. He looked at me for a moment, his face still hard, and then nodded and picked up one of his bagel slices and chomped it down in three big bites and then ate the disgusting lox by itself, with his fingers, rather than on his bagel. "D-Dad," I said, "what about the b-b-butter and c-cream cheese?" He frowned and gave me a look and picked up the plastic container of Philadelphia Chive and Onion Cream Cheese Spread and dipped his right index finger in it and shmeared it on his other bagel slice and devoured that in another three big bites.

Before starting the movie, I had to use the bathroom. When I raised the seat, I saw that Dad had earlier peed but not flushed. I saw that his urine seemed cloudy and was a strange darkish color, and that it smelled bad. I thought nothing of it and just flushed to get rid of the odor.

The movie I'd chosen was *Horsefeathers*. Soon came the scene where Groucho as Professor Quincy Adams Wagstaff, new president of Huxley College, is having a meeting in his office with two black-robed professors as he's cracking walnuts with his telephone handset. He tells the professors that he thinks the college is neglecting football for education. "What would this college be without football?" Groucho asks. "Have we got a stadium?" One of the professors says yes. "Have we got a college?" Yes. "Well, we can't support both. Tomorrow we start tearing down the college." I looked over at Dad. No laughter, not even a chuckle. Soon Wagstaff's secretary enters and says that the Dean of Science is there to see him and is impatient with having to wait. Groucho ignores her and continues kibitzing with the two professors, and she exits but soon re-enters. "The dean is *furious!*" she insists. "He's waxing wroth!" Groucho leers at her. "Is Roth out there too?" he asks. "Tell Roth to wax the dean for a while." That was one of our favorite Groucho lines of all time and my father and I'd unfailingly guffawed at it for years. Not now. He just stared at the screen, his gray eyes blurry and his face a mask.

We watched the rest of the movie in silence. My father found no humor in anything, not even the classroom scene where Groucho says to Harpo, as Pinky the dogcatcher, "Young man, you'll find as you grow older that you can't burn the candle at both ends," and Harpo pulls from the inside pocket of his oversized topcoat a candle doing just that and Groucho wags his painted-on eyebrows and says, "Well, I was wrong. I knew there was *something* you can't burn at both ends. I thought it was a candle."

Harpo. If I were ever going to be an actor, which I'm certainly not, I'd want to be like him. He never had to talk.

When I told Dad I had to go, he didn't say anything at first. Then, after a moment, he looked at me and smiled slightly and said, politely and in a firm voice, "Thank you for the bagels, son. They were especially good today. I certainly appreciate it." I nodded and told him he was welcome. As I was about to open the door to leave, my father stood up from his chair and grimaced a bit, probably because of his back, and stared at me again, as though he wasn't sure who I was at first, and said, barely audibly, "Let me not be mad, son." He paused and looked directly into my eyes and then down at his ugly feet. "Not mad. *Please*, Tom."

NINE

BENJI MUST HAVE been glad for the chance to get the hell out of the house today to go to Saturday lunch at Izzy's. Naomi and Elise were going at it full-bore because Elise came home after her midnight curfew last night, her breath stinking of beer and make-up a bit smeared. "I can't believe what a goddamn little *slut* you've turned into!" Naomi screamed. "Oh, go *fuck* yourself, Mom!" Elise shot back. It degenerated from there. When I knocked softly on the door to Benji's room to ask if he was ready to go, he opened it right away and cocked his head to the right and opened his eyes wide and arched his eyebrows and nodded enthusiastically.

We got there before Herschel and the other guys did and took one of the bigger tables, near the kitchen. To the left of the kitchen door, mounted high, was a big black-framed painting, that had been there for as long as I could remember, of an elderly rabbi, gray-bearded and bespectacled, seated and holding an opened scrolled Torah, his blue-and-white tallis wrapped around his shoulders and covering his head and also wearing *tefillin*, those small, black, cube-like boxes with leather straps, with one set wrapped around his left hand and arm and another around his head, with the black box square in the middle of his forehead. He appeared very serious, maybe even uncomfortable. He may have been constipated. I wondered if he would have laughed at "Tell Roth to wax the dean for a while."

Next to that painting was an equally large framed head-and-shoulders color photo of Izzy in his younger days, when he had more hair and bushier eyebrows. He was smiling hugely in the photo, showing somewhat crooked teeth, and it occurred to me that I couldn't remember the last time I'd seen Izzy smile like that. At best, any more, he'll crinkle his nose and the corners of his mouth will move north in a sort of half-assed quasi-smile, but his lips stay closed and teeth never make an appearance. His wife, Sadie, died two years ago of metastatic breast cancer, so maybe that's it. She used to come to the deli regularly and would make the rounds of every table and booth and everyone seated at the counter. "So your pastrami is *good?*" she'd ask.

"So you'll have some *cheesecake?*" She was a short, pleasant-looking woman who always wore her gray hair in a bun.

I noticed Benji staring intently at the painting of the serious rabbi. "What are those straps for?" he asked. "And those funny little cubes?" I thought for a moment but couldn't remember the explanation. It's all complicated. There's a lot to know about the hundreds of customs and traditions and rules and expectations, as to tefillin and davening and everything else. It's hard for the average person to get a handle on. Many rabbis spend their lives studying the Torah and the Midrashim and the Talmud and whatnot, trying to get all the rules and details and interpretations straight that other rabbis and Jewish scholars—Maimonides and Hillel and those guys—have agonized about over the centuries. Herschel even told me once that Orthodox rabbis and scholars have spent many tedious hours poring over the texts to figure out when it's okay or not okay for a man to touch a menstruating woman—not just intimately but at all, like on her elbow. Yikes! "Well," I said after a bit, "it's to show d-devotion to G-G-God." That pablum answer hopefully covered the territory, and I guess it did because Benji nodded and seemed satisfied.

Soon Magda brought a basket of the lovely rye bread with caraway seeds and small, foil-wrapped pats of butter and asked if we wanted anything to drink. "And who is dis young man?" she asked. I tried to think of how to explain our relationship but couldn't easily, so just said, "This is B-B-Benji. He came just to m-meet you. He's heard a l-lot about you."

She nodded and patted his shoulder. "Only goot things, *ja?*" I noticed that Benji was staring at Magda's big face, his mouth slightly agape like a simpleton, and kicked his leg just a bit. He immediately looked down and blushed.

I ordered two chocolate phosphates for us and told Magda, jokingly, not to skimp on the Bosco. She looked confused but said nothing.

Soon Herschel and Jake and Howie arrived. Herschel'd met Benji before, of course, and gave him a high-five. I'd worried that Herschel would badmouth Naomi in front of Benji, but he didn't. He never mentioned her. I was glad of that. What would be the point? My idea was for Benji to have time away from his mother and sister and not have to think about them or be reminded of them. All Herschel said, as Benji studied the menu, was, "What are you gonna have, kid? I highly recommend the Hear-O-Israel. It'll make you happy all day and for some of tomorrow." Benji looked at him and smiled subtly and shrugged. But when Magda came to take our orders he said he wanted the Son of a Brisket Melt. I'd thought of getting that sometime, if I ever have the courage to vary from my usual. It has seasoned, slow-cooked beef on grilled challah bread with grilled onions and melted Swiss cheese. Yum!

Benji again stared at Magda's face as she was taking Jake's and Howie's orders. I didn't stop him. I didn't blame him. I had the fantasy that she'd pause from her order-taking and come over to me and stroke the back of my head with her large white hand. "Julius," she'd say, "I must tell you dat you are really quite da man. Da rest of dese gentlemen, including da runt here wit da blue beanie, are just … how do you say? … ordinary. *Common*, dey are. But you are not. If you vish me to run away wit you to anyvhere in da world, you have only to ask." She'd pause and look at each of the guys in turn and hold her gaze, with those amazing pale-blue eyes. "And," she'd say, "I vill be happy to cook for you many vonderful meals, anyting you like—kielbasa, bigos, potato soup wit sour rye, golouka—and ve vill have amazing, uh, copulation, *ja?* I am sure you are *quite* vell-endowed and skilled." The other guys would look up at her with mouths agape and then at me, with new respect. Benji would, too. Magda would again stare directly at each of them in turn. "And," she'd then add, addressing the crowd, "dat stutter don't matter. He is much man."

When our food arrived, Herschel, as usual, doused his Hear-O-Israel with Dijon Grey Poupon and took his customary huge bites, dripping the mustard and Thousand Island dressing onto his shirt sleeve and the formica-topped table. I noticed that Benji was staring at Herschel, wide-eyed, and stifling a grin. "How's your melt?" Jake asked. Benji's mouth was full with his own sandwich so he just nodded. Jake smiled. Benji, after swallowing his mouthful, asked him what he was eating. "It's called The Epiphany," Jake said. "Grilled pastrami, Swiss and sauerkraut between potato pancakes. I don't know why it's called that, but it's magnificent." *Sauerkraut!* I thought, grimacing. Yuck!

Benji had a look of delight on his face as he downed his Son of a Brisket Melt and then took sips of his phosphate through a transparent plastic straw. It was good to see him happy. After a moment, I asked if I could try his sandwich and he smiled and nodded and pushed his plate toward me. I took just one bite, a small one. It was wonderful. The grilled challah and beef together were sublime. I had the thought that I'd tell Naomi that *I'd* ordered the Son of a Brisket, to show her that I could vary my routine, but immediately thought better of it. What if she interrogated

Benji and he told her the truth? Then I'd have to try to think of a way to worm out of my lie. Or, I could ask Benji to lie to his mother about my lunch selection if the occasion arose. But that's probably not a good way to go; better he should stay uncorrupted for as long as possible.

Soon Izzy came over to our table and wiped away some of the spilled mustard and dressing near Herschel's plate. His apron wasn't improved since our last visit. He lightly slapped the back of my cousin's head with an open palm. "What are you, for God's sake, a three-year-old, spilling everywhere? Ach!" I noticed Benji staring at Izzy's face and then at the big color photo near the kitchen door and then back at Izzy.

"Hey, Iz," Herschel said, hunching his shoulders and crossing his arms in front of his chest and bending forward a bit. "It's cold in here. Can't we get a little *heat?*"

Izzy kept wiping. "*Nu?*" he said after a moment, shrugging. "It's colder outside, yes? So you should count your blessings." He touched Benji's shoulder and asked, more gently, "How is your lunch, young man?"

Before Benji could answer, I said, "Izzy, is it t-true you use B-Bosco syrup in your phosphates? That's what I told B-B-Benji."

He shook his head and said, "You bet."

I was confused. "So you *d-do* use B-B-Bosco?"

"NO," he answered, looking impatient. "*You bet.*" I must have still looked confused because Izzy furrowed his brow and muttered, "Oh, for God's sake!" and stalked into the kitchen.

"Way to go, *putz*," Jake said. "You irritated the man."

In less than a minute Izzy returned, carrying a large, dark-brown plastic bottle in his right hand. Magda was behind him. "*This!*" he said loudly, holding up the bottle. "Do you see?" The label identified it as Fox's U-Bet Premium Chocolate Flavor Syrup. "All the great delis use this," Izzy said. "Your Carnegie's, your Katz's, the old Rascal House, all of them, they use this. Not that Bosco *chazzerai*. You shouldn't show your ignorance so much." Herschel and Jake laughed out loud, and Benji stared at them for a moment and followed suit. "It's the best for egg creams, too," Izzy added.

"Sir," Benji said to Izzy, "why is The Epiphany called that?"

Izzy again patted Benji's shoulder. "So, finally from someone a sensible question. Good boy. I had the idea maybe eight years ago when my wife, may her memory be a blessing, was making *latkes*, potato pancakes, for Chanukah. I was eating a pastrami with Swiss on rye, and had the idea of this. I told Sadie. 'Nu,' she said, 'that sounds good. An *epiphany*, you've had.' I had to look up that word." He paused and rubbed the top of Benji's head. "My wife was a teacher, you know."

We were all quiet for a few moments. I looked over at Howie, finishing his Izzy's Chicago Dog. It took a while, because he took small, careful bites and always chewed with his mouth closed. After each few bites, he put his hot dog down on the plate and delicately wiped the corners of his mouth with his cloth napkin. There were no crumbs in his vicinity. I was grateful he hadn't ordered another of those disgusting pickled tongue sandwiches. Howie'd said little during lunch. He's quiet, always polite. I noticed how well-toned his arms and shoulders and chest looked, even under his shirt. I remembered that he'd said that he'd worked out at a gym before and during *King Lear* because he was practically naked so much in his Poor Tom scenes in Act III on the heath, in the storm, and also in Act IV, in the Dover scene, and he wanted to look okay. That worked. Good shoulders and pecs.

I had the thought that he'd now be a decent choice for *Naked and Afraid*, whereas before the play he'd been good-looking enough, I guess, though maybe a trifle soft and flabby around the edges. Howie's survivalist partner would, now, be quite impressed with his physique and would certainly want to snuggle with him during the cold scary nights in their fragile temporary shelter of branches and vines and foliage, with the manic monkeys yelling and the relentless mosquitoes buzzing.

I remembered Howie onstage at the dress rehearsal and performances, during Act III, in his Poor Tom persona, clad only in a loincloth, the thunder sheets booming to simulate the storm, talking crazy—"The foul fiend bites my back!"—and singing snatches of one of his bizarre songs— *"But mice and rats and such small deer have been Tom's food for seven long year ... "*—and huddled into himself, arms crossed against his chest, shivering, because of the supposed rain and wind. "Poor Tom's *a-cold!*" He'd been great. Finishing the last bites of my potato salad, I remembered thinking, during those rehearsals and performances, that acting just seemed so easy for this guy, so effortless, and he was so talented throughout, not just as innocent Edgar in the early scenes but also as mostly-naked Tom on the heath and then later, still in madman beggar disguise, helping and protecting his poor father, blind Gloucester, and keeping him from offing himself, jumping off a cliff. I admired him, but was also jealous. If I could've done Edgar half as well as he did—if I *could* act at all, which, of course, I can't, what with the damned stutter and my lack of any talent—I think I could feel that I'd actually done something with my life.

A mensch, Howie is.

Well, I'd taken good photos with Howie in them for my father's damned *King Lear* album, I'll say that for myself. My favorite picture was that eleven-by-fourteen framed one hanging at the end of the hallway between the living room and the bedrooms—the one from the dress rehearsal storm scene in Act III when Dad, as mad Lear, wild-eyed and wild-haired, looks at naked, shivering Poor Tom, in his loincloth, and says, "Thou wert better in a grave than to answer with thy uncovered body this extremity of the skies … Thou art the thing itself! Unaccommodated man is no more but such a poor, bare forked animal as thou art." That stuck with me. That's maybe one of my best photos, not just because of the interesting subjects but also because of my craft in the exposure; I'd used diffused fill flash, mounted on a bracket so as to lower the shadows, and slightly underexposed to enhance the dramatic strangeness of the situation. So there's that.

As we were finishing our coffee and dessert—the cheesecake for Benji and me—Herschel looked at me and said, "So how's Uncle Herb doing?"

I didn't answer right away. I wanted to answer, to tell my cousin that his uncle was behaving strangely, that he'd been having trouble sleeping, was in pain from his back injury, had said he felt like a failure at playing Lear but that some other guys he'd mentioned—Scofield and Jacobi, for two—hadn't failed. They'd gotten it right, he'd said. I wanted to tell him that his uncle wore his horrible green bathrobe, which has symbolism for me, and didn't shower or shave much anymore and that he smelled bad and now he wasn't even always flushing the damned toilet. Part of me wanted to tell him about all that, to get it out. Maybe Herschel would have insights. But I just couldn't manage all that talk. All I said was, "I g-guess he's okay."

I don't know if the old man's back is, really, better or worse. He stills winces when he moves and it sometimes seems to take him longer than usual to stand up straight when he gets up from his chair. He told me he's still gobbling Ibuprofen. I asked him recently how his back was and he thought for a moment and then gave his usual answer: "I guess it could be worse." He noticed me staring at him. "Well, he said, "actually I think that those Salonpas patches, and maybe the cream, are helping, at least a little."

Thank God he says he's sleeping a little better. I'd refilled my Ambien prescription from Ansfield and had given the full bottle to Dad.

Magda brought our checks just then. "You come again, young man," she said to Benji. "Ve give you more chocolate phosphate." She furrowed her brow and gave me a look and shook her head and then winked at Benji. "But not vit dat cheap Bosco, *ja?*"

Benji smiled. "You bet!" he said.

Herschel looked up at her and grinned hugely. "Magda," he said softly, putting his short arm around her waist, "you're a hell of a woman. You've captured my poor heart, I can tell ya that. Oh, absolutely!" She giggled and walked away.

As we were driving home, Benji asked me what an egg cream is. "Well," I said, "An egg c-cream is seltzer, m-milk and chocolate s-syrup. Sometimes v-v-vanilla syrup." He nodded and asked why it was called that, since it includes neither eggs nor cream. It was a good question, and I was surprised that I'd never thought about that before. Here I've lived a life for forty years and never once pondered that issue, and here Benji's just twelve and hasn't started shaving yet and, right off, he does. "Listen," I said, "We'll g-g-get egg creams sometime soon, okay? I p-promise."

TEN

MY CELESTE MITZVAH was lovely. Her parts worked fine, and so did mine. She didn't say so, but I'm sure she was happy with the outcome; she found out what she needed to find out. I don't know if the encounter resulted in blissful sensations for her, but it did for me.

I'd been nervous as hell beforehand. I couldn't sleep most of the night before our rendezvous. In my nervousness, I wanted to clutch on to sleeping Naomi, but wasn't sure that would be an okay thing to do. For one thing, I was on the verge of sleeping with another woman. For another, she was upset about the scratch on the back of her car. She'd asked me to get her Acura washed, what with all the winter slush lately, and I agreed. She said to take her car to the carwash attached to the local convenience store and gas station, Kelley's Market, where you sit in the car as it's getting washed. But I said I couldn't do that. I can't sit inside a non-moving car that's in a small enclosed building, with the car windows closed and the powerful streaming water and soap and those huge mechanical brushes pounding at the front and sides and back of the car, and the steam and the horrible nonstop noise, and sometimes you can't see out the windshield because it's covered with soap, and you have to just sit there, helpless—getting out of the car is absolutely not an option— and wait for the scary ordeal to be over, wait until the green EXIT sign flashes and the big door opens and you can finally—*finally!*—drive out into the open air and can open the windows. I did that stay-in-the-car option just once, and it was a nightmare. I sweated like a pig and could barely breathe. I was quite verklempt. I may have screamed. Thank God I was alone.

So I told Naomi I couldn't go there but would go to Mermaid, where you pay more but can get out of the car while it's going through the wash and just calmly stroll through a corridor and watch the procedure through huge windows that have little signs letting you know what's happening on the other side of the glass—"Chassis Bath," whatever that means, is one— and can observe your car moving down the line and getting all nice and clean but not be involved, can blessedly be a spectator rather than a panicking participant, and can then casually saunter over and ease yourself into your clean car when the Mermaid guys, all in dark-blue coveralls, have finished drying the exterior with those little folded light-blue towels they always hold, one in each hand, and one of them has gestured you over with a beckoning index finger. Naomi gave me a look of disgust and shook her head, but conceded.

After the car wash, I stopped at Home Depot to buy furnace filters and, when backing out of the parking space, turned the steering wheel a bit too tightly and got too close to a concrete barrier and scratched the right rear fender of Naomi's Acura. I felt sick when I heard it happening. It wasn't big or deep, but it was noticeable. I didn't tell her about it. I hoped that Naomi wouldn't notice right away, wouldn't be aware of the scratch until she'd driven the car herself so she'd think it had happened on her watch. But no. "How the fuck did *this* happen?" she growled within an hour of my return home. I looked at the scratch and drew my finger along its length and shook my head. "I have n-no idea," I said. "Some b-bastard must have gotten too c -c-close." I shook my head in disgust. "People are *so* c-c-careless! And they didn't even l-leave a n-n-note!" She gave me a look, studying my face. I don't know if she believed me, but she didn't say anything. Still, she was pissy the rest of the evening and said nothing as we got ready for bed.

By the time I got to Celeste's condo in mid-morning, I was so nervous that I was trembling. My mouth was dry and my face felt flushed. My heart was beating fast. I wondered if she'd be nervous too, but she didn't seem to be. She greeted me at the door with a little closed-mouth smile and arched eyebrows and touched my right forearm and squeezed just a bit. Then she leaned up and kissed my cheek, very briefly. She looked good, wearing tight jeans and a soft light-green sweater. Her pretty short hair was clean and had a lemony smell. She had an elastic support on her right wrist. "I'm having some wine," she said. "Chablis. Want some?" I nodded. I wanted to say something more, to thank her, to tell her how amazing it was to be here with her this day, how I couldn't believe my luck to be here with someone like her, a woman like her, who'd played wonderful Cordelia, but my mouth was still too dry.

Celeste brought out some stone-ground-wheat snack crackers and assorted cheese on a plate, as well as a blue bowl of Trader Joe's trail mix, with not just the almonds and cashews and cubes of chocolate that she likes but also pistachios, cranberries and tiny cherry bits, and we ate and drank and I tried to muster saliva so I could say something and wouldn't come off as any more of an idiot than I could help. But when I could finally talk, all I could think of to say was, "I was so s-sorry you g-g-got hanged. That was too b-bad." She looked at me strangely. "I mean, n-not *you*," I went on. "C-C-Cordelia." I was embarrassed, but Celeste smiled and nodded.

"I understand," she said. "Yes, too bad."

After a bit, she went to the kitchen to refill our glasses. "You know," she said when she returned, "there was a revised version of *Lear* that was the standard for about 150 years, until the mid-1800s. A guy named Tate wrote it. Nahum Tate. Cordelia and Lear don't die, and he continues being king and Edgar and Cordelia get married and they take good care of Lear, who eventually dies happily, of old age, and then Edgar and Cordelia rule the kingdom together. It's a nicer ending. Then, for whatever reason, someone changed it back to the original tragic ending, with all the deaths."

After that, my memory is foggy. We ate some more cheese and Celeste drank a third glass of wine and I noticed that her pretty blue-gray eyes seemed a bit glazed and her cheeks flushed, and somehow we wound up in her upstairs bedroom and soon her jeans and sweater were off and she unbuttoned my shirt and undid my belt buckle and we kissed gently, not at all passionately. She handed me a beige condom from the top drawer of the nightstand. I felt like that guy on *Jerry Springer*: "We was kissin' and stuff and next thing I know I'm, like, all naked in her bed." I don't specifically remember our doing it, any details, other than that it was wonderful and that she kept the wrist support on as we made love. She wasn't closed up down there. For a moment, I tried to fantasize that it was Cordelia I was with. I imagined her saying that line I liked—"Unhappy that I am, I cannot heave my heart into my mouth"—as we were doing the deed. But that nice fantasy didn't last long.

I remember that, afterward, Celeste went "Whew!" and got out of bed and stood up and, with her back to me, raised her arms high and straight and entwined her fingers and stretched, doing a deep side bend to the left and then one to the right. She had a narrow waist. I could see her spine and ribs as she stretched. There was a little dark-brown spot on her lower back, just above her sweet bottom. Probably it was just a mole, but maybe, I thought, it was something worse. It occurred to me that she perhaps didn't know about the spot and I should tell her about it, suggest that she see a doctor. But I didn't. Then she turned to me and smiled and touched the tip of my nose and whispered, "Be right back," and then walked briskly to the bathroom. I watched her walking away.

While she was gone, I lay on my back, my head on one of her large fluffy pillows, covered with a flower-patterned pillowcase, my hands locked behind my head. I felt fine. I couldn't remember when I'd felt so fine. My world, for once, seemed just right. Naomi and my father and any other worries, even poor Benji, weren't cudgeling me. Later, maybe, they would, but not now. Later, probably, but not at the moment. I felt grateful to Celeste, but at the same time, just then, wished that she'd stay in the bathroom for as long as possible so I could just be there alone in her bed, lying still and feeling good, and not have to talk or interact, not have to say anything or do anything. I just wanted to savor the moment.

I noticed a nice framed print on the wall to the left of the bed, and recognized it from my high school Introduction to Art class. It was *Christina's World* by Andrew Wyeth, and showed, from behind, a young woman in a pink dress and plain shoes in the left foreground, semi-reclining in a field of grass, leaning on her spindly right arm, staring upward at a distant farmhouse on the horizon, in the right background. A few smaller outbuildings were near the farmhouse and there was a barn some distance to the left of the house. All the buildings were gray and looked old or weathered. The sky above the horizon was also gray. The woman, who must be Christina, seemed tense or maybe just very alert. Her hair was slightly disheveled, or maybe blowing in the wind. Her face was turned away. That bothered me; I wanted to see her face, her eyes, her expression. *Who is she?* I wondered. *What's going on in her head? Is she longing for something? If so, what? How is this her world?* I had the thought that she looked, from the back, like Lydia: same small body and thin arms and nice dark hair.

I thought just then that I wouldn't have minded if it'd been Lydia I'd shtupped instead of Celeste, though, of course, shtupping Celeste had been quite lovely. I closed my eyes and conjured Lydia's sweet heart-shaped face with the cute freckled nose and big eyes and full lips, framed by that poufy black hair. I briefly imagined that she was here with me in Celeste's bed, naked and relaxed and happy. Naked and unafraid.

When I opened my eyes, I glanced back toward *Christina's World* and then a strange thing happened: the grass in the painting seemed to sway back and forth gently, as though blown by a nice breeze. The woman, Christina, stayed still in her tense repose and the buildings on the horizon were still, too, but the grass swayed. I could almost hear that soft swishing sound. The hallucination lasted for just a moment and then everything was static again. But that was a special moment.

When Celeste returned from the bathroom, she was wrapped in a lavender terrycloth robe. Her hair was a bit askew and her face was still flushed. "Want some more wine?" she asked. I shook my head. I didn't want to risk Naomi smelling alcohol on my breath and asking questions. "Okay," she said. "Well, I'm going downstairs to get another glass. Be right back." Her demeanor seemed a bit cooler than before. Her voice was slightly nasal and she spoke in a bit of a monotone. I hadn't noticed that before. I remembered that Lear, at the end of the play, said of dead Cordelia that "her voice was ever soft, gentle and low—an excellent thing in woman." That seemed a nice thing to say about your tragically deceased daughter—sad but nice. I guess it was true of Celeste's voice in the play, but not so much in real life. Still, I thought how good it would be to hear her say my favorite Cordelia line—"No cause!"—preferably in her soft, gentle and low stage voice. I had the idea that she could certainly do that much, considering the favor I'd done her.

So when she returned, wine glass in hand, I said, "Hey, Celeste, any c-c-cause?" She looked at me strangely and furrowed her brow and scrunched her face. I tried again. "I kn-know you have c-cause to hate me. Your sisters have n-none." She stared at me blankly and shook her head, as if to say "What the *hell* are you talking about?" I thought about trying again and saying that if she had poison for me to drink I'd take it, but decided to let it go. "Well, I said, "I better get d-dressed and get g-going."

As I was getting ready to leave, I noticed a nice silver-framed photo of Celeste and Andrew on a hutch in the living room. They were both smiling and looking directly into the camera and had their arms around each other. I had the impression that the photo'd been taken at a wedding. She was wearing a pretty yellow-and-green patterned dress and he a dark-gray suit and white shirt and a blue-gray tie. He was taller than she and thin, with black-framed glasses, perhaps a bit nerdy-looking. If I hadn't known that Andrew was a certified public accountant, I might have guessed that from his appearance. I'm not sure what a certified public accountant does, but it certainly sounds like a nerdy occupation. Still, there was something about Andrew's facial expression—a gentleness, maybe—that I liked. But they looked good together, and, I guess, happy enough. What do I know?

A good thing was that Celeste gave me a nice hug before opening the front door to let me out. I held her close, maybe closer than I should have, and kissed her cheek. I was hoping our lips would meet again, but they didn't. Nor did she return my cheek kiss. Nor did she thank me for my mitzvah. I wasn't sure if it was okay to expect that. It should have been me thanking her, really, expressing huge gratitude for the chance for someone like me, a schlemiel such as myself, to spend part of a morning in bed with a beautiful and sexy and talented woman like her. I should have dropped to my knees and raised my grateful eyes heavenward and tightly encircled her sweet creamy thighs with both arms and loudly proclaimed, sans stutter, "Thank you, thank you, *thank you*, Celeste! Today was absolutely the high point of my pathetic life! It was my, my … chance of a *lifetime!*"

I also thought, just then, of going ahead and asking her why she'd chosen me instead of Donny or some other stud from the play. But I wasn't sure how that question would go over, so let it go.

Well, I thought as I was driving home, *what if Celeste dies young from melanoma skin cancer from that brown spot on her back that she never knew about because I didn't tell her about it when I could have?* How would I feel then? What kind of person am I that this lovely, amazing woman lets me—*me!*—have sex with her, a once-in-a-lifetime experience, and then I don't open my stupid mouth to warn her about a potentially deadly health hazard, the possible result of which is that she expires way before her time and all that beauty and talent are gone forever, and now poor gentle Andrew is alone with just his accounts to keep him warm? Not a good person. Certainly not a mensch.

While at a stoplight, I felt worried about seeing Naomi later, worried that she'd read guilt on my face. But that worry faded for the moment when I looked in the rearview mirror and noticed a nice-looking red-haired young woman taking advantage of the pause to put on lipstick. She was staring into her own downward-tilted rearview mirror, chin raised, and, with her right hand, carefully applying lipstick to her puckered lower lip. She seemed very intense about the whole procedure. Then she smooshed her lips together and studied her image in the mirror, her head cocked to one side and eyes opened wide. The light turned green and I had to drive on, but I wished that we'd been stuck at a railroad crossing and waiting for a slow-moving two-mile-long freight train to pass so I could have just spent ten or fifteen minutes watching that pleasant young woman do her lips, her eyebrows, her makeup, brush her hair, whatever other grooming, without ever having to talk to her or otherwise interact. No expectations. Usually I would, under such circumstances, have felt trapped, unable to move forward or backward. But watching my sweet little redhead would be a happy enough distraction that I don't think I would have panicked. I appreciated the chance to briefly observe that beauty do her face, but felt sad thinking that I'd likely never see her again my life long.

ELEVEN

NAOMI WOKE ME up at three in the morning, though not on purpose. She was sleeping soundly, on her left side, and I was asleep too and then I heard her little *"m-m-m"* moan, not just once but over and over. I turned on the table lamp on my side of the bed, low beam, and leaned over to look at her face and saw that she was smiling in her sleep. She must have been having a nice dream. I, too, had been having a good dream, in which I was at Starbucks and that interesting woman with the ponytail and the scrunchie noticed me staring at her and smiled back but said nothing and then, a few minutes later, just before leaving, she stopped at my table and smiled again, showing perfect white teeth, and handed me a breakfast sandwich— sausage, cheddar and egg. "I thought you might enjoy this," she murmured. Then she bent down and, her face close to mine, whispered in my ear. "I really do hope you'll … *enjoy!*"

Hearing Naomi moan and seeing that little smile, just then I felt warmth—affection, but also lust. Part of me wanted to put my arms around her back and maneuver her sleeping body to face me and to hold her tightly and deposit numerous kisses on her lips and face and neck. If she remained unconscious during all that, it would be fine; it would be good to just have contact with her sleeping body. She didn't need to be awake. If she regained consciousness, though, I hoped to even get her excited and amorous.

But another part of me didn't want to take a chance on that. If I awakened her, even with friendly intentions, maybe Naomi'd be warm and loving back but just as likely she'd be irritated about being aroused from her sleepy ecstasy and lash out. "Jesus Christ!" she might snarl. "What the hell are you doing? Leave me the fuck *alone!*" So I contented myself with gently spooning against her and very softly stroking her right shoulder and upper arm. She was wearing a pink-and-white-checked flannel nightgown.

But then I couldn't get back to sleep. I knew I wouldn't be able to for a long while, and resigned myself to yet another long winter's night session of worries and ruminations. My first thought, though, was that at least the winter solstice had come and gone and now the nights won't be as long as before that blessed event. The darkness versus daylight difference maybe won't be much, but at least the movement will on the positive side of the ledger. So there's that.

One thing that popped into my brain was a wedding I'd helped Liz with in July. I'm not sure why. It might have been related to seeing that photo of Andrew and Celeste at her condo, which may have been done at a wedding. The reception for the July wedding was at a Marriott near the freeway. Liz, as usual, left early. Thankfully, there were no disasters or tragedies other than the father of the bride going on and on tediously for fifteen minutes during his toast speech, with the aid of a stack of three-by-five blue index cards with his notes in purple ink. Between each long-winded anecdote about his beloved daughter, including one in which he proudly took credit for teaching her to ride a red Schwinn bicycle with training wheels, he raised his head to pause and grin hugely at the audience, showing long yellow teeth. The bride, Shelly, alternated between smiling sweetly while dabbing at her eyes and looking like she wanted to kill her father for going on and on. But she definitely loosened up later in the evening, during the dancing.

After the obligatory dances—the couple's first dance, the wedding party dance, the parent dances—Shelly and her bridesmaids, all well-lubricated with alcohol, danced together with big enthusiasm. I stood to the side taking candids of them dancing, most with the bride in the center of the frame. I knew she'd like such pictures. Then, while the DJ blasted "Mony Mony" and everyone on the dance floor raised their arms and yelled "*Yeah! ... Yeah! ...* " on cue, Shelly suddenly turned around and bent over and raised her gown above her waist and exposed her butt—bare except for beige thong panties. All the bridesmaids howled with laughter. I perfectly, though unintentionally, captured the moment with my camera.

Later, when selecting which pictures to give to the couple, at Liz's request since she was "unusually busy," I agonized about what to do. Would Shelly want a picture of her drunkenly exposing her tush on her wedding day? Would she think it was embarrassing or think it was cute? After agitating about it, I decided the former and deleted that photo and decided to not mention it to the bride. But then when I called, again at Liz's request, to tell Shelly that her pictures were ready, her first question was, "Oh, did you get me flashing my ass to the ladies? I *really* hope you did!" I didn't answer for a moment. "N-No," I finally said. "I don't r-r-remember that." There was a pause. "Oh," she said softly. "Well, okay." So, I guess, yet another unfortunate incident of Julius Dickman failing a female.

I liked that Marriott. I had the idea that maybe a job I'd like would be vacuuming the hallways and ballrooms and meeting rooms of a big hotel like that. That's probably a job that a person does alone, operating a large and very powerful vacuum cleaner and being quite thorough. I wouldn't have to talk with anyone, except maybe some of the other housekeeping staff. I could just do my job every day, and it would be good to see the results, the clean carpets. Maybe there'd even be an outside chance of seducing one of the female housekeepers. If she didn't speak English, that would be okay. I wouldn't have to talk much, if at all, and thus wouldn't need to agitate about my stutter.

Holding onto sleeping Naomi, I thought also about what Celeste had said about that guy Tate's alternate version of *King Lear*. I like it that Cordelia didn't get hanged in his version. That was a good change. That was certainly the best thing Nahum came up with. Her horrible death was the saddest part of the play. Cordelia and Lear had finally reconciled after going through so much, and he, finally calm and sane, talked nicely about their going to prison together and singing like two caged birds and telling each other stories about who loses and who wins at the royal court, who's in and who's out, and take upon themselves "the mystery of things as if we were God's spies," and then, *KA-BLOOEY!*, she gets murdered at dickhead Edmund's behest. Lear killed the captain, another nasty prick, who was hanging Cordelia but he got there too late to save her. What was the damned point of her being murdered, after all the horrible crap that she and her father had gone through? No point that I can see. It seemed like too much, just adding a layer of gratuitous misery on top of all the other sad layers. Just random cruelty. *Vey iz mir!*

Then, a few minutes later, Lear himself gave up the ghost, probably from the strain of all the high emotion. Too much for his old heart. It makes a person question what's up. It was almost as though God or Shakespeare, or maybe both those guys, was sneering and pointing at dead Cordelia and dead Lear, to say nothing of poisoned Regan and self-slaughtered Goneril, and going, "So, schmuck, you thought the world makes *sense?* That there's some kind of moral order? Justice? That love triumphs? *Redemption?* HAH! Well, take *this*, putz, and pull your fluffy head out of your ass!"

Well, maybe life *is* just one damned random and absurd thing after another, and that's all. Nothing more. It seems that way sometimes. Maybe Twersky's wrong.

Well, it was just a play, not real life, so why am I so farmisht? It's silly. Still, I can't get past it, lying awake in the middle of these quiet, endless winter nights. All those corpses. Lear's death and Gloucester's, too, were sad, I guess, maybe even tragic, but at least they were old farts who'd had their lives. And Goneril and Regan turned out to be nasty women who did unspeakable things. But not Cordelia. She was young and good and beautiful. Her life was ahead. Celeste had said that Tate changed the plot so that Cordelia and Edgar got married and lived contentedly for a very long time and took good care of Lear until he died of old age—a blessed and fortunate old geezer, unburdened at last. So maybe that's a more satisfying ending. It was definitely a *happier* ending. But what's more realistic—a happy ending like that or the original bleak, hopeless one with stiff corpses, lifeless eyes opened wide in final horror and mouths agape, strewn every-where, including Cordelia's? *Especially* Cordelia's. Maybe bleaker is truer, in some great scheme of things. What do I know?

Cordelia's demise puts me in mind of that question in *Love Story*: "What can you say about a twenty-five-year-old girl who dies?" Maybe the answer is: *Nothing.* What's there to say? Just get her in the ground before she ripens and move on.

Maybe sometime I'll ask Celeste what she thought of Cordelia's death. Celeste. I can't get her out of my mind, our little adventure. I don't know if it was the right thing to do, but I'd sent her a text message after our time together saying that I liked seeing her and thanking her for the cheese and crackers. I was trying to be cute. I suppose I could have said something more direct:

> *Thank you for making love with me, dear Celeste. It was sublime! I'm glad I could do a mitzvah and help out with your understandable concern about your parts. Hope you and Andrew can now have that make-up sex and then keep happily shtupping.*

Maybe she'd have gotten a kick out of that. I didn't think I'd hear back from her, so was happily surprised when I got a return text: *You're welcome for the cheese and crackers, Julius. You were a fine lover.*

Thinking of Celeste, my mind went back to watching that redhead doing her lipstick in her car after our adventure. I had the fantasy that she, the redhead, might have noticed me watching her in my mirror and got upset and inadvertently accelerated while working on her lower lip and crashed hard into the back of my Honda. Maybe I would have had painful whiplash. If so, I'd contact Lydia and ask her to represent me. We'd meet in her well-appointed office and she'd go over options. "Don't worry, dear Julius," she'd say. "I'll make sure we get some well-deserved justice for you." Maybe she'd be wearing that sexy little black dress again. She'd advise me to see a doctor, of course, to get evaluated. Maybe she'd have a particular one in mind, someone more likely to give the opinion she'd prefer. That doc would hopefully be a Jew, a competent one, but, I guess, *could* be a gentile—as long as he or she testified convincingly in my favor.

I'd get to see a side of Lydia that I've not seen: the tough-minded professional personal injury lawyer with a big rep. Maybe seeing her in action would make me love and admire her even more, would add to her charm. Or it could go the other way. Maybe I'd be so impressed by her confidence and abilities and determination that I'd be intimidated, over-whelmed, would maybe feel that the chasm between us was even greater than I'd thought and that there was even less chance than I'd imagined for a *shlub* like me to have a chance with someone like her.

But either way, I'd hopefully get some money out of the deal. If so, I'd consider inviting the redhead to a nice lunch as a token of reconciliation, if she wasn't too bitter about being sued. Maybe Olive Garden or even Luigi's. As she was delicately taking small bites of her pasta with shrimp, I'd tell her how much I'd enjoyed watching her apply the lipstick in her car. "That was a very l-l-lovely shade f-for you," I'd say.

It's funny what goes through a guy's head when he's wide awake in the middle of the night. For some reason, lying comfortably next to Naomi, I thought of someone I've seen around town now and again for years, usually in the warmer months. He's a young guy, probably in his mid-twenties, with severe cerebral palsy, I believe, and gets around in an electric wheelchair. He's thin and misshapen, with his skinny arms permanently bent and fingers clawed, and has close-cropped hair. He usually has an agonized facial expression, with his brow furrowed and eyes a bit wild. His pinched face and short hair puts me in mind of a Holocaust survivor. His tongue hangs out of one corner of his mouth and he usually drools. He can make his chair move by operating a little stick handle with his tortured right hand. He can't talk, but communicates by spastically touching a wooden board with letters and some key words and phrases—"*Thank you*" is one— on the tray of his chair. There's also a small plastic tag on the upper left corner of the tray that says "CARL" in all caps. I always see the board, but have only seen him use it once or twice.

I've seen Carl at the weekend farmers' markets and at street festivals in the summers, and once when I was with Herschel and Ajax on one of my cousin's cockamamie seduction quests. It's good that he gets out. He sometimes wears a yellow T-shirt with an image of Fidel Castro in his khaki fatigues, scruffy-bearded and wearing his customary military cap with the short bill and flat, wide top. Fidel could have balanced a medium-sized pizza on top of that cap. Another time, the guy was wearing a T-shirt with an image of, I believe, Lenin—bald pate with dark hair around the fringes, wide-set and intense brown eyes, neatly-trimmed goatee. Carl must admire communists. Always alone, he is. Poor guy. What a life. What must it be like? I'm sure he needs constant big help with eating, washing, going potty, dressing and whatnot just to get through one tedious day after the next. I wondered if he was able to get out much in the winter, like now. It must be hard to maneuver that damned wheelchair through the snow and ice and slush.

And I wondered, too, as I did with Big Art, whether this poor guy has ever known the joy of a high-quality kosher hot dog, like an Izzy's Chicago Dog. If not, he should. I'm sure Carl deserves *some* good things in life.

I wondered what Dad would say if I told him about the cerebral palsy guy. Maybe he'd say, "Count your blessings, son." That would be a good point. Whatever my problems and issues, at least I'm better off than Carl. My body works okay. So at least there's that.

I thought, too, about yesterday. I'd watched part of a movie on a DVD, *Quest for Fire*, with Benji in his room. It was about a prehistoric tribe, the Ulam, who somehow have fire but don't know how to actually create it. So they just keep a fire going all the time in their cave and hope for the best. Unfortunately, the Ulam get attacked by a nasty and ugly apelike tribe, the Wagabu, who want to steal their fire. They have to flee from the cave carrying what's left of their fire, which they call *atra*, in a flimsy bone basket. Sadly, it gets accidentally extinguished in a marsh and the tribal big boo-hoo assigns three guys, Naoh and Amouka and Gaw, to find more atra. So they wander around in the vast and harsh wilderness searching for fire and have various difficulties with mastodons and saber-toothed tigers and other bands of grunting primitives armed with spears and clubs, some of whom are cannibals. I only saw about half of it, so didn't know the outcome of their quest until later, at dinner. "How'd it t-t-turn out?" I asked Benji. "Did they get f-fire?"

"Who?" Elise asked. "Did *who* get fired?"

Benji ignored her. "Yup," he said. "They steal fire from the Kzamm tribe. And then Naoh gets a girlfriend, Ika, from a more advanced tribe and some guy from that tribe teaches them how to make their own fire." He paused and grinned slightly at me. "And Ika teaches him *other* things, too."

"What the hell are you talking about?" Naomi asked. She turned to me. "What kind of *mishegas* are you filling his head with? *Kzamm* tribe, for God's sake. Don't be encouraging such crap!"

I had a hard time looking Naomi in the face during the meal. Spooning against her creamy buttocks at night while she's asleep is one thing, but looking at her awake face just then was quite another. I worried that she'd read my guilt over Celeste and start asking questions. I'm not sure, any more, if I'm smart enough to lie well to her. If I thought she was suspicious, I'd try to change the subject before she started in on me. That sometimes— not always— works. "So," I'd maybe say, "what's up with D-D-Dorinda? How about R-Ramona?" Naomi and Elise like to watch *The Real House-wives of New York City* and they prattle nonstop. "Oh, that Sonja is, like, *so* obnoxious!" Elise will hiss. "Yeah?" Naomi will counter. "Well, what about Luann? She's the most self-centered cow on the show. She says she's a countess. Oh, countess, my *ass!*" So maybe starting in with the house-wives can be my fallback if my girlfriend suspects that I've shtupped another woman. It's worth a try. The alternative is gloomy.

I'll say this about Elise and Naomi: I sort of like them now and again when they're snarking about silly TV shows together. I feel fondness, affection even, for the two of them—pains in the ass though they often are otherwise. They like to eat potato chips—usually Lay's Sour Cream and Onion, from a family-sized bag—and they chatter and critique. It's endearing, in a twisted sort of way. It's interesting how they can be screaming insults and obscenities at each other, faces contorted and bodies tense, and then ten minutes later be together on the couch, Elise usually barefoot and sitting cross-legged, happily watching this crap, munching chips. I have little use for Elise otherwise, and she certainly has little for me, but I like hearing her go on about those silly housewives.

I had the thought that maybe my father'd like that show. Maybe he'd like the infinite supply of drama on *Real Housewives of New York*. "It's all theater, high or low," he'd said. Maybe he'd appreciate seeing those chatty Upper East Side women strutting and fretting their hours upon the stage, such as it is, puckering their lips and administering bilateral air-kisses to each other every two seconds while going *"mmm-whah!"* and consuming vast quantities of spirits, vodka gimlets and banana daiquiris and the like, and scarfing down hors-d'oeuvres, including cantaloupe balls, and huge steamed lobsters with melted butter, and crème brulee, and comparing plastic surgeries and Gucci bags, and heading off for long weekends in the Hamptons or Berkshires, and huffing and quarreling over endless trivial grievances and supposed slights. Dispensing and reacting to infinite petty offenses seems to be the driving dramatic force of the show—"Ramona said *what* about me? Oh … my … *God!* I cannot believe that she could be so insensitive! And here I thought we were *friends.*" It isn't Shakespeare, but it's certainly drama. We could watch it together while eating Doritos or Cheetos and maybe even comment and critique, like Naomi and Elise.

Maybe the old man'd particularly like Bethenny, the part-Jewess who used to be one of the New York housewives, if they show reruns with her. I like her too, and have even had occasional fantasies when, now and again, I've watched the show with Naomi. Bethenny's small, a spinner, like Lydia and Celeste. She's thin and not tall and dark-complected and pretty, and even named her company after her physique. So she's my preferred type physically, but, of course, there'd be no chance for me with someone like her. It's unthinkable. She's rich and successful and beautiful and smart and talks well. She's another who's way out of my league. Well, who knows? Celeste was out of my league, too, and look what happened there. So maybe I'll get a text message one of these days from Bethenny, who'll have decided to return to the show:

> *Listen, I'm just very tense from having to put up with drunken Sonja and overbearing Dorinda and obnoxious Ramona, flirting with everyone who owns a schwantz, and that giganto countess and her ridiculous cabarets. And Leah? Don't get me started. On top of all that aggravation I'm trying to run Skinnygirl, and there's a lot of damned stress everywhere, and I truly need to do a little hankie-pankie with a real man like you who won't blab or go wacko on me. Are you available?*

That would be nice.

TWELVE

NAOMI KICKED ME out this morning. She saw the text message I'd sent to Celeste and hers back to me. I'd intended to delete both texts, but forgot. She's been checking my phone regularly since Thanksgiving, since her suspicion that I'd been having an affair with Lydia. That's what she told me as I was making our morning coffee. I've never seen Naomi so angry. Her nose looked bigger than ever and her whole face, not just her shnoz, had a purplish hue. "We're DONE!" she hissed. "Get your bony ass out of this house, and I mean NOW!" After a minute, her lower lip started quivering and her face softened and she started weeping. "I can't believe you *did* this to me!" she whimpered, more softly. "How *could* you?"

The specific reason she was checking my phone was to see who'd called me in the middle of the night, at three-fifteen. It was my father. I'd had yet another bout of my damned insomnia but had finally—*finally!*—fallen asleep when I was startled by the ring. I went into the bathroom to answer. "Hey, son," he said right off, without even a hello. His voice sounded hoarse. "Can you bring some Kentucky Fried Chicken? Original, not crispy. Make sure it's mostly drumsticks, and a few breasts. Mashed potatoes and baked beans for sides. Potato wedges. Alright?" I told him it was the middle of the night and I'd bring it tomorrow. There was a long pause. "Oh," he said. "Okay. I guess so. *Damn* it, anyway." There was another pause, and I thought he'd hung up when he growled, "Okay, goodbye." I didn't know that Naomi had heard the phone ring or me talking—until this morning, that is.

After Dad's call, I was up most of the rest of the night, agitated. *What was that all about?* I wondered. *Is he nuts?* That's not all that was bothering me. Yesterday I looked up *Christina's World* on Wikipedia and learned that Christina was a real woman and that she'd had something called Charcot-Marie-Tooth disease—at first I thought it was some sort of dental problem—and couldn't walk. They originally thought she had polio. She had to scoot around. I'd been thinking all along that the pretty, thin woman in the painting was just reclining peacefully in the grass, looking up longingly at that gray farmhouse on the horizon, and looked tense or alert because she was absorbed with her thoughts or longings or dreams. And maybe that part was true enough. But it was startling to learn that it was *more* than just that, that poor Christina was crippled. The article said that Wyeth had, from his window, seen her crawling across a field and that's what inspired him. I don't know why the whole deal affected me as it did. The reality of the situation was just different from my notion, from what I'd thought when I saw the print on the wall in Celeste's bedroom, where she and I'd just shared a few lovely erotic minutes.

I was still thinking about Christina this morning when Naomi started yelling at me in the kitchen. Benji and Elise had heard Naomi screaming and came into the kitchen. Elise stared at me harshly, jaw clenched, but said nothing. Benji looked scared, though. His eyes were moist and his chin was trembling a bit. It hit me just then that I was going to have to move out and not live with him anymore.

I was thankful that Naomi, after reading the text on my phone, didn't scream, "Who the fuck is this bitch *Celeste?*" I'm not sure if Naomi made the connection as to who Celeste actually was. I'd brought Naomi and the kids to the premier of *Lear*, and of course she'd seen and read the program with the names of the actors, but I don't know if she connected the name on the text message with the woman who'd played Cordelia. I don't believe that I ever mentioned Celeste to Naomi, feeling as I have about her and not wanting Naomi to read my face or thoughts.

Nor did Naomi ever have occasion to meet any of the actors other than Herschel and Dad. She didn't want to go to the cast parties. She's never had much use for Shakespeare and said more than once that his plays are "a pain in the ass" and that she can't understand "all that confusing old language, all those damned '*thee's*' and '*thou's*'" but went with me anyway to the premieres of *Macbeth* and *Death of a Salesman* and *Othello*, to be a good girlfriend. She napped through half of *Othello*. She prefers musicals—*Oklahoma* and *The Music Man* and *Cats* and the like. Marian the librarian's her favorite character. After we saw *The Music Man* she went around the house for weeks singing "Being in Love," the one where Marian says that all she wants is "a quiet man, a gentle man, a straightforward and honest man" to live with in a cottage somewhere in Iowa. I'm quiet enough, I guess, what with the damned stutter, and maybe or maybe not gentle, but I admit to falling short on the honest and straightforward parts. Well, now that she's apparently done with me, I hope Naomi finds a guy with *all* of her desired qualities.

I had the brief impulse to explain to Naomi that my tryst wasn't personal, that I was just trying to do a mitzvah, a good deed, which helps a guy become a mensch. But I thought better of it. I doubt she would have been sympathetic.

On the other hand, maybe it would have worked to my advantage for Naomi to know that someone like Celeste had reached out to me, carnal-wise. Maybe it would have elevated her opinion of me. "Wait, what?" she'd maybe say. "Are you telling me that a beautiful, sexy, talented actress actually *asked* you to sleep with her? *You?* I can't believe it!" She'd look at me askance, brow furrowed and maybe her hooked nose prominent. She'd stare at me in a way she's never done before. "Well, maybe there's more to you than meets the eye, Julius Dickman. Maybe I've underestimated you all along." She'd pause and nod. "Hell, maybe I've been wrong about this schlemiel thing."

As to my father, Naomi's never much liked him. She's resented him for expecting me to be his photographer for so many years—"his Boswell," as Celeste said—and also for his wanting me to help him memorize his lines. As to the photography, it's bothered me that Dad's never once thanked me for all the time and bother. And I, too, resent the years I've had to sit with him on evenings or Sundays and go through each play he was about to be in, reading the lines of the other characters that preceded his lines, as cues. "The t-trick of that voice I do well r-remember," I recall reading in preparation for *Lear*, doing one of Gloucester's lines from the Dover scene. "Is't not the k-k-king?" From his La-Z-Boy, Dad squinted and closed his eyes while concentrating. "Ay," he intoned, "every inch a king. When I do stare, see how the subject quakes … " It was tedious. He'd always insisted that he felt anxious if he didn't memorize all his lines before the rehearsals started for each play. He said that he wanted to know the text before rehearsals so that he could worry less about that and "be able to concentrate on weightier matters as to my character."

I'm absolutely *thrilled* that all of that cueing's over now.

That said, I wouldn't have minded so much if it'd been Celeste whom I was helping to memorize her lines. Maybe she could have sat on my lap, warm and relaxed, in just her bra and panties, or even naked, with one arm around my shoulders. "How, n-now, C-C-Cordelia!" I'd read. "M-Mend your speech a l-l-little lest you may m-mar your fortunes." She'd smile and arch her eyebrows slightly and maybe deposit a sweet little kiss on my cheek. She'd nod, to show that she had this one down pat. "Good my lord," she'd respond in her soft, gentle and low voice, "you have begot me, bred me, loved me. I return those duties back as are right fit … " *That* would be lovely.

But it wasn't just the photography and the memorizing. Naomi's had a grudge against Dad since the Passover Seder she hosted the first year we were together. To be a good girlfriend, she'd invited him. Lydia was there, too—the first time I met her. Passover's always been important to Naomi; she's said many times that she has warm memories of childhood Seders at her Bubbeh Harriet's home—the family being together; the good food; the kids hunting for the hidden matzo, the *afikoman*; the telling of the Exodus story; the Four Questions. But I feel differently. For one thing, we never had a Seder after my mother killed herself when I was twelve. For another, it's a problematic holiday, in my opinion. I'm happy, of course, that the Israelites were finally released from bondage in Egypt, where they had to make bricks without straw, and finally got to go to the Promised Land, but I don't like it that Moses or God, or maybe both of those guys together, came up with the nasty idea of killing the firstborn males of the Egyptians to finally convince the damned pharaoh to let the people leave. That's what I said during that Seder at Naomi's. She'd been going on and on about how wonderful Passover is and how grateful we, as Jews, must feel about finally having been released from slavery and about being God's chosen people, blah blah, and for some reason she asked if I agreed about that whole deal and I said, probably foolishly, that I was okay, sort of anyway, with the early plagues—the frogs and the boils and the locusts and the waters of the Nile being turned red and the others—but had a problem with the final plague, with the whole idea of the Hebrews shmearing lamb's blood on their doorways so that the Angel of Death would pass *them* over but then go on to inflict horrible death to the firstborns of families who didn't have the happy benefit of knowing about that blood-on-doorway deal. "Well," I said, "it s-seems to me that if you celebrate P-P-Passover, you're sort of s-saying, 'Ha ha, *your* k-kids are dead but *m-mine* are okay.'" I didn't say so, but I also had an issue with slaughtering all those poor lambs just for their blood.

My comment didn't go over well with Naomi. Her face darkened and she gave me one of her looks. "Oh, what bullshit!" she snarled. "That is *so* sacrilegious! You should be *ashamed* of yourself."

Dad furrowed his brow. "No, he shouldn't," he said. "He's expressing his opinion. I think he has a point. For that matter, why couldn't God just have whisked the people out of Egypt on some kind of magic carpet instead of going through all that bother, all those damned plagues, to unharden the pharaoh's heart? Wouldn't that have been easier, less painful, for everyone?" Naomi didn't like that at all. Her heart's been hardened against Dad ever since.

Lydia's reaction was interesting. She said nothing during all of it, but sat there quietly, serenely, taking it all in, now and again maybe smiling subtly. She definitely smiled, briefly, when I said what I did about the dead Egyptian firstborns. I had no idea what was going on inside of her sweet head, then or later. I remember wishing that I would have asked her to share her thoughts about the Angel of Death and the lamb's blood and all.

I think maybe I first fell in love with Lydia a bit later when we were all seated at the table and Benji, as the youngest, asked the Four Questions as to why this night is different from all other nights—*Why do we eat reclining? Why do we eat only bitters?* and so on. I watched Lydia's face as she placidly looked at Benji and then as she listened to each of Grampa Morris's tedious responses. At one point, during his long-winded recitation of why, on this night, we only eat matzo, unleavened bread—because the Jews were in such an understandable sweat to leave Egypt that they couldn't wait for their bread to rise, so they didn't put leavening in it and, of course, it turned out flat, and matzo thus symbolizes the humility of poverty and slavery—Lydia turned to look directly at me and held her gaze for a moment, just as she did this past Thanksgiving when Naomi was going on about Arthur. Those were both nice moments. I tried to imagine what she was thinking: maybe *Good for you for standing up to my bigmouthed cousin. You're a good man, and I'd like to, uh, get to know you better. Much better.*

So I wonder how Dad will react when I tell him that Naomi's done with me. Unlike Herschel, my father's never said a bad word about Naomi. He's never quite said a good word, either, as far as that goes. I don't think he's given her much thought.

Seeing Naomi's tears, along with hearing her "How *could* you?" I found myself very much wanting to hold her, to comfort her, even in that dire moment. But I didn't. Maybe I should have. Or maybe that would have been a sick thing to do under the circumstances. I'm not sure how it would have gone over, in any case. She might have hoisted the Keurig and smashed it into my skull. Or she might have forgiven me and whimpered that we should try hard to find a way to move past this horrible indiscretion because, despite our difficulties, deep down we love each other and want to have a life together. But I just went upstairs and started packing.

THIRTEEN

EDGAR SAID, "O gods! Who is't can say 'I am at the worst'? I am worse than e'er I was." That's how I was feeling my first night at Dad's, sleeping in my old room. I'd called Herschel to see if I could stay with him for a few days. He said he has just a small one-bedroom apartment, which I knew, but I could sleep on his couch. I thanked him but, after briefly considering his offer, declined. That couch has seen better days. It has huge indentations and the springs are a menace. Plus, there're suspicious stains on the cushions, perhaps an outcome of my cousin's erotic life—solo or otherwise. But he said the offer stood if I changed my mind. When I told him that Naomi'd kicked me out, he just said, after a pause, "Okay." I expected to hear more—maybe "Well, you're better off without her," or "Hey, this is tough, but you'll get through it,"—but "Okay" was all he said.

That's fine. On the one hand, I'm good with Herschel and it would have been okay to be with him for a while—a short while. On the other hand, it would likely have been an ordeal to have to listen to that damned Thersites squawking out "Lechery! Lechery!" and "Chuck you, Farley!" day and night. A little of that obnoxious green-feathered bigmouth goes a long way.

I'm down on myself for not deleting the text messages from my phone. That was stupid and careless and now I'm paying for it. I should have anticipated that Naomi would look at my messages after I caught her with my phone on Thanksgiving. So now I'm done with her, I guess, and it's because of my own damned idiocy. If I had a board, I'd smash it over my head.

I should feel guilty because of sleeping with Celeste, considering the outcome, and I do a little bit, even though I was just doing her a favor, but not as hugely as I would have thought. I'm not sure why. I mostly feel bad about getting caught.

Another reason I'm down is that it just occurred to me that now I won't get to be a photographer at Benji's bar mitzvah this spring. That's something I was looking forward to. I wanted to do something good for him, take pictures that he'd like, mostly at his party in the evening. I'd just do it on my own because I knew Naomi wouldn't hire Liz. There was some issue that Naomi had with Liz about the photography for Elise's bat mitzvah. I was there, of course, assisting, but don't know what their disagreement was. Naomi may have mentioned the particulars the first year we were together, but I don't recall the details; I probably stopped listening to her after the first two minutes of her diatribe. I know that Naomi's been critical of Liz's blond wig and her dog-choking-on-a-bone laugh, so maybe that's it. Anyway, I wanted to do a special good thing for Benji, even though he told me that he's not looking forward to his big day. In fact, he said, he can't wait to get it over with.

I can relate. I felt the same about mine. That was a horrible time. My mother was six-months dead and my head and heart weren't in it, weren't in all the preparation I had to do: working on my *maftir*, getting all the singsong Hebrew down pat, and memorizing my silly speech that Rabbi Shapiro, Twersky's predecessor, had given me, which included a spiel about the lesson we Jews learned from my Haftorah portion—some silliness about Joseph and his coat of many colors. I don't recall all the details; it had something to do with Joseph's eleven brothers being mean to him for various reasons, including jealousy because their daddy loved him best, and some grievances as to Joseph's dream interpretation ability, and throwing Joe into a pit and selling him to Arab merchants, Ishmaelites, and dipping his many-colored coat into goat's blood as a ruse and then lying about it to their father. The whole story was violent and, it seemed to me, fairly petty. And on top of that, there was yet more killing of animals—a goat, in this case—just for its blood. *Very* irritating. But I guess there must have been a life lesson there somewhere—maybe similar to whatever lesson there was in *Lear* about how a father shouldn't love one child more than his others because it causes resentments, which can lead to murderous outcomes. Or at least he shouldn't say so out loud, like Lear did and maybe Joseph's old man did as well.

I never, at the time, thought much about what the point of the Joseph spiel was because it was a canned speech for any bar mitzvah that took place around the same time of year as mine, featuring that particular Haftorah portion. I had no choice in the matter and that part of my speech had nothing to do with me personally. I was so nervous that I couldn't sleep a wink the whole night before my blessed event, and then I threw up three times before we—Dad and I—left for Beth El, and then puked again as soon as we got to the temple. I don't remember much, but I must have somehow muddled through. I guess I was finally a man in the eyes of our religion, but definitely didn't feel much like one. I felt like a nervous, sick-to-his-stomach little boy.

And maybe the worst part of my bar mitzvah was when, stuttering through my speech, in English, I had to say the part about how grateful I was to my beloved parents for all they'd done for me over the years, in my journey to Jewish manhood. When I got to the part about "my dear mother, may her memory be a blessing," I choked up and almost couldn't go on. A wave of incipient nausea swept over me, but I took a deep breath and somehow finished the silly speech. Herschel later told me that my face looked green when I finally got to sit down.

So I can understand how Benji feels. Still, I'd like to take good pictures for him. I would have liked to have done that little personal mitzvah on his big day. Well, I guess someone else will have to do that. I won't be there.

Another reason I'd wanted to do a good job taking photos at Benji's bar mitzvah was to make points with Naomi. That'd been on my mind a lot since the Luigi's fiasco. If I did a good job, I'd thought, maybe she'd be grateful and stop giving me crap for a while, yelling at me and belittling me and the like, especially for minor transgressions, and would cut me some slack. And who knows? Maybe she'd even show her gratitude with an erotic episode or two, as she did shortly after I'd first met her when I helped Liz with Elise's bat mitzvah. Well, that's all moot now.

Poor Benji. I wonder if he feels bad that his mom kicked me out. I wonder if he misses me. I'd like to think he does. What if I don't get to see him anymore? That would be horrible. I was just getting to know him better.

I didn't tell my father about my plight right away when I called him before coming over to tell him I was bringing his requested Kentucky Fried Chicken. "What are you talking about?" he said. "I didn't ask you for KFC. I mean, that's great, but I never said anything about that."

"You c-c-called me in the m-middle of the night," I said. "You t-told me exactly what to b-b-bring—the d-drumsticks and baked b-b-beans and all. Original, not c-crispy. Don't you remember th-that?"

There was a pause. "No. No, I can't say I have that recollection. Not at all. Well, hell, bring the damned chicken. You can have a piece." He paused again. "Are there potato wedges?"

I still didn't say anything about my situation when I got there. "What ho, Brabantio?" my father said by way of greeting. I handed him the KFC bag. His eyes widened. He didn't say thanks, just grabbed it from my hands without a word and hustled to the kitchen and tore open the bag and went at it with gusto while standing beside the counter. It was a sight. There was my father, dressed as usual in that damned green robe, barefoot, his white hair long and uncombed, bewhiskered, eyes a bit wild, holding a drumstick in each hand and taking big chomps first from one and then from the other. I half-expected him to toss the bones over his shoulders, like Charles Laughton as Henry VIII. When he'd quickly devoured both drumsticks he picked up a breast and held it delicately, almost lovingly, with both hands and stared at it fondly for a moment and then chowed it down in three huge bites. "Scrumptious!" he muttered. Then he looked around for the potato wedges, a worried look on his wrinkled face. "Ah!" he intoned when he located them. "Excellent!" He downed all but two of the wedges, and then noticed me staring at him. "Julius," he croaked, "have one." He handed me one potato wedge, and then stuffed the last one in his mouth. I think he swallowed it whole. "Let us not be greedy," he muttered. "All things in moderation, eh? Enough is as good as a feast." He quickly scarfed down another drumstick and then the entire container of baked beans and then a biscuit, sans butter. For the first time since commencing his meal, he wiped his chin and mouth with one of the paper napkins from the bag. That was a good sign; at least the old man still had *some* couth. Then he again noticed me. "Oh," he said, "Julius. Yes. Well, son, have a drumstick." But there were none.

After he'd finished he lowered himself slowly into his La-Z-Boy and turned on the TV, high volume. *Judge Judy* was on again and the judge was berating the plaintiff, a clean-cut, husky young Latino guy with black-framed glasses. "Don't tell me what her daughter *told* you," she yelled. "That's *hearsay!* Get over it! Show me some evidence—documents, photos!" The young man said nothing, just glared at Judge Judy. I wondered what was going on inside his head. I supposed that his thoughts weren't generous.

"D-Dad," I said after a bit. "I have to t-tell you something. N-N-Naomi kicked me out this m-morning. Can I stay with y-you for a while? Just t-till I get a p-place of my own?"

"Oh, sure," he replied. I waited to see if he'd ask what had happened, but he didn't. He just sat there and happily watched that loudmouthed

Jewess and now and again nodded as she enthusiastically dressed down both the plaintiff and the defendant, a thin older woman with wispy whitish hair and watery pale-blue eyes whose chin was trembling and who looked to be on the verge of a nervous breakdown. At one point the Latino guy held up a piece of paper, a document of some kind, and the judge directed her bailiff, Mr. Byrd, to bring it to her. This guy was a tall, older, slightly pot-bellied black man wearing a uniform with a tan shirt and dark-brown trousers, with a salt-and-pepper goatee and a wooden facial expression. He, too, wore black-framed glasses. Mr. Byrd wordlessly sauntered over to the young man, retrieved the paper, and, stone-faced, sauntered back to hand it to Judge Judy. He seemed in no hurry on either leg of his journey. It was maybe three steps for him to get the document and another three steps back to the judge, but the round trip seemed to take a week. I found it amusing, but then was startled to hear my father loudly yell, "C'mon, Byrd, move your *shvartze* ass! We don't have all *day* here, for Chrissake." He turned to me and furrowed his brow and nodded. "I guess I told *him*, huh?"

Without any warning, he then jumped up from his chair and tore off the green robe and tossed it almost violently into one corner of the living room. He was wearing just a pair of yellowish-green pajamas. Then he grinned hugely and assumed a sort of cheerleader pose and, in a high-pitched falsetto voice, loudly intoned, "Byrd, Byrd, he's our man. If *he* can't do it, *nobody* can!"

But by dinnertime my father seemed more normal, less weird and hyper. He said he wanted Hamburger Helper, the one with beef stroganoff, so I went to Piggly Wiggly to get a box of the Hamburger Helper and a pound of ground round and made our meal. As we were halfway through, he stopped eating and put down his fork and said, softly, "Okay, Julius, tell me what happened with you and Ms. Naomi." I didn't go into detail. I didn't mention Celeste. I just said we hadn't been getting along and decided to go our separate ways and that was that. He listened and nodded now and again. "I'm sorry," he said.

I asked him how his back was feeling, having noticed how delicately he'd lowered himself into his chair. He shrugged. "Better, I think." He paused. "I guess it could be worse."

It felt strange sleeping in my childhood room, in my old bed, alone, on a cold, dark mid-winter night. There was no Naomi to snuggle against. I missed her body. I missed touching her hip through one of her nice flannel nightgowns. I couldn't say that I missed *her* yet, Naomi the person, though.

I wonder if I will. She'd been a royal pain in so many ways and I've wondered so often why I've stayed with her. But there were good times. We had some nice things together, and I can't deny having warm feelings despite all the bullshit. I've liked our morning talks, except when she was too tedious or annoying with her kvetching about Arthur.

I finally fell asleep around midnight, pondering such thoughts, but then popped awake just after three-thirty and for a minute didn't know where I was. I reached over for Naomi but, of course, she wasn't there and I felt disoriented and turned on the bedstand lamp, and after a moment remembered where I was and why. Just then I felt strange, weepy even. *Here I am,* I thought, *a forty-year-old schlemiel fuck-up who's somehow managed to screw up my relationship and lose my girlfriend and maybe lose poor Benji in the bargain, and now here I am living in my barren childhood home with my maybe-wacko father.*

I fell back asleep, but then popped awake around seven and, as usual, my damned brain immediately started agitating and ruminating. At least it wasn't dark out. I wondered what's ahead. *I don't want to stay here for too long,* I thought, *particularly with my old man being weird at best and maybe nuts at worst, at least sometimes.* I still didn't understand what's up with him. Doing *King Lear* somehow threw him for a loop. He said he thought he failed at his big role, but I still don't know just what that meant. I wish I could talk with him, try to understand, but that doesn't seem to be in the cards. I'd like to know better what's going on inside his head. I want to try to understand his decline, his being so ... *diminished* from who he was, and not that long ago. That scares me. I'd like to be a good son, if possible. I need to help him with that damned back pain. I've tried, and still will. That's one thing. We've never talked together much, at least about anything important. I stopped trying after he blew me off about Mom's suicide. That soured me. We've watched the Marx Brothers on our Sunday mornings together and eaten bagels and cream cheese and, for him, lox, and laughed a lot—mostly at Groucho, less at Harpo and Chico, and not at all at Zeppo.

Part of me wants to stay here for a while to help, if I can, but part of me doesn't want that and wants to move on. Staying here feels like being stuck. Part of me wants to go back to living by myself if Naomi and I are definitely done. I was glad to move out of here after I turned eighteen, and Miriam was, I believe, glad to see me go.

Living alone again wouldn't be too bad. I can handle that. I handled that fine for almost twenty years before I met Naomi. On the one hand, it was lonely sometimes and the long winter nights alone in my bed, with the insomnia and the ruminating, were hard. On the other hand, looking back, I liked it that I didn't have to worry about trying to please anyone or about aggravating anyone. When you live alone you can load the dishwasher any way you want and start it whenever you want to, whether or not it's full, and you can empty it whenever you're so inclined—as soon as the dishes are dry or a week later or even a *month* later. You can wait until twenty seconds before the garbage guys come before putting the cans to the curb. When you live alone you can burp, mouth agape, as often and as loudly and disgustingly as you want to and you can pass gas from morning to night and not have to worry about anyone being grossed out or giving you bad looks. You can talk to yourself if you're so inclined, stuttering or not, and no one will look at you askance. You don't ever have to worry about ordering takeout for some woman and inadvertently screwing up her order, horribly upsetting her, and then have to listen to her ranting to some poor innocent restaurant manager. When you live alone you can happily cut your spaghetti rather than doing that pompous twirling it around your fork, and not have to live in fear of rebuke.

Miriam. I've now and again wondered where she is these days. She tolerated me at best, and I'm pretty sure that she wanted me out so she could have Dad all to herself. She never said as much, but the vibes were there. They'd been together for four years by the time I moved out, and were married for two of those. I'm sure I resented her for taking my mother's place in the house, particularly considering the circumstances of Mom's demise, and I'm sure she picked up on that. We didn't have a mutual admiration society. She threw out cold pricklies when Dad and I would have our monthly Sunday morning brunch sessions. She rarely actually said anything but her face would harden and the corners of her mouth would turn down and she'd give us looks that silently screamed disapproval, even when we guffawed. I remember once when we watched *Monkey Business* and, near the end, all the brothers are together at the Old Barn to rescue a kidnapped young woman and Chico says, "You call this a barn? This looks like a stable," and Groucho replies, "Well, if you look at it, it's a barn; if you smell it, it's a stable," and Chico says, "Well, let's just look at it." My father and I slapped our knees and broke up over those lines, but Miriam just gave us bad looks and crossed her arms and shook her head and looked peeved and finally muttered, "Well, *honestly!*"

So I was glad to leave. Dad helped me pay for my two years at one of the second-tier state colleges, and maybe Miriam resented that too. Who knows? I tried not to think about her too much after I left. All I know is that I was happy when they split up ten years ago. I never knew just why they split, and, now, don't much care. They went their separate ways, and I'm glad.

The one nice thing Miriam did say was when she asked me what I wanted to major in at that college. I had no idea—nothing much interested me—so I just said, "M-Maybe c-cultural anthropology." She nodded her head and said, "Well, that's just a *fine* idea. Great choice! Good for you." I had no interest in anthropology at all, and had just said that because a girl I coveted when I worked on the high school yearbook, Robin Cohen, had said that she wanted to study that. She said she was fascinated with the Inuit and their culture in the frozen North and especially liked it that they were almost always cheerful and helpful to each other—unlike, she noted, her own family. I remember that I asked her who the Inuit were and she curled her lip and gave me a look of disdain. "Uh, *Eskimos?*" she sneered. "Duh!" If I hadn't quit college because of total boredom, maybe I'd have actually gone ahead and studied anthropology. Maybe those Inuit are interesting, being so cheerful and eating whale blubber and sharing their women with guests and all.

My interest in Robin came, of course, to nothing. She had zero interest in me and, I'm sure, saw me as just another nerdy nothinghead on the yearbook staff. I don't know what happened to her after high school. Probably the closest she ever got to the Inuit was watching *Nanook of the North.*

I'm not glad that Dad put a framed photo of Miriam on the dresser in my bedroom. It's one of two such photos in the house; he has another such on the dresser in his room. I took the one in my room down as soon as I saw it and put in in the bottom drawer of the dresser, face-down.

I'd like to ask my father which of his wives he preferred, but I'm afraid to hear the answer.

I must have dozed off because I had a bizarre dream in which I was at the county fair, alone, and decided to go on the Ferris wheel—something I'd *never* do in real life. I was in a car by myself and, sure enough, the damned thing suddenly stopped at the very top. I looked down at the cars below me, swaying back and forth. There were young couples in both, each kissing passionately, lovingly entwined. I waited patiently for the Ferris wheel to start moving again. But it didn't, and after a few moments I started to panic. I had zero control. I was sweating and couldn't breathe well. I was verklempt. I couldn't stand up, of course, which was horrible, and I was pinned in by the steel safety bar. My car, too, was swaying, and I had the sensation of feeling nauseated. I had the fleeting thought that I couldn't vomit, though, because my puke would likely land on one of the kissing couples. That wouldn't be good. But I felt more and more sick. Then I looked all the way down, at the people on the ground, indifferent to me and my plight. Some were walking about and some were laughing heartily and some were just standing still and swilling drinks, probably beer, from plastic cups. I saw Big Art, his huge gut extended, wearing his tattered blue baseball cap, standing by himself and, bug-eyed, staring at women passing by and taking gulps from a bottle in a brown paper bag. "Artie!" I yelled. "Help me. *Please!*" In my dream, he looked up at me briefly, squinting, but then just shrugged and walked away, still grasping his bag with the rotgut inside.

After what seemed like an eternity, the damned Ferris wheel made a loud creaking sound and started to move again, slowly. Finally, my car made it to the bottom and stopped and the guy opened the safety bar and I scurried out and fell to my knees and hugged the ground. I was still a bit nauseated and looked around for a restroom in which to vomit, and just then I saw Miriam walking along in the middle of a group with four other stern-faced elderly Jewish women, all well-coifed and with heavily-made-up faces, including too much rouge, and all nicely dressed, one even sporting a dark-brown fur stole. Miriam was glaring at me, her brow furrowed. "You need to man up, Julius," she said sharply. "This is simply *not* acceptable!" All four of the other stern women nodded in agreement.

Forty years old and kicked out by my girlfriend and back to living in my meshugenah father's house. Sleeping in my childhood bedroom. Tough dreams. *Vey iz mir!* That damned Edgar was on to something: I feel worse than e'er I was.

FOURTEEN

FORTUNE'S WHEEL has, I hope, turned upward for me again, thanks to what my cousin told me about sweet Celeste. Yesterday morning Herschel called to see if I wanted to go out for Chinese—"Chink grub," as he put it—after I was done with work. I was glad to hear from him. I'd been at Dad's for four days and needed a break. My thought was that I'd welcome the chance to talk with someone who's not out in left field so much of the time, or at least on the border, and have some soup and lovely sweet and sour chicken and maybe an eggroll or some pot stickers and drink tea from one of those delicate little white cups with no handle.

The most worrisome thing with my father started two nights ago. I'd fallen sleep around eleven and then just after two was awakened by what sounded like a noise coming from the kitchen. I thought about getting up to investigate, but then decided that the better part of valor was not to. What if there was a large, nasty burglar who, in addition to being a lowlife criminal, was anti-Semitic? That could result in a bad outcome. The noise didn't last long, so I pulled my head out from under the blanket and went back to sleep.

But when I went to the kitchen in the morning, the place was a mess. My father's Metamucil container was opened, the lid fallen to the floor, and some of the orangish powder had spilled on the wet countertop and was now a messy paste. An opened loaf of bread and a carton of eggs were on the counter, as well as a pint of Half-and-Half, also opened, on the kitchen table. There was a pan on the stove and a yellow-crusted plastic spatula and I could see that someone had made scrambled eggs. I looked in the sink and, indeed, there were remnants of cooked eggs and toast crusts on a dirty plate. I thought maybe the Jew-hating burglar had made himself at home and cooked some eggs for himself before ransacking the house and searching for the non-existent safe, and thought it interesting that he, too, had apparent digestive issues and needed Metamucil for regularity. But then I noticed the plastic Heinz ketchup bottle, white plastic lid opened and coated with dried ketchup, on the far edge of the counter and immediately suspected that it was my father who'd been the feaster. He's always doused his scrambled eggs with ketchup. Mom used to hate that he did that. She'd make a face, with a very scrunched-up nose, and turn away in disgust. I remember that she once said that she couldn't stand seeing the red of the ketchup mixed with the yellow of the eggs.

When Dad came to the kitchen for his coffee, I immediately noticed that there was something that looked like dried ketchup on the left sleeve of his ratty green bathrobe. "D-Dad," I said, "did you come d-down here l-l-last night to make some eggs?"

He looked around the kitchen, brow furrowed, and yawned. "No," he said, "I don't believe so. I don't have any recollection of doing that." He cocked his head and stepped closer and looked at my face, his gray eyes mostly clear. "Are you sure *you* didn't do it but just don't remember? Sometimes that happens, you know." He paused. "Are you sure you're okay, son?"

He poured his coffee and plopped down into his La-Z-Boy and turned on the TV without waiting for me to answer. The *Today* show was on and jovial Al Roker was standing in front of his fancy-schmancy digital maps, telling about a nasty snowstorm that was sweeping across part of the northern tier of the country. Dad pointed at him and said, snidely, "What the hell kind of a king wears glasses with ordinary blue frames? Tell me *that*. It doesn't smack of royalty, does it? They should be *purple*." I again didn't answer; I didn't know what to say. Then Roker grinned hugely, white teeth gleaming, and said, "Now here's what's going on in *your* neck of the woods." Dad glared at the TV, his gray eyes hard. "Oh, the hell with *that!*" he said loudly. "You don't need a weatherman to know which way the wind blows, right?"

He snatched up the remote control and changed to the History Channel. It was a documentary about the rise of Hitler and there was that hateful maniac mass murderer orating to a huge crowd in Nuremberg, wearing his Nazi uniform with the stupid swastika on an armband around his left upper arm, with that childish haircut and bizarre mini-mustache, gesturing wildly and wagging his right hand, index finger now and again thrusting at the masses. He was speaking German, of course, but there were subtitles. He was all exercised with his big grievance about how Germany had gotten screwed over at the end of the Great War and how we must—*must!*—return *das Vaterland* to its former glory. Dad pursed his lips and shook his head. "Look at that Nazi bastard," he muttered. "Strutting away. He has that audience eating from his hand, though. Say what you will about the guy, he's got the groundlings slobbering. When he comes out for his curtain call, they'll no doubt give him a long standing ovation—maybe two or three minutes, huh? Impressive!"

Shortly after that was when Herschel called about our getting together for dinner. I was happy to hear from him. Enough mishegas for one day.

I had to go to the bathroom before leaving. When I raised the lid I immediately, again, noticed my father's cloudy and foul-smelling urine in the toilet. *What the hell's this old fart been drinking?* I wondered. *Raw cabbage juice?*

After I cleaned up the kitchen, I showered and dressed and got ready to go to work. "Do you *have* to go, Julius?" my father asked pitifully, subdued now and barely audible, as I was ready to exit. I looked at him sitting in his chair in the living room, alone, wrapped in his ancient green robe. His white hair was longer than ever, almost down to his shoulders, and unruly. I didn't know when he'd last washed it. He had a real beard going. His feet were bare and his toenails were a horror, particularly both big toes. His eyes, just then, were murky, watery even, and seemed much lighter than their usual medium-gray. He again looked smaller than he had been. At least the discoloration from the clunk to his head was mostly gone, except for a little bit around his eyes. That purple robe from *Lear* was still draped over the back of his La-Z-Boy, and I noticed that the gold-colored scepter Lear'd toted in the first scene, when he had his kerfuffle with Cordelia and impetuously banished Kent, was on the sofa. There was an opened bag of Cheetos on the floor next to his chair and an opened jar of the Planter's Lightly Salted Dry Roasted Peanuts on the coffee table.

I nodded. "I have a p-p-painting job I have to g-go to, Dad. Perry's expecting me to b-be there."

My father sighed and scratched the top of his head and waved his hand dismissively. "Well, okay, then," he said. "Bless thy five wits."

The painting job Perry'd asked me to do was a vacant one-bedroom apartment on the west side, in the complex that he had a contract with. It was vacant because the renter, an eighty-nine-year-old widow, Mrs. Weinstein, had sadly departed this world following a stroke. Her two children had cleared out the apartment. Perry'd told me that the old woman had been taken to University Hospital, and she expired there.

While preparing the surfaces—washing the walls with a sponge mop with a cleaning strip, using a solution of one-quarter cup of TSP per gallon of water, and carefully fixing cracks and patching holes before sanding—I remembered the last time I'd been at that hospital. It was with Naomi, six months ago. We went there to visit her friend Fern, who was recovering from total knee replacement surgery. Rivkah's always-smiling husband, silver-haired Dr. Berliant, had done her operation. Fern never liked me much. She once told Naomi that I was "beneath" her. But I went along on the visit, to be a good boyfriend. The hospital entrance has a gigantic revolving door, divided into two even sections by a thick glass divider, each section big enough for eight or ten people, and then a smaller regular door off to one side, probably for people in wheelchairs and the like. There's a prominent sign that reads "PLEASE USE REVOLVING DOOR, IF POSSIBLE." But I couldn't possibly do that, and headed toward the smaller door. I couldn't take a chance on being trapped inside that damned big door if, for whatever reason—electrical outage, hand of God—it stopped revolving. "Where the hell are you going?" Naomi said. I told her that I just preferred the smaller door, but she knew the truth. She threw me a look of big disgust and entered the revolving door alone.

Fern wasn't thrilled that I'd come, I could tell that. And then, of course, Naomi had to tell her that I was too scared to use the revolving door. "Can you *believe* that?" she practically hissed. Fern gave me a look and sighed and shook her head. "Oh, Naomi!" she whispered. "Naomi, Naomi."

My girlfriend's mood didn't improve the rest of that day. After visiting Fern, we went to the hospital cafeteria for lunch. She ordered a cheeseburger from the grill and I just got a chicken Caesar salad. I paid. We didn't talk at all. That was okay. Watching Naomi eat, though, I thought of Rivkah and her fondness for cheeseburgers. I had the thought, just then, that I wished it were Rivkah I was with at lunch instead of Naomi. That would have been fine. I would have bought her two desserts, carrot cake or whatever her sweet little heart desired, one to eat and one to take home in a box.

Naomi didn't talk to me at all on the drive home, nor for much of the rest of the day. That was okay, too. I wondered if she was reflecting on Fern's opinion of me. I couldn't think of anything I needed or wanted to say to her, and was glad of the silence. I remember that I sat with Benji for a few minutes in his room while he played on his X Box. We didn't speak much either, but that was comfortable.

Naomi. I haven't heard from her since she kicked me out and don't know when, or if, I will. I miss her now, I'll say that. Despite all, I can't deny that I miss the woman. It's not just her body at night that I miss, though there is that. There's definitely that. Now I think that I miss her, Naomi the person. I miss her face, the sound of her voice, even when that voice was ripping me a new one. I miss sitting with her two mornings a week for our couple's check-in. Maybe that's sick. It seems sick. What do I know? I even miss her tears. I'll miss watching *It's a Wonderful Life* with her next December, on or around Christmas Eve, and maybe hoping to get laid that night.

And, of course, Benji. That's what really tears me up inside.

I hadn't remembered to bring my Sony CD player to the job, so couldn't listen to any play while I painted. That was okay. I was fine with the silence. I liked just concentrating on my work: assembling all my tools and supplies, carefully taping off moulding and windows and doors, putting down my drop cloths, preparing the surfaces, priming the walls and ceilings and sanding down bumps and ridges, stirring the paint, cutting the edges and corners with a beveled sage brush, rolling beige paint on the walls and white paint on the ceilings while being careful to not spatter much, cleaning up the room, storing the unused paint, cleaning my brushes and rollers. It was good to just do my work, my craft, being deliberate and thorough, working at my own pace, and not have to talk with anyone.

In mid-afternoon, I took a break and sat in a corner of the empty living room, on the floor. I hoped to get a feel for the recently-deceased occupant of the apartment, that poor Mrs. Weinstein. I didn't know anything about her. Perry'd said that she'd lived there for twelve years after her husband died. Maybe she'd had lonely times, being there alone in her final home. Maybe she, too, had insomnia and popped awake in the middle of long dark nights and immediately commenced to ruminating and obsessing about things. Or maybe she was mostly happy and slept soundly. Maybe she was a social queen and had a rich, full life with family—children and grandchildren and siblings and nieces and nephews—and loads of friends. Maybe she'd played mah-jongg four afternoons a week. Maybe she'd been active in Hadassah, and was even a muckety-muck—president, treasurer, or just recording secretary. Maybe she'd volunteered at a food pantry or at the temple resale shop.

But, either way, I couldn't get a feel for her. There was no presence, no spirit, of Mrs. Weinstein that I could detect. She was just gone. She'd lived alone in those rooms for twelve years and had her stroke there and was taken out of the apartment, most likely on a stretcher, and put in an ambulance and hauled to the hospital, where her long life ended, suddenly or otherwise. I don't know if she was conscious when they took her out the door of her apartment, probably horizontal, for the final time. I don't know if she'd had a chance to say goodbye to her cozy little home. And now she's gone and soon someone else will move into the freshly-painted apartment and it will be their home for a while, maybe until they, too, have a stroke or heart attack or ruptured aneurism or other cataclysmic medical event, and have to exit the apartment suddenly and forever, maybe in great pain, perhaps unconscious, and then their life, too, will be over and the next mediocre painter—me or Perry or whoever—may or may not be able to commune with their departed spirit.

And what's the point of it all? All that strutting and fretting. All those good times with the grandkids and those mah-jongg afternoons. All those hours spent sorting out donated clothing and then folding and attaching price tags to acceptable items in the annex room of the temple resale shop. All those evenings alone in her second-story apartment, with the door surely locked, maybe double-locked, eating a Lean Cuisine Spaghetti with Meat Sauce frozen dinner and then going to bed right after the local news. I suspect that Mrs. Weinstein turned off the TV right after hearing about the weather in her neck of the woods, and cared not a fig about the sports. Hopefully, her sleep was untroubled.

I met Herschel at five-thirty at China Palace. He immediately ordered a pot of hot tea from our server, Mei-Lin. I did too. I noticed that my cousin looked much better than usual. No sloppy gray sweatshirt. Instead, he was wearing a white button-down dress shirt and a cardigan sweater, the same shade of blue as his yarmulke, and gray slacks. His short hair was nicely combed and he was clean-shaven. He'd trimmed his sideburns. Even his fingernails were cut short.

I didn't quite understand his transformation until Mei-Lin returned with our tea, in delicate little white pots, and asked if we were ready to order. Herschel cocked his dwarfy head and looked up at her, grinning foolishly like a mooning teenage boy. "Well," he said, in an exaggeratedly polite tone, his eyes opened innocently wide, "I'm considering the shitake mushroom beef. Do you think that's a good choice, Mei-Lin?" I thought it was a silly question. What's she supposed to say? "No, the shitake mushroom beef is *horrible*. I wouldn't feed it to my dog. Get something else." But Mei-Lin just smiled and said that was "a great choice," that that selection was definitely one of *her* "very favorite dishes." I studied her during this interchange. She was taller than most of her China Palace ilk and bustier, too. She wore a frilly white blouse and a tight, short black skirt. Her ebony hair was pulled straight back and gathered at the rear in a severe bun and she had a pretty face with porcelain skin, dark eyes and a small red-painted mouth. Her cheekbones were sublime. She had what looked like perfect makeup, and a lot of it, including pleasant bluish-green eyeshadow and huge eyelashes, probably false ones. Her calves, I noticed, were unusually muscular.

I noticed Mei-Lin staring at Herschel's yarmulke. I wondered what he'd say if she asked what it was.

I ordered a cup of wonton soup and my usual sweet and sour chicken and an appetizer of grilled pot stickers for both of us. We both watched Mei-Lin walk away, toward the kitchen. When she was out of sight, Herschel whispered, "I hope my fuckin' fortune cookie says 'You will score with your server tonight.' That'd be okay, huh?" I just nodded.

When Mei-Lin brought our orders, she smiled, subtly but sweetly, as she placed my cup of soup in front of me. Herschel again mooned at her, a silly grin on his face. "Oh, thank you *so* much," he said. "Say, I wonder if I might get some chopsticks, if it isn't too much trouble. I, uh, *prefer* using chopsticks, you know."

She nodded and turned to me. "Chopsticks for you as well, young man?"

I shook my head. "N-No thanks," I said. "I d-d-don't know how t-to use them."

She gave me another sweet smile and nodded. "A very honest response," she said softly. Then she looked at Herschel and held her gaze for a moment before walking away. He didn't look pleased.

I ate my soup first, but had a difficult time cutting the wontons into manageable-sized bites. I dished my chicken and white rice and a few onion slices and carefully separated the yucky cherries and pineapple and green peppers from the good parts and pushed them to one side of the plate and then poured the sweet and sour sauce over the rice and chicken and onions. Herschel noticed. "So you order a nice dish and then immediately trash half of it?" he said. "What the fuck's the *matter* with you?"

I looked at him and arched my eyebrows. "I guess I'm j-just a schle-miel," I said. "What can I t-t-tell you?"

He gave me a look and shrugged and went back to eating his shitake mushroom beef. I noticed that he was competent with the chopsticks. He maneuvered them perfectly with the stumpy fingers of his right hand, pressing the wooden ends together to perfectly grasp pieces of not just the beef but the mushrooms and pea pods and onions, as well as a pot sticker, and then lifting them to his mouth nicely. I noticed, too, that he only took normal-sized helpings and chewed with his mouth closed and never once dribbled food back onto his plate or the white tablecloth.

The reddish sweet-and-sour sauce on my rice and chicken put me in mind of the ketchup my father'd poured over his scrambled eggs in the middle of the night. He'd said that he didn't remember making the eggs. He also hadn't remembered calling me in the middle of the night and asking me to bring him KFC. I felt worried, maybe even depressed. Herschel noticed. "What's up, cuz?" he asked. I told him my concerns. I told him about Dad's appearance and his strange behavior. I told him what Dad had said about feeling like a failure at playing King Lear but that some others, and I named them, hadn't failed. Herschel stopped eating and put down his chopsticks and listened.

I asked him if he knew who those other guys besides Scofield were—Ian McKellen and Derek Jacobi and Holm and Gielgud. He nodded. "Actors," he said. "Limeys. They all played Lear one time or another." He paused and stared at another attractive female server, four tables down. "Jack MacGowran played the Fool in Peter Brook's great play and movie of *King Lear* with Scofield," he went on. "Not as amazing as me, of course, but, you know, okay."

I didn't respond to Herschel's comment about Brook's unbelievably depressing movie, which my old man had also, I guess, liked. I just remember that damned Scofield and everyone else talking like they had a mouthful of sand-encrusted marbles.

Herschel could see that I was worried. "Listen," he said, quietly, "if Uncle Herb goes batshit, give me a call. I'll do what I can."

Just then Mei-Lin came over and asked if we wanted anything else. Herschel looked up at her and immediately picked up his chopsticks in his right hand and resumed eating his dinner. He made a point of competently grasping a tiny onion and delicately bringing it to his mouth and then murmured, "*Yum!* Quite delicious, Mei-Lin." Whatever reaction he hoped to get from her, it didn't work. She stared at him for a brief moment, her perfectly plucked eyebrows arched, and then turned to me and smiled again, just a bit. "Was your sweet and sour chicken good today, sir?"

I blushed but nodded. "Yes," I eventually answered. "Quite g-g-good, th-thank you."

We both again watched Mei-Lin walk away, with interest. Her slim hips swayed. After she was out of sight, Herschel sighed and put down his chopsticks and picked up a pot sticker with his fingers and shoved most of it into his mouth. Remnants dribbled onto the tablecloth. "Oh, well," he said, still chewing. "What the hell, huh? Nothing ventured, nothing fuckin' gained." He paused. "Oh, by the way," he added, "speaking of women, remember Celeste from *Lear?* Played Cordelia? I heard that she split up with her husband."

FIFTEEN

I COULDN'T SLEEP the night after China Palace. I slept a little, I think, but not much. I was too excited. Sweet little Celeste had broken up with Andrew! How amazingly *wonderful!* What a turn of events. Lying in bed, I couldn't help wondering if it was because of me, because of our little adventure together. Maybe there was something about our encounter that charmed her, moved her, made her realize that she wanted, needed, to be with me rather than with her blah accountant husband. I wasn't sure what that something could be, but still.

I wondered whether she'd call me or if I should take the initiative and contact her. What would I say? "Hey, Celeste," I'd maybe murmur, sans stutter. "Hey, sweetheart, I heard about you and Andrew. And guess what? I'm done with Naomi, too. Can you *believe* it? Oh, I've dreamt about this— you and me together, finally. I'll take good care of you, I promise. We have our lives ahead of us now."

Maybe that would be too weird.

I should have asked Herschel if he knew whether Celeste had moved out of their condo or if Andrew did. If she stayed and if I was right about her wanting to be with me, I wondered if she'd want me to move in. That would be okay. It would be wonderful to make love with her again, and again and again, in that nice upstairs bedroom, with poor crippled Christina, in her rustic little world, hanging on the wall to the left of the bed and gazing longingly at that gray weathered farmhouse on the horizon.

It was nice, for a change, to lie all warm and comfy in bed in the middle of a long, cold winter night and not be plagued by worries and negativities, to not ruminate about my issues. There was just my happiness about Celeste. The wheel of my fortune had, at last, circled upward to its apex, like that damned Ferris wheel car in my dream. But this time would be a good dream. *Finally in my ridiculous life*, I thought, *some big-time nachas.*

I wondered whether I should call Naomi and tell her about Celeste and me, to get it out in the open, to maybe even stick it to her a bit for kicking me out. "Hey, N-Naomi," I might say. "Do you r-remember that t-text message that you s-saw on my phone? From Celeste? The one that you k-k-kicked me out over? Well, g-guess what?" But maybe that would be mean.

But after wallowing in such bubbly thoughts for a time, it occurred to me that I could be wrong. Maybe Celeste's leaving Andrew has nothing to do with me. Maybe she hasn't given me a thought since I did my mitzvah, since I helped her out with her ladyparts concern. I guess that's possible. Maybe there were long-simmering issues between the two of them that have nothing to do with me. Maybe they'd had another horrible argument about money, with another violent push-her-down-the-stairs ending and another sprained wrist. I'd like to think that Celeste thinks about me and longs to be with me, where she'd be safe and cherished, and I hope that's the case. But who knows what's really going on inside that sweet head?

Around three, I tried to stop thinking about Celeste so that I could relax and maybe even sleep. I tried to think about other things. Magda was one. I conjured her big pale Polish face, her blond pageboy haircut, those sturdy shoulders, her tinkling giggle. I had the fantasy of being with her in a rowboat on a lagoon. I'd be rowing and she'd be sitting in the rear seat, dressed in a tank top and tight denim shorts. She'd be telling me her story of growing up on the outskirts of Krakow, living in a big white-painted house with her loving parents and five siblings, three boys and two girls. On Sundays, they'd all gather together for dinner, perhaps white borscht and roast duck. Mom and Dad and each of the six kids would talk about the events of the past week and their hopes and plans for the week ahead. They'd discuss issues of the day. Everyone would listen respectfully and not interrupt. Maybe some grandparents would be there. It would be like that annoying multi-generational family of cops on *Blue Bloods*, gathered together for Sunday dinner. I wouldn't have to talk at all. I'd just row, steadily and with masculine strength, and listen to my Magda. I might nod here or there or say "Um-hmm" or "That s-s-sounds very n-nice." It would be a sunny summer day, not like this long, cold, dreary winter night. Now and again I'd stop rowing and close my eyes and just listen to the sounds: the birds singing, the creaking of the oars from other boats, children laughing on the shore, Magda reciting her happy history. "Oh, ve had such *goot* times!"

After we'd returned the boat, she and I would get hot dogs and Pepsis at the refreshment stand and sit at a picnic table near the shore and eat quietly. The hot dogs wouldn't be up to Izzy's standards—they wouldn't be those great Nathan's Hebrew National Kosher Beef Franks—but we wouldn't care. My Magda and I would be together on a lovely summer day, and that would be good enough.

Maybe later we'd go back to her place and make sweet love. She could call the shots. "I vant to be on top, *ja?*"

I thought, briefly, of little Lydia as well. I had the fantasy that she'd call me on my cell while I was at a painting job, maybe still at Mrs. Weinstein's apartment. "Oh, Julius," she'd say, "I just heard about you and Naomi. I'm *so* sorry! Are you, uh, okay?"

"Well," I'd answer, "it's been a p-pretty tough t-t-time." I'd pause. "F-Frankly, Lydia, I don't think I'm d-doing too well. I miss N-N-Naomi."

I'd hear a little sigh at the other end of the phone. "Do you want to get together and talk?" she'd ask. "Maybe grab some coffee?" Perhaps we'd then meet at Starbucks. I'd get my usual tall white chocolate mocha and Lydia would order something more exotic, perhaps a caramel macchiato or a chai crème frappucino. We'd sit at one of the smaller tables along the wall and she'd ask what happened. I'd probably tell her the truth, though maybe sparing certain intimate details out of respect to Celeste. Lydia'd listen quietly but intently, chin in hands, those big, dark eyes focused directly on mine. I'd likely stare at that cute, feminine upturned nose with the dusting of freckles and maybe at her black poufy hair as well. It would be good. But if I did tell her the truth, how would she react? Would she be upset that I'd cheated on her cousin? Or would she understand things, be sympathetic to my perspective? Would she slam down her cup and walk out on me or would she take one of my hands in both of hers and nod her sweet head and say, "Oh, Julius, you've been through a lot and I truly admire and respect you for it. Maybe we could, uh, you know … "?

But I'd avoid talking about my father with her. Nor would I tell Lydia my hopes for a future with Celeste. After all, if things don't work out with Celeste, maybe Lydia could be in the bullpen. I'm sure that Naomi wouldn't like my taking up with her cousin, if it came to that, but she kicked me out, after all, so she doesn't get a lot of say-so as to my doings.

But I don't think it'll come to that. I don't think I'll have to choose between my two women. The more I thought about it, lying in bed in the middle of the long night, the more confident I felt that Celeste, now that she was free, would want to be with me, inept and ineffectual noodnik though I am. Maybe she even thinks of me as an artist, like herself, because she'd noticed that I did the photos at the table reads and dress rehearsal and cast party. That seemed to interest her. I don't at all think of myself as an artist, but if she does I'm okay with that. I'll take any positive thoughts from a woman I covet, any non-schlemiel assessments.

Perhaps Celeste's long dreamt of being with a fellow artist rather than with a boring certified public accountant. Maybe she even has the fantasy that I'd be *her* photographic Boswell, that I'd take many lovely pictures of her in our years to come. Perhaps she'd somehow intuited, from when I first photographed her at the *Lear* table read, that I knew how very special she was as a subject, that I realized that she was one of those rare women whom the camera loves, and was flattered and wanted me to memorialize her magnificent little face with those delicate cheekbones, framed with that short light-brown hair, for years to come. That could happen. That could be my project now that I'm happily finished doing the photos of Dad for his damned albums and to adorn his damned walls. Maybe I could even do a book of pictures just of my love, taken over the years we'll have ahead of us, and call it *Visions of Celeste*. Or perhaps *My Very Own Cordelia*. That could maybe be the big accomplishment I've not yet had.

Well, maybe all this speculating about women gets a guy nowhere. Again I had the thought that you think you know them, think you have a handle on them, but you can be so wrong, deluded, like Othello was about Desdemona or Albany about Goneril.

Goneril and Regan—some pair! On the one hand, a person could say they were just horrible, evil, scheming women who did terrible things and deserved their bad outcomes. On the other hand, maybe you can have some sympathy for them, at least at first. Maybe they're not just one-dimensional characters. Their father was a self-centered, impulsive, hot-tempered old tyrant who'd no doubt lorded it over them when they were kids, ordering them to bring him his slippers and his robe and a slice of Dutch apple pie á la mode at night and to be seen but not heard, except when he wanted them to stand erect in a neat little row in front of him and belt out "How Great Thou Art." When Cordelia was born, he drooled over her and blathered endlessly that she was his favorite. I'm sure *that* went over splendidly with the older sisters. And then he grew old and decided to retire and give away his kingdom so he could crawl unburdened toward death and he childishly demanded that his daughters tell which one loved him best, so he could reward the winner with the biggest dowry land portion. Regan and Goneril each flattered him, laying it on thick—"I am alone felicitate in your dear highness's love!"—but maybe they were just going along to get along, playing the game he'd probably often forced them to play, because they knew what he was like, knew that he needed constant phony praise to bolster his outsized ego, knew that he was a very difficult and self-important old geezer who'd "ever but slenderly known himself."

Then, after he impetuously banished Cordelia for refusing to flatter him, he announced that he'd stay with each of the other two on a rotating monthly basis, and they'd have to also host his hundred knights for that month. The sisters grudgingly accepted that at first, but after a while started kvetching that the knights were behaving badly. Well, maybe they had a point. I'm sure it would be one thing to have to put up with two or three riotous knights tearing around the palace and breaking the china and leaving empty ale glasses and overflowing ashtrays and used condoms everywhere, and taunting the servants and feeling up the scullery maids, and generally being obnoxious. But a *hundred?* Yikes!

So maybe those sisters, nasty though they were, deserve some sympathy. Granted, they turned into murderous monsters later on, but maybe a guy needs to cut them a little slack at the start of the play. Then again, I could be wrong. Maybe Regan and Goneril really *were* just nasty cartoonish horror stories from first to last and don't deserve any benefit of the doubt. What do I know? When it comes to women, not much.

I decided to stop thinking about them, women, for a while. What does it get a guy? Except that I really liked thinking about having hot dogs and Pepsis with Magda at the refreshment stand. That was good. That was uncomplicated. Or maybe she'd have preferred a bratwurst. I dislike brats, but maybe Magda finds them enchanting. They typically have that tough skin and you have to bite down hard to pierce the skin with your teeth, and sometimes hot juice flies up against the roof of your mouth, maybe burning you, or dribbles down your chin.

Last Memorial Day, Herschel and I went to Bratfest at Washington Park. He ate three bratwursts but I had none. I remember that we saw Tunnel Terry, alone as always, ambling toward a bench near the shore of the pond with those long strides of his. The guy's six-seven or six-eight and rail-thin and has narrow, hunched shoulders and a concave chest. He has a long, narrow head with a big mop of unruly brown hair, parted in the middle, and always stares straight ahead with almost lifeless green eyes, unblinking, as he lopes along with huge strides, torso inclined forward. His shock of hair bounces as he walks. He always wears raggedy blue jeans, rolled up at the bottoms, and a long-sleeved flannel shirt, always untucked.

When the temperature approaches ninety degrees, he'll sometimes roll up the sleeves of his shirt, too, showing bony blue-veined forearms. He lives in the big tunnels of the university heating system, and supposedly knows where all the entrances and exits are. It's cool there in the summer and warm in winter. Herschel told me that the security people tried many times to evict him from the tunnels but he always sneaked back into them, so eventually they decided to just hire him to keep an eye out and let them know about any tunnel problems, but that Terry declined the offer. "Too much bother," he'd said. Herschel also said that Terry has a history of silently emerging at odd times from the tunnel openings on campus, a six-seven emaciated and ghostlike figure, startling the bejesus out of young coeds on the way to their Victorian literature or women's studies classes.

When we saw him at Bratfest, Tunnel Terry was carrying a white-paper-wrapped brat in each big hand as he loped toward the bench. I remember wondering what was going on inside his head. I asked Herschel if he knew Terry, as he had Snowball, and he said he didn't but hollered a greeting anyway. "Terry," he shouted, "how's it going, man?" Terry glanced at us and nodded, subtly, but said nothing and continued on his way. It was sad to see. Almost everyone else at Bratfest was either paired off or in happy groups, many inebriated on beer or on the way, and here was this bizarre isolato sitting alone on a green bench, munching on one brat and grasping its twin and just staring out, expressionless, over the brackish pond water.

Snowball. When we were at China Palace, I'd asked Herschel if he knew what the man's real name was. "Eugene," he said. "He answers to either name. He doesn't much care one way or the other."

It would be nice to take Benji to Bratfest in a few months, on Memorial Day weekend. That would be good. I have no idea if Benji likes bratwursts. Maybe he does. Maybe Herschel would want to go again, and it could be the three of us. I've seen fathers and sons together there, munching on disgusting brats, juice spurting out when they take a bite, and it seems nice. I've felt envious. So I'd like to go there with Benji. Maybe Celeste would want to go, too, assuming we're indeed together then. I don't know if it would be okay for me to reach out to Benji. Probably Naomi wouldn't like that. I suspect she wouldn't. Well, Miriam, in my dream, said I needed to man up, so maybe I shouldn't worry too much about what Naomi likes or doesn't like, and just do something that's a right thing to do.

Celeste! How did a schlemiel like me get so lucky?

SIXTEEN

I MAY GIVE UP helping Liz with photography. Yesterday I did a wedding that wound up depressing hell out of me, and was physically and emotionally exhausted when I got home after midnight and fell asleep pretty quickly, though still troubled by the reception, and then was startled awake an hour later by a loud noise in the kitchen. I jumped up and went to check it out, and there was my father trying to take apart the Honeywell thermostat on the living room wall with a pliers and a screwdriver. At least he wasn't wearing the green robe. Instead, he was attired in pale-blue boxer shorts with six images of smiling bunnies, three on either side of the fly opening, and a white V-neck T-shirt. I myself was wearing only my briefs; I'd felt too verklempt to put on my bathrobe. Dad had the outer white plastic cover of the thermostat off and was farting around with the innards. He didn't even notice me entering the room. "This will work," I heard him mutter to himself. "I *know* it will."

I didn't want to startle him, so tapped him gently on the shoulder. He was startled anyway and jumped six inches. "*Zounds!*" he practically shouted, watery bluish-gray eyes wide and looking startled. "Is't the fiend?" He winced noticeably and rubbed his lower back. After a few moments he calmed down and seemed to be studying me. I wasn't sure he recognized me. Then he furrowed his white brow and his eyes seemed to focus better and he pointed at me and nodded. "Sirrah!" he whispered. "Naked fellow. Is't truly you? Poor Tom, my philosopher?" I shrugged but had to stifle a chuckle because he looked so ridiculous standing there in those boxers with the six bewhiskered bunnies staring out, devilish grins on their little rabbit faces, and spouting his nonsense. My father's thin, white, old man calves and his ugly bare feet, with those horrible toenails, were center stage. He still had a somewhat bewildered facial expression.

He stared at me for the better part of a minute and soon his eyes turned grayer and more clear and he smiled just a bit. "Julius," he said, "what the hell are you doing standing there in your underwear?"

"I was g-going to ask you the same q-q-question. And what were you d
-doing with the thermostat?"

He furrowed his brow and turned to stare at his handiwork. "I don't
know," he said. "I don't remember."

I nodded. "Well," I said, "are you okay n-now?"

He shrugged and stared at the screwdriver in his right hand. "I guess
so," he finally answered. He scratched the back of his head. "I'm fine,
Tom."

"Okay. Go to b-bed, D-Dad."

I couldn't sleep for a long time after that. I couldn't stop thinking
about the wedding. Liz had, as usual, left the reception early, just after the
cake cutting, and I'd stayed. Her blondish wig had slipped a bit to one side
during the formals photos and I'd considered telling her about it, but didn't.
I probably should have. The couple's first dance, to "At Last" by Etta
James, was next on the agenda. It was a careful dance because the bride,
Sandy, was noticeably pregnant; it looked like she had only a month or less
to go. That's why, I supposed, they were having a winter wedding: to make
their little muffin-in-the-oven legit. The groom, Johnny, was a handsome
guy: moderately tall, stocky, muscular, curly brownish-blond hair, strong
facial profile. I suspected he was a jock of some sort.

As it turned out, their first dance was also their last of the evening. As
far as I could see, the couple didn't talk much to each other the rest of the
night or even spend much time together.

All in all, Sandy and Johnny's wedding reception was the most joyless
event I'd ever been to. I don't remember anyone in the crowd laughing or
even smiling much. Johnny's stepfather fell asleep at his table for about
fifteen minutes, chin in hand, with the groom's mother sitting silently
beside him, looking unhappy, slogging down gin and tonics. I counted four,
maybe five. It was almost as if the guests were going through their motions,
playing their roles, pretending to be interested and even happy for the
couple, when what they mostly wanted, it felt like, was for the damned
event to be over with so they could go home and crawl into their beds and
pull the blankets over their heads. That's how I felt, too.

Even the DJ was joyless. This guy was an obese, fleshy, pasty-
complected individual with plastered-down bleached-blond hair and multi-
colored designer glasses with purplish lenses—a very poor man's version of
Elton John. He announced events, such as the bouquet toss, in a dread
monotone, with all the enthusiasm of a past-her-prime spinster somberly

declaring that the library would be closing in ten minutes. People danced for the first hour or so, and then less and less as the dreary evening wore on. I dutifully took what photos I could, but the opportunities for memorable ones were few and far between.

Toward the end of the evening, the DJ played a slow song, "I Will Always Love You," but nobody ventured forth onto the dance floor at first. But when the song was maybe a third of the way through, the groom's soused mother stood up from her table and unsteadily walked over to the bar, where Johnny and three of his friends were shlurping tap beer from plastic cups. She wordlessly took her son's hand and led him to the dance floor and snaked her arms around his neck and pressed so closely against him that you couldn't have slipped a tissue between them. She closed her eyes while dancing with Johnny, her head resting against his chest, and had a look of near-ecstasy. I watched, but didn't memorialize the moment with my camera. I give myself credit for that. I saw her run her hands slowly over his muscular back as they danced. For a brief moment, she caressed his right posterior with her left hand and may have even squeezed a bit. During all this, Johnny had a neutral facial expression; he neither smiled nor grimaced. When the music stopped, she stood on her tiptoes and touched Johnny's cheek with the fingers of her small right hand and kissed him on the lips. Her eyes stayed closed; his didn't. The kiss didn't last long, but there seemed to be a certain ardor, perhaps alcohol-fueled, on her part. Then she grasped his hand and squeezed and let go and turned around and carefully, so as not to stumble or weave, walked back to her table, chin raised and eyes moist and glazed over, staring straight ahead, and sat beside the somnolent stepfather and downed a healthy gulp of her gin and tonic.

Johnny said nothing but, from the dance floor, stood still for a moment to watch his walking-away mother and then calmly strolled back to the bar to resume imbibing with his buddies. I had no idea, from watching him, how he felt about the whole deal.

What was equally interesting, though, was that I noticed Sandy watching her new husband and his drunken mother during all this. She was sitting at a table near the far side of the dance floor with two of her bridesmaids, perfectly still, calmly taking it all in. Her blank facial expression never changed. I wondered what the bride was thinking, what was going on inside her head. I wondered what she and Johnny would talk about later, on their wedding night. I wondered how things would go when Sandy had her baby in a few weeks and her mother-in-law toodled into the hospital room, all smiling and warm and, hopefully, sober, to meet her new grand-child and congratulate the new parents. Vey iz mir!

The whole experience made me question my photography career, such as it is. I've been okay with doing the weddings and bar and bat mitzvahs, overall, and never stopped wanting and hoping for an erotic episode with a bridesmaid or other female attendee, but I keep having bothersome experiences at those events that keep me up, uncomfortably ruminating, at night. I can't seem to balance that out by conjuring a lot of happy moments. Do I need that?

But, I thought, lying in bed, doing the painting is okay. No drama there. I had the thought that maybe I'd see if Perry needed me more often for painting stuff. If not, I even had the idea to start my own painting business. I wouldn't call it *Dickman's Fine Painting*, though. Maybe *Julius's Mediocre Painting*. Or even *Poor Tom's Painting*, with no descriptor one way or the other. I'd be a one-man operation. I don't want to work together with anyone or manage or supervise anyone else. I don't want to have to make conversation. I just want to do my work alone, preparing the surfaces and applying the coats of paint with brushes and rollers as carefully as I can, not making messes, and cleaning up thorough-ly, and maybe listen to my CDs of plays while I did my work—just the comedies, though, and maybe some of the histories, but not those damned corpse-strewn tragedies anymore. I'd like to line up enough jobs to keep my wallet from being too thin and to buy a few Swissburgers or cod fillets and root beers at Culver's, as well as those very lovely cheese curds that a guy can dip into a plastic container of ranch or barbecue or honey mustard sauce, though never again—*never!*—via the damned drive-through lane.

Of course, if I have a possible future with Celeste, I'm going to have to be serious about earning gelt. Andrew probably brought in a steady paycheck, doing whatever it is that he does. I don't even know who certifies those accountants or how that happens. It's an impressive job title—*certified public accountant*—but what does such a person actually do, besides taxes? Maybe I'll ask Celeste when I see her soon. Or maybe it would be best for me not to mention Andrew at all and for the two of us, Celeste and me, to just concentrate on our bright future together and to put Andrew and Naomi in the rearview mirror.

I finally fell asleep around dawn, but it was a troubled, uneasy sleep.

When I woke up, I heard the TV in the living room blasting and knew that Dad was watching *Springer* again because I heard that "JER-RY! JER-

RY!" I wondered if my father was again pumping his upraised fist and chanting along with the other meshugeners. I tiptoed into the living room, without him seeing or hearing me, and stood behind and to one side of his La-Z-Boy. He was pumping but not chanting. I happily noticed that he'd cleaned up a bit. He must have showered and washed his hair since our earlier encounter. He'd pulled his now-long white hair back into a ponytail and tied it close to his head with a piece of brown twine. He didn't, thank God, smell bad. He was wearing neither the ratty green robe nor the smiling bunny boxer shorts, but, instead, nice blue jeans and a gray long-sleeved hoodie. He even had on white sweat socks and a pair of brown dress shoes. I appreciated not having to look at his horrid feet. He was watching the show intently, hands clasped together and held tight against his sternum, leaning forward, his brow furrowed with concentration.

Jerry was talking with a chubby guy with a dark-brown mullet who'd admitted to sleeping with both of his fiancée's younger twin sisters, though *not*, he insisted, at the same time. "What can I tell you, Jerry?" the guy said. "You only live once, know what I'm sayin'?" Jerry, brow furrowed, bemused, holding in his right hand a large lime-green note card with JERRY SPRINGER in black block letters on the side facing the camera and grasping his microphone in his left hand, nodded. "Sure," he said, "that's an interesting perspective. So, tell me, do you love your fiancée?" I couldn't hear the guy's answer because my father was nodding and pointing at the TV and saying, "Now *that* is the question, isn't it?"

I quietly left to go to the bathroom because I didn't want to witness the inevitable confrontation between the chubby guy and his fiancée, likely with tears on her part and "How *could* you?" and then her charging at him with the wild overhead swings and then the "JER-RY! JER-RY!" Maybe one or both twins would emerge from backstage, horribly agitated, and they and their older sister would go at it as well. Or maybe all three of the women would turn on the chubby guy with the mullet. Oy gevalt!

When I returned, a new segment was on, featuring a tall, rail-thin black guy in a powder-blue suit and pink tie, with close-cropped hair and a perplexed facial expression, standing in the background, hands clasped behind his back, while two black women went at it in the foreground. One was a tiny woman in a bright-red dress and the other was a taller, large woman with massive bare arms and a huge head of curly orangish hair. It turned out that her hair was a wig, because the smaller woman adeptly swiped it off the other's head during one of their tussles and it fell to the floor. The small woman immediately noticed and delicately picked up the wig with her right thumb and forefinger and held it at arm's length in front of her and strolled assertively to the front of the stage and raised her chin victoriously and tossed the wig to the fourth row of the audience, a smug look on her little face. The audience, of course, howled and immediately commenced with the "JER-RY! JER-RY!"

My father nodded and even grinned, just a bit. "Tom," he whispered. "Act II is quite the juicy little drama, wouldn't you agree?" I just nodded and asked if he wanted coffee. He immediately sat up very straight and his gray eyes brightened and he grinned hugely and nodded enthusiastically.

When I returned from the kitchen with our coffees, Jerry was alone on the screen, in close-up from the waist up, attired in his usual sport jacket and dress shirt but no tie, and looking directly into the camera, brow slightly furrowed, perfectly serious. A sign on the bottom of the screen indicated that he was delivering his "Final Thought." This was a brief life lesson on relationships, apparently based somehow on the second segment. "In a perfect world," he intoned, "those we love would love us back in return. But sometimes they no longer have the intent. We've all been down that road, and it hurts. Sometimes a new love happens. But at other times, someone wants you back. If so, don't give them mixed messages. Say what you really want." Then, after a brief pause, Jerry finished with a hyper-sincere, "Until next time, *please* take care of yourself … and each other." During all this, Dad listened intently, his hands clasped together as in prayer, and nodded vigorously here and there. "That's *right!*" he exclaimed when Jerry said that a new love sometimes happens. "*Tell* it, Jerry," he said, fairly loudly, at another point. Following Jerry's exhortation for us to take care of ourselves and each other, Dad raised both hands, open palms facing the screen, and nodded his head vigorously and exclaimed, "You've got it, Jerry. You've got it, buddy boy."

As depressed as I'd felt about Sandy's wedding, I couldn't help chuckling at the absurdity of it all—provocative yet bemused middle-aged Springer, his young guests with their convoluted relationship issues, the young blood-lusted audience members constantly shouting "JER-RY!," the big black-shirted security guys who sometimes had to stifle a giggle as they separated the combatants, and, then, particularly, Jerry's oh-so-sincere Final Thought, apparently to attach a sliver of meaning and credence and sanity to balance out the preceding fifty-nine minutes of nuttiness and violence.

And there was my father, the well-regarded Yale-trained actor, done now with his wonderful stage career and reduced to this, sitting alone at home day after day like a meshugenah recluse, watching this low-level drama. *Well*, I thought, *at least he's not yet reduced to watching Roadrunner cartoons.* There's that. Maybe I can get him off this crap and on to something better—not necessarily a huge amount better, but at least somewhat. Maybe, as I'd thought, he'd like those well-heeled Upper East Side chatterers from *The Real Housewives of New York City* and their slightly higher-level drama.

Or, maybe I can try to get him to watch news and current events stuff again. He used to like to watch the evening news shows and, now and again, CNN or MSNBC and the like. But not lately. I remembered when Dad and I were watching some boring politician in a segment on one of those shows, giving a speech, and there was a skinny older guy in a checkered sport jacket, with wire-rimmed glasses and a bushy mustache, below and to left of the politician, doing sign language interpretation of what the guy was saying, with the usual mouthed words and exaggerated hand and facial gestures, including a lot of raised eyebrows and intense facial expressions. I recall thinking that I might like such a job. A guy can be up there on a stage and never have to actually *talk* to anyone, but just do those wonderful animated expressions and gestures. It seems a useful thing to do.

SEVENTEEN

I THOUGHT I was at my lowest point—my "worst," as Edgar said—when Naomi kicked me out, but I was wrong. I'm lower now. I don't know how I could get much lower. Now I'm *really* at my worst, because Herschel told me that Celeste and Donny are together now—"an item," as he put it. He told me that when I called to see if he wanted to do lunch at Izzy's on Saturday. This will be Benji's weekend at home rather than with his father—I keep track—so I had the idea of setting up a lunch and asking Benji to meet us there, hopefully without Naomi knowing, so he could again enjoy some menschkeit.

Naomi. Her face, for some reason, came into my head after Herschel told me about Celeste. Not right away, because I was way too verklempt for a time, but later. I remembered her looking up at me, wet-faced, from her seat on the couch in December, the day before Christmas Eve, when we watched the ending of *It's a Wonderful Life*, just before she suggested that we make love. I remembered her face when she told Fern about my being scared to use the revolving door at the hospital. And I recalled her sarcastic expression, with the corner of her upper lip curled, while watching *The Real Housewives of New York City* with Elise, munching Lay's Sour Cream and Onion chips and snarking about Countess Luann or Sonja or Ramona. Her habit was always to scoop a healthy handful of chips with her left hand and store them in her open palm and then delicately select one chip at a time with her right thumb and index finger and raise the chip high before depositing it, with a delicate feminine gesture, into her gaping mouth.

I fondly recalled Naomi going on and on during our morning coffee couple-check-in sessions in the kitchen with her petty grievances about Arthur. I even conjured the image of her big purplish nose when she was upset with me, which was often. Just then I missed my Naomi's face, in all its iterations.

Celeste and Donny! Herschel's news hit me over the head like a card chair swung by a hulking, scowling, big-bellied professional wrestler—the Iron Sheik, say, or Sgt. Slaughter. Or maybe "Stone Cold" Steve Austin.

Who saw that coming? How could I have been so stupid? was my thought. *How so naïve?* I shook my head and slapped my forehead with an open palm. Schlemiel? The word doesn't do justice. Putz? Schmuck? Shlub? Shlimazel? Schnook? *Shmegege*, even? Idiot? Those words neither. Here I'd had soaring fantasies of being with Celeste, of being her lover, of moving in with her and being her man, making her feel safe, taking care of her, maybe being her photographic Boswell, and now those fantasies have shattered in an instant and look who she's with instead—pretty boy Donny, for God's sake, with his wavy hair, muscular torso, nice tenor voice, and handsome face! It's just hard to believe. It was *his* damned character, that scheming lowlife Edmund, who was responsible for wonderful Cordelia's being hanged. So now I find out that Celeste's taken up with the guy who played the despicable cocksucker who'd ordered *her* lovely character's sad death! How could she *do* that? Does the woman have no self-respect? If she'd taken up with Howie, who played Edgar, that would at least be more understandable. Edgar was a good guy, a definite mensch. Or she could have chosen Jake—another mensch. Nahum Tate, I'm sure, would have approved of either of those matches.

"Stone Cold" Steve Austin. Now there's a name. Stone Cold Julius Dickman doesn't have quite the same ring. Maybe *Mushy Lukewarm* Julius Dickman.

Some man I am. I wondered if Celeste's given me so much as a thought since our little morning of passion. I even wondered if she was fantasizing about Donny when she and I were doing the deed. If so, I at least appreciate that she didn't moan out his name in a moment of passion.

I wondered if Donny will move into Celeste's condo, assuming she stayed and Andrew moved out. If so, they'll surely shtup in the very bed where she and I had our little moment of bliss, with poor crippled Christina on the wall to the left of the bed, tensely reclining in the grass of her little world. Maybe Celeste would have one or several of those arched-back multiple orgasms that Herschel's gone on about.

So now, in a twinkling, I've gone from big nachas to big tsoris. The wheel of my fortune's flipped yet again. *Vey iz mir!* Just then I think I understood how poor verklempt George Bailey felt that Christmas Eve, perched desperately on the bridge in Bedford Falls, grasping a snow-covered railing, looking down at the cold, swirling water. I briefly imagined myself on such a bridge staring, wild-eyed like George, at the raging icy river, ready now to jump in and get this disappointing life over with at last.

The freezing water would blessedly envelop me and soon my troubles would end and I'd just be history. My strutting and fretting would be over; I'd be heard from no more. Out, brief candle. I'd pass and be forgotten with the rest. I had no illusions that there'd be a Clarence the guardian angel to jump in the river instead so as to save me by my saving him and to show me that I was so very wrong to think of suicide, that it would be a terrible mistake to throw away the precious gift of life, to help me understand that I'd really had a wonderful life after all, that I'd made a positive difference in the lives of many, that I still had much to live for.

Crap! Good old George loaned money at decent interest rates to many poor working stiffs, some of them Italian immigrants—"a bunch of garlic caters," Mr. Potter had called them—so they could have a roof over their heads and a pot to piss in and not have to come crawling to Potter for housing. There was even a whole neighborhood named after him, Bailey Park, of the modest houses he'd helped build. That's definitely something. George had a lovely wife, who'd adored him since they were children, and four winsome kids. He'd made his widowed mother happy and proud. People loved and respected him and eagerly gave him their money when they thought he needed it. What have I done with my life?

Well, I thought, *what do I care?* Let Celeste and Pretty Boy be as happy as two larks singing hymns at break of day. Let her wallow in the marvelousness of his tall, masculine physique and chiseled face and sparkling blue eyes and, no doubt, his huge *shlong*. Let them know many years ahead of unabated joy and erotic bliss, wedded or otherwise. What do I care? I have my own worries.

My father, for one. He's back to poor hygiene after his brief hiatus. Yesterday he removed the brown twine holding his long hair in a ponytail and now it's dangling and straggly again, though clean enough, and he's back in the damned green bathrobe, and again I have the supreme pleasure of seeing his feet, with those toenails. Yikes! I'd been hoping that he'd put that phase behind him, but I guess not.

And that's not the worst. Last night I thought I heard the garage door opener motor whirring in the middle of the night. I didn't want to get out of bed to check it out, fearing another possible nasty anti-Semitic intruder. But after a bit I screwed my courage to the sticking place. Dad's Ford Escape wasn't in the garage. I didn't know where he'd gone. Maybe, I speculated, he just went to Kwik Trip to get a gallon of milk and a loaf of bread. Or maybe he'd decided to drive to Alaska. I didn't want to think about what was going on with my father, just then. *Enough of this old man's loopiness,* was my thought. Still, I was concerned. I didn't want to be, but had to. I'm Herbert Dickman's son, his only child.

I only wanted, just then, to be alone with my grief over Celeste, even over Naomi, and not to be bothered with filial obligations. I wished I had a sibling, maybe a brother—a Leonard, an Arthur—to call on to help out.

I had the thought, though, that if Dad didn't come back in a reasonable amount of time, I should call the police. I didn't want to have to do that; I didn't want to be bothered. I didn't want to talk to any authority figures or have to answer their probing questions—"So, Mr. Dickman, has your father been behaving *strangely* lately?"—or endure their pitying facial expressions. But I'd have to.

I sat down in Dad's La-Z-Boy and crossed my arms and huddled into myself. It was a bit cold, so I covered myself with his luxurious purple Lear robe. I picked up the gold scepter and waved it about. "I am a K-K-KING!" I shouted. "A *r-royal* one." It was the first time I'd sat in his chair for years. I couldn't remember the last time. That was my old man's chair, no one else's. It was a long-time part of him and he was part of it. Sitting in it felt like an invasion of his space. But it also felt like I was sharing something with him, bonding with my father, in a strange way. I felt comfortable, and the purple robe was warm and soft and comforting. I started to feel sleepy.

But before I could fall asleep in the chair, I started weeping. It just happened, out of the blue. I couldn't remember the last time I'd cried. I don't know why. Probably everything was, just then, too much. And now my weird father was AWOL in the middle of the night, with no explanation. One damned random thing after another! I felt depleted. I had the brief thought that I should fight the tears, should buck up, should try to be a man. *Oh, the hell with that,* I thought after a moment. I reclined all the way back in the chair and pulled the purple robe snugly around me and sobbed like a urine-soaked baby for what seemed like a long time. Afterward, I felt drained but better, relieved of something.

I decided that I'd better drive around for a while and look for my father before calling the police. In his loopiness, an encounter with the authorities could go badly. Suppose he went apeshit—"You're stopping me? *Me?* Know you not who I am? I am Herbert *Dickman*, the great classical actor. I just finished playing Lear. I've done Romeo and Antony and Hamlet and Claudius and Macbeth and Iago and Willy Loman. How *dare* you, peasants?"—and they had to arrest him for resisting. Maybe he'd extend to his full height, long white hair blowing amok in the night air. "What?" he'd intone. "A prisoner? I am even the natural fool of fortune. Come, and ye get it, ye shall get it by running!" And he'd flee the scene on foot and the officers who'd tried to arrest him would radio for help and soon every beefy cop in the county would be chasing after my poor wacko father, sirens screaming in the winter night and red and blue lights strobing. Yikes!

Before going to look for Dad, though, I decided to just relax for a few minutes and slow down my fevered brain and try to think pleasant thoughts. I thought about Benji; I found that calming. I really hoped he could come to Izzy's on Saturday. He'd liked it before, and hopefully would again. I wondered if he'd again stare, slack-jawed, at Magda. That was a nice moment. Magda seemed to like him. I missed Benji. I had the idea that maybe he and I could watch all of *Quest for Fire* sometime soon. That would be good, something we could share. I wanted to know what it was that Naoh's new girlfriend, Ika, from that more advanced tribe, had taught him.

I thought, too, about Lydia. Now that Celeste's out of the picture, I briefly wondered if she and I could ever be "an item." But I quickly dismissed that thought. It's out of the question. It's ridiculous speculation. I've clearly been a dismal failure with women and there's no reason to think that things could ever be different, particularly with a clear winner like Lydia.

On the other hand, anything's possible. Maybe Lydia has a higher opinion of me than I think I deserve.

I decided to look at some of my father's albums. I pulled the *Othello* one from the oak bookcase in the living room and paged through it. Dad looked fine in the photos—my photos, that were nicely crafted—as Iago. He'd perfected a sort of hunchbacked physique and a perpetual curled-lip sneer. I remembered his final line: "From this time forth I never will speak word." I liked that one. It occurred to me, not for the first time, how proud my father'd felt about his career, how much a part of his identity it was. I felt jealous.

I must have fallen asleep in the La-Z-Boy because next I knew there was my old man standing in front of me, looking concerned, gently shaking my shoulder. "Son," he said, gently. "Are you okay?" I looked out the window and saw that it was still dark outside. My father was dressed in the same jeans and sweatshirt as earlier.

"Dad," I said, "where the hell were you? Where'd you drive to in the middle of the night?"

He pursed his lips and looked confused. "Drive?" he said. "I don't think I drove anywhere. I don't remember doing that." He looked at me askance. "Where's all this coming from, Julius?"

I just shrugged. "Okay, Dad," I said softly. "Just go to bed. I will, too."

But then I couldn't sleep. I was too farmisht. Thoughts raced through my mind. One was that despite how crappy my life is just now, at least the days are definitely getting longer. The sun comes up earlier and goes down later; now it's light outside until after five. There're still way more hours of darkness than light, but the direction of change, though subtle, is positive. No one can alter that. None of these women can. They don't have *that* power over me. They have other power, but not that. Even if my father goes way wacko and even if Celeste and Donny live happily ever after and shtup blissfully day and night and her parts work wonderfully and she never gives me a thought, the days between now and the summer solstice, which is far away but coming, will get longer—gradually, but surely. And by mid-June there'll only be eight hours of scary darkness. So there's that. Maybe that's just enough to keep me from jumping off some icy bridge—at least for now.

I also thought about Scanner Stan. I hadn't seen him since last fall, but, for some reason, he came into my mind. The last time I saw him he was sitting on a bench downtown, his usual bench, alone as always. It was a nice autumn afternoon, though a bit cool, and Stan was in his usual attire: dirty white undershirt, baggy black cargo pants, and ancient red tennis shoes—Keds, perhaps. Those shoes were worn-down, filthy and stained, and the left one had tears in the fabric near the heel. He had his usual five-day growth of brownish whiskers, and I remember noticing the start of gray streaks, mostly around his weak chin. He has a distinct underbite. His hair was unruly and, as usual, appeared not to have been washed for a fair while. I noticed, too, that his hairline had definitely receded since the last time I'd seen him. He had on the same brown-framed glasses with thick Coke-bottle lenses that he'd always worn, and I noticed that there was gray duct tape wrapped around the hinge of the right arm temple. Both lenses were, as usual, smudged and filthy. Stan's always been short and stocky, but looked heavier still than when I'd last seen him. His gut had noticeably expanded. He had his usual one-liter bottle of Mountain Dew beside him on the bench and was holding his ancient black police/fire scanner, with a slightly bent antenna, in his right hand. His habit's always been to sit quietly on his bench and to look around, first to one side and then the other, calmly surveying the landscape—eyes squinted, mouth hanging slightly open, a bit buck-toothed—and now and again to raise the scanner to his mouth and speak quietly into it in a guttural monotone. Once I was close enough that I heard him say, in a low voice, into the mouthpiece, "Everything's quiet on lower Main Street. Over." I've never known if he's actually connected to the authorities or if it's just his delusion.

When I saw him last fall, Stan was eating a Hostess Twinkie. There was also an unopened package of Hostess Ho-Hos on the bench, to his left. He washed down bites with huge gulps of the Mountain Dew. Watching him, I had the same thought I'd had before as to Big Art and others: *Has this poor sumbitch ever had the pleasure of eating a truly high-quality hot dog on a quality bun?* It seemed a trivial thought, though. What do I know about Stan's life? He could be mentally ill, tortured by delusions and hallucinations, maybe overwhelmed with paranoid thoughts or fears. He could be homeless, could be an alcoholic or a hopeless drug addict. He could be pathologically lonely. At best, he's yet another sad isolato. I doubt that he eats too healthily, especially if he routinely feasts on those Twinkies and Ho-Hos and maybe Ding-Dongs as well, with their twenty-five-year shelf lives.

So I'm guessing that experiencing a Nathan's Hebrew National Kosher Beef Frank, grilled, on a poppy seed bun, with all those hoity-toity condiments, isn't high on his list of life priorities. It's probably not among the items on his bucket list, if he has one. I doubt he's ever given it any thought. Maybe he has. Maybe while sitting there alone on his bench day after tedious day, always alone, grasping his maybe-fake scanner, glancing up and down the street for possible real or imaginary scofflaws or trouble-makers to report to the cops, or maybe looking for telltale flames in an abandoned building, doing his supposed civic duty, even if he's delusional, he's happily fantasized about someday eating a high-quality dog, something a step above the usual cheap low-grade boiled wieners on run-of-the-mill white bread buns—a package of six such buns wrapped in cellophane going for $1.09—that was all he's likely ever experienced in his sad little life so far. That's possible, I suppose. What do I know?

I had the thought that I wish Herschel had been with me when I last saw Stan. He'd have made small talk with him, made him feel okay. "Hey, Stan," he'd have maybe hollered out, not condescending or sarcastic. "How's it going, buddy? Everything quiet on Main Street?"

Thinking about Stan, I had the same thought I'd had about Carl: *At least I'm better off than he is*. I should count my blessings, like Dad advised. Maybe I have my woman troubles and maybe I don't have much going for me these days, maybe fortune's wheel is at a low point now, more tsoris than nachas, but on the great scale of things I'm still more fortunate than Scanner Stan or Tunnel Terry or poor Blanche or even Big Art. I think I am, anyway. So there's that.

Lying in bed, I thought, too, about my mother. I very much wanted to listen to "The Whiffenpoof Song" with her, that part about the stupid little lost lambs. I wished I could talk with her about Celeste being with Donny instead of with me. I wished I could tell her that I missed Naomi and wanted to see Benji, to be in his life. I'd tell her that I've missed her. That would be a good thing to say. I don't know what she'd answer. Maybe she'd just listen and nod and encourage me to have a positive outlook, to be optimistic. Maybe she'd remind me that Edgar had also said, "The worst is not so long as we can say 'This is the worst.'" That would, I guess, be a comforting thought. I'd consider her wise words and purse my lips and nod my head. "Thanks, M-Mom," I'd say. "So, as c-crappy as things are, they can always be c-crappier, huh?" She'd arch her eyebrows and purse her lips and lean her head to one side and subtly nod and look into my eyes. She'd reach over and, with her thumb and index finger, grasp the point of my chin and raise it just a bit. "Don't let the pygmies get you down, son," she'd murmur in a gentle, soft and low voice. "They, too, will turn into fleshless Yoricks."

Edgar. That guy certainly knew what he was talking about as to "the worst." There he was, a guy with status and standing, wealth and privilege, and then, in a twinkling, all that was gone and he had to disguise himself as a beggar madman, Poor Tom, and blather crazily about being tortured by fiends and drinking ditchwater and eating mice and rats for seven long years and being "whipped from tithing to tithing," whatever a *tithing* is, just to stay alive in a cruel world turned suddenly absurd. His poor father, old Gloucester, was another sad case who'd experienced "the worst" in that damned play—having both eyes ripped out by Cornwall and horrible Regan, and in his own *house*. Yikes! "As flies to wanton boys are we to the gods; they kill us for their sport," blind Gloucester said. Even though he'd said that in a moment of horrible despair, maybe his jaundiced view was right and Twersky's isn't. What do I know?

"Let me t-tell you," I'll maybe tell my father, "there's no d-d-divinity shaping our ends, even our r-rear ends."

I'll have to look up what a "wanton" boy is. Is it different from the wonton soup I'd had at China Palace? I recalled that Mei-Lin had given me a sweet, almost mysterious, little smile when she'd put that soup on the table in front of me. I'd had the brief thought that maybe she liked me. It was good, that soup—not as lovely as Izzy's matzo ball soup, of course, but good enough, warm and comforting. Those wontons were big. I like the China Palace wontons, particularly the fillings—ground pork, minced mushrooms, chopped green onions—but it's not easy to cut them into smaller pieces with just a soup spoon, so a guy can consume them easily enough without choking. A matzo ball is soft and cuts easily with a spoon, but not a wonton. They usually aren't soft, with that harder doughy shell— at least the ones from China Palace. You have to try to pin the middle of the wonton to the side of the bowl with the edge of your soup spoon and try to cut into it before it slithers away to the middle of the bowl. You almost have to use a knife to cut them, but I didn't want to do that because Herschel would have looked at me askance and curled his lip in disdain. "What the fuck kind of pathetic pussy loser uses a *knife* to cut a damned wonton?" he might have scolded—good-naturedly, but still. "Jesus Christ, I can't believe what I'm seeing!"

So what was Mei-Lin's little smile about? Was it personal? Did she indeed like me, maybe even *want* me? Or was she just being affable so as to get a bigger tip? I guess I'll never know.

Well, no matter. I'm done with women for now. I think I am.

I hope Naomi and Celeste are sleeping peacefully right now, untroubled by worries or disturbing thoughts or dreams. Rivkah and Lydia, too. I'm sure I'm not making an appearance in any of their dreams or imaginings. Still, I wish them nachas.

The menschkeit at Izzy's should be good, though. There's that.

EIGHTEEN

AS DAD AND I were driving to Izzy's, I had the random thought that maybe I should call Donny and ask if he'd noticed that brown spot on Celeste's back and, if so, if he'd mentioned it to her and advised her to see a doctor. Maybe that would save her life. But then it occurred to me that he might wonder how I knew about the spot. What could I say? Could I tell him that Celeste and I had shtupped, though it wasn't really personal, at least on her part? That probably wouldn't fly. Maybe I could lie, perhaps tell him that I'd heard about it from some woman I know who'd seen Celeste naked in the gym locker room. But that wouldn't fly either because I don't know if she even goes to a gym. So I dropped the idea. I don't want to talk to Donny, anyway.

Dad was with me because he'd overheard me, after our dinner last evening, calling Benji to see if he wants to come to Izzy's on Saturday and asked if he could go too. It was pathetic but amusing. "Oh, Tom," he practically whispered after I'd hung up, looking up at me from his beige La-Z-Boy. "Can I go? *Please*, Julius?" His eyes, again a murky, pale bluish-gray, were opened wide as he looked up at me pleadingly, like a little boy begging his daddy to take him to the mall to see Santa so he could ask for a train set for Christmas. Dad's mouth and tongue and whiskers were again orange-stained from the Cheetos he'd been shoveling into his mouth. I had to turn away and stifle a chuckle at the absurdity of it all.

I didn't answer him right away. I had mixed feelings. On the one hand, I thought, maybe it'd be nice to have my father there with Benji and Herschel and even Magda. On the other hand, I didn't want him to go. I wanted to keep the various parts of my life in their own little compartments. But I took the high road. "Sure, Dad," I replied—reluctantly, but still.

At least I'd had a smile earlier because of my father. I'd seen him go into the bathroom and heard him grunting and then, after several minutes, heard the toilet flush, twice, and a few moments later he opened the door and saw me and grinned hugely. "Ah," he said, "let me tell you something,

Julius. There's nothing in this world more satisfying, and *rare*, than a good dump!"

But I'd also had a fright because of Dad—not because of anything he did but because of what he'd been watching on TV a bit later yesterday. It was a movie with subtitles, *Das Boot*, about a German submarine in World War II, with the dramatic focus on the handsome, craggy-faced captain and selected crew members and their poignant life struggles. One of them, Johann, has a short-lived nervous breakdown. Toward the end, the submarine gets attacked by a British fighter plane and they have to dive, but there's big damage and the sub can't level off and commences to sink. The crew's trapped. Just before the boat's in danger of being crushed by the pressure of being at a worrisome depth, it lands on a sea shelf. The crew members work frantically to make repairs before their oxygen runs out, and after many hours their efforts bear fruit and they somehow surface and limp toward the German-controlled French port of La Rochelle. They arrive and are overjoyed to have made it there alive, a triumph after all their adversities, but then Allied planes suddenly zoom in and bomb the sub and many of the crew are wounded or killed and then the damaged submarine sinks in the dock, and the good-looking captain—lying badly wounded on the dock, blood oozing from his mouth—watches his beloved boat being destroyed and sinking, just before he tragically expires.

It was a sad ending, I suppose—they were Nazi bastards, but still—but what distressed me most, watching, was just the thought of being on a submarine in general and particularly one that's far under the surface and sinking. Oy gevalt! What kind of eternal idiot, I wondered, would ever volunteer to be on a damned submarine, a boat that goes *under* the water, where you can't leave if you want to, can't escape, where you can't ever be by yourself much, where you have to sleep in a tiny metal bunk with a side rail in a stack of three bunks in a crowded and low-ceilinged room with dozens of other snoring and farting guys, where you rarely see the sky and open air, where the enemy wants to bomb you if you're surfaced or drop nasty depth charges on you if you're not, where you could die a horrible death—gasping for air, lungs collapsing—and then your corpse is ensconced for eternity in a rusting tin can at the bottom of the ocean?

Then last night I lay awake for at least an hour, again obsessing about being trapped and out of control in a damaged submarine far below the surface. My face felt flushed. I imagined being one of the crew members in our desperate predicament and my colleagues, though scared, are in control of their emotions and competently working hard to fix the ballast system. I'm huddled in a corner, not helping, having a panic attack—breathing hard, sweating profusely, heart pounding, probably weeping, maybe praying— and one of the guys hears me sniffling and pauses from his labors, grasping a formidable sixteen-inch-long steel wrench in his manly and gnarly hand, and glares at me, shaking his head slowly, a look of contempt and disgust on his sweat-streaked face. "Pathetic!" he mutters. "Another freakin' Johann. What a *schlemiel!*"

When we got to Izzy's, I happily saw that Benji was there already, seated alone at one of the larger booths. He must have taken the bus. He stood and politely greeted Dad and shook his hand. "Mr. Dickman," he said softly, "nice to see you again." At first, I wasn't sure that my father knew who Benji was; his brow was furrowed and his eyes, now a light-gray, seemed a bit murky and he appeared vague. But then he seemed to recognize him from the long-ago Seder at Naomi's and nodded and mumbled, "How are you, young man?"

A few minutes later, Herschel and Howie walked in the door together. "Magda," Herschel bellowed, "I need coffee immediately. It's *freezing* out there, for Chrissake. Let's *go*, huh? Chop, chop."

She gave him a look as he took off his coat and sat down. "'Chop, chop'? Little people wit no good manners have to vait for coffee," she scolded. "Maybe long time, *ja?*" She glanced at Benji and smiled. "But young men wit polite ways get phosphate right away." She noticed Dad. "And who is dis nice-looking citizen?" she asked.

"This is my f-father," I said. "H-Herbert."

She studied Dad for a moment. "Iss goot to meet dignified gentleman. You vould like nice hot coffee on cold day, Mr. Herbert?" My father just nodded, and I noticed that Benji was again staring at Magda, his mouth slightly agape, with the same simpleton expression on his face as before. I felt momentarily happy seeing that, but kicked his ankle a bit anyway.

"Magda," Herschel said, sitting up straight, eyes opened wide in feigned innocence. "I sincerely apologize for my, uh, my *insensitivity*. I truly do. But you have to know that my little heart is thumping away just to see your magnificent face again. My palms are all sweaty, my knees are weak. They might buckle. I can barely speak, I'm telling ya. It must be love, huh? Am I wrong?"

She looked at him and giggled. "Vell," she said, "if you can barely speak, please do not bother. And let us hope dat your knees don't buckle so den you fall flat on your face, *ja?* Dat little face can't stand much more punishing, you know."

Herschel said nothing at first, but glanced at Dad and nodded. "She's got a point, Uncle Herb," he finally said. "I'm hardly handsome old Edmund, huh?"

Thanks a lot, cuz, I thought. *Thanks for bringing that up.* Here I happily hadn't thought about Celeste and Pretty Boy for the last half-hour and now damned Herschel has to bring it up!

I noticed Benji studying the menu. He tapped me on the arm. "Julius," he whispered, "I'd like to try something different than the last time. Something other than that Son of a Brisket Melt. That was good, though. Maybe I'll try The Epiphany, like Jake had. Or something else. What do you think?"

"Sure," I said, "whatever you want. The Epiphany would b-be okay. Or maybe c-corned b-b-beef on rye. That's my favorite. But you should d-definitely get matzo b-b-ball soup, too, Benji. A c-cup or a bowl. It'll warm you up."

The corned beef on rye is what I wanted and had planned on ordering. But then I had the thought that I'd like to get something that Naomi would approve of. I thought of ordering a Cobb salad with a grilled salmon add-on, like that bluehair Big Art had so rudely stared at through the front window. Herschel told me once that women like it when men order salads in restaurants, though he didn't say why. It probably had something to do with his "game plan" theory. So Naomi'd probably approve of that. She hadn't commented one way or the other, though, that time I ordered a chicken Caesar salad when we visited Fern in the hospital.

But then my thought was: *Hell, why try to please that woman, considering that she kicked my ass out and we're no longer a couple and now I'm living with my wackadoodle father?* So I decided to order corned beef hash. I'd hugely enjoyed Izzy's hash twice before—once before I moved in with Naomi and then once again after that—and it was to die for each time: cubed potatoes, diced onions and peppers sautéed, slowly, with chunks of juicy corned beef trimmings, mixed with egg, and scrambled into a crisp omelet that's marvelously moist in the middle. I'd told Naomi, the second time I had it, that I just loved that hash and planned to get it again. That was a mistake. She gave me one of her looks, with the downturned mouth and crinkled nose, and made very clear that she disapproves of corned beef hash, or *any* kind of hash, loudly opining that it's "just totally *disgusting*." She said she couldn't kiss me for at least a day because I'd eaten the hash. So the hell with her! I'll order Izzy's lovely hash and eat it very slowly and deliberately, savoring each mouthful, and think of her while savoring, and if I ever have the chance I'll tell Naomi that I'd ordered it and loved it and that I plan it get it again the *next* time I go to Izzy's, and not only that but I plan to stack my father's kitchen shelves with family-sized cans of Hormel Mary Kitchen Corned Beef Hash and open a damned can whenever I was so inclined, for breakfast or lunch or dinner or even as a bedtime snack. So there.

Big Art. I recalled my one personal encounter with him, last May. I was walking downtown, on Main Street, and saw Art—grasping his usual paper bag with the rotgut, his squeegee pole beside him on the ground—leaning heavily against one of those big red-white-and-blue mailboxes, probably waiting for walking-by women to harass. He was wearing a filthy black sweatshirt and his tattered blue baseball cap. His gut protruded hugely, as though he was eight months pregnant. Half of that gut, including his belly button, was visible between the bottom edge of his ragged sweatshirt and the top of his equally-ragged khaki pants. It was an overcast day. I thought it would be friendly to say something to him. "Hey, Art," I offered, "d-do you think it's g-g-gonna rain?" He turned his head and glared at me for a few moments, his unblinking eyes bulging, but said nothing. Then he shrugged and pursed his lips and tilted his huge head to one side in a dismissive gesture. "How the hell do *I* know if it's gonna rain?" he growled. "If it rains, it rains. If it don't, it don't. I ain't a goddamned weatherman, for Chrissake."

When Magda set down the usual basket of rye bread with caraway seeds and small foil-wrapped pats of butter, my father immediately grabbed a slice and devoured it in huge bites, without buttering it, and then immediately chowed down another slice in similar fashion. I noticed Benji staring at him as he stuffed the bread in his mouth.

Just then Izzy came into the dining room from the kitchen. I noticed right away that he didn't look well. His face was thinner and more drawn than the last time. He seemed more hunched-over and his eyes were a bit sunken. He looked exhausted. But he was still wearing the stained white apron. "Iz," Herschel said, "you okay? You look like warmed-over shit."

Izzy brushed a speck of dirt from our table with the corner of his apron. Then he tapped the back of Herschel's head with an open palm, not gently, causing my cousin's blue yarmulke to slide a bit to one side of his head. "Nu?" Izzy said. "So now you're a *doctor?* Ach! Don't *drei mein kop* with your mishegas. I'm a tired old man. I'm worn out. So maybe I'll even see my Sadie soon. Who knows? You young people, you need to have respect for us frail senior citizens." He looked at Dad and his eyes softened. "Herbert," he said quietly, "it's been a while. *Wie gehts?* How've you been?"

Dad shrugged. "What can I tell you, Isadore? I'm still taking breaths in and out. I retired from the theater, you know. So I'm no longer a poor player treading the boards. I'm tired, too." He paused and looked at Benji and then at me. His eyes were that murky blue-gray. Under the fluorescent lights, I noticed that his face seemed more lined. He looked older. "I failed at the big one, Izzy. That's all there is to it." He scratched his head. "I mean, what more can I tell you?"

Magda brought chocolate phosphates for Benji and me and coffees for Dad and Herschel and a Dr. Brown's Cream Soda for Howie. Benji stared stupidly at her again. I nudged him in the ribs. "Oh, thank you," he murmured to Magda, smiling. "Thank you very much." He took a sip of his phosphate and smiled up at her and then at Izzy. "*Wonderful*, huh? You bet!"

"Iss nice polite young man wit good manners," Magda said. "And vat you will have today, young man?"

Benji picked up the menu and studied it for a moment. "Well," he said, "I think I'd like to try the Izzy's Chicago Dog. And, absolutely, a cup of matzo ball soup." He looked to me. "Would that be okay?" I nodded.

Izzy nodded too and patted the back of Benji's head. "*Ess gezunt*," he said. "Eat well, young man."

Dad was studying the menu, his brow furrowed. "Isadore," he said, "what do you recommend?"

Izzy looked thoughtful. "Well," he said after a moment, "I recommend the Sadie's Pastrami on Dark Rye. That was my wife's favorite, you know. Sadie, may her memory be a blessing, insisted we carve the meat the right way." He put his hand on Benji's shoulder and rubbed lightly. He seemed more animated. "You see, first, you have to steam the pastrami for at least three hours, till the meat's ready to fall apart. Then you have to cut it by hand, always. We used to use the slicing machine, you know, but Sadie finally said no to that. 'It's a *shonda* to cut pastrami with that thing,' she said. She was right, no? So now we hand-carve it. But you gotta work with the meat. You have to read the navel and meet the grain."

He paused and looked at Herschel. "It's hard to get a good cutter, though. I've been through three of them in the last two years. The last guy before the one now, a bad-tempered diabetic goy, was a goddamned pain in the toochis. If a customer ever kvetched about the pastrami or the corned beef, he'd go crazy and get all red in the face and wave a knife around and threaten to quit." He looked at Magda. "You remember that putz?"

"Oh, *ja*. Big pain in da ass, sure. But goot cutter."

Izzy shrugged. "I suppose," he said. "But finally I had enough with his mishegas. '*Again* you're going to quit?' I told him. 'You can't quit, and you know why? Cause I'm going to *fire* your bony goy ass.'" He turned to Benji and put a hand on his shoulder. "You should excuse my language, young man."

Benji nodded and glanced at me. "I've heard worse, sir."

Maybe being a cutter here at Izzy's would be a good job, I thought. You have a skill, a set of high-quality knives that hold their edges, and your work has a good outcome: it can make hungry people happy. I wasn't sure, though, if a cutter has to talk much with people—customers, servers, others. If so, maybe I wouldn't like that so much. If a guy could competently carve the pastrami and corned beef and brisket and whatnot, reading the navel and meeting the grain, whatever that means, and keep his knives sharp and clean and just do his craft and not be too bothered with human interaction, except maybe with Magda and even Izzy now and again, that would be good. And I don't think I'd go nutso on Izzy, like the diabetic goy did.

As we were sipping our drinks and waiting for our food, Benji asked my father why he thought he'd "failed at the big one." I was surprised to hear him, a twelve-year-old kid, ask that, but it was certainly a right question. I'd asked that, too, but, of course, hadn't received much of an answer. Dad pursed his lips. He looked at Benji and then, briefly, at me and looked thoughtful. "Too big, young man," he said, barely audibly. "Too complex. Lear was just too large a role. I didn't think it would be, but I was ... wrong." He paused and stared up at the painting of the maybe-constipated old rabbi on the wall above the doorway to the kitchen and then at the photo of Izzy. His face softened. "All that huge, roiling emotion—just so many layers, too many peaks. His descent into madness. I could never get a handle on all the, uh, the range of emotions—all that anger, pathos, self-pity, madness. Lear's *huge,* rash anger that happened so quickly in the first act! His temper, the nuttiness. Too much! I couldn't master it. I tried, I did. I got close now and again, I think, but … " He paused again and nodded his head. "Plus, I think I waited too long."

"How do you mean?" Howie asked.

Dad looked at Howie. His eyes were almost glazed over but at least he wasn't, for the moment, out in left field. He thought for a moment and then nodded. "Too physically demanding. All that yelling, right from the start, and particularly in the storm scene where I had to shout to be heard above the goddamn rain and thunder and wind sounds, to project to the back of the theater. My throat hurt and my voice got hoarse. I realized early on, probably after the first three performances, that I wasn't up to it, physically. I felt *so* exhausted. Maybe I could have done Lear when I was sixty-five, even sixty-eight. But, you know, I waited too long. I didn't have the … the energy, the stamina." He glanced in my direction. "I can't believe how much it took out of me, Julius."

He paused and looked down at his lap and rubbed his chin with one hand. "I wanted to be as close as possible to Lear's age in the play when I did it, you know, but maybe that was … a mistake." He shook his head and looked at me and then at Benji. "You can't do Lear when you're not yet old enough to understand approaching death, but you can't wait till you're so goddamn old that you don't have the energy, the strength. Ach!" He picked up his coffee cup and raised it to his lips but then put it down without drinking. He again stared at Benji. "Lear is the greatest role ever written, young man, for sure, but also the most … impossible. For me it was." He vigorously scratched the top of his head. "Well," he practically whispered, "what the hell's the difference, anyway? It doesn't matter, in the long run. Am I right?"

No one said anything for a long minute. Then Benji asked, "Well, did you do anything in the play that you thought was good, that you're proud of?"

Dad again pursed his lips and seemed surprised at the question. I was too. It was something that never occurred to me, but, I suppose, should have. "Hmm," he said, sitting up straighter and pursing his lips. "I have to think about that." He took a sip of his coffee and furrowed his brow. "Well," he said after a few moments, "one thing was that I decided, early on, to give Gloucester a big hug when I suddenly recognized him in the Dover scene, where my line is 'I know thee well enough. Thy name is Gloucester.' I thought at first it might be too schmaltzy, but then decided to do it anyway. And you know what? I'm damned *glad* I did. It was a good thing—two sad old men who have a history, who love each other, and have both been through hell and driven to … to madness by their nasty, ungrateful kids." He paused and looked down at his lap and nodded. "So, I suppose that was a good thing, huh?"

"Yeah," Benji said. "Totally."

"I thought it was good that you wore a loincloth instead of being naked in the storm scene," Howie, finishing the last bite of his Big Dipper, said. "Both Ians, Holm and McKellen, went naked. I thought that was too much."

"Yeah," Herschel added. "Besides, if you go nude every doofus critic would probably comment on the size of your dingus. You don't want that, right?"

"Hey," my father said, grinning just a bit, "every *inch* a king." Herschel and Howie giggled.

Benji nodded. "I remember that hug. That was nice. And you know what else was good? I liked it when the daughter, I forget her name, was dead at the end and you were kneeling over her, all sad, and you pulled a white hair from your head and held it to her mouth to see if she was still breathing. That was, like, *so* perfect. It made me feel weepy."

My father stared at Benji and, after a bit, nodded thoughtfully.

When Magda brought our orders, I felt happy as I watched Benji happily spooning his matzo ball soup and devouring his Izzy's Chicago Dog. I looked over to the table, three down from ours, where Rivkah and I'd sat after our divorce was finalized. I conjured her sweet olive-complected face with those big dark eyes, framed by that glossy black hair, and imagined sitting with her again at that table, she chowing down her hot dog and then quickly following with a second, stuffing fries into her gaping mouth between bites of Chicago Dog. She'd perhaps be thinking ahead to carrot cake for dessert—one to eat immediately and another to take home.

If things had worked out differently, Rivkah and I might have been regulars at Izzy's for the last ten years. Maybe we would have gone there with our son. We'd have sat at that same table each time—a little family tradition. Maybe the kid would follow his mother's lead and get Chicago Dogs or maybe he'd even emulate me, his doting father, and get matzo ball soup and corned beef on rye and that nice potato salad. I'd tell my son about how Izzy always double-bakes his rye bread and describe the process, in detail, so as to get him to appreciate the craftsmanship. We'd share a love of chocolate phosphates with U-Bet syrup, never that lesser Bosco. Maybe Rivkah would have to gently remind him to put his napkin in his lap.

If Rivkah and I'd had a son, I'd definitely have considered naming him Leonard or Arthur. I'd have consulted her, of course, and hopefully she'd have been okay with one of those. Either is better than Julius. Or maybe she'd have insisted on a more traditional Israeli name—Mordecai, perhaps, or Dov. Dov would be fine. I like that one. It's not a pussy name, like mine; it's short and masculine and unpretentious. I'd be fine with that name for myself: Dov Dickman. It would be good. I suspect I'd have been more successful at getting women with a name like that.

If we'd disagreed on naming our son, though, I'm sure Rivkah would have prevailed.

As I watched my father eating his pastrami sandwich, I suddenly felt a wave of queasiness because of the color of the meat—too ruby, almost surreal. It seemed like something that a person should look at, maybe admire, but not actually consume. I had to look away, and took a few deep breaths, in through the nose and out through the mouth, so as to try to avoid feeling more nauseated. The last thing I wanted to do was to throw up all over Benji. But, thank God, the breathing worked.

"Dessert for anyone?" Magda, after clearing away the main course dishes, asked. "Ve of course have da cheesecake, also da pecan squares, rugelach, lokshen kugel—all goot things, *ja?*" She noticed Benji looking up at her, again with the simpleton stare. "How about you, young man?" she asked.

I tapped Benji's shoulder. "How about you and I get egg c-c-creams?" I whispered. "Would you l-like that?"

His eyes brightened and he nodded enthusiastically. "Two egg c-creams, M-Magda," I said. "With ch-chocolate."

My father leaned over toward me. "Can I have one, too?" he asked softly. "I haven't had an egg cream for years." He paused. "*Please*, son."

I had to again stifle a chuckle. "Sure, D-D-Dad," I said.

As we waited for our egg creams, I noticed a small, stout woman sitting alone at the counter, her back to me. I couldn't see her face but saw that she had dyed reddish hair and was wearing a dark hat with a narrow brim. The skin on the back of her neck appeared unusually pale. There was a closed paperback book on the counter near her, but I couldn't tell what it was. She was eating something from a bowl, and from the faint smell, slightly sweet and slightly sour, it may have been cabbage borscht. I thought that it might be Blanche, and felt thrilled to see her. I very much wanted to go over and hug the little woman and offer to pay for her borscht.

I was about to call out her name, but just then she turned her head to look out the front window and I could see that it wasn't the sad little woman from Starbucks. This one had dark, hard eyes and her upper lip was curled in an almost disdainful way.

As we were paying at the counter, I had the thought that I'd like to buy two Joyva Halvah Bars—one marble and the other chocolate-covered—and send them home with Benji to give to Naomi. "Tell your m-mom that it's a little advance b-b-birthday present," I thought of saying. "Tell her that it's a t-token of my esteem." But I didn't do it. Naomi couldn't know that I'd been at Izzy's with her son.

I felt briefly ashamed of myself, just then, for my earlier petty thoughts about my Naomi—my silly idea of telling her that I'd ordered Izzy's wonderful corned beef hash and *loved* it and was going to eat tons of it at home, too. *You're a better man than that*, I thought to myself.

Well, I don't know about that.

NINETEEN

THE NEXT DAY, Sunday, I woke up exhausted. I'd fallen asleep easily enough but then popped awake at two-thirty and commenced ruminating and couldn't get back to sleep for close to two hours. Lydia's sweet face, for some reason, immediately came into my tortured brain. I had the sudden thought, on awakening, that she was a lesbian. I wasn't sure if I'd just dreamt that I'd seen her happily walking down the street arm-in-arm with another woman and then, at a corner, the two of them exchanging a sweet and prolonged kiss, or if I actually *had* seen her recently. Either way, it was worrisome because it meant that, given her preferences, I was definitely out of the picture. I felt glad that Lydia was happy, that she had someone, hopefully a soulmate, but sad for myself. My chances of a future with sweet Lydia—always slim to begin with—now seemed out of the question.

Then I worried about Izzy. I remembered how worn and frail he'd looked, how he'd said that he was "a tired old man." He'd said something about seeing his Sadie soon. *Well, what if Izzy tips over?* I wondered. That could happen. The possibility hadn't seriously occurred to me before. I'd been so farmisht about the deaths of Cordelia and Lear and the Fool and Ophelia and other characters in the damned plays that the deaths of real people that I care about hadn't been on my mind. I'd certainly miss Izzy if he went. *If he goes*, I thought, *what will happen to the deli? Will it close? If that happens, where would I meet up with Benji?* A life without Izzy's would be a bleak one. For that matter, where would I get such wonderful high-quality matzo ball soup?

But I was immediately ashamed of myself for wondering all that. Here someone I know and care about feels poorly and might even expire sooner than I'd thought and what I mainly think about is how that might affect *me*. So maybe I'm not just a run-of-the-mill schlemiel, but a pathetically self-centered one.

And what about my father? He's another *alter kacker*, and, it seems, another frail one. What if he goes? He said he wanted to crawl unburdened toward death. But will that be a long crawl or a shorter one?

Well, I thought, *it would absolutely be good to see the old fart actually laugh again before he goes.* Since *Lear* ended, the most I've seen him do is half-assedly titter or chuckle a bit or, at most, mildly giggle now and again, maybe at *Springer* or *Judge Judy.* But no guffaws or healthy belly laughs. It's felt frustrating. Lying in bed in the middle of yet another long and dark night, yet again awake and alone, no Naomi or Celeste to reach out to, no Magda or sweet Lydia, I decided to try to elicit from my father, the great Herbert Dickman, something more than just a smile or a pathetic titter. I missed hearing him actually laugh out loud—healthy, heartfelt. I thought about trying our old standby again, Groucho and his brothers. But neither *Duck Soup* nor *Horsefeathers* had worked out. Maybe I could try *Monkey Business* or *Animal Crackers*—my dead mother's favorite—or *A Day at the Races* or *A Night at the Opera,* but most likely the result would be the same and I'd end up more frustrated.

I heard the wind howling outside and got up to look out the window and saw that it was snowing steadily, big fluffy white flakes. *Great!* I thought. *Now I'll have to shovel in the damned morning.*

The other thing on my mind was that Liz had called to ask if I'd photograph a wedding coming up that she couldn't do because she'd be going out of town that weekend to visit her daughter and grandchildren. I told her I'd think about it and get back to her soon. But after her call, I wished I'd just said no. I wished I'd have been upfront and told her that I just didn't want to do any more weddings or bar or bat mitzvahs. All they do, it seems, is agitate me more than I'm already agitated. Enough, already, with such aggravation.

I was going to get up and get dressed and assess the snow situation, but fell back asleep. I had a decent dream shortly before waking up. In it, I was living by myself in Mrs. Weinstein's apartment. It was a beautiful summer evening, warm and balmy, and I remember that I looked out the second-story living room window and noticed that the sun was almost down. I saw, down on the street, that young woman with the ponytail and the lime-green scrunchie walking by herself, clutching her Macbook Pro tightly against her chest with both arms. She had a serious, concerned expression on her pretty face and her brow was furrowed and her chin was trembling; she may have been crying, or about to. I wondered what was going on. I saw Carl in his electric wheelchair going very slowly in the opposite direction. They passed each other and looked into each other's faces but neither acknowledged the other. His face was, as usual, tortured and his tongue was hanging out of one corner of his mouth and his torso was bent over to his left. His right hand was clutching that little stick that propelled his wheelchair. Big Art was leaning against a nearby brick wall, wearing his tattered blue baseball cap and holding his squeegee pole in his left hand and a brown paper bag in his right, staring at women walking by.

And I saw white-bearded Snowball—*Eugene*—and Blanche, with her tattered-at-the-collar lacy blouse and the funny little black hat. They were walking along together and Snowball, still dressed in his railroad stripe overalls and his puffy beige parka with the faux-fur hood and the heavy brown work boots, was grinning hugely and talking and gesturing enthusiastically with one hand. He looked happy. I could even see the gaps between his white teeth. Blanche was looking up at him with a serious facial expression, watery pale-blue eyes wide, and nodding now and again but saying nothing. I wondered what he was telling her. I felt glad— *thrilled*—that the little woman wasn't alone as usual.

In the distance, I glimpsed Tunnel Terry from the back, in his usual blue jeans and flannel shirt, loping along with his wonted long strides.

But strangest of all, I saw Rabbi Twersky walking along by himself, briskly, brow deeply furrowed, his nose wart prominent, wearing one of those severe long black coats and black open-crown hats with rounded edges that the Hasidim favor. He was furiously chewing gum, maybe Juicy Fruit. He was carrying a blue cloth tote bag with a large yellow Star of David symbol and I could see a green package of Depend Guards inside the bag. As I watched him, he looked up and saw me in the window and just stared for a moment and then shook his head, as if in disgust. "*Shmuck!*" he shouted. "Enough with the ruminating and obsessing already! It's very irritating. What would Abraham, Isaac and Jacob think of such self-indulgence?" Remembering my dream when I awoke, it occurred to me that the coat and hat were unusual because Twersky isn't a Hasid. Still, overall it was one of my better dreams because it didn't leave me feeling *too* verklempt.

Abraham, Isaac and Jacob—the muckety-mucks of our faith. We're *constantly* singing out their names at shul. That damned Abraham was willing to sacrifice Isaac, his beloved son, when God said he had to. But then God, for whatever reason, backed off from that demand and Abe sacrificed a ram instead. If there's really a God, and I ever see Him, I'm going to give Him a piece of my mind about insisting on all those damned animal sacrifices.

It was still snowing by the time I stumbled out of bed, a bit groggy from my dream. Dad must have been exhausted from our deli excursion because he was still asleep at nine-thirty. Before going out to shovel the walk and driveway, I made a cup of coffee and, while shlurping, studied the photographs of my father in the living room and hallway, the pictures of him in his big roles. I thought about what Dad had said at Izzy's, again, about having failed. He said he'd waited too long to play Lear, that you can't do it when you're too young to understand coming death, but you also can't wait to do it when you're too damned old and don't have the energy and stamina. He maybe could have added that a guy shouldn't wait until his brain starts turning to dust and blows out through his earholes. *What a freaking dilemma!* I thought. *How can a guy know when's the right time?* I wondered if Scofield or any of those other guys, Jacobi and Holm and McKellen and Gielgud, had had similar dilemmas. If so, did it make them looney-tunes too?

I thought, too, about Howie. It'd been nice to see him again yesterday. I again had the thought that he'd been a wonderful Edgar, especially as Poor Tom, although I had the same fleeting but petty thought I'd had before: I doubt I can ever be as good a son to my father that Edgar was to his. But I also remembered having noticed that Howie looked a bit softer, maybe a bit more fleshy, than at our last Izzy's outing. His chin definitely appeared weaker. Maybe he'd stopped going to the gym, now that *Lear* was over and he didn't have to be practically naked onstage as Poor Tom. I had the idea that if I'd been blessed to play Edgar—an impossible fantasy, but a pleasant one—I would have buffed up like Howie did, and thought about the gym routines I'd have done: curls, reverse curls, bench presses, lat pulls, squats, leg lifts, pull-ups, sit-ups, others. But, unlike Howie, I'd have kept up with all that after the play'd ended so as to enhance any chances of impressing women.

Maybe I'd even go to the beach now and again when summer came. Maybe Celeste would be there on the sand with Donny. They'd be lying together on an oversized blue blanket, she wearing a skimpy pink bikini, and there'd be a cooler at one edge of the blanket with beers for him and a bottle of Chablis for her. There'd be a round Tupperware container with her favorite Trader Joe's trail mix. Maybe she'd have to keep that container in the cooler to keep the chocolate cubes from melting. He'd be napping. After a bit she'd notice me and maybe smile a warm little greeting. I'd maintain eye contact with her and stand up very straight and puff out my chest and square my shoulders and flex my muscles. She'd notice my sinewy shoulders, my bulging biceps and triceps, my rock-hard pecs, my six-pack abs, my firm glutes, my well-defined quads, my gnarly calves. Her face would flush. Maybe she'd sigh and glance down at sleeping Donny, his mouth open and a bit of spittle gathered in one corner, and then back at me. "*Damn!*" she'd mutter softly, looking up at me with big eyes. "I guess I missed my chance with *you*, dear sculpted Julius."

Maybe I'd kneel down next to Celeste. "Uh," I'd maybe say, "I n-n-noticed that you have a b-brown spot on your l-lower back, my d-dear. M-M-Maybe it's something, uh, b-bad. D-Do you think so?" She'd look at my face, eyes warm and moist and a sweet smile on her pretty face, feeling cherished and protected.

If Donny looked at me askance, I'd ignore him, pretend he didn't exist.

Then I had the brief fantasy of my walking away from Celeste and Donny, strong and manly, a contented smile on my face, and seeing, some distance away on the beach, Naomi and Perry Schwartz sitting together on green cloth beach chairs, drinking wine coolers. Their backs were to me, but I could see their facial profiles as they stared at each other adoringly. She was looking up at him seductively and then she leaned toward him and coyly raised her face and sweetly rubbed the tip of her big hooked Yid nose against the tip of his also-hooked shnoz. *Great!* I thought. *I knew it would come to this.*

The snow was deep, but not quite deep enough to prevent my pushing open the front door to go outside. So, at least, I wasn't trapped.

After I'd finished shoveling, I felt exhausted and my body ached. It'd been a heavy, wet snowfall. It was still snowing, though less, when I came in, but at least I'd gotten most of it off the sidewalk and driveway and it would be easier to deal with the rest later. Then I had an idea. I opened the freezer and took out two bagels to thaw, an onion and a sesame, and set out the butter and cream cheese and made fresh coffee.

When my father came out to the living room just after ten-thirty—again in that damned green robe, long white hair askew, shoulders a bit slumped, eyes murky—I directed him to plop down in his La-Z-Boy and brought him his coffee and sesame bagel, which I'd defrosted in the micro and then buttered and slathered with cream cheese. I didn't want to chance his again not schmearing the cream cheese and I didn't want to hear him, confused, kvetching about what kind of bagel was *really* his favorite. There was no lox, but he didn't seem to notice. "Let's watch something d-different today, D-D-Dad," I said, and slid a DVD into the machine.

It was the season seven disc of *The Mary Tyler Moore Show* boxed set and I selected episode six, "Chuckles Bites the Dust," in which WJM kiddie show host Chuckles the Clown, dressed in his Peter Peanut costume while leading a circus parade, gets stomped on and killed by a rogue elephant. In the TV newsroom, Lou Grant, sad and shocked, says that the elephant tried to "shell" Chuckles. Lou and Murray Slaughter joke about the absurdity of his death and Lou says that it's fortunate the elephant didn't go after more people. Murray nods in agreement. "You know how hard it is to stop after just *one* peanut," he jests and he and Lou laugh heartily. They crack wise further and Sue Ann Nivens, the station's perpetually horny "happy homemaker," joins in. Mary thinks it's terrible that they're making light of Chuckles's tragic demise and scolds them for their lack of respect for their deceased colleague. Lou tells her that their laughter is just an emotional release, that everyone does it to try to ease the pain of a tragedy. "*I* don't," Mary insists.

Then there's the memorial service and the minister, Reverend Burns, delivers a eulogy, warmly recalling Chuckles and the wonderful characters he created in addition to Peter Peanut: Mr. Fee-Fi-Fo, Billy Banana, and, the minister's favorite, Aunt Yoo Hoo. Mary, despite herself, giggles at the mention of each. Her work colleagues and others turn to stare at her and she's embarrassed. Reverend Burns recalls Mr. Fee-Fi-Fo's catchphrase when he was knocked down by his "arch rival," Señor Kaboom: "I fell down and hurt my foo-foo." Mary chortles noticeably, and more people turn to glare at her. "Life's a lot like that," the minister goes on. "From time to time, we *all* fall down and hurt our foo-foos." Mary can't contain her increasingly loud laughter, and the audience is shocked. But the minister asks her to stand up, which she, mortified, does, and he tells her that Chuckles would have appreciated her laughter. "He *lived* to make people laugh. Tears were offensive to him, *deeply* offensive. He hated to see people cry. So go ahead, my dear, laugh for Chuckles." And Mary bursts into uncontrollable sobs of grief.

My idea was that no feeling, warm-blooded human being could watch that episode and *not* laugh out loud.

But I was wrong. I laughed heartily on cue. My father, on the other hand, watched the episode and smiled weakly here and there, always with closed lips, and nodded twice—once when Lou said, "We laugh at death because we know that death will have the last laugh," and again when the minister said what he did about how we all hurt our foo-foos. But that was it.

The hell with this difficult old man, I thought. *I'm done.* I recalled one of Herschel's favorite epithets: "Hey, fuck you and the horse you rode in on." I never knew what that meant—what horse?—but it sounded good. I thought of snarling it at my father, but controlled myself. Instead, I just left him sitting in his damned chair and, without a word one way or the other, stomped to my room to take a nap. I didn't even clean up the cups and dishes.

But I couldn't sleep. I was still agitated. I closed my eyes and tried to think of something pleasant. What came into my mind was yesterday at Izzy's when Magda'd brought Benji and Dad and me our egg creams. Mine was sublime, creamy and rich, with the U-Bet syrup. It was the best thing I'd tasted in a while. Benji loved his, too. He'd even closed his eyes, briefly, while sipping. "Oh, my God, Julius," he said at one point. "This is, like, *so* good." My father drank his dutifully but said nothing. When I asked him if he liked it, he just shrugged. "Not bad," he said. "Okay, I guess."

After a while, I went back to the living room to watch a little television and, hopefully, calm down. Dad was sound asleep in his La-Z-Boy, head tilted to his right and mouth slightly opened. He was snoring lightly. I covered him with his white afghan and turned on the TV, with the volume low. There was a Sunday marathon of *Naked and Afraid* on Discovery Channel. I got to see the last part of an episode featuring a duo, Samantha and Adam, who'd been schlepped to some barren African desert where it gets to 110 degrees during the day and where there are huge scorpions and jackals who make scary high-pitched sounds at night, as well as a tribe of large predatory baboons with prominent red bottoms who scream constantly and wag their bushy eyebrows and display their big canine teeth in a menacing way. Samantha had a better-than-average ass and a narrow waist, but, as always, it was frustrating that the production people blurred her breasts and genital area.

The next episode was more interesting. It featured Jason and AK. He was just okay—tall and skinny and blond and bearded, with tattoos featuring some obscure Chinese characters on both upper arms and shoulders. But AK was stunningly beautiful, with dark, thick hair and incredible huge dark-brown eyes. Her face reminded me of Rivkah's.

They're in a dense jungle area in Guyana, near the ocean, and there's tension between them. They've built a shelter near a river but she thinks that they need to construct a "secondary shelter" on higher ground, just in case, and gets to building one. He strongly disagrees that they need another shelter, and criticizes her because he thinks that she's wasting time on it and also because she eats too much of the meager food that he's been able to provide. He complains that she's not carrying her load—at least not in a way that *he* approves of. Then he's successful at spearing a sting ray in the ocean, which they cook and eat some of and plan to save the rest to eat later.

They both feel more relaxed after they've eaten and start getting along better. That was nice. But soon a huge scary storm blows in to the neighborhood—sheets of rain and roaring wind and scary lightning and nonstop peals of loud crackling thunder—and the pair huddles together, shivering, and watch in horror as the river rises rapidly and tree branches crash to the ground around them. They soon have to abandon their original shelter and, soaking wet in the pouring rain and slipping and sliding in the mud, frantically make their way uphill to the secondary shelter. They have to leave behind the remainder of the cooked sting ray. But they're finally relatively safe in AK's sturdy little shelter, which has survived the fierce storm, and Jason has to eat his nasty words of rebuke to her.

I was quite absorbed in Jason's and AK's little drama and didn't notice that my father was awake until I heard him exhale loudly. "Oh, my," he murmured. I looked over and saw that he was sitting up very straight, eyes opened wide, hands clasped tightly in his lap, and staring transfixed at the screen. Jason and AK were huddled together in her secondary shelter on the higher ground, still shivering while the rain poured down around them and the wind whipped foliage and branches all around. They were, understandably, frightened—quite naked and afraid. Who wouldn't be? They were helpless to do any more for themselves and were totally at the mercy of the harsh elements. They looked very small and insignificant there in the big jungle, with the storm raging around them—indifferent to their peril—and the trees bending to their breaking points from the fierce wind and the river below still rising. Dad seemed fascinated. I didn't remember the last time I'd seen him more alert and interested in anything. He slowly shook his head and leaned forward and stared even more intently at the screen. "Poor *wretches!*" he muttered.

"What, Dad?" I asked.

He glanced at me and then back at the television. "Poor wretches," he repeated, more loudly, now sitting up very erect and alert. "Poor naked wretches, wheresoe'er you are, that bide the pelting of this pitiless storm, how shall your houseless heads and unfed sides, your looped and windowed raggedness, defend you from seasons such as *this?*" He covered his face with his hands and rubbed vigorously and then turned to glare at me and stared, eyes now a sharp and hard gray, for maybe twenty seconds. Then he slowly shook his head and looked down at the floor and then once more at the screen. "Is man no more than *this?*" he asked, now barely audibly, pointing at Jason and then at AK "Thou art the *thing* itself. Unaccommodated man is no more but such a poor, bare, forked animal as thou art."

He suddenly sprang up from his La-Z-Boy. "Oh, I have taken too *little* care of this!" he practically shouted. Then he ripped off the ratty green robe and furiously wadded it and unceremoniously tossed it to the floor, startling me. He had on a pair of old, worn blue pajamas. "Off, *off* you lendings," he intoned. Then he glared at me, eyes snapping. "COME!" he yelled, in a commanding tone of voice. "*Unbutton* here." I felt frightened. When I didn't move or say anything, he shook his head in apparent disgust and ripped open the pajama top, popping off at least three buttons. One flew and struck the TV screen. He tore the top off and wadded it and tossed it on top of the discarded robe. I'd never seen my father so exercised, in real life as opposed to in a play. Then he ripped off the pajama bottoms and threw them against the far wall. There was my seventy-two-year-old father, the famous classical actor, naked as a jaybird—whatever that is—wild-eyed, his pasty-white and wrinkled skin hanging loosely around his neck and arms and torso except for around his slightly bulging belly, his pale legs spindly, his long white hair and white beard scraggly and disheveled, his feet a horror story with those toenails, and his pathetic circumcised and somewhat shriveled schwantz … right there, sort of, and my immediate thought was: *I guess it was good, like Howie said, that the old man didn't go nude in the storm on the heath scene.*

All that was disturbing enough. But then he marched to the front door and opened it wide and, barefoot and unaccommodated, stepped out onto the snowy stoop and looked to the gray sky and raised both arms high and straight. "You SEE me here, you *gods*," he shouted at the top of his lungs, "a POOR old man, as full of grief as age, wretched in *both!*" He paused and turned his head to glare at me, his face tight with raw emotion. Flakes of snow were gathered on his head and shoulders. I wasn't sure whether he even recognized me. "Oh, Tom," he murmured after a few moments, now more calm, "my wits begin to turn. Art cold? I am cold myself."

I gently took his hand and pulled him into the house and closed the front door behind him. He was shivering noticeably. I got a big dark-green towel from the linen closet and patted him dry and retrieved his robe and helped him into it. "Thank you, son," he said softly. "Oh, I should have become wise before I became old. Don't you agree?" I just shrugged but said nothing and led him to his chair and sat him down. I covered him with his white afghan and tucked it in around him. As I started to walk toward the kitchen, he asked me to come back for a moment. When I did, he looked up at me, his face now softer and eyes murky and back to that watery and pale bluish-gray. "Julius," he whispered, "let me not be mad. *Please!* Keep me in temper, sweet heaven. Not *mad*, son."

TWENTY

SITTING ALONE in the living room of my father's house after I'd watched the local evening news, I felt angry because of the stupid hospital rules. I could have gone to Izzy's and bought some of their wonderful matzo ball soup in a takeout container to bring to Dad, but thought it would be more special, more personal, if I actually made him soup and brought it to him in the hospital. So earlier today I'd gone to the tiny kosher section of the grocery store and bought three boxes of Manischewitz Matzo Ball and Soup Mix and made a batch of soup from one. It was easy enough. You combine two eggs with two tablespoons of vegetable oil in a small bowl and mix that up with a fork and then add the contents of Package #1, the dry matzo ball mix, and stir the whole thing together with the fork and stick the bowl in the refrigerator to chill for at least fifteen minutes, and then pour ten cups of cold water in a big pot and add the contents of Package #2, the dry chicken soup mix, and bring that to a boil, and then wet your hands and form the batter into one-inch balls and drop them into the boiling broth, and then turn the heat down to let the whole deal simmer for twenty minutes. That's it.

I wasn't sure if I'd made the matzo balls too big or too little, but my efforts produced nine full-sized balls and one mini-sized one and they all looked okay, firm and round. I remember thinking that it was too bad I was using vegetable oil instead of schmaltz. I hoped Izzy wouldn't think less of me if he found out. Or my sweet Magda.

Unlike Izzy's great soup, my matzo balls were sinkers, not floaters—a minor disappointment on the great scale of things.

But when I brought the soup to the psych ward later this morning, in a dark-blue thermos container, the head nurse, Suzette, said they had a rule that visitors weren't allowed to bring in food for patients. I asked her why not. Our eyes locked as she told me, in a soft and melodic voice with just the hint of a lisp, that there was nothing she could do, that not allowing visitors to bring food to patients was a long-standing rule in that ward, that they had to be careful about such things, and she was sorry to have to bear such news. I was briefly upset and momentarily considered mentioning the incident to my father when I saw him, but thought better of it. In his nuttiness, he'd perhaps blow it out of proportion or maybe even suspect a conspiracy.

Even though I didn't like what Suzette had told me about the food rule, I was quite smitten with her. She was short and a bit zaftig and had a perfectly round face with lovely smooth pale skin dotted with dozens of brownish freckles, amazing huge green eyes with golden speckles, and a magnificent head of reddish-brown curls. She could have told me that they had a strict rule against allowing Jews to visit patients and I wouldn't have objected. I thought of offering her the matzo ball soup as a gift. "Maybe you could take it home for your family," I might say, sans stutter, hoping that she'd then reply that she lived alone—no husband or boyfriend—but wouldn't mind having a considerate and caring man in her life to share some delicious hot soup with on a cold, dark winter evening instead of having to always, *always* eat alone.

But I just asked her how my father was doing. She nodded and told me that they were giving him meds to calm him and he seemed better than when he'd been admitted yesterday. They were, she told me, doing some tests. She said he was asleep now and it would be best not to wake him. She said he'd be in a single room "in our quiet area" for the first day or maybe longer.

I was glad to hear Suzette say that Dad had calmed down. He'd certainly been a mess when Herschel and I'd brought him to the hospital yesterday afternoon. After the *Naked and Afraid* fiasco, after he'd relaxed in his chair for a bit I'd led him to his bedroom and had him put on a pair of flannel pajamas and helped him lie down and covered him with an extra blanket because he was still shivering and went to the kitchen to make him a mug of Swiss Miss hot chocolate with mini-marshmallows. I felt numb. Dad drank the cocoa too fast and had a coughing fit and spat out three of the little marshmallows. I told him to try to sleep for a while. He nodded and closed his eyes.

I went back to the living room to think, but within a few minutes heard my father call out. "Julius!" he squealed. "Oh, *Tom*, wherefore art thou?" He was sitting up straight in bed, arms crossed in front of his thin chest. He seemed to be staring at the photograph of Miriam on his dresser. "Blow, winds," he commenced to croaking, still staring at the photo, raising both arms high above his head, "and crack your cheeks. *Rage!* Blow, you cataracts and hurricanos, spout till you have drenched our steeples, drowned the cocks! *Rumble* thy bellyful!" He paused and stared at me, gray eyes wild. I again wasn't sure he recognized me. "Here I stand, your slave," he went on, more softly and deliberately, now again staring at Miriam, "a poor, infirm, weak, and despised old man."

Thank God, he slept then. I was glad. I plopped down in his La-Z-Boy and covered myself with his purple *Lear* robe and tried to think about what to do. I was unsure. I felt quite verklempt. After a while, I felt that I had to get up and do something active and give my overheated brain a hiatus and went outside to shovel the rest of the now-concluded snowfall. I wasn't sure if I should have left Dad alone, but it felt good to be doing something physical. When I was done, I went in the front door and there was my father, awake, again totally nude, standing in the hallway and holding his empty cocoa mug in his right hand, a bit bent over, and staring at me with what seemed a bewildered look. "How dost, my boy?" he asked yet again. "Art cold?" He crossed his arms on front of his white, bony chest and shivered hugely from head to toe. "I'm *cold* myself, Julius."

I got him dressed and back into his bed and covered him with his comforter and again threw an extra blanket on top of that and then called Herschel. He came over right away and listened to my story and talked a bit with Dad. "Uncle Herb," he said, softly, "how're you doing today?"

"My Fool!" my father said, grinning hugely at his nephew. "How dost, boy?" He paused and again started at the photo of Miriam and then back at me. "How am I doing?" he said, barely audibly. "Truly, boy, if I were doing any better, they'd have to give me the keys to the kingdom."

Herschel said he wasn't sure what we should do. "Maybe let him rest for a while and see if he comes out of it."

But a bit later, Dad woke up and noticed us and beckoned me over. "May I please ask you a question?" he said, again very softly. I nodded. Dad glanced suspiciously to one side of the room and then the other. "Knowest thou the way to Dover?" he whispered. I recognized that as one of blind Gloucester's lines to his son, Edgar, in disguise as Poor Tom.

"Yeah," I answered. "I guess so."

Dad nodded and moved his face closer to mine and touched my right hand and went on, in a soft voice that I had to strain to hear. "There is a cliff whose high and bending head looks fearfully in the confinéd deep. Bring me but to the very brim of it and I'll repair the misery thou dost bear with something rich about me." He moved his face closer yet to mine. "From that place," he whispered, "I … shall …. *no* … leading … need."

Herschel looked concerned and gestured for me to follow him into the kitchen. "Listen, cuz," he said, looking concerned. "We better call a doctor right away. Your old man's talking about jumping off a freakin' cliff. I think he needs to be somewhere." I phoned Dr. Ansfield and got his answering service, being a Sunday, but he called back within twenty minutes. I talked to him briefly, but then asked Herschel to take over so as to not subject Ansfield to my pathetic stutter on his day off. The doctor said he'd call the hospital and request authorization for Dad to be admitted.

I didn't think Dad would go willingly. But then I had an idea. I gestured Herschel over and whispered in his ear. He scrunched his dwarfy face and gave me a look, but then shrugged his shoulders and nodded. "Uncle Herb," he said, "some people we know very much want to hear you do Hamlet's well-known soliloquy. We can bring you to them. Would that be okay?"

I wondered, then, if my ruse idea was problematic—maybe it wasn't that wise to ask a guy who's just made a reference to suicide to impress people by reciting a passage about whether or not to kill yourself. But it worked. While we were sitting in a room waiting to be admitted, my father looking confused, Herschel asked one of the staff members to tell his uncle that he wanted to hear Hamlet's famous soliloquy and Dad smiled and stood up and bowed and perfectly recited that one—"To be or not to be, that is the question … " and so on. When he got to the part where Hamlet wonders why a guy should struggle so hard against all the harsh and difficult things in life " … when he himself might his quietus make with a bare bodkin"— meaning a dagger—I winced a bit. Then the old man bowed again and Herschel and I and the staff guy and one of the admitting nurses applauded and Herschel loudly shouted out an enthusiastic "Bravo!" and Dad laced his fingers and raised his joined hands to his sternum and furrowed his brow and tilted his head to his right and smiled humbly and bowed and mouthed, "Thank you! Oh, thank you *so* much!" and blew three kisses, and after that my father was happy and satisfied and meek and went along happily with whatever the hospital staff wanted.

Today, even though Dad was still asleep, I decided to sit with him for a while. I felt sad that he couldn't have the soup I'd prepared. Lying in his psych ward hospital bed, my father looked small and fragile, older than his years. I thought about him in his role as Macbeth three years ago. That seemed, now, like a long time ago. He'd been in his late sixties then, but was still fit and hearty and quite masculine in that role, particularly at the start of the play when Macbeth and Banquo have helped Duncan, the Scottish king, win some silly battle and then they encounter the three dissembling witches, who tell Macbeth that he's now Thane of Cawdor, in addition to his already being Thane of Glamis, which is good but unknown and unexpected news to him, and prophesy that he'll be King of Scotland down the road, which sets off the whole bloody mess that follows—all those hairy Scots in kilts strutting and fretting.

That damned *Macbeth*. I recalled three years ago when Dad did that role and he got angry with me—and not just normal anger, but out-of-left-field and totally off-the-wall anger. It was just after the dress rehearsal had ended and Dad, still in costume, was calmly talking with pretty smoky-eyed Elspeth, Lady Macbeth, also in costume. He noticed me hanging around with my camera and asked me to take a posed photo of the two of them. I did, and then casually said, "You know, Elspeth, I think that *M-M-Macbeth* is my f-favorite p-play." Dad's face hardened and immediately turned bright red and his jaw muscles commenced to working. "HEY!" he yelled loudly. "What the hell's the *matter* with you, Julius? You *can't* say that name in the theater, unless it's *during* a rehearsal or performance. You have to say 'the Scottish play.' You want us to have bad luck? Jesus Christ, Julius! You should *know* better!" Then he stalked away but returned in a minute or so, still red-faced, and shoved a three-by-five index card into my chest. "Now say this line right *now*, so we don't have bad luck, and then spin around and brush yourself off. It's a goddamn *cleansing* ritual." I wanted to sink through the floor in embarrassment, but looked at the card and read the line he'd written down—"Angels and ministers of grace defend us!"—and then spun around and brushed myself off.

I don't hold a ton of grudges against my old man, but that's definitely one. I couldn't look Elspeth in the face after that.

I thought of asking Suzette if she and her people could try to persuade Dad to let them cut his hair and maybe trim his beard or, better yet, shave it off while he was their guest. I wasn't sure if he'd allow that, but hoped he would. Maybe he'd be as enchanted with Suzette as I'd been and would happily agree to anything she suggested. I would if I were him. But I didn't ask.

Watching Dad sleep, I remembered him so intently watching *Naked and Afraid* and getting so bent out of shape, referring, in his nutty state, to AK and Jason as "poor naked wretches" and "unaccommodated man." I don't know if they were wretches, but AK and Jason were certainly naked—mostly, anyway. That nakedness was fine with me, at least in her case; her ass was sublime. But it had sure set off my old man. He, too, had seemed, at least for a time, a poor naked wretch when he tore off his green robe and blue pajamas and stood outside the doorway screaming crazily. *Well,* I thought, *if even an accomplished old fart like Herbert Dickman can diminish into wretchedness, maybe no one's immune.* Hell, maybe even a woman as bright and successful and beautiful and wealthy and seemingly solid as sweet Bethenny could now and again decline into extremis, despite all that gorgeous clothing and makeup and hair.

Bethenny. I visualized her sweet face. But what do I know about someone like her? I have no idea if she's ever felt wretched, but I definitely wouldn't mind seeing her naked. I'm sure it would be a less horrifying sight than seeing my naked old man yesterday, particularly with that pathetic shriveled schwantz. Then I recalled that I *did* get to very briefly see Bethenny naked last year when she drunkenly jumped into a swimming pool on a rerun episode of *The Real Housewives of New York City* that I'd watched with Naomi. It probably happened during one of their housewifely excursions to the Hamptons or Berkshires. But it wasn't as satisfying an experience as it could have been because, of course, they blurred her good parts, except for her excellent little bottom, just like they do on *Naked and Afraid.* Are all these TV people afraid that seeing female parts will drive men mad? Well, if so, maybe they're not wrong.

Seeing what I did of sweet Bethenny almost made me crazy—partly with lust, but also with yet again contemplating the wide and deep chasm between that little woman and me.

Well, maybe that chasm isn't *really* all that wide or deep. Who knows? I guess it's at least possible that little Bethenny lies awake at night like I do, worrying and ruminating and dwelling on her failures and regrets and worries—whatever those might be. Maybe she's really, deep down, a quivering mass of neuroses. It doesn't seem likely, from seeing her on TV, so capable and self-confident and seemingly in control of her busy and multi-faceted world, with the Skinnygirl and the Bravo and her charity work and whatnot, but who knows? Snowball—Eugene—wears a big parka and heavy work shoes in sweltering heat, and I'm sure he's not rolling in paycheck stubs, but maybe—who knows?—he sleeps better at night and is happier overall than Bethenny or Dorinda or Ramona or any of those well-off, well-coifed, well-dressed, accomplished and famous housewives, with all their strutting. Maybe that bizarre isolato Tunnel Terry, warm and cozy, though always alone, in one of the huge university heating tunnels on a freezing winter night, sleeps contentedly and innocently too, untroubled by worries or bad dreams. What do I know?

Well, if Bethenny ever calls or texts and wants to get together for a stress-reducing carnal episode, she and I could, after doing the deed, maybe have a few vodka gimlets or banana daiquiris and, still naked, share our worries and concerns and fears and anxieties. Maybe she'd tell me that she routinely pops awake in the middle of the night and worries and obsesses about her love life and business doings. I'd practice Naomi's active listening skills: "Um-hmm" and "Help me to understand … " and the eye contact and the furrowed brow and the nodding and the like. Maybe Bethenny'd be more sympathetic than Naomi was as to my anxiety at the Culver's drive-thru. "Oh," she might say, "I can *totally* understand how you feel about being trapped, with no control. I've been there. It's *terrible!*" I'd like that. It would be a different kind of intimacy than the erotic loveliness we'd just shared, but it could be good. Maybe I'd find out that, even with all her attributes and successes, she's actually *more* screwed-up than I am, that her life is as messy—or more, even—than mine. I'd probably be surprised if that were the case, but maybe not *too* surprised. There'd be a certain satisfaction in learning that—twisted satisfaction, to be sure, but still.

Watching my sleeping old man, I wondered if I should let Naomi know about him. She certainly isn't one of his fans, but maybe she'd be concerned, if not for my father then perhaps for me, for old time's sake. Still, I wasn't sure how she'd take it if I contacted her. Maybe she'd like it that I reached out and would ask me how I was doing with all of it and would be concerned and even comforting. Maybe, being a social worker, she'd have thoughts or suggestions. Or maybe she'd say that she could care less about my father and would again rake me over the coals for sleeping with Celeste. Maybe she'd even start in again with the tedious tears and the "How *could* you?"

I again remembered that Naomi's birthday is coming up soon, in mid-March. I'd like to at least send her a birthday card, if not also a present, but I'm not sure how she'd take that gesture either. I harkened back to my vision of seeing Naomi with Perry Schwartz at the beach, rubbing noses, and a thought occurred to me: *How in hell can I go on working for Perry if he's now, as I suspect, with my ex-girlfriend, for whom I still have feelings?* I like Perry and I've definitely liked doing painting for him, but a guy has to have limits if he's going to have any self-respect.

Celeste. I hoped that she was doing fine with Pretty Boy and was happy enough. My idea of buffing up and impressing her was, I realized, a silly one, a fruitless one, and I dismissed it. I don't have the discipline to go a gym often enough to see real results. I'm too lazy. That boat has sailed. Sitting there in that quiet hospital psych ward room, watching my father breathing in and out evenly, his mouth a bit open, I decided to stop torturing myself by thinking any more about Celeste. Enough, already. Where does it get a guy? Thinking about Cordelia would be okay, though. She's wonderful, though not a real woman and, thus, can't touch me.

But then, sitting there next to my sleeping father, I had a random thought. Maybe sweet little Cordelia *wasn't* as wonderful as I'd been thinking she was. She was definitely still some woman, almost too good to be true, but it occurred to me that maybe she was really almost as petulant and rigid as her father early on, in Act I, though in a different way, when she'd refused to flatter Lear the way Goneril and Regan had. "Love and be silent," she'd said in an aside. On the one hand, that's fine, even admirable. On the other hand, would it have been *so* terrible for Cordelia to have just played along with her father's childish request, to humor him a bit, like her older sisters did? What would the harm have been for her to indulge the eighty-year-old geezer a little? Instead, she stubbornly stuck to her integrity guns and refused to say anything falsely flattering, and he flew into a rage, and that was the start of all the drama, all that strutting and fretting, that led to such sad outcomes. Maybe there's a case that darling little Cordelia should have known how her father'd react to her silence and could have just harmlessly placated him and lived to fight other, more meaningful, battles. Sure, she was kind and caring and loving later, when her old man went bonkers and she rescued him and took care of him and they'd reconciled and she said "No cause, no cause," and was again loving and caring when they were taken prisoners and he talked about their going to the hoosegow together and singing like two caged birds and telling stories about who's in and who's out, like God's spies, but she still might have been too rigid earlier. Maybe honesty and integrity aren't all they're cracked up to be—sometimes, anyway.

I wondered, too, whether or not I should tell Benji about Dad. On the one hand, I thought that it would be nice to include him in what was going on, particularly since he knew my father and seemed to like him and had asked Dad whether there was anything he did as Lear that he was proud of and had said what he did about how he liked it that Dad had pulled a white hair from his head to see if Cordelia was still breathing after she'd been hanged. I liked it that he'd offered that observation, and certainly admired him—a twelve-year-old smooth-faced kid—for being astute enough to notice something that subtle. But *I* hadn't noticed that gesture, and I'd seen the damned play, including rehearsals, several damned times. Nor had I noticed or been moved by Dad's hugging Gloucester in the Dover scene. But Benji'd noticed and liked *that*, too.

On the other hand, I thought that maybe it wouldn't be fair to involve Benji in my father's craziness. The poor kid's got enough going on, what with his mother and sister and their horrible obscenity-laced screaming matches, and having to visit his father on alternate weekends, and getting ready for his bar mitzvah and whatever else may be going on with him that I don't know about. I feel like I want to protect him, as much as I can, from my adult mishegas. He's got enough travails of his own now, and, no doubt, more ahead after he's been bar-mitzvahed and becomes a man in our faith. *Hah!*

My father appeared to be sleeping soundly, so I decided to go home for the day. As I was walking down the corridor to the elevator that led to the parking ramp, Lydia again came into my mind. I had the out-of-the-blue hope that she was more inclined to being bisexual than to being a dyed-in-the-wool lesbian. If so, I'd at least have a chance with her—not much of one, to be sure, but still a chance. It was a comforting thought because it meant that all hope wasn't lost.

I thought of taking the elevator, but couldn't do it. I walked the four flights of stairs down to the parking ramp. So far, I'd done the stairs each time I visited. I felt a bit ashamed that I was such a meshugenah wuss about such matters, but then told myself that it'd been a rough couple of days, all things considered, and it was okay to be a wimp over such a minor matter. Maybe that was letting myself off the hook too easily.

I turned off the TV after the local news—right after the weather, in fact, like poor Mrs. Weinstein—and, after stewing about the matzo ball soup issue for a while, had the thought that I should do something to honor my poor brain-sick father, alone tonight in a strange bed in a hospital psychiatric ward. After a bit I went into the kitchen and opened one of the lower cabinets and found an unopened large bag of Cheetos. I sat in Dad's La-Z-Boy and covered myself with his purple robe and waved the gold scepter around and ripped open the bag and scarfed down every morsel and then tossed the empty bag unceremoniously to the floor. I thought of eating an entire jar of Planter's Lightly Salted Dry Roasted Peanuts and not caring if some nuts found their way to the floor, but dismissed the idea. A guy has to have *some* self-control. It was maybe disgusting to eat all that Cheetos junk, but it tasted good. Before going to bed, I carefully washed all the orange residue from my face and hands and gargled with Listerine to try to cleanse the orange powder from my lips and tongue

TWENTY-ONE

I DON'T KNOW if I'm happy or unhappy that Dad's out of his single room in the "quiet area" of the psych ward and now has a roommate. His name is Ralph but he wants everyone to call him *the Admiral*. He's an older guy, as short as me and with bright blue eyes and close-cropped silver hair and, usually, a gleeful and boyish facial expression. He talks constantly and rapidly and seems to have endless energy. He says he had a career in the navy as a chief warrant officer and had hopes and plans to achieve higher rank, and still does, but I don't know if all that's true or just a psych patient's delusion. He also told Dad that he's some kind of a secret CIA operative but that he can't talk about that, can't give out details, because he swore a sacred oath not to. My father seemed impressed with that one.

When he's not spouting such, the Admiral loudly sings snatches of seagoing songs, always extending his right arm and waving his right index finger as a sort of conductor's baton. The first ditty I heard from him was one that starts with a question: "What will we do with a drunken sailor?" It went on and on and included verses with creative options for what to do with such a sailor: "shave his belly with a rusty razor," "stick him in a longboat until he's sober," and, my favorite, "put him in bed with the captain's daughter." In between such poignant verses, The Admiral raised both arms high, fingers stiff and straight and outspread, and belted out the chorus at the top of his lungs:

> *Way hay and up she rises*
> *Way hay and up she rises*
> *Way hay and up she rises*
> *Early in the morning*

When I came to visit Dad yesterday morning, the Admiral grinned hugely and waved at me as I entered the room and loudly said, "Hey, *there* he is! What's *your* name, matey?" I introduced myself and he giggled. "Julius!" he intoned. "It's a *great* name. It's a *wonderful* name! I knew a petty officer named Julius when the fleet was in the Philippines. Great guy! Marvelous fella! And he wasn't petty either, I can tell you that. Not petty at all. He spoke highly of everyone, including the idiot captain. *Very* generous guy. If he got cookies from home, he always shared them. Macaroons, they were. Wonderful macaroons!" Then he turned to Dad. "Herbie," he said, "you didn't tell me you had a son. That's wonderful, Herb. That's absolutely lovely. I'm sure you're proud of good old Julius. You *must* be, Herbie. Am I right?"

My father nodded. He looked better than he had the day before. His eyes were more clear and alert. He even smiled. "Yup," he said, "I definitely am. He's a good kid."

"You know, fellas," the Admiral went on, "I once had a girlfriend named Julie. She was nice to look at and good in bed, as you might say, but she had a bad temper. She threw away my golf clubs because she said I spent too much time on the links. That was balderdash, though, because I hardly ever golfed. She was exaggerating, Herbie. She was *stretching* it, is what. Oh, very much so. She always went barefoot, and then complained that her feet hurt. 'Julie,' I finally said, 'you're a great little broad, but you're making me crazy. Adios, Julie. I wish you the very best of luck in all your endeavors.' That was before I started working for the government."

I liked the Admiral. *He may be nuts*, I thought, *he may be manic, but at least, damn it, he's fun.*

After a bit I excused myself to use the bathroom, but I didn't really need to go. I just wanted to see if Suzette was on-duty, and—if so—talk with her, maybe, but definitely look at her. I'd been up for at least two hours in the middle of the night, thinking about Suzette much of that time and conjuring that round freckled face with the big green eyes and that lovely head of reddish-brown curls. That slight lisp. But, sadly, she wasn't working.

When I returned, the wall-mounted TV was on and Dad and the Admiral were, surprisingly, watching an episode of *The Real Housewives of New York City*. "They show reruns all day today, Julius," the Admiral explained, speaking loudly and talking fast—so rapidly, almost forced, that it was hard at times to understand him. "And then tonight, Tuesday night, there'll be a new episode. I can't wait! I love this show, I'm telling you! Dorinda's my favorite, fellas. She's the most beautiful woman I've ever seen. I'm telling ya, fellas, I've never seen a more exquisite woman. She's *charming*, is what. Well, okay, she's maybe a bit high-strung, but so what?

Who isn't? Hell, I might even marry her sometime. I'm sure she'd agree to that. Why wouldn't she? I just might do that, by George. What do you think of that, Herbie?"

Dad nodded and pursed his lips and looked thoughtful. "I see the appeal," was all he said.

I sat in the chair next to Dad's bed and watched with them. The drama *du jour* was that the housewives were horribly upset with Ramona because she'd left early from some social gathering that Luann had organized— maybe one of the countess's cabaret affairs, in which she stands straight and tall and enthusiastically belts out songs, not always quite on-key—to go to another party elsewhere. Leah and Luann and Dorinda were all in a huff, claiming that Ramona'd "done this stunt before" and that she was really more interested in going places where she might meet a new man than she was at socializing with her friends. Luann towered over Dorinda, and both of their faces were set hard with anger. Sonja was three sheets to the wind. She said nothing, just nodded her head in apparent agreement with the others and scarfed down at least a dozen green grapes and assorted cheeses from a silver platter and poured herself another drink and downed the entire glass fairly quickly. Her eyes were starting to glaze over.

"Quite the strutting and f-f-fretting, huh, D-Dad?" I said.

"I guess," he said, shrugging his shoulders again. I noticed that he wasn't even paying much attention to the program and that he seemed subdued. "I don't know about that," he added, very quietly.

Well, I thought, *there goes that idea.*

Later that morning, just before the patients' food trays were on the way, I told Dad that I was going to trot down to the hospital cafeteria for lunch. He looked at me soulfully, his eyes that pale bluish-gray again, and looked like he was about to cry. "Do you *have* to go?" he murmured.

"He'll be back, Herbie," the Admiral said loudly. "Don't worry, Herb. Kids have to eat, you know. Kids are *always* hungry, you know. They have to eat a lot so they can grow. It's a natural thing, Herbie. It's true the wide world over. I've been all over the world, and it's true everywhere. You just have to accept it. Am I right, Herb? Have a good time, Julius. Have a lovely feast and don't worry about a *thing*. Your father and I will have a high old time with Dorinda and them other fancy New York broads and we'll be here when you get back. I *guarantee* it, Julius! Right, Herbie? Am I right? Of course I am. So march your butt down to the mess and have yourself a wonderful lunch, kiddo. Eat hearty, matey!"

The cafeteria had a huge salad bar and another section with oatmeal and various flavors of yogurt and bran muffins and assorted fruits and other healthy selections, but I opted for a hot dog and fries from the little grill that was tucked away in one corner. I wanted to see what their hot dogs were like. I sat down with my tray at a small table near the far wall and looked around at the crowd. There were a few doctors, some in white lab coats and some in light-blue V-necked scrubs, with stethoscopes around their necks, and a smattering of other assorted health care types: nurses of various ranks, physician assistants, lab technicians, and whatnot. I noticed that a lot of them were eating the oatmeal or fruits or other of the healthy options.

Then I was pleasantly surprised to see Mei-Lin and an older Asian women seated at a table on the other side of the aisle from mine, a little way away. The older woman was thin and tiny and had a wrinkled face and short wispy gray hair. Her face was expressionless. She was using chopsticks to eat from a bowl of brown rice with broccoli or some other kind of unappetizing green vegetable mixed in. The two weren't talking. Mei-Lin wasn't eating, just staring, unblinking, at nothing that I could detect, cradling the point of her delicate porcelain-like chin between her right thumb and index finger. She looked very serious, maybe preoccupied. She wasn't wearing much makeup, and no false eyelashes. Before I could think, I stood up and trotted over to their table. "M-Mei-Lin," I said, "Hi. Remember m-m-me?" She looked up at my face and studied it for a moment and then shook her head. "I was at China P-Palace a l-little while ago with my c-cousin, Herschel. I had sweet and s-s-sour chicken. And w-wonton soup."

She again shook her head. "No," she said. "I'm sorry. I don't recall."

"Oh, well, th-that's okay." I couldn't think of what else to say and felt foolish. "Are you h-here to s-s-see someone?" I finally asked.

She nodded and looked at the older woman, who hadn't acknowledged my presence at all and was still eating from her bowl of rice. "My father's upstairs. He has pancreatic cancer." She paused and looked down at her lap. "Stage four."

"Oh," I said. "Well, I'm s-sorry." I couldn't think of anything else to say and muttered a weak goodbye and walked back to my table. I regretted that I hadn't been able to sneak a peek at Mei-Lin's muscular calves.

The hot dog was just okay. It was grilled, but tasted bland. The bun was some kind of fluffy white bread, also just okay, nothing special. I squeezed the contents of little plastic packets of both ketchup and mustard on it, but they didn't much improve the experience. I wished that I'd ordered grilled onions. I thought again about my idea to prepare high-quality hot dogs—Nathan's Hebrew National Koshers—for Carl and Scanner Stan and Blanche and Tunnel Terry and Eugene and whatever other poor wretches, so to speak, who are out there, even including that surly big-bellied Art. It would be a mitzvah. "Hey, Artie," I'd boom, sans stutter, as I handed him his dog. "I hear it might rain today. What do *you* think?" And then I'd laugh heartily before he could sass me back. "Here ya go, pal," I'd say, more gently. "Have some relish and grilled onions. Have some sport peppers and tomato pickle. Good, huh? How about a sprinkling of celery salt?"

It occurred to me that I'd have to provide something for people to drink, to wash down their dogs with, and had the idea that it would be good to stock, instead of the usual Pepsi or Coca-Cola products, something more high-class—maybe those Dr. Brown's sodas that Izzy's features. He has several good flavors, including not just the cream soda that I prefer and the Cel-Ray Tonic that Herschel likes but also black cherry and root beer—all in hoity-toity brown glass bottles with twist-off caps. I suspect that Carl or Blanche never had the pleasure of drinking one of those. Stan always drinks his liter-sized Mountain Dews.

I had the idea that it would be nice if Herschel or Benji, or even both, could be there with me to help with the cooking or serving the hot dogs and drinks. They could do most of the talking, exchanging pleasantries. Given my awkward encounter with Mei-Lin and, I suspect, her mother, I probably need to keep my social intercourse to a minimum.

Mei-Lin. *Well,* I thought, *so much for that warm little China Palace smile.* I guess she was just being affable to get a fatter tip.

When I got back to Dad's room, Herschel was seated next to his bed, visiting. He nodded to me and pointed toward his uncle and gave me a look. The TV was off. My old man was lying in his bed—posture rigid, hands clasped behind his head—and talking loudly, quite animated. His gray eyes were sharp and opened unusually wide, unblinking, focused on the ceiling, as he went on and on. He didn't acknowledge my return. After a few moments of listening, I had the idea that my father was reciting his life story. The Admiral, in the other bed, was listening intently and nodding now and again and asking questions here and there. I wasn't sure at what point of his life Dad's recitation had started, but by the time of my return from lunch he was remembering grade school.

"There were only eleven of us in my class at Elmwood Elementary," he was saying, "and I was the best speller. I won most of the spelling bees in fifth and sixth grade, except when Darlene Johnson beat me one time when she spelled 'boulevard' after I got it wrong. I screwed up the 'ou.' I never much liked Darlene after that. She . . ."

"Whatever happened to Darlene, Herbie?" the Admiral interrupted.

Dad furrowed his brow. It was then that he seemed to notice that I was there, and looked at me and nodded slightly. "Well," he went on, "I believe she became a kindergarten teacher. She married a cop. His last name was Cooper. I don't think it lasted, though. Anyway, after that I went to Monroe Junior High and started to be interested in theater. In ninth grade we read *Romeo and Juliet* and I loved it. We watched a movie of the play, the old one with Barrymore and Leslie Howard and Norma Shearer, and I thought, *Hey, maybe I can do that.* I wanted to be Romeo, wanted to kiss Juliet. They didn't have a drama club there, though. In gym class we had to do endurance runs, run around the gym until Mr. Steffan said we could stop and walk for one lap. One lap! Steffan would stand in the middle of the gym clapping his hands to set a tempo and he'd pull out a white handkerchief and mop his brow, as though *he* was all tired out from our exertions. Hah! There was this guy, Phil Kosinski, who was real big and loud and he used to snap his towel at guys' butts in the locker room. That really hurt, you know."

"Why didn't you stand up to Phil, Herb? Ya gotta stand up to a bully, am I right? Did you stand up to Phil? Did you knock him on his ass, Herbie?"

Dad thought about that. "No," he went on. "I didn't. Maybe I should have. Anyway, I had my first girlfriend in junior high. Nancy, her name was. She wasn't Jewish, you know, but she was cute. She had long blond hair, very straight, and braces. I remember she had braces. She kept her mouth closed when she smiled because she was embarrassed. She was a good kisser, I can tell you that, but I was always worried about those damned braces cutting my lip. When her parents found out I was Jewish, they said she couldn't see me anymore. I was sad about that."

"Did you still see Nancy after that, Herbie? Did you try to get in her pants?"

Dad furrowed his brow and shook his head. "No, I never." He paused for a moment and kept staring at the ceiling. "That never crossed my mind." He nodded and seemed to be thinking. "Maybe I should have."

Well, it went on from there and after a bit he got around to his high school days. One memory was that he had another girlfriend, Rosalind, who, this time, was Jewish and in junior year they started "going steady" and four months after that he lost his virginity to her in her bedroom at home, when her parents were out for the night and her older sister, a waitress, was at work.

"Was she a virgin too, Herbie?" the Admiral asked, his blue eyes bright and mischievous. "Did you bust her cherry?"

Dad furrowed his brow and squinted. "I think so," he replied. "She cried a little when it happened and there was some blood on the sheet. So I guess so."

I felt embarrassed to be hearing about my father's early sex life, from him, but was also interested.

Then followed a fairly long recitation about his high school theater days. He'd joined the Drama Club and ascended rapidly and had a big role in *The Fantasticks* and played the stage manager in *Our Town*. In his senior year he got to play Lysander in *A Midsummer's Night's Dream*, his first Shakespeare. Rosalind did theater, too, but only small roles, and they broke up right after graduation because he was going away to Northwestern to be an undergraduate and she was staying home to attend technical college and become a licensed practical nurse.

"Well," the Admiral noted, "if a broad's gonna be a nurse she might as well be a practical one. You wouldn't want someone handling a bedpan whose head's in the clouds. Am I right?"

On the one hand, all this was interesting stuff and I was hearing it for the first time. On the other hand, it was getting tedious and I found myself less interested. But when he started talking about his days at Yale Drama, I perked up. "I auditioned for the lead in *Richard III*, but didn't get it. I got to play Buckingham instead. My big role was James Tyrone in *Long Day's Journey into Night*. I met Sarah my senior year. On our first date, I took her to Morey's in New Haven on a Monday night to hear the Whiffenpoofs. That was her idea. She loved those guys, and knew the words to a lot of their songs, including, of course, the big one. She even knew the lyrics to 'Shall I Wasting' and sang them to me later that night as I was walking her home: '*Shall I wasting, in despair, die because a woman's fair? …* ' I'm telling you, I fell in love with her right off."

"So what happened to Sarah, Herbie?"

There was a long pause. "We stayed together and got married after a few years. That was good. After a while, Sarah wanted to start a family, but I didn't want to yet because I wanted to get my theater career going first. She was pretty unhappy about that, and we quarreled. I wasn't making much money, either. You know how it is. Finally, after we'd been married for five years, she gave me an ultimatum: have a child or split up. So I agreed, reluctantly, and a year later our son was born."

"Your son, huh? That's Julius, right? Was that son Julius who's sitting over there, Herbie? Or someone else? How many kids did you have, Herb? I never had no kids, Herbie. Not that I know of, anyway. For all I know, though, there might be a few little midshipmen out there somewhere. I wouldn't be surprised, Herb, I can tell you that."

"Yes," Dad said. "Yes. Julius. He was our only child. Quiet little guy. I named him after Groucho. Sarah liked the Marx Brothers, too. I don't recall her favorite. It might have been *Horsefeathers*. We'd seen all their movies when we were dating. We laughed a lot. She didn't like the name Julius, but I insisted." He paused. "Maybe I shouldn't have done that. Sarah wanted more kids, but I was lukewarm about that." He paused again. "Maybe it would have been okay to have another kid or two. Too late now, though."

During this, he never looked at me, just stared straight ahead. I'm not sure he even knew I was still there, he was so wrapped up in telling his story. Herschel, though, nudged my arm with his elbow.

"Julius. That's an okay name, Herbie. That's a fine name. You made a good choice there, in my humble. So are you still with Sarah, Herb? Is she still in the picture? Or did she ditch you for someone better? Oh, just *kidding*, Herb."

Dad hesitated and furrowed his brow and didn't say anything at first. "No," he said softly. "No, I'm not with her. She died a long time ago. She, uh, she took an overdose of pills."

"*Really?*" the Admiral intoned. "An overdose, huh? Died, huh? Well, that's a shame. That's too bad. It certainly is too bad, Herbie. A terrible tragedy, for sure. Why'd she do *that*, Herb?"

Dad paused again and looked down. He didn't say anything at first. Then he said, "Well, I guess she got depressed. Pretty much. She thought I was having an affair, see. She thought I was going to leave her and our son for someone else. I told her I wasn't, but she wouldn't believe me. Miriam and I were just friends. She was in theater, too. But we weren't … involved then. We just got together for drinks after performances, that sort of thing.

Sarah was taking medicines for depression and anxiety, and she, uh, she ... just overdosed. They called it an apparent suicide. I don't know if Sarah meant to die. Maybe. I don't know. I've never known, for sure. No note. I came home very late one night and she was on the floor, unconscious. I called an ambulance." He paused. "She died later in the hospital. They couldn't revive her."

"A terrible thing, that is. A tragedy, Herb. What happened then, Herbie? What'd you do?"

"Well, it was hard. I was a single parent, trying to establish my career. I got my first big break when I played Romeo. And then, of course, *Hamlet*." He brightened noticeably. "You play Hamlet when you're young, right? But Miriam and I stayed friends." He pursed his lips and looked at the ceiling. "She was helpful, you know. And she was a good listener." He paused. "So, after a while, we got married."

"Which of your wives did you like best, Herb?"

My father sat up straight and, for the first time, looked directly over at the Admiral in the other bed. "Oh, that's easy. *Sarah*, for sure," he said, much louder than before. "*Absolutely!*"

TWENTY-TWO

I TOLD LIZ that I'd do that wedding she asked me to photograph. I don't want to, but I don't want to disappoint her. She's been good to me over the years and I owe her that much. It'll be my last hurrah, though. Enough with all the drama at these damned weddings. I'm already worried about what kind of mishegas will transpire at this one.

Well, maybe at my last hurrah I'll finally score with an inebriated bridesmaid. Maybe that dream will finally come true. After all I've been through with my father lately, on top of all my woman troubles, I think I deserve some nachas there. I'm not sure, though, if *deserves* enter into any such equations. It'd be *nice*, I guess, to believe that there's really some big boo-hoo—Yahweh or whoever—who's keeping tabs as to deserves and who decides about whether or not to inscribe us in the Book of Life for another year on Yom Kippur. But you either believe that stuff or you don't.

At least the old man seems better. He was released from the hospital two days ago, on Thursday, and since then he's mostly been sleeping a lot. And when awake he's been more or less okay. With Dad not bonkers, I'd asked Benji if he'd like to come over this afternoon to visit. I asked him to bring his DVD of *Quest for Fire*.

I miss the Admiral, though. When I went to the hospital on Thursday to pick up Dad, I could hear Ralph singing loudly as I approached their room:

> *We come on the sloop John B*
> *My grandfather and me*
> *Around Nassau town we did roam*
> *Drinking all night*
> *Got into a fight*
> *Well, I feel so broke up*
> *I want to go home.*

The Admiral, sitting up in his bed, blue eyes bright and mischievous, grinned hugely and waved enthusiastically as I entered the room. My father was sitting on the edge of his bed, facing his roommate, and waving his outstretched hand, index finger extended, along with the lyrics. And he was actually smiling, a big healthy grin. He even made a half-assed attempt to mouth the lyrics along with the Admiral during the chorus:

> *So, hoist up the John B's sail*
> *See how the main sail sets*
> *Call for the captain ashore*
> *Let me go home,*
> *Let me go home,*
> *I want to go home, yeah, yeah.*
> *Well, I feel so broke up,*
> *I want to go home.*

After the final verse—the one in which "the poor cook, he caught the fits and threw away all my grits, and then he took and he ate up all of my corn"—the Admiral abruptly stopped singing and greeted me. "*Julius!*" he practically shouted. "Great to see you today. Isn't it a splendid day? The sun is shining, Julius, I can see that out the window. It's a *lovely* day! It might be cold out, though. Your dad's ready to go home. Isn't that right, Herb? He feels so broke up he wants to go home." He giggled and slapped his knee. "You take good care of him now, Julius. Your father's a great guy, a *wonderful* actor. Herbie, you're better than any of them, better than Olivier or any of those guys. Better than *Brando*, for Chrissake! Am I right, Herbie?"

Before the hospital people wheeled Dad, in a wheelchair, out of his room for his exit, I shook the Admiral's hand and told him that it had been a pleasure to meet him. "I, uh, certainly w-wish you the b-b-best of luck, M-Mister Admiral," I said. "I t-truly do."

He nodded and patted the back of my right hand with his left. "That's alright, son," he said, calmly and more slowly than before. "I appreciate the good thought. Take care of your dad. He's a great guy. I have to stay here a bit longer to, uh … "—and here he lowered his voice and darted his eyes back and forth from one side of the room to the other—"to be sure there's no skull*duggery* going on in this place. You know what I mean, right?"

At least I got to briefly see Suzette before we left. She gave me Dad's discharge summary and told me about his medications that I'd have to pick up at the pharmacy. She said that, in addition to psych meds, he'd be taking an antibiotic, amoxicillin, for a urinary tract infection that they'd found out about in a routine urinalysis. "UTIs can be tough for older folks," she'd said quietly, while Dad was saying goodbye to one of the other nurses. "They can cause agitation or confusion or even, uh, delirium." I nodded but said nothing. I was having trouble concentrating on what she was saying because I was lost in that round freckled face and lovely green eyes with those golden speckles and that melodic voice with the lisp. When she told me to be sure that my father drinks a lot of water, as well as daily cranberry juice, all I could do was nod again. "I w-w-will," I mumbled.

"And," she went on, "we did a blood test and saw that he'd been taking Ambien. He doesn't have a prescription for that, though."

I looked down at my shoes and shrugged. "I d-do," I said, weakly. "M-Maybe he's been t-t-taking some of m-mine."

Suzette studied my face for a long moment. "I see," she said. "Well, Ambien can be a big problem, particularly for older people. They can do things in their sleep that they don't remember later. If he's going to take that medication, he has to have his own prescription and be carefully monitored by a doctor. *Very* carefully monitored." She paused. "Okay?"

I nodded, but wanted to evaporate into the air.

At least Herschel'd been a comfort. After Dad's manic recitation of his life history on Tuesday, my cousin'd invited me over to his place. He ordered a pizza from Papa John's and, while we were waiting for it to come, asked me what I thought about what my father had said and how I felt about any of it. I shrugged. "I d-don't know," I said. "I'm n-not sure what t-to think." I didn't know what more to say. Ajax was right there at my feet, looking up at me with big chocolate-brown eyes, and I scratched him behind his ears. It was comforting.

Herschel nodded. "Did you know most of what he was saying, about your mom and Miriam and all? I know I didn't."

"N-N-No, I didn't either. It was n-news to me." Just then I felt weepy, but didn't want to fall apart in front of my cousin. So I was glad when Thersites, in his cage in the corner of the living room, commenced to loudly squawk "Kiss my ass, Ajax! Kiss my *ass*, Ajax!" followed closely by both of his other brainless selections—"Lechery! Lechery!" and "Chuck you, Farley!" He repeated that last one five or six times, with a brief pause between each tedious recitation. Herschel's face tightened and he glared at the parrot. "SHUT the *fuck* up!" he yelled. "Show a little goddamn respect!" Just then I stopped feeling weepy. *Thank you, dear Thersites*, I thought to myself. *I apologize for all my bad thoughts about you.*

"Well," Herschel said after a few moments, "at least he said that he liked your mom better than Miriam. That's something, huh?"

I nodded my head. "Yes," I said. "Th-that was s-something." I stroked the top of Ajax's head with my open right palm. "That was d-d-definitely s-something."

The pizza was fine—hand-tossed with sausage and extra cheese. Herschel and I didn't talk much, other than to giggle about the manic but joyful Admiral.

Since that evening, I've had mixed emotions. On the one hand, I'm glad that my father was taken care of so well and was now taking medication and, so far anyway, seems okay—no further worrisome episodes. On the other hand, I'm still not sure what to think. I was happy— *thrilled!*—to hear that he preferred Mom over Miriam. That was an absolutely lovely thing for me to hear, and I silently said a prayer of huge thanks to the social -boundaries-off Admiral for asking such a direct question. But the old man also said that my mother had overdosed because she thought he was having an affair with Miriam. He'd denied that he was, but I'm not sure whether or not to believe him. I've been angry that I had to hear all that—and for the first time—from my father while he was wackadoodle in a hospital psychiatric ward, telling his story not to me but to another psych patient. That wasn't right. "People have their demons." Hah! "The heart is a lonely hunter." My *ass!*

Part of me wants to confront the old man, to ask him directly what the truth was. But another part doesn't want to raise any further issues. Maybe he's still too fragile to deal with such things. But maybe I'll have a chance down the line to find out what's what. I hope I will.

I was glad that Benji was coming over. I hadn't seen him since Izzy's. I was looking forward to seeing the movie with him and Dad. Maybe it would be a nice bonding experience. And I was looking forward to finding out what Naoh learned from his new girlfriend, Ika. But then I thought that maybe watching that particular flick wouldn't be such a great idea. Maybe Naoh and those other cavemen guys would be mostly naked—I couldn't remember their state of dress or undress from my initial watching of part of it with Benji—and that would set Dad off again. Maybe he'd get weird and start in again with the "poor naked wretches" and "unaccommodated man" mishegas, and maybe even again take to ripping off his own damned accommodations again. I couldn't deal with that. *Maybe*, I thought, *we should just watch something bland in which everyone is always fully dressed from head to toes and stays that way and behaves properly and there are no scary storms.* Maybe *Downton Abbey.*

Dad was glad to see Benji. "Hello, young man," he said. "Good to see you again. Had any egg creams lately?"

Benji just smiled. "No, sir," he answered. "Not lately. But I look forward to that again."

Dad nodded. "Me, too" he said, softly, after a moment. "Me, too."

I noticed Benji looking strangely at Dad, studying him. It occurred to me that maybe I should have told him in advance that Dad looked different than when he, Benji, had seen him at Izzy's. The hospital people had, as I'd hoped, somehow persuaded my father to let them cut his hair and shave his beard. They'd even cut his horrid toenails. He'd eaten well at the hospital, and now he looked more like the old handsome Herbert Dickman. His posture was even better, more erect. His eyes weren't murky.

I had the idea that Suzette had taken the lead in getting Dad to agree to be groomed so as to make points with me. I again conjured her sweet face, and had the thought that maybe I'd call her to thank her for helping my father, for being kind and competent and caring. Or maybe she'd initiate a call, to ask how Mr. Dickman was doing following his release and if he was taking his meds as prescribed. Either way, I'd maybe ask if she wanted to get together—outside of the hospital, of course—to have coffee. I'd suggest my usual Starbucks. But then I thought that might not be a good option. What if that lovely Macbook Pro woman was there at the same time? I might have a hard time giving due attention to Suzette because I'd likely be staring more than I should at Ms. Lime-Green Scrunchie, probably having lustful imaginings. Suzette would notice. "*Men!*" she'd maybe mutter. "You're all alike." Then she'd stomp out without another word.

But then, remembering Suzette's scolding, if that's what it was, about the Ambien, I dropped the idea. As much as I'd love to see that sweet, sweet freckled face again, I'd be embarrassed.

I made sweetened potato pancakes for the three of us, from a Manischewitz box. It was easy. You beat two eggs with a fork in a bowl and add one-and-a-quarter cups of cold water and the pancake mix and stir it all up and let the batter thicken for a few minutes and then put some vegetable oil in a large skillet and drop tablespoons of the batter into the hot oil and brown both sides of each pancake. There were six or seven for each of us. I set out little bowls of both applesauce and sour cream. Dad generously schmeared both on his pancakes but Benji just did small dollops of the sour cream. "Wow," he said when he was done, "that was *great*. Thanks so much, Julius."

After we ate, I had Dad sit in his La-Z-Boy and put Benji's DVD in the player. I again felt momentarily worried that the damned movie would throw my father into another wacko tizzy, what with any nudity or violence or other perturbations that he'd likely enlarge to cosmic significance, like bonkers Lear. I particularly didn't want that to happen with Benji there.

But it didn't. Watching the movie made me a bit nostalgic, though, because I again fondly recalled the first time I'd watched part of it, with Benji in his room, while Naomi and Elise were downstairs, probably watching the housewives and trashing Luann or Dorinda or Ramona while scarfing down Lay's potato chips from a family-sized bag.

Naomi. I hadn't thought much about her for the last few days, what with all my father's crazy stuff, but now I did. I again remembered our morning couple check-in sessions, drinking coffee and listening to her work grievances, mostly about Arthur, and, later, her rote "How did that make you feel?" and the like. I thought about her lovely pot roasts, with tiny boiled potatoes. I recalled being in bed with her, she asleep while I was wide awake with my insomnia, and listening to her little "*m-m-m*" sounds and reaching under the cover to stroke her flannel-covered right hip. I even, strangely, fondly recalled her splotchy face and her weepy "How *could* you?"

But *Quest for Fire* was fine. The Ulam guys—Naoh and Amoukar and Gaw—were mostly covered with furs and animal skins. They had a tough go of it, though, on their journey to find fire—atra—to bring back to their tribe. But after they rescue lithe and naked little Ika—painted blue per the custom of her tribe, the Ivaka—from captivity by the cannibalistic Kzamm tribe, she introduces the three guys to several new experiences, broadening their limited cavemen horizons. At one point they're all lying around resting and a medium-sized stone rolls down a hill and chunks Amoukar in the head. Ika laughs loudly and heartily, startling the guys. Laughter is foreign to them; they've not experienced it before. They just stare at Ika, not sure what to make of this new thing they're seeing and hearing. *Is this blue bare-assed chick crazy?* they're maybe wondering. I worried, when she came on the scene, that her lovely nakedness would set Dad off, but happily that didn't happen.

She's also the catalyst for teaching them to make their own fire. That happens when Ika joins forces with the three Ulam guys but then realizes that she's near her home village and heads off in that direction. Naoh, by now smitten, follows her and is soon captured by the Ivaka, all similarly painted blue. After hearing them, like Ika, chatter constantly and laugh out loud a lot, Naoh watches in amazement as one of them creates fire, using a crude hand drill. Later, Amoukar and Gaw rescue Naoh and they, too, get to witness the perpetually laughing Ivaka. Ika leaves with the guys.

The other big new experience Ika offers is the missionary position. The Ulam only know doggy style, and Naoh forces himself on Ika a few times in such manner. He's not big on foreplay. Later, on their return journey, Naoh feels amorous and again initiates sex, employing his customary doggy. But skinny little Ika wriggles around and maneuvers herself so that she's on her back, beneath him. He's surprised by the novelty, but soon seems to like the face-to-face intimacy. "See what I mean?" Benji whispered to me while they were going at it. "I told you she teaches him *other* things." I was embarrassed that we were watching a sex scene with Benji. Even though he'd seen it before, I felt embarrassed.

Also on their return journey, they're all again resting and Amoukar glances down from a height at sleeping Gaw and mischievously drops a rock on his buddy's noggin, startling him awake. It causes quite a gash, and his head begins to bleed. Naoh and Ika and Amoukar howl with raucous laughter, and after a bit Gaw, despite his pain, joins in too.

That was all cute enough, but the absolutely incredibly *wonderful* thing was that my father suddenly commenced to loudly guffawing along with Ika and the cavemen and kept at it for maybe two minutes. He was slapping his knee and pointing at the screen and laughing heartily—mouth opened wide with a bit of spittle drooling out of one corner, gray eyes sparkling, almost doubled over, belly jiggling. Benji and I just stared at him for a few moments and then happily joined in with our own laughter. All seven of us carried on with big joy.

Hearing my poor father finally laugh so heartily was an unexpected but delicious moment of nachas that, at least just then, went a good way to balancing out all the damned tsoris.

The only sad thing about *Quest for Fire*, for me, was seeing the cannibalistic Kzamm guys. Every one of them had a thick mane of long straight red hair, and seeing that put me in mind of the redhead whom I'd watched applying her lipstick at the stoplight after my memorable mitzvah morning with Celeste. It made me sad to think that I never knew who that redhead was or what she was like or if she and I might have a future, and I had no control as to whether or not I'd ever see her again. If I do, it would likely just be by chance, maybe at another stoplight, and then the light would turn green and we'd again go our separate ways. That chance seems unlikely. But if it did happen and I could at least get to watch her doing her pretty face for a while, that would be something good—a warm memory for my sleepless nights ahead.

Celeste. Hopefully she and Donny are happy together and hopefully he takes good care of her and her theater career proceeds splendidly. *If I ever hear about him pushing her down any stairs,* I thought, *I won't tolerate it.* Maybe I'll hire a thug to punish him, if I can figure out where a guy goes to find a thug.

Soon Dad excused himself to go to the bathroom and Benji got up to look at the framed photos in the living room and hallway, studying each. "Hey," he said, "these are *great* pictures." He seemed particularly fascinated by the one of Dad as Macbeth, where he's all weirded out and startled at seeing the ghost of murdered Banquo at the banquet scene. "Where's this one from?" Benji asked. I told him, and he nodded. "Oh, yeah," he said. "I remember. That was the one where the guy's wife made him murder the king, right? He had second thoughts, but she said he had to do it and then he did." He looked up at me, forehead wrinkled. "Maybe he shouldn't have listened to her."

"M-Maybe," I said. *Some kid,* I thought again. I thought of warning Benji to never say the word "Macbeth" if he's in a theater, except while that play is in a rehearsal or a performance, but to say "the Scottish play" instead. But then I thought that explaining the reason for such a ridiculous thing would be too tedious, so dropped the idea for the moment. *But,* I thought, *I'll definitely warn him about that some time.*

After my father hadn't emerged from the bathroom for a while, I felt a bit worried and walked over to the closed bathroom door and listened. I heard a sigh and then some light moaning and grunting. "D-Dad," I said, not loudly, "are y-you okay?"

"Yes," he answered after a moment. "I guess so."

"Listen," I said after a moment. "D-Don't forget to take your M-M-Metamucil. Okay?"

TWENTY-THREE

THAT NIGHT I fell asleep around eleven but then popped awake three hours later and my brain immediately commenced to churning. I thought about what Benji'd said about Macbeth, that he didn't want to murder Duncan but that his ambitious wife had talked him into doing it. I remembered that she, Lady Macbeth, had played the *you're not a real man* card with her husband, so that he felt he had to do the murder to show her that she was wrong, that he certainly *was* a real man, quite willing to do horrible things, including assassination, to advance his career and her queenly ambitions. And that deed then led to him, Macbeth, succeeding Duncan as king and then becoming a vicious tyrant and going on to order the deaths of lots of people, including his buddy Banquo and his son, Fleance, and his former buddy Macduff's wife and kids. Macbeth quickly turns into a very nasty guy whom everyone hates, and eventually they all turn against him and there's a battle and Macduff kills him and slices off his head and parades the severed noggin around the castle. Yikes!

Well, maybe all that horror and all those corpses littering the stage could have been avoided if pussy-whipped Macbeth had just stood up firmly to his pushy wife. That had been Benji's thought, and he was probably right. "Now, listen, *Elspeth*," Mac could have said early on, his face hard and jaw set and looking directly and unblinking into her lovely smoky eyes and speaking in a firm, masculine tone of voice. "I am NOT going to kill this guy. Okay? I do not care what your stupid ambition is for us. And forget that 'you're not a real man' bullshit. Offing Duncan would be a *rotten* thing to do, a huge shonda, and there is absolutely NO chance in hell! Do you hear me, Elspeth? Do you hear me loud and *clear?* Good! So get that idea out of your pretty little head, *Elspeth*, immediately and forever. *Fershtaist?*"

All that strutting and fretting didn't turn out well for Mrs. Mac either. She got wacko after a while from guilt about Duncan's murder, and took to hallucinating that her hands were bloody and she couldn't get them clean. And then she expired, shortly before her husband did. "The queen, my lord, is dead." At the end, someone said of Lady Macbeth that "as 'tis thought," she "took off her life." So they *thought* she did herself in, but that may or may not have been the case. Same with Ophelia in *Hamlet*. A lot of strutting and fretting there, too. Ophelia was all verklempt about her old man's inadvertent death at the hands of her boyfriend and how haughtily Hamlet had treated her, and then the last straw for her was that nasty Claudius sent Hamlet out of the country, to England, and she was awash with grief from all that drama, and next we hear of her, from Gertrude, she was perched on a tree branch, clutching a bunch of flowers, but the branch broke and she tumbled into the water and drowned, clothing waterlogged, while singing snatches of melancholy songs. But it wasn't clear whether her sad demise was an accident or a suicide. She was definitely distraught and had likely gone round the twist, what with one stressor after another, but that's all we know for sure.

So now I find out from Dad blathering to the Admiral that my mother's like Lady Macbeth and Ophelia: maybe a suicide but maybe not. All this time I'd thought she'd killed herself and wondered how she could have done that to twelve-year-old me, and now I learn that perhaps her death was a suicide but perhaps not. At least that's my old man's version. "*Apparent suicide*" is what, according to him, some suit had concluded. And I'll likely never know the truth. That's what's hard. If I knew for sure one way or the other, at least I'd have that and could get my head around it, whether or not I liked it. So now, unless my father knows more than he's said, I'm *still* in the dark.

Damned old fart.

I at least hope that my father appreciates my having used the hospital elevator. I avoided it as much as possible when I visited him, and avoided, too, that big revolving door at the hospital entrance. But I couldn't avoid it when he was discharged and an aide wheeled him out of the psych ward and into the elevator to go down to the ground level, and I was with them, holding a white plastic bag with my father's stuff. The elevator was crowded, and, of course, I was farmisht. I may have been sweating. My face felt flushed. My heart was beating fast. I even considered doing alternate-nostril breathing, weird as that would have looked. There were maybe eight or nine people in that elevator, including one cute little thing with a pixie face and warm hazel-colored eyes and straight medium-length brown hair. Her name was Emma Grace and the badge hanging around her pretty slender neck also identified her as a *BSN*—whatever that is. I tried to avoid eye contact with her on our elevator journey, but I guess I must have stared too much.

Emma Grace got off on the floor just before ours and, as she started to exit the elevator, turned her head to look directly into my eyes for a long moment. It seemed like a long moment; it might not have been that long. In that moment, part of me was embarrassed for having stared but another part felt like pleading with her, sans stutter: "Take me with you, Emma Grace. *Please!* Let me be with you for a while, just a few minutes. We can sit on that nice bench in front of the main entrance. I'll buy you a nice cup of steaming hot chocolate with marshmallows, maybe Swiss Miss, to help you warm up. Could we maybe just hold hands for a minute or two? I won't say anything, and I won't bother you after that." Then the moment passed and Emma Grace was gone.

So I was wide awake in the middle of the night with all those ponderings, Macbeth and Lady Mac and Emma Grace and every damned thing else, plus wondering about my poor mother, my fevered brain obsessing.

But, on the other hand, I was fine with Benji. I like trying to be a better father to him than his own old man apparently is. It's a snide satisfaction, maybe, but it's how I feel. And Benji seems to like me well enough. I introduced him to egg creams, after all. If I tip over today or tomorrow or any time soon, hopefully he'll at least remember me fondly for that. And if Benji has a son, down the road, maybe he'll introduce the kid to egg creams and think well of me, whether or not I'm still around.

Lying awake, I again had the thought that at some point I'd like to live alone, maybe in Mrs. Weinstein's apartment if still available. Maybe I could ask Perry to pull strings to get me that place. I even thought about how I'd furnish and decorate it. I'd like to get my own La-Z-Boy, a different color than Dad's beige, and also a big comfortable couch, with fluffy cushions, that I could lie on in the evenings and fall asleep while watching TV, maybe covered with a white afghan, like Dad's. Like the chair, that couch would be new and unsullied, unlike Herschel's couch, assuming I could afford new stuff. I had the thought, too, that I'd like to get a print of *Christina's World* to hang on the wall of my bedroom, in a spot where I could see it from my bed. It's a comforting painting, with that enchanting crippled young woman gazing longingly at those weathered farm buildings on the horizon. But it's also disturbing, particularly the mystery of what's up with poor Christina, what might be going on inside her sweet head.

That print would also remind me of my lovely time with Celeste. That would be pleasant because, I'm quite sure, I'll never again have such a lovely interlude; gazing at the print would balance out that sad realization with remembering that at least I had that morning. There's that. And maybe while staring at *Christina's World* sometime, alone in my bed, I'll again have that lovely, albeit brief, hallucination of the grass swaying in the foreground.

Maybe I'll follow Herschel's example and hang some quotes—printed in nice script, framed in black metal—on the living room wall of my apartment. I'd probably start with some or all of Macbeth's gloomy "Tomorrow, and tomorrow, and tomorrow … " spiel—if not the whole deal, then maybe just "Out, out, brief candle" or perhaps "It is a tale told by an idiot, full of sound and fury, signifying *nothing.*" I might soften that one to say "It is a tale told by a *schlemiel* … " Or maybe I could hang "Unaccommodated man is no more but such a poor, bare, forked animal as thou art" in my bathroom and look at it each time I step out of the shower. That should help a guy stay humble.

Well, I thought, *I can't really think of getting a place of my own right now. My old man will need me to take care of him for a while, anyway.*

I wondered, too, if I should ask Rabbi Twersky to visit my father. I'd briefly considered asking him to visit Dad when he was in the psych ward, after he got out of that "quiet area," but decided against it. Twersky probably wouldn't have been a fan of the Admiral. I can just imagine him walking into the room and hearing the Admiral manically belting out "The Sloop John B" and Dad sitting on his bed grinning like a fool and waving his arms and trying to sing along—*"Well, I feel so broke up, I wanna go home."* Twersky would likely furrow his brow and grimace and shake his head in disgust. "Herbert!" he might insist. "This is *not* part of God's mission for us as Jews! Stop this *at once* and come to your senses." But now that Dad's home and seems saner, less of a raving meshuggener, maybe a rabbinical visit would be okay.

At least Dad's back seems to be better since he was in the hospital. He's not bent over so much and hasn't complained of pain. I haven't noticed him wincing as much when he gets up from sitting or lying down. And I noticed that he hasn't been gobbling Ibuprofen. Just yesterday, when I asked him about his back pain, he didn't give his stock answer—"I guess it could be worse"—but actually nodded and said, "You know what, Tom, I think I'm doing okay." So that's a step in the right direction. Maybe those

Salonpas patches I gave him, and the Blue Emu cream I've rubbed on his back, have helped.

Lying awake, I thought, too, about what Suzette had told me about Dad having a urinary tract infection. She'd said that a UTI can cause confusion and delirium in an old fart. If I hadn't been so childishly infatuated with Suzette when she told me that, I could have been a better son and asked questions: Was that infection maybe part of the reason he'd been acting so bonkers lately? Or other things? What do I do if he starts getting wacko again?

I felt ashamed that I hadn't made the connection between noticing his cloudy foul-smelling urine and his having a possible infection. Edgar would, I'm sure, have made that connection with Gloucester even when he, Edgar, was in disguise as Poor Tom and worried sick about his own dire peril. And then he surely would have done something about it. I don't think they had antibiotics back then, but … something. *Well,* I thought, *I guess I can try to be sure that the old man drinks enough damned water and cranberry juice.* At least I can do that, hopefully, without screwing up.

I again remembered that Naomi's birthday's coming up, in mid-March. I had the thought that I'd really like to get her something nice, in addition to sending a card. I want her to know that I still think about her. Maybe that'd make her want to get back together. Perhaps she'd like something practical, like a high-quality nonstick frying pan. I remember her now and again kvetching that the coating on the largest of her current frying pans was wearing down, causing more sticking than when it was new. I'm not sure if you can buy just one frying pan or if you have to get a whole set of the damned things. Or maybe she'd like a less-practical but more personal present, such as a silky negligee or a sexy teddy or a bustier or the like. On the one hand, she might like something like that and feel flattered that I, her former boyfriend and lover, still thought of her as an attractive, sensual, and desirable woman. On the other hand, she might think that I was presumptu-ous and out-of-place to be giving her something so intimate now that we're no longer together, especially since she'd discovered that I'd shtupped another woman and so horribly betrayed her and she'd kicked my pathetic toochis out of the house. "The nerve of that schlemiel!" she might complain to Fern or even to Perry, if they were now, as I've speculated, an item. "He just wants to get in my pants again!" Well, maybe I'll compromise and just get her another comfortable and warm flannel nightgown, perhaps one with neutral black-and-white checks that she couldn't read too much meaning into.

Valentine's Day is coming soon. Maybe I could even send Naomi a Valentine with a nice sentiment and then a little question on the bottom: *"Any chance you'll take my ass back?"* I'd like to do that. But I'd worry that she'd send it back with RETURN TO SENDER!! in huge black Sharpie letters on the envelope. That'd be a downer.

I wondered, too, when Magda's birthday is. I'd like to at least get a nice card for her. I'd get one with a nice but not-too-schmaltzy sentiment on it and sign it "Your Friend and Admirer, Julius." It probably wouldn't be okay to sign "Love, Julius," even though that's the case. Maybe I could go to Izzy's to give it to her. I'd sit at the counter, either before or after the lunch rush so she wouldn't be too busy, and hand it to her as she took my order. She'd study the card and nod her big Aryan head and smile. "Oh, dis is so *nice*," she'd maybe say. "I am glad you are my friend, and I admire you too, you know. You are goot man." Maybe she'd even lean over the counter and plant a sweet, neutral little kiss on my cheek. That would be lovely. Maybe she'd grasp my hand in one of hers and squeeze. "Listen," I'd perhaps say, still holding hands with her, "when it g-gets warmer out, would you l-l-like to go on another b-boat ride? We could have hot d-dogs and P-Pepsis again. Would you l-like that, M-M-Magda?" She'd smile warmly and nod. "Oh, sure," she'd say, "dat vould be nice."

I'd check on Izzy while I was there. Poor guy. He's maybe going downhill. If I didn't see him right away while I was sitting at the counter, I'd ask Magda if he was working that day. She'd slip into the kitchen. "Dat nice guy Julius vants to see you," she'd say. "Iss handsome young man, *ja?*" He'd come out and right away wipe any crumbs off the counter with the corner of his stained apron. "Iz," I'd say, "how are you d-doing today?" He'd shrug. "Ach. Not too good," he'd maybe answer. "I'm still a tired alter kacker." If he again mentioned that he might see his Sadie soon, I'd perhaps bring up Edgar's line to his father when Gloucester, blind and helpless and in despair, talked yet again about wanting to die. "Men must endure their going hence even as their coming hither," Edgar said. "Ripeness is all." Izzy'd pause and look at my face and, after a moment, furrow his brow. "Ripeness? What kind of mishegas is *that?*" he'd ask. "Well, no matter. Seeing you again makes me feel much better." He'd turn to Magda. "Bring this man a double order of corned beef hash," he'd say. "On the *house!*"

TWENTY-FOUR

I'D BEEN HORRIBLY worried about the wedding that Liz asked me to do, assuming that it would somehow turn to doo-doo like so many others. But it was okay—*more* than okay. There was some big-time uncomfortable drama, to be sure, but that drama led to one of the best moments of my life.

I was exhausted even before the wedding began because I'd been up most of the night before. My mind was churning. But, for a change, it wasn't all worrisome stuff. A nice thing was that I recalled running into Snowball that morning. I was getting ready to check out at the grocery store, where I was stocking up on Manishewitz products—a few more matzo ball soup mixes, potato pancake mix, egg and onion matzo, soup nuts, Tam Tam crackers, and even a jar of borscht with diced beets for Dad—and staring straight ahead when I heard someone cheerily saying, "Well, well, if it isn't the world-class photographer, Mr. Julius." I looked to my right and it was Eugene, dressed in his usual attire, with the hood of his parka covering most of his white hair. He was pushing a grocery cart with three twelve-roll packages of Cottonelle toilet paper and maybe fifteen cans of Campbell's Cream of Tomato soup and a single lemon. He was grinning hugely. "Well bless my soul, what a pleasure it truly is to see *you* again," he said. "This old world, it just keeps on turning. Isn't that a truism, sir?" He took off his gray mitten and stuck out his hand, which I grasped and shook. My hand felt lost in his. Then he enveloped my right hand in both of his big ones and pumped up and down. I hadn't noticed, the one time I'd met him at Lieberman's Bookshop with Herschel, how large his hands were.

His saying that reminded me of my idea. "L-Let me ask you s-something, Eugene," I said. "Do you l-l-like nice hot d-dogs, very g-good ones, like N-Nathans Hebrew National K-K-Kosher Beef Franks? With hoity-toity additions, like g-grilled onions and sport p-peppers?"

Snowball furrowed his forehead and cocked his head to one side and thought for a moment. "Why," he said, "I don't believe I've had that particular honor. No, Mr. Julius, I can't say I have. But it certainly sounds enticing. May I ask why you're inquiring?"

I told him about my dream to start a hot dog stand to give high-quality dogs on high-quality buns to "f-folks who may not have h-had the opportunity t-t-to so indulge." I thought of mentioning how I wanted to do a mitzvah, a good deed, to help in my quest to become a mensch, but let that pass.

Eugene leaned his big head to one side and giggled. "Well," he said, "count me in, Mr. Julius. Please do, indeed. I've not indulged, no sir. And I admit to being intrigued by those 'hoity-toity additions.'" He gave me his cell phone number—I was surprised, for some reason, that he had a phone—and again vigorously shook my hand before we parted. "And I'll say this," he said, "I'm quite sure you're much more than just a *mediocre* housepainter, as your diminutive cousin said. I'm certain you're world-class *there*, too."

When I got home, my father was in the bathroom, with the door closed. I could hear him straining and softy grunting. "Dad," I said, through the closed door, "are you okay? Have you been taking your stuff?"

"Yeah," he replied, in a somewhat muffled voice. "I'm okay. And yeah, I've been taking that tasteless crap. Mostly." When I finally heard a flush, followed shortly after by another, and he emerged from the bathroom a minute later, a bit pale, his face flushed, I was so hyped-up about my conversation with Eugene that I told him about my hot dog stand plan. He listened politely and said that he thought it was "a splendid idea." He asked what I planned to provide "as far as liquid refreshments go" and I told him my idea about the Dr. Brown sodas. "*Excellent!*" he intoned, more animated. "You can use my Foreman Grill if you want to. And I'll pitch in with some financing, too."

I went into my bedroom to lie down for a few minutes. I felt fine. I hadn't felt so fine in a while. Then I had the idea that some Sunday soon we'd have one of our bagels and lox and Marx Brothers brunches and watch *Duck Soup*. I wanted to see if Dad, since he'd so unexpectedly guffawed aloud at Amoukar dropping the rock on Gaw's head, would also again laugh heartily at some of our favorite scenes, especially the "gal a day" one with Groucho and Margaret Dumont. I decided not to tell him in advance about our watching that particular flick; I'd just stick it in the DVD player and see what happens. And I'd offer him his choice of a sesame or onion bagel and see which way he went on that. Or maybe it would be best to not give a choice, so as to avoid any consternation, and again just give him his sesame.

I hoped to hell he *would* laugh at Groucho. I'd be thrilled to see my father fully back to his pre-*King Lear* self—the old self-satisfied, rod-up-his -ass Herbert Dickman wearing dark-colored turtlenecks, the great and accomplished classical actor, no longer spouting his scary *nothing* mishegas nor ripping off his clothes and standing naked and shivering in the winter cold and raging to the elements about "poor naked wretches, wheresoe'er you are" or kvetching about being "a poor old man, as full of grief as age, wretched in *both*." I've had enough of all *that* for two lifetimes.

But, I thought, *I'll never really feel secure about the old man.* He was bonkers and now, just over a week after his psych ward time with the Admiral, he seems better. For *now*. But who's to say he won't again go off the deep end if things degenerate? Things can always degenerate. He'll hopefully get that damned UTI under control with the antibiotic I picked up for him at Walgreens, and now I'll have to try to be aware of indications of future possible infections, with the smelly urine and so on, and I'll be sure he takes his psych meds and antibiotics, which he has to finish the whole container of even if his symptoms improve, and drinks a lot of water and daily cranberry juice. I've doled out his meds to him each day, the right dosages at the prescribed intervals. And no more damned Ambien for him! I picked up some over-the-counter sleep stuff at Walgreens—Zzz-Quil and Somnapure. Maybe I'll try one of those. Maybe that would help. At least his back seems to be feeling better; he's not grimacing in pain all the time. And now the old man will hopefully see Ansfield and maybe also a shrink at regular intervals and, if necessary, get whatever other meds he needs to not be bonkers.

And, hopefully, he's past his angst about feeling like a failure as Lear. He hasn't mentioned that since our Izzy's excursion. On the one hand, I don't feel like bringing it up with him. On the other hand, maybe it would be helpful for the old fart to at least talk about difficult feelings. If so, I'd use the silly listening skills I learned from Naomi: "Help me to understand why you felt like such a complete and total fuck-up at playing your lifelong dream role." Or maybe I can get Benji to bring it up with Dad; he seems to have a talent there that I don't. But that's probably not a good idea.

But will all that be enough? The old man had said he wanted to crawl unburdened toward death. Maybe he's more unburdened now than he was before, at least in some ways, but could that change? What if he slips and hurts his damned back again? He's done with carrying Cordelia's corpse onstage, thank God, but he could fall down the stairs while carrying laundry to the basement. He could even break a hip, always a bad thing for an old fart. Or he could clunk his noggin again on the cabinet with the detergents and fabric softeners and lint traps and the like. Or maybe his poor old brain will deteriorate and he'll get some kind of dementia. Maybe he won't recognize me anymore.

At least he liked my idea as to the hot dog stand. I wasn't sure he would. So there's that.

The wedding started out fine. The couple weren't going to see each other until the ceremony, scheduled for noon in the chapel of an old white-painted country church. I was to arrive early and take a series of agreed-upon pictures: the exterior of the church, the snowy grounds, the bride and her bridesmaids, and the groom and groomsmen. I did most of the basic exterior shots fairly quickly. When I went to the room where the bride and the bridesmaids were getting dressed, the maid of honor, Miranda, told me that the bride, Heidi, hadn't arrived yet. She looked worried.

I said I'd come back in a while and went down a corridor to another room, where the groom and groomsmen were getting ready. There were five of them altogether, including the groom, Kenny, who was in a playful mood. He was grinning and kidding around and practicing saying *"I DO!"* in an artificially loud and hyper-sincere voice. I did their pictures, including candids and a few posed ones, one with Kenny and his best man, Lanny— both of whom were short and stocky types—and a few with all five guys. There was the usual kidding around and good-natured insults. There was no drama at all and, as usual, I found the menschkeit comforting. I even learned that Kenny and Lanny worked together, as carpet installers. I found that interesting, since I knew that Heidi was a muckety-muck executive of some kind at a local credit union. Liz had mentioned that she supervised a bunch of people and earned a pretty penny.

After I did pictures of the guys, I went back to do the photos of the bride and bridesmaids. As soon as I walked into the room, though, I sensed tension. I didn't see Heidi. One of the bridesmaids, a short, pretty little blue-eyed thing with dark, short hair, looked to be on the verge of tears. Her eyes were moist and her cute little chin was trembling a bit. She was looking down at her shoes. "Uh," I said, "I'm h-here to do the p-p-pictures."

No one said anything right away. Then Miranda looked at me and held her gaze for a moment. "Heidi's not here," she said. "She's still at home.

She's, uh, kind of upset." I asked her if she thought I should just snap a few pictures of her and the others, and then do the rest when the bride arrived. She shook her head. "No," she muttered, "not just now."

It was, then, just thirty minutes until the ceremony was scheduled to begin. I left the room and sat on a card chair in the corridor, where I could see the door to their room and would know when the bride made her appearance. There wouldn't be much time for the photos of the ladies, but I'd do what I could. Sitting there, I had the idea that maybe I'd have a chance, later that evening, with that cute little blue-eyed bridesmaid. She was certainly way younger than I, but maybe, when inebriated after the reception, she'd be … needy and interested in an older man with experience—a little, anyway.

Ten minutes or so later, Miranda and the other three women came out of the room and walked to another room just down a corridor from the chapel. I followed. The whole wedding party, except for the bride, was gathered there, along with the white-haired minister and two older women whom I knew to be the wedding planners. I'd met them earlier that day, when I first arrived with my equipment. One was Bev, but I couldn't remember the other's name. The air was heavy with palpable tension. The bride's personal attendant, Becca, had been dispatched to the corridor to intercept Heidi, if she showed up, so that she wouldn't barge into the room and see her groom before the ceremony.

Soon it was just five minutes before the ceremony, and the bride still hadn't arrived. I was standing near Kenny and Lanny. No one was talking much. The poor minister looked confused. Bev was on her cellphone. Then she put the phone down and walked over to Kenny, a concerned look on her face. "Uh, I hate to say this," she said, softly, "but Heidi's still at home. She's very upset about … well, she's having a kind of, uh, meltdown."

"But she's coming, right?" Kenny asked.

Bev shrugged. "I don't know, Ken," she said, more softly. "She's pretty emotional." She paused. "Maybe not."

Kenny's face was expressionless. He just stared at Bev and held his gaze for a moment, and then looked down at his shoes and pursed his lips and furrowed his brow and, after a moment, subtly nodded his head. Then he raised his face and arched his eyebrows and looked into Bev's eyes. He shrugged his shoulders. "Well," he said, "what*ever*."

Hearing that groom say what he did just then, at that particular moment, gladdened my heart immensely. I'm not sure why. But it felt, somehow … *perfect*. It seemed one of those absolutely lovely but rare transcendent life moments, when all the stars are perfectly aligned. Hearing Kenny's "what*ever*" and seeing his neutral facial expression in that moment made me feel happier than I could remember feeling in a long time—as happy, or maybe even happier, than hearing my father guffawing at *Quest for Fire*. I must have grinned hugely and maybe even giggled a bit because Bev and the other planner and Becca and Miranda and some of the other bridesmaids, though not the blue-eyed object of my desire, looked at me askance. Bev's facial expression was hard and she didn't look pleased. I should have felt embarrassed, but didn't. I locked eyes with Bev for just a brief moment and then turned back to Kenny. He stared back at me and saw my joyful facial expression and then nodded his head and gave out with just the briefest of subtle smiles in return.

Heidi, surprisingly, waltzed into the church almost ten minutes later, in her gown, holding her bouquet, and the ceremony went on, a bit later than scheduled. Her face was somewhat red and splotchy even through her makeup, as though she'd been crying, and stayed that way throughout the ceremony, including on her journeys down and then back up the aisle. She had a somewhat pissed-off look in general, which stayed on her otherwise-pretty face on and off throughout the day and evening.

The verklempt bride's look aside, the ceremony went fine and Kenny delivered his ringing "I DO!" just as he'd practiced. The receiving line and other post-ceremony/pre-reception events went as planned also, including the wedding party stopping at a local bar while I snapped pictures. The reception at a fancy country club went swimmingly, too, and there was a lovely meal and the usual toasts and good dancing.

Still, there was certainly a chill in the air all day and all evening among the wedding party, particularly the ladies. While the groomsmen were at the bar, I overheard one of them, a tall and lanky black guy named Oscar, telling someone that Heidi was horribly upset with one of the bridesmaids, though he didn't say which one other than that it wasn't the maid of honor. Nor did he say why she was upset; I'm not sure he knew that. I certainly never learned the reason. I suspected that the object of the bride's ire was my cute little dark-haired attendant who'd been all emotional earlier. I found out that her name was Renee. I thought it must have been she, because I noticed that Heidi didn't say a word to her nor, I don't believe, even made eye contact with her. But I did notice the bride now and again briefly glaring at Renee, her face hard and tense. And during the dancing at the reception, Heidi did fast dances with Miranda and the other brides-maids, but not with Renee.

I was in a good mood all day and all evening. I felt fine. It was tiring having to do all the photo stuff by myself, but I didn't care. This was my final photography event, unless I somehow manage to be Benji's photographer, and Kenny's response to Bev had made my last hurrah the absolute *best*, though unexpected, way to go out that could have happened. Every time I conjured that delicious moment of nachas, I couldn't help smiling.

As for Renee, she sat by herself much of the time at the reception. She didn't have an escort, as far as I could see. She didn't take part in the bouquet toss, just sat alone. She certainly seemed an outcast. During a lull in the events, I cautiously sauntered over to where she was sitting alone. "Excuse m-me," I said, "I have the idea that you're n-not having a good d-d -day. Would you l-l-like to t-talk?"

She looked at me for a few moments, her face expressionless, and then shook her head. "No," she said, "I'm fine."

"Are you sure, R-Renee?" I asked, looking directly into her eyes. "I'm a g-g-good listener. Whatever's t-troubling your soul, I c-care."

She gave me a hard look then, her forehead wrinkled and blue eyes snapping. "I said *no*. I'm fine. Now fuck off and leave me the fuck *alone!*"

"Sure," I said after a moment. "What*ever*."

TWENTY-FIVE

THAT NIGHT, I slept better than I had in a long time. I was exhausted when I got home from the wedding reception, but it was a good exhaustion. I drank a glass of White Zinfandel and went straight to bed and fell asleep quickly and slept untroubled. I didn't once pop awake and commence to ruminating and worrying and obsessing.

When I woke up, I still felt fine. I actually felt happy and even optimistic. I decided to just lie in bed for a long while and let my mind wander before I had to get up and start in on our bagels and lox and *Duck Soup* brunch. One thing I thought about was Benji's upcoming bar mitzvah. I decided to contact Naomi about that. I didn't feel brave enough to actually talk to her, so sent her a text:

> Hi. Hope you're well and happy enough. Benji's big day is coming up! I'd be very glad to do the photos—gratis, of course. Let me know.

I considered adding a red heart emoji or two, but thought better of it.

I decided, too, to definitely go ahead with my idea of starting my own painting business. I'd seen Perry at a painting job before Dad went into the hospital and had to endure yet another of his damned seduction narratives. In this one, he'd gone to the condo of a middle-aged woman to look at her place before submitting a painting bid. After talking about her painting needs and discussing possible colors and options for the sheen on the walls and ceilings—flat, semi-gloss, luster—she looked up at his face and asked, softly, "Would you like to see my vagina?" He was, he said, taken aback. "Sure," he replied, after a few moments. She smiled and took his hand and led him to a corner of the living room and showed him a medium-gray sculpture that she'd done of a female lower torso, from the waist down and showing just the tops of thick thighs, with a mildly hairy vulva at the juncture of those thighs. She murmured that it was modeled on hers. Perry said he told her that he liked it but was disappointed. "I was, uh, hoping to see the *real* thing, not cold clay." He said that the encounter led to, yet again, "a memorable fornication," right on the living room floor, near the sculpture.

I didn't want to hear it. Enough, already. For one thing, I was envious that, yet again, a female client had thrown herself at my boss. Or so he *said.* Aside from Celeste reaching out for help with her parts, nothing like that has ever happened to me, not remotely, and I briefly imagined how I'd have reacted if it did. Would I have been suave and quick-thinking like Perry, or would I have been my usual schlemiel self? "Uh," I'd have probably said, "that's a v-very nice v-v-vagina, m-ma'am. You s-say you m-m-made it yourself?" She'd nod. "Well," I'd go on, "I certainly admire your artistic sk -skills. What k-kind of c-clay did you use?" She'd probably have shrugged and shook her head in disgust and huffed to the kitchen, muttering under- neath her breath, to pour herself a stiff drink.

For another, it occurred to me that if Perry was out there seducing or getting seduced by all these women, maybe Naomi was, indeed, in his sights, or had been. She's always found him attractive—liked his looks, including that chin with the manly Kirk Douglas dent, and that he was taller than she and that he was so refined and polite, blah blah—so I imagined that it wouldn't take much effort on his part to lure her into the sack, if he hadn't yet. Maybe my fantasy about seeing them together on the beach sitting on those ugly little green chairs and rubbing the tips of their damned hooked noses together wasn't that far-fetched.

But poor Arlene, with her purple-streaked hair. Here she has her own tough issues, what with the anorexia, and now her horndog husband is out there boffing every female client he can. If I ever see Arlene, at temple or wherever, I'll try to be extra nice and considerate. Perhaps Benji and I could treat her to a delicious egg cream or two at Izzy's, to maybe fatten her up a bit.

So, all things considered, I decided to go ahead with my idea to end my professional relationship with Perry and start my own painting deal. It won't be easy, and I'll have to work harder than I've been doing, but it would be good. Probably Perry won't like that I'll be a competitor. But if he's going around shtupping my former girlfriend, why should I care?

I'll have to buy my own equipment and supplies—vinyl gloves and coveralls and hats; painter's tape in various colors and drop cloths; caulking stuff, sandpaper, and steel wool; sponges and mops; an assortment of professional-grade brushes, with both natural and synthetic bristle; rollers and sprayers; trays and pails, including a few five-gallon ones; a ladder or two; cleaning materials; and whatnot. I'll have to start an account at Sherwin-Williams or someplace to buy my paint and supplies. I'll have to figure how to do the business stuff: setting up paperwork, advertising, keeping records, billing, and the like. I'd have to figure out how to get clients. I'll have to get a bigger vehicle to haul my crap around. My idea is still to work alone and to paint vacant apartments or offices between tenants, so as to interact with my fellow human beings as little as possible. It'll be a lot of work and a pain in the ass, but, now, with Dad seemingly better, I feel up to doing it. I think I do. I hope so.

I'll likely have to get some help with my business taxes. I wondered if gentle Andrew might be interested in taking me on as a client. Maybe we'd even get to be friends. I'd neglect mentioning to him that I'd done the deed of darkness with his wife, or note the circumstances. I wouldn't tell him that making love with his wife had been the absolute high point of my life. I still don't like it that he pushed Celeste down some stairs and hurt her shoulder and wrist, but, I suppose, that's between them. Maybe after discussing tax issues for a while we'd push the documents aside and have a few glasses of wine and talk about Celeste. "D-Do you m-m-miss her?" I'd ask. "Are you s-sad?"

Maybe he'd furrow his brow and look thoughtful for a few moments. "Yeah," he'd perhaps say, "but, you know, life goes on. She made her choice." He'd pause. "Well, hell, I hope she's happy enough with that hunky actor asshole."

I'd nod in understanding. "L-Listen," I'd maybe say, "I'm g-going to do a hot dog stand when it g-gets warmer out. It'll b-be high-quality stuff, N -N-Nathan's Kosher B-Beef. If you s-stop over, I'll give you a f-f-free hot dog. Would you l-like that?"

Andrew would smile. "Sure," he'd say, "that would be *great*."

Maybe he and I could be friends and I'd invite him to Izzy's some Saturday to join Dad and Benji and Herschel and Howie and me. Maybe Jake would come. It would be good menschkeit. If Andrew's never had Jewish deli food before, Benji and I would educate him. We'd offer suggestions. I'd extoll the virtues of Izzy's double-baked rye bread and corned beef sandwiches and his corned beef hash and, of course, that lovely matzo ball soup. I'd note Izzy's schmaltz preference for the soup. Herschel would undoubtedly go on and on about the Hear-O-Israel and Isadore's Mishmosh. Perhaps we'd ask Izzy to step over. "Iz," Herschel'd say, "what do you recommend for this goy?" Maybe Andrew's never had a good chocolate phosphate in his life. Benji could tell him about U-Bet. I suspect that Magda would like him, but I hope not too much.

Magda. I can't imagine her ever being a drama queen like Heidi was yesterday, getting all in a snit and not showing up for her own wedding until the last damned minute and agitating everyone. Heidi would fit right in with Ramona and Sonja and Luann and even, sometimes, Naomi; they all strut and fret and carry on with high emotion over minor matters. Oh, *big* drama! But I've never seen such from my darling Magda. I wondered if she might be willing to help me with my hot dog stand. I have some ideas and visions but not a lot of common sense, but I'm guessing that she's different. I suspect that she's way more practical than I am, which would be good. She could help me with some of the planning, like getting a permit and buying supplies and equipment and preparing the food and the like. Plus, Magda's always affable in a sincere way, unlike lovely Mei-Lin. She could talk nicely to guys like Tunnel Terry and Scanner Stan and even Big Art. She'd be kind to Carl and Blanche, never condescending or mean.

Well, who knows? All I care about now is trying to look out for the old man and doing my thing, handing out free quality dogs, those lovely Nathan's Hebrew National Kosher Beef Franks, grilled, on poppy seed buns, hopefully with the usual condiments—the relish, onion, sport peppers, tomato pickles, and celery salt. With a Chicago Hot Dog that stuff is usually slapped on automatically, but I'm thinking that I don't want to go that route. I'd rather make them available as options, so that people could decide for themselves what to slap on. Not everyone, I'm guessing, likes sport peppers. I don't. I'd also, of course, have high-quality ketchup, Heinz most likely, and both yellow and Grey Poupon mustard available; and little bags of high-falutin' potato chips and, of course, an assortment of Dr. Brown's sodas, for the poor wretches who've likely never indulged.

Wretches. Hah!

As to the bags of chips, I have some options in mind: Pringle's Original Potato Crisps, Cape Cod Original Salted Kettle Potato Chips, Terra Sweet Potato Chips, and perhaps Miss Vickie's Sea Salt and Vinegar Potato Chips. Naomi and Elise always stuffed their faces with those Lay's Sour Cream and Onion ones so I'd certainly stock those, hoping that my former girlfriend would show up and appreciate my foresight and thoughtfulness.

Lying there in bed, hands locked behind my head, staring at the ceiling, feeling fine, I thought about who else might come to my stand. The day would be warm and sunny. There'd be lovely cumulous clouds floating along. It would be great if not just Magda but also Benji and, hopefully, Herschel could be there to help out and to do most of the interacting. That would be fine, though I'd maybe have to try to be aware of Benji yet again staring, slack-jawed, at Magda's big pale face instead of tending to his duties. But if he did, I'd certainly understand; I've been there. Still, I might have to nudge him and say, sans stutter, "C'mon, son, close your mouth so the flies don't fly in and pay attention to your job here."

I'd of course want the old man to be there, too, if he felt up to it, particularly since he'd offered to help finance the deal and offered his George Foreman Grill. As long as he wasn't wackadoodle and ripping off his clothes and being all "Oh, poor me!" like Lear, it would be nice to have him there with me. I'd like that, and, hopefully, he would too.

Herschel could even bring Ajax, to help break the ice with any folks who were shy or uncomfortable with their fellow humans.

If Herschel asks, though, I won't go along any more with taking pictures of him and his mutt as a ruse to seduce women. Enough, already, with that.

Maybe Big Art would be one of my first customers. He'd show up with his gut hanging out between the bottom of his filthy sweatshirt and the top of his also-dirty khaki pants. "Artie," Herschel'd say, "How's it going, big guy? Want a dog?" He'd nod, bug-eyed, and I'd use stainless steel tongs to pluck a hot dog from Dad's Foreman Grill and stick it in a bun and hand it to him and gesture toward the little trays of the condiments. He'd probably hold the hot dog in his big dirty right hand and examine it closely, maybe sniff it, and then pour on disgusting quantities of ketchup and mustard and maybe some relish and onions and devour it in three huge sloppy bites. Ketchup and mustard would likely drip onto his sweatshirt. He'd purse his lips and nod his big buffalo head. His gut would still be hanging out. "*Good!*" he'd intone after a short while. "Yup, that's damned good."

Perhaps Scanner Stan would show up, with his usual five-day growth of whiskers, dirty white undershirt and black cargo pants and tattered red Keds, hair unwashed and unruly, brown-framed glasses with the smudged lenses, carrying his black real-or-not scanner in one hand and maybe his liter-sized Mountain Dew in the other. "What's up here?" he'd ask quietly, suspiciously, glancing furtively from side to side to spot any scofflaws or pyromaniacs. Magda would smile at him. "Ve got goot hot dogs," she'd say. "You vant?" Stan would look around with a furrowed brow and ask how much one costs. "Iss *free*," Magda would happily intone. *"Really?"* Stan would say. "That's great." He'd look over the tray of condiments and, slowly and carefully, deposit some on his dog. He'd maybe like the onions and even the celery salt, but not the tomato pickle. Maybe he'd prefer the Grey Poupon. I'd hand him a small bag of Cape Cod Original Salted Kettle Potato Chips. Benji would politely ask him if he'd like a nice Dr. Brown's soda, perhaps a cream or a black cherry. Stan would shake his head and point to his Mountain Dew. "You can save that for later, sir," Benji'd say nicely. "Wouldn't you like to try something new?" Stan would shrug his shoulders and nod. He'd perhaps choose the black cherry and twist off the top and take a cautious sip. Then he'd take a large bite of his hot dog and then another, larger, sip. After a moment, he'd glance at Benji. "Oh, *man,*" he'd maybe say, "this stuff is, like, amazing! *Thank* you." After he finished, he'd walk away a few steps and maybe lift his scanner to his mouth and mutter into it, something that none of us could hear. I'd like to think he was saying, "Everything is just *wonderful* here on Main Street. *Yummy!* Over."

Soon Snowball and Blanche would arrive together. Maybe I'd have called him on his cell. He'd be attired in his usual beige parka with the faux fur hood and scuffed brown work shoes. He'd be gesturing and talking to her enthusiastically, though I couldn't hear him, and she'd seem to be listening and would now and again nod. She'd look unsure of herself, though glad to be safe with Eugene, and likely wouldn't say anything, but he'd be his usual loquacious self. "My oh my," he'd loudly intone, grinning, and looking directly at me. "What have we here, Mr. World-Class Painter? Is this the manna from heaven for poor folk who've not indulged, about which we so pleasantly discoursed?" I'd nod. "Well, well," he'd go on. "Blanche, my dear, this promises to be a repast for the ages. May I procure for you a lovely Mr. Julius Chicago Dog, with the works?" She'd look around cautiously and then back at Snowball, and shrug her shoulders just once.

Just then Herschel would notice Snowball and trot on over. "My friend!" he'd say, extending his hand. "Time and the river still wait for no man, eh?" Perhaps they'd vigorously shake hands, and Eugene would introduce Blanche. She'd stare down at the ground while Herschel took her hand to gently shake it. Maybe she'd notice Ajax nearby and her face would brighten and she'd kneel down and stroke his neck and pat his head and smile up at Herschel, just a bit. "What's his name?" she'd murmur, barely audibly.

I suspect that Snowball has to be careful about eating, though, what with several of his front teeth missing. He'll likely have to hold his hot dog carefully and bite off a piece on one side of his mouth rather than in the front, and chew on just one side or the other as well. Eating soup wouldn't be a problem for him, though. If my ship ever comes in, I'll buy Eugene some nice top-of-the-line front teeth.

Tunnel Terry would perhaps unexpectedly emerge from around the corner, loping along silently, a six-seven concave-chested specter, his shock of dark hair bouncing, dressed in his usual raggedy blue jeans and a long-sleeved, untucked flannel shirt. He'd look around, expressionless, vacant green eyes unblinking. Maybe I'd take a dog off of the Foreman and stick it in a grilled bun and silently hand it to him and point to the condiments. Terry would accept it without a word but would then raise the index and middle fingers of his right hand. I'd probably not understand at first, but would then remember Bratfest. I'd nod and immediately procure for him a second hot dog and stick it in a bun and wordlessly hand it to him. Or maybe I'd wrap each dog in white waxed paper. He'd very briefly make eye contact with me, or maybe not, and then would turn and amble away, firmly grasping his two Chicago Dogs, one in each big hand. I'd watch him turn the corner and slip silently out of sight, an emaciated and outsized ghostlike figure.

In a bit, Carl would roll up in his electric wheelchair. He'd have his usual agonized facial expression, with the furrowed brow and wild eyes. Maybe he'd be wearing either his Castro T-shirt or the Lenin one. I'd notice him staring, tongue hanging out and drooling, at the hot dogs on the Foreman grill. "Would you l-like one?" I'd ask. Carl would nod, just once. I'd turn to get a dog from the grill but then I'd see Benji and Magda approaching, she holding a hot dog in one hand and a Dr. Brown's Cream Soda in the other. She'd gently place both on Carl's tray. "I hope you vill enjoy, young man," she'd say. Carl would spastically point to the "Thank you" on the wooden board on his tray. Carl would look at the hot dog and the cream soda on his tray and then up at each of us in turn. Magda would immediately understand that he couldn't easily feed himself and would jump in. She'd pick up the dog and hold it to his mouth and let him take a bite off of one end. Then she'd hold it away while he chewed and swallowed. "Dat's fine, young man," she'd say quietly. "Iss goot, *ja?*" Benji would work the top off of the brown bottle. "Would you like something good to drink?" he'd ask. Carl would look up at him and nod again, just the once, and Benji would hold the bottle to Carl's mouth to let him take a few swallows, though being sure not to hold it there too long so that the guy didn't choke. If Carl dribbled his food or drink, Benji or Magda would dab his face with a paper napkin.

Perhaps others would show up as well. Maybe Kenny and Lanny would come by, perhaps during their lunch break from a carpet-laying job. I'd greet Kenny enthusiastically, grasping his hand and pumping his arm. "Hello, b-b-brother," I'd say. I'd give them free hot dogs, and ask what condiments they'd like. Kenny would shrug just a bit. "Hey," he'd say, grinning. "I'm just peachy keen with … what*ever!*"

Who knows who else might come? Maybe sweet Amanda or Suzette or Sylvia or even Robin Cohen. "Robin, my dear," I'd say in a deep voice, sans stutter, "do you suppose those cheerful Inuit ever get to enjoy tasty treats like *these?*" Maybe my lovely redhead would even be driving by and see the goings-on and park her car and check us out. How lovely would that be?

Perhaps Twersky would even come by, perhaps after another shopping trip to Walgreens. He'd be dressed normally, not in the ridiculous Hassidic coat and hat. He'd be carrying a plastic bag with Depends and Colgate's Ultra-White Toothpaste. He'd stare at the hot dogs on the Foreman Grill, his brow furrowed. "Oh, they're f-fine," I might assure him. "They're Nathan's Famous Kosher—not k-kosher-*style*. All beef. No p-p-pork at all." He'd look over to Dad, standing nearby. "This is true, Herbert?" he'd ask. "No pork?" Dad would nod. "That's what my son said, Rabbi. My son doesn't lie, you know." Twersky would purse his lips and shrug. "So," he'd say, "that's okay with me then. Could I have with a *bissel* mustard?"

My father would, I'd hope, enjoy the whole experience. He said he's done with his strutting, so even if he still thinks that "it's all bullshit," he'd like just hanging out and getting to know my maybe-bizarre friends and enjoying a Chicago Dog and some chips and a Dr. Brown's. He and I could clink our brown bottles together before drinking. "You've done a good thing here, kid," he'd say. "A *mitzvah*, is what."

Maybe Celeste would even come by, probably with Pretty Boy. I'd take the high road. "How've you been?" I'd ask her, in as masculine a voice as I could muster, sans stutter. "Sorry we don't have any Trader Joe's trail mix, which I recall your fondness for, but we have top-of-the-line hot dogs and the highest-quality chips extant." If Donny asked what flavors of soda we had, I'd ignore him, pretend he wasn't there. Maybe that wouldn't be much of a high road. Still, it would be lovely to see darling Celeste. As they were leaving, she'd mumble something that I couldn't quite hear. "Cordelia," I'd intone loudly, with an exaggerated dramatic gesture, grinning hugely. "Stay awhile. Ha! What is't thou sayest? Thy voice was ever soft, gentle and low—an *excellent* thing in woman." I suspect she'd either be impressed or think I was nuts.

I recalled that I'd considered offering a free hot dog to Andrew. I hoped that he wouldn't show up while Celeste and Donny were there, though. That could be ugly. Otherwise, I'd be happy to see him. Maybe I'd introduce him to Kenny and Lanny and tell them that if they were ever looking to hire a top-of-the-line certified public accountant, Andrew's their man.

Maybe Lydia would even show up, probably arm-in-arm with her new lover. Perhaps her cousin would be with them, and even Elise as well. If so, I'd give Lydia a big smooch and a warm hug. Maybe I'd even pat her butt, if I could get away with that. "Lydia!" I'd say, still sans stutter, "How absolutely *lovely* it is to see you. Are you, uh, happy enough with what's-her-name?" I wouldn't worry if Naomi or Lydia's lover seemed bothered, or even if Naomi's face turned purple.

Still, it would be so good to see my Naomi again. Oh, sweet Jesus! I'd hug her warmly, too, if she'd allow, and prolong the embrace as long as possible. I'd be sure to give her a very special, grilled-to-perfection Chicago Dog. Maybe she'd like a Cel-Ray Tonic. I can't deny that I still have feelings for that woman, despite anything that happened with us—despite her having been a nag and a scold, despite her having discarded me—and I'm grateful to her for what time we had together, whether or not I ever see or hear from her again or even if she hires a skywriter to spell out, in huge letters, JULIUS DICKMAN IS A PATHETIC SCHLEMIEL WITH A LITTLE SHLONG across the heavens.

I'd even try to reach out to Elise. "D-D-Dog?" I'd say to her, smiling brightly. She'd stare and furrow her brow, unsure of my meaning, but eventually nod just once. I'd hand one to her. "A p-p-perfect treat for a l lovely, refined *shaneh maidel.*"

And if Rivkah came along, I'd of course happily give her a freebie also. I'd stop whatever I was doing and just watch her as she ate her dog.

Maybe she'd close those big dark eyes and make that nice little moaning sound that I recall so fondly from when we went to Izzy's after our divorce.

After a while, I got out of bed and got dressed and started getting ready for our bagels and lox brunch. I put the bagels on a plate and got the butter and cream cheese from the refrigerator, and set out the lox for Dad, and started the coffee. I put the *Duck Soup* DVD in the machine. I truly hoped that, finally, my old man'd yet again guffaw out loud at Groucho, particularly in his classic scenes with imperious Margaret Dumont. I knocked on his bedroom door. "D-D-Dad," I said, just a bit loudly, "time to w-wake up." I heard him groan a bit, but he didn't answer.

After a few minutes, my father, wrapped in his ratty green bathrobe, stumbled out of his bedroom. I noticed that his face seemed unusually pale and drawn. His eyes were that watery light bluish-gray. He went straight to the bathroom and closed the door behind him. I heard him moan and groan and make what sounded like straining sounds. I heard him coughing and clearing his throat. I went to the door and listened. "D-Dad," I said after a bit, "are you, uh, okay? Have you been t-taking your M-Metamucil?"

I waited for my father to answer.

He didn't.

TWENTY-SIX

RABBI TWERSKY said that he thought we should do three nights of sitting shiva following the funeral tomorrow, Tuesday, but I told him that two were enough. That's all I can deal with. One would be okay, as far as that goes, and maybe that's what I'll insist on. I don't even know who'd come to the house for the damned shiva other than Herschel and Howie and Jake and maybe a few others from the theater or the temple. Perry will likely show up, and would maybe shlep his poor little malnourished wife along. We'll have to have at least ten guys for a minyan to recite the Mourner's Kaddish. That might not happen. Izzy will surely come if he feels up to it, and Magda too, out of respect, even though she's not a Yid. Twersky told me that anyone can come, whether or not they're a countryman, but only Jews can do the Kaddish. If Rivkah and Arnie come, he'd definitely be part of the minyan.

I don't believe, though, that Benji can be part of a minyan until he's been bar-mitzvahed and is officially a man. A man. *Hah!*

If Izzy does show up, I'll be sure to keep an eye on him to be sure he's okay. I'd want him to be comfortable and not exert himself. If he seems tired or frail in any way, I'll lead him to Dad's La-Z-Boy, in which I'm now comfortably ensconced, and have him sit. If he seems cold, I'll cover him with the white afghan. If he wants to take a little nap, fine. I'll tell everyone else who's there to keep the fucking noise down. I'll probably say it better than that, though.

I think I'd like it if Celeste came. She was, after all, Dad's favorite daughter in Lear. They reconciled at the end and were all lovey-dovey before she sadly bought the farm. I'll give her a sweet hug and hold her tightly for as long as she'd allow and sniff her hair to see if it still has that nice lemony smell. "Th thank you, again, for that m-m-memorable m-morning," I'll maybe say. If I can manage to squeeze out a tear or two, I will. That might soften her a bit. And if she wants to shlep conceited Donny along, I won't say no.

When I called Twersky yesterday afternoon to tell him about my father and how he'd expired, he didn't say anything for a moment. Maybe his thought was the same as mine: *Here's this famous classical actor who's played all these high-falutin' characters who all went out in high style, oh-so tragically—Romeo, Hamlet, Lear, Macbeth and so on— and here the old man checks out alone of a heart attack while sitting on the toilet, boxer shorts bunched around his ankles.* And the strange thing was that he even had a subtle little smile on his dead face! I didn't mention that to the rabbi

Herschel'd actually tittered, briefly, when I called to tell him, though he immediately apologized. "Hey, I'm sorry," he said, "It's just so, I don't know, *off-script* for old Uncle Herb." I nodded, though of course he couldn't see that.

"You know," I told Herschel, "I c-can't *believe* D-Dad is gone. I could k-kick myself for not actually b-being sure he was taking his damned b-bowel stuff. He c-could have stuck around l-longer. I wanted him t-to, you know, be there to help with my hot d-d-dog stand."

"I hear you, cuz," Herschel replied, "but don't sweat it too much. Remember what Kent said: 'Vex not his ghost. O, let him pass. He hates him that would, upon the rack of this tough world, stretch him out longer.' Anyway, some guys who have heart attacks *feel* like they need to take a dump, but they really don't. Like that bloated Elvis."

Herschel offered to come over to be with me, but I declined. I wanted to just be alone in the house yesterday and, now, today. It's strange being here alone, though, struggling to come to terms with the idea that my father is gone and will *never* be here again, ensconced in his La-Z-Boy, wearing that damned green robe. I wanted to just let my mind wrap around that change.

I'll have to let Miriam know, I suppose. She deserves to know. If she wants to come to the shiva, okay. I suspect she will. I'll leave the photo of her on his bedroom dresser, but won't put the one in my room back. It stays in the drawer. If she does come, I'll try hard to take the high road and be cordial. I probably won't reveal to her what Dad said in his psych ward room to the Admiral about which of his wives he liked best—that amazingly *delicious* moment in my life. It would certainly be petty of me to tell her that, but definitely satisfying.

As to the Admiral, I'd *love* it if he showed up at the shiva. The guy may be wackadoodle here and there, but at least he's upbeat. Maybe he gets all down in the dumps when not manic, but, if so, I haven't seen it. Perhaps at the shiva when Twersky announces that, since we have a minyan—if we have enough for a minyan—we'll now recite the Mourner's Kaddish, the Admiral would sit up straight. "Kaddish?" he'd maybe say. "What's that? Is it anything like cottage cheese? I like cottage cheese with those little green chives. I prefer small curd. Large curd, in my humble, doesn't cut the mustard. Isn't that something? Did Herbie like cottage cheese? I bet he did. A true gentleman he was, one of the greatest actors of all time—better than Scofield or Lunt or Welles or any of those guys. Better than Gielgud or McKellen. Well, we're all going to miss old Herbie, aren't we? Hell of a fella he was, by God." Miriam would no doubt glare at the Admiral disapprovingly and probably *tsk-tsk* at him. I'm sure the Admiral wouldn't care. If he noticed her clucking at him, he'd probably heartily laugh out loud, blue eyes twinkling, and maybe break out in "The Sloop John B" or "Drunken Sailor" or even "The Wreck of the Edmund Fitzgerald." I'd like that.

Maybe after the Kaddish, the Admiral would beckon me over. "Now don't forget what your dad said, Julius. He said you were a good kid. I heard him say that. Do you remember when he said that? He said it. He *did*. So that's something right there, huh?"

"Yes," I'd reply. "Yes, that's s-something."

One of the paramedics who came yesterday after I'd called 911, Petersdorf, was an older no-nonsense guy with thick shoulders and practically no neck. He had a tattoo on his right forearm that said "Betty" in very nice blue cursive. The other, Ms. Robinson, was a sweet-faced black woman with tight dreads. She was shorter than I and solid, slightly zaftig. After Petersdorf matter-of-factly announced that Dad was gone, she looked up at me with big, liquidy, chocolate-brown eyes. "I'm very sorry for your loss." she murmured. "It's a hard thing to lose your father." Her eyes moistened. "I lost mine two years ago, you know." I wanted to put my arms around Ms. Robinson and hold her close and comfort her. "There, there," I thought of whispering softly, sans stutter. "I'm sure he's looking down and taking care of you." I thought of also saying, "Help me to understand why that affected you so much," but quickly decided that would be a stupid thing to say. Instead, I'd just gently kiss her cheek and whisper, "It'll be okay, sweetie." She'd look up at me and gaze into my eyes and nod, just once, and then rest her wet face briefly against my chest. Maybe there'd be a tear or two, or at least a sniffle.

After Petersdorf and Ms. Robinson had left with my father's corpse, I sank into his chair and wrapped myself in his purple Lear robe and took delicate bites of my onion bagel, with the usual butter and Philadelphia Chive and Onion Cream Cheese Spread. Sitting there alone, eating, I had the thought that I wished he'd waited to expire until after we'd watched *Duck Soup* so that I could finally know whether or not he'd again laugh at Groucho wagging his black painted-on eyebrows and saying, "Well, a gal a day is enough for me. I don't think I could handle any more." I realized that it was a weird and petty thought—a *very* petty thought, considering—and felt ashamed of myself. *But still*, I thought, *now I'll never know*.

Sitting in Dad's chair again today, a jangle of thoughts have paraded through my mind. One was the food at the shiva. The general rule is that the guests bring food. At shivas I've been to, people brought things like babka, challah, rugelach and, commonly, bagels. But I'd like to have some control. I'd like to be sure that if there *are* bagels, they definitely at least include our favorites, onion and sesame, and also, absolutely, cinnamon and raisin in honor of Mom, and also that there'd be a supply of our favorite cream cheese. Maybe I could ask Magda to bring a tray of cheesecakes from Iz-zy's. If Naomi comes, I hope she'll bring one of her lovely baked tuna casseroles, all golden brown on top and moist in the middle. I'd worry, though, that someone would bring something disgusting, like gefilte fish or pickled tongue. That would make me gag, which wouldn't be a good look at my father's shiva. Twersky would no doubt give me one of his disapproving looks, his nose wart bright red and maybe throbbing.

I don't know whether or not it would be sacrilegious, but I'd like to set out big bowls of Cheetos and Doritos and even Planter's Lightly Salted Peanuts, to honor my dear departed. Then, if Pretty Boy came with Celeste, I'd urge him to try the Cheetos. "That was my p-poor father's favorite s-snack," I'd tell him, dabbing the corner of my eye with a handkerchief. "He'd b-be honored if you'd have s-some." He'd gobble down a few, to be affable, and my hope would be that soon his mouth and lips and tongue and fingers would turn orange and he'd look ridiculous and Celeste would be disgusted and maybe even turned off.

When Celeste was getting ready to leave, I'd insist on speaking to her in private for a moment. "Listen, kiddo," I'd say, softly but firmly, sans stutter, "are you aware that you have a brown spot on your lower back?" She'd probably furrow her brow and shake her lovely little head. "Well," I'd go on, "you *do*. You DO! Maybe it's nothing but maybe it's something bad. Now listen, you *absolutely need* to see a doctor to get this checked out, Celeste. And *soon!* You can't wait. You *need* to call tomorrow. *Tomorrow!* Fershtaist?" She'd nod. "Oh, thank you," she'd murmur, eyes warm and soft, and maybe hug me briefly. "You're a mensch, Julius Dickman." I'd nod my head. "And," I'd insist, "I want you to call me *right* after your appointment and let me know what the doc says. Okay?"

I'll definitely set out all of the albums, with their 72-point boldface titles, and some of the framed photos of Dad from his plays, in the living room. I'll certainly set out the last one I did, from *King Lear*—the one from Act III with my father as the wild-eyed mad king in that miserable hovel with the Fool and almost-naked and shivering Poor Tom—in the most prominent place. I'll tell people that my father felt that playing Lear was the capstone to his long career treading the boards, that he was so proud of doing that great role in that magnificent play, which he considered "a treasure of Western literature," and that he'd deliberately waited to do it until he was close to Lear's age in the play, old enough to understand approaching death. I wouldn't mention, though, that he thought he'd failed or that he felt he'd waited too long. And if anyone commented favorably on the quality of the photograph itself, the lighting and exposure and composition and the like, I'd just smile humbly and nod. "Oh, thank you so m-much," I'd say. "I r-really appreciate that."

Now that my father's passed, it happily occurred to me that I could finally stop worrying about going up with him in that damned tiny single-engine airplane—one in which a guy can't stand upright—to tour the summer countryside. What a *huge* relief! It's one thing I can now cross off of my list of topics to worry and ruminate about when I have my damned insomnia. I'm in shock and incredibly sad that my dad's gone, and I know I'll always miss him horribly, and I'm sorry that he missed out on that experience. He was looking forward to it. But I'm glad that *I* don't have to worry about it anymore.

When people are ready to leave the shiva, I suspect they'll play their parts and utter the usual departing words to me: "May God comfort you among the other mourners of Zion and Jerusalem." That's a nice enough thing to say, I guess, but maybe it would get tedious and rote after a while. Even if it does, though, I'll have to play out my little role in response. "Th-thank you so m-much," I'll say, my face sincerely drawn and sad and eyes possibly moist. "And thank you for c-c-coming. It was a comfort. My dear D-Dad would have appreciated your b-being here. *Zay g-gezunt.*"

Whether I stay here or move to a place of my own—maybe even Mrs. Weinstein's apartment—I hope to have Benji come over now and again. He and I could watch, or re-watch, DVDs of cavemen movies—*Quest for Fire* again, certainly, and *Clan of the Cave Bear* and *One Million Years B.C.* and the like. Maybe we could do Sunday morning bagels and flicks here and there, when he didn't have to go to one of his sad weekends with his "gaping asshole father," as Naomi so nastily said. I suspect he'd like Groucho and his brothers; I bet he'd laugh at Groucho telling Margaret Dumont, ". . . but I can't see the stove." That should appeal to an adolescent. It appeals to me. I hope he's not a fan of lox, though. Enough of *that* chazzerai in this household. Maybe Benji and I will even watch *Springer* and *Judge Judy* together now and again. Maybe we'll even pump our upraised fists and sing out "JER-RY! JER-RY!" together. And, certainly, we'll listen very closely and attentively to Jerry's Final Thoughts to learn what we can about relationships. Maybe that'll help Benji down the road. It may be too late for me, though. Then, when the show was over, I'd turn off the TV and we'd discuss. "So, Benji," I'd say, "what d-did you get out of what J-J-Jerry s-said?"

And maybe he and I would listen to "The Whiffenpoof Song" now and again, maybe on my parents' June anniversary. On the other hand, that might not be a good idea. If I get all misty at "Baa, baa, baa," Benji'd maybe have a lesser opinion of me.

Sitting in my father's La-Z-Boy, absorbed in thoughts and memories, I heard a ping on my cellphone. It was a text from Naomi: *I already hired another photog. Maybe I'll send you an invite.* I immediately texted back: *Oh, thank you so much. I'd LOVE to come.* After I sent it, though, it occurred to me that she hadn't said she *would* invite me, only that she *might*. So maybe my message was presumptuous. I considered texting her back, but decided not to for now. If she comes tomorrow night, we can talk about it then.

I hope to Christ Naomi does come.

My father's La-Z-Boy. I decided then that I'd keep it, whether I stay here or move elsewhere. It was his and now it'll be mine, for as long as it lasts or I do. I want that link, that bond, to my old man. Maybe I'll keep the purple Lear robe and the gold scepter in a plastic box next to the chair and cover myself with the robe and wave around the scepter now and again and think of my poor father. And, of course, I'll keep and always treasure the white afghan.

I had the thought, just then, that I really hope my hot dog stand idea isn't just a pipe dream. I want to do that for Carl and Blanche and Stan and the others, as a mitzvah, but just then I worried that I don't really have it in me to plan and carry out such a big deal. It's really a lot to think about and actually make happen. I don't know if I'm up to it. I hope I am. But if I'm not, I'll at least maybe buy some Chicago Dogs at Izzy's and keep them warm in a thermal container of some sort and walk around on Main Street and other streets and hope I run into Scanner Stan or Tunnel Terry or Big Art or some of the others and just give them a free hot dog. All the condiments will be on the dog, and they won't be able to choose for themselves what they prefer, but that'll have to be okay. And I'm not going to shlep around sodas or bags of chips; the wretches will have to do without.

I decided, sitting comfortably in Dad's chair, to call my new business *Poor Tom's Okay Painting.* Or maybe I'll zap the "Poor." Either way, the title has a nice ring to it, and it isn't all self-praising. It doesn't set expectations too high. If a guy says he's going to provide "fine" painting, there's no direction to go but down from that lofty standard. But "okay" sets a more reasonable bar. When I'd finished a job and asked the client if she was satisfied with the results and she looked around at the walls and ceilings and thought for a moment and furrowed her brow and said, "I guess it's *okay*," I would, after a moment, nod and say back, "Well, s-sweetheart, that's all I p-p-promised, r-right?"

If possible, I'll try to specialize in painting the empty houses and apartments of people who've recently tipped over. At each such job, I'd maybe take some quiet time and try to get a feel for the spirit of the now-stiff former occupant. Hopefully, I'd now and again have more luck in that regard than I did with poor Mrs. Weinstein.

Maybe someday I'll even be able to commune with my father's spirit. That would be lovely. I'd like to ask the old fart whether or not he finally felt unburdened there at the end, at least a little. I hope he did.

At least my old man died wearing his ratty green robe. Even though that damned robe saddened me, I suppose I'm glad of that; it was a Chanukah present from my mother and he'd kept it all those years. That's something. Maybe, instead of keeping it, I'll request that he be buried in it. Probably that wouldn't fly, though. Probably Twersky, irritated with me as usual, would strongly object. "We have many *traditions* in our faith, Julius," the rabbi'd say. "We must always do things the *proper* way, as God has commanded us." He'd likely furrow his brow and purse his lips and shake his head and glare at me. "Bury Herbert in his bathrobe! Where in hell do you come *up* with this mishegas?"

I won't push that one, though. I don't want to vex the old man's ghost.

Well, it'll be May before too long. Memorial Day's at the end of that month, and that means Bratfest. I hope I can take Benji. I'd love it if my sweet Magda would come, too. The three of us would surely have a lovely time, and, hopefully, Magda and I would hold hands. Maybe we'd even walk along lovingly arm-in-arm, like Lydia and her damned girlfriend. If we saw Tunnel Terry, I'd certainly buy him a nice pair of brats. I'd be fine if he doesn't thank me, just nods. Or not even that much. It'd be a nice little mitzvah. Maybe Benji and Magda and I could stroll down to that brackish pond with Terry and just sit quietly beside him on his green bench while he silently munches on his brats and stares, unblinking, at the still water. We wouldn't have to talk.

And, of course, the other lovely beauty of May is that June, featuring the summer solstice, is right around the corner. The summer solstice is, blessedly, the longest day of the year, the day with the least amount of scary darkness. On the one hand, that's wonderful because there's all that lovely daylight. On the other hand, it means that the days will start getting shorter, a little less light each day, between then and the winter solstice in December.

That strange little smile on my poor dead father's face—I can't get it out of my mind. Maybe he was remembering Lou Grant's wise words: "We laugh at death because we know that death will have the last laugh."

What do I know?

About the Author

Poor Tom is Martin Drapkin's fourth work of fiction, following *Now and at the Hour, Ten Nobodies (and their somebodies),* and *The Cat Tender.* He's also a photographer, specializing in black-and-white street photographs and portraits of mothers and daughters. He still uses film. He and his wife, Erica, live in rural Cross Plains, Wisconsin, with several mildly neurotic rescue dogs.

For more information, please visit www.drapkinbooks.com.

CPSIA information can be obtained
at www.ICGtesting.com
Printed in the USA
JSHW011937080123
35725JS00008B/247